A GARRISON CHA... ...LLER

NIGHT
NIGHT
KILLER

CRAIG N. HOOPER

Connect with Craig:

Website: http://craignhooper.com

Email: craig@craignhooper.com

We humans, you see, have an infinite capacity for self-rationalization.

CHARLES WENDELL COLSON

ONE

THEY CAME for me at six minutes to midnight on a foggy, abandoned stretch of Highway One.

They'd picked a decent spot to run someone off the road. Vandenburg Space Force Base was five miles in my rearview mirror, and the lights from that sprawling complex had all but faded to black. With the cool Pacific Ocean to the west, and hot inland temperatures to the east, the fog was pea-soup thick on this muggy summer night. You could force a car off the road, blitz the vehicle with bullets, then be on your way unseen and unheard.

Earlier, I'd been in Lompoc, California visiting a former client. When I left the man's house, I spotted the dark sedan with three occupants pulling out to follow. I wasn't sure if the tail related to that brief client meeting, or if it was about something else entirely.

The pursuing vehicle suddenly killed its lights. Following that, the engine's throaty burble jumped an octave higher, which told me things were about to get serious. My dog, Ranger, who sat in the passenger seat, also knew something was wrong. He swiveled his head backward and gave a low decibel growl.

For a second, I thought the driver was crazy for going dark and pinning the gas pedal. But then I realized the car could navigate using my headlights and taillights.

So, I did something crazier: I went dark, too.

That didn't last.

As soon as I killed the lights, I knew it was a mistake. With no ambient light, it was like driving into a black abyss. The slightest turn in the road and I'd be in the ditch, eating my steering wheel, so I flipped my lights back on and played it smart.

The fog came at the Caprice heavy and fast. Ranger didn't like the view from the windshield, so he slinked into the passenger footwell. Instinctively, I let off the gas since I could only see thirty feet down the road. Slowing down like that caused the approaching vehicle to draft tight against my rear bumper.

Before I could squint and get a look at the driver, the dark sedan shot into the oncoming lane to pass. My first thought was to hammer the gas. That way I could race this fool and make sure he didn't force me off the road or spin the Caprice with a PIT maneuver.

But I decided on a different strategy, something unexpected: I jammed the brakes.

"Hold on, Ranger!"

As the seatbelt strained against my chest, the sedan rocketed past on the left. Ranger was curled up tight in the footwell and whimpered at the sudden G-force strain.

I tried my best to keep the wheels from locking and fishtailing the car off the road. When the Caprice slowed to a near stop, I cranked the steering wheel to the right and put four tires on dirt, then slammed it in Park. I kept the car running.

Ahead I saw the glow of taillights and heard the sedan's brakes squealing. I fished a set of keys from my left pocket and used the smallest one to unlock the glovebox. A Savage Stance handgun was tucked under the car owner's manual. Reaching across, I grabbed the gun with my left hand and used my right to open the passenger door.

My dog wasted no time, hopping out and scampering into the dark.

"*Ranger*," I hissed after him.

He didn't listen.

I flattened my body and shimmied across the seat, then slipped onto the dusty ground. Staying crouched, I eased the passenger door shut. At this point, the sedan's engine whined as it hurried in reverse. I used the moment to roll into the shallow ditch to my right. When I popped up, I was deep in a fog layer. All I could see were the sedan's red taillights, which looked like sinister animal eyes tracking my direction.

I climbed the far side of the ditch and backed away, moving slowly between the trees for cover. With the compact 9mm handgun at my side, I picked a tree to hide behind, then waited and listened.

The sedan skidded to a stop, then shut off. My '86 Chevy Caprice had the upgraded V8, so the 5.0-liter engine burbled away in the background. I'd left it running to muffle any sound I made.

Two car doors opened and closed, then two sets of steps scraped against the pebbled dirt. The third man must've stayed in the vehicle. The other two men didn't talk. By the slow pace of their steps, I knew they didn't rush toward the Caprice either. Moments later, when they both yelled "Clear," I knew I was dealing with trained men. My guess: either former law enforcement or ex-military guys.

Suddenly I heard, "He's hiding out there somewhere."

A different voice said, "Use his car."

I listened to my car door open and the Caprice back up. The man parked perpendicular to the road. That way the headlights pointed in my direction. But there were trees and dense fog, so I remained easily hidden.

"Nothing," said one of the men. "I can't see jack beyond the ditch."

"I'll stay here, you go look for him. He can't be far. Remember, he has that German shepherd with him. I'd take your piece."

So, they are armed.

I released my gun's safety and sidestepped to the north, closer to where the sedan was parked. I heard one man tromping around to my left. The other dude, the one in the Caprice, played with the high beams for a bit. But when he realized they didn't help with the low visibility situation, he exited the vehicle.

I heard a window rolling down, followed by two men talking. Since I couldn't make out their words, I moved closer, crawling all the way into the ditch. In between the shifting layers of fog, I glimpsed the car.

No wonder I can't hear. The man outside the vehicle was leaning into the open rear window and speaking with the third man in the back seat.

To my left, I heard some scuffling steps, followed by heavy breathing. The man looking for me suddenly emerged from the fog. He tried to navigate the ditch too fast and tripped, smacking his face on the ditch's upside. Fortunately, he was too distracted by his clumsiness to spot me. When he stood to brush himself off, I noticed his stature. He looked close to six foot six, a good two inches taller than me. Though he had some height, he was paper-clip thin and nothing but a set of gangly limbs. I bested him by at least thirty pounds.

Mr. Gangly proceeded to the other side of the car and leaned into that open window.

I edged up the ditch, now just fifteen feet away, and strained to listen. I heard, "You need to find him, gents. Now. And we need to press him hard. We need know what he knows."

"Got it, sir," said the fella closest to me. Though he was bent over, I could tell that man was average height and weight.

"We need to implore him to leave Stanley alone," the back seat man said, "and not get involved."

Stanley was the former client I'd just visited. *So, this is about him.*

Back Seat Man continued, "We need to do whatever it takes. Understood?"

Hearing enough, I rose and proceeded quietly toward the sedan's rear passenger door. Along the way, I placed the Savage Stance flat against my right palm. The Stance was considered a concealed weapon, so it was only a tad over six inches long. My big hand shielded most of the weapon from view.

The man in the back seat saw me first. I figured he was startled by my sudden appearance since he didn't say anything. All he could do was point in my direction.

Mr. Average scrambled backward and banged his head trying to extract it from the vehicle. When he got his head out and witnessed my purposeful stride, he reached for his hip. Before he could get his right hand on his weapon, I clobbered him squarely on the left side of his face.

The impact made a dull but loud crack. The hit was so flush and hard I imagined the gun's imprint was momentarily outlined on his cheek.

He moaned and dropped to his knees in a mild daze.

After shaking his head, the man collapsed onto his hands. With my forearm, I hammered the back of his neck until he pancaked onto his chest, then I used my left boot against his side and fed him to the ditch.

By this point, Mr. Gangly was scrambling around the sedan's hood. As he passed the front passenger tire, I used my left hand to discreetly open the back door. I slid my hand up and grasped the corner of the window frame. Just as the man bent to lunge at me, I wheeled the door open and stepped back and watched him tackle a swinging door.

Bone and flesh and metal collided.

The impact caused the door to slam shut. Mr. Gangly fell face first to the ground in a tangle of limbs.

"Enough!" yelled Back Seat Man. He cowered, and I saw no gun, so I focused on the real threats. Mr. Gangly spit dirt and fumed and cussed and tried to stand. After some wobbly moments on his legs, he fell onto all fours.

I opened the back door again. This time I used both hands on the open window frame. Like a battering ram, I smashed the door against his head. Twice. The second blow flattened him. Then I stepped onto his shoulder blades and leaned into the car, placing my palms flat on the seat.

"No!" screeched Back Seat Man. He held an iPad in front of his face for protection.

Before I could say or do something, I heard rapid movement behind me. Thinking it was Mr. Average back for round two, I retreated from the car and spun.

Not Mr. Average, it was Ranger!

My dog tore into the vehicle and chomped onto the man's lower right leg. Ranger shook his head violently. So fast, in fact, I couldn't tell if he had the man's pant leg or his actual leg in his jaws. By the squealing sounds, I assumed Ranger had contacted bone and/or skin.

My dog easily dragged the man across the back seat.

"Stop, stop," he yelled. "Call him off. Please!"

I didn't. Ranger's training had finally paid off, so I praised him. "Attaboy," I said. "Good job. Now out."

Ranger pulled Back Seat Man from the vehicle. His body dropped just to the left of Mr. Gangly, and his head bounced off dirt, which stopped the incessant screaming.

I tucked the Stance away and straddled him. "Wanna know what I know? Is that right? I know you messed with the wrong man, that's for sure."

The man blinked repeatedly. I assumed he was concussed from the impact on the back of his head. I cradled his skull with my left and smacked him with an open right palm.

Not hard, but not soft either.

A moment later, he refocused. "Wait," he said. "Just wait. You have it wrong."

I scoffed. "*I* have it wrong. Really?"

He held up his hands with his palms flat toward me. "Please just wait. I work for . . ."

When he paused too long, his nose met my fist, which was an unpleasant meeting.

"You were saying," I encouraged him.

"I work, I work," he stammered. After a big swallow, he managed, "I work for the government."

Laughing, I said, "So the government sends armed goons in an unmarked vehicle to run me off the road, and then do who knows what?"

I balled my fist and held it out.

"Sorry, I meant hired by the government."

"Oh, that makes it better, more understandable. Forgive me."

Before he met my fist again, he blurted, "Okay, okay, I was hired by someone big, someone high up in the government. I'm telling the truth."

"Who?" I demanded.

"Someone very high up."

As soon as I scowled, he said, "Fine, it's ..." He squinted and didn't finish the sentence.

I sighed. "Last chance, pal. Who?"

The man opened his eyes, then swallowed. "The AG. The Attorney General of the United States."

TWO

"Don't hit me. Please!"

I couldn't believe the recently appointed attorney general, a man named Ernesto Tuchek—and Stanley's father, by the way—hired these goons. I was so deep in thought about that I hadn't realized my fist still wavered over the dude, threatening another unpleasant meeting.

A familiar ring broke the tension, which snapped me out of it. I relaxed my hand.

"That's him there," the man said, thumbing toward the car. "I've been trying to reach him."

The familiar ring came from the iPad on the back seat. For years I'd resisted buying a smartphone. But recently my mother remarried, and my young son was visiting Grandma in Mexico on a two-week summer trip. To keep in contact with Simon, I'd broken down and purchased an iPhone so we could video chat.

That familiar ring was a FaceTime call.

"I'll answer it," I said, scuttling into the back seat. Ranger hopped into the back seat with me. I commanded him into the front driver's seat.

Grabbing the iPad, I said, "Ernesto would probably love to see my face. He'll be a little surprised, though."

"Wait!" the man said. He scrambled to his feet and stepped toward the car door.

"Not so fast." I reached over and closed the door. To keep him at bay, I extracted the Savage Stance and placed it on my right knee, pointing the barrel directly at the rear passenger door.

He held up his hands. "May I approach?"

I nodded. Ranger, however, took issue, barking the moment the man moved.

"Easy, boy," I said.

Back Seat Man inched his way to the car. Cautiously, he leaned onto the window frame and said, "Please don't answer that call."

"And why not?"

"It'll just muddy the waters."

"The waters are pretty murky already, pal."

As I turned back to the iPad, he blurted, "Don't! Please. The AG doesn't know about you. He—"

"He certainly knows who I am."

"I mean, the attorney general doesn't know you showed up at Stanley's place and that we went after you. He has no clue, and he probably won't be too pleased we were so..."

"Aggressive?" I offered.

"Fair enough," he said.

I declined the FaceTime call and turned toward him. His hired hands were standing by the ditch, probably conferring over what to do about my presence in their car. After placing the iPad on the seat, I said, "Tell me more."

The man took a deep breath. "It was my judgment call to chase after you. I've been trying to reach Mr. Tuchek ever since you showed at Stanley's. He wants to stay apprised of every detail, so I tried to reach him for an update and to get some guidance on your sudden appearance, but he's not exactly at my beck and call, especially since it's so late on the East Coast. The way you abruptly left Stanley's got my attention. I wanted to know what happened between you and the kid, so I made a snap decision. For all

I know, you might've killed Stanley or beat him and left him for dead, and I wasn't about to let you get away."

"So, Ernesto Tuchek hired you to protect his son?"

He eyed me. "How'd you know that exactly?"

Because it was a classic Ernesto move. But I wasn't about to get into the weeds with this guy. He didn't need to know that five years ago Ernesto Tuchek hired me to do the same thing: protect his son, Stanley. At that time, Ernesto was the California governor, and I was a suspended FBI agent. Stanley had received some death threats, and I was tasked with protecting the kid.

Instead, I said, "Lucky guess. What's your name, anyway?"

The man smoothed out his wavy hair. "Griffith Murphy, local PI out of Santa Maria. Might've heard of me?"

"Might've not."

"People call me Griff."

He leaned into the car a little, like if I got a closer look maybe I'd recognize ole Griff. I didn't. Neither did Ranger. He growled, causing Griff to back up.

I studied the man as he straightened. He reminded me of a midforties washed-up surfer. Griff didn't have the vocabulary of a surfer, just the look. His thick hair had a brackish hue about it, as if he'd been out in the ocean this morning but had yet to wash out the salt. Since I was follicly challenged and kept my head shaved, I tended to fixate on people's hair.

"Listen, Griff, I'm gonna call Ernesto back. I wanna talk with the man and—"

"Can I talk with him first? Sorry to interrupt, I just want to explain things."

"I get it, Griff, I do. Probably a little embarrassing for you if I make the call since you were hired for protection, and I got the one-up on you. Plus, like you said, you don't want your employer—the chief law enforcer of our nation, mind you—to find out you employ armed men who won't hesitate to run someone off the road."

I paused since Mr. Gangly and Mr. Average were moving toward the car. Ranger sprang into the passenger seat and barked ferociously out the window. I played it a little more subdued. My eyes flashed to the handgun on my leg, then back to Griff.

He waved his men back.

"How about," I continued, "you tell me everything you know. Starting with the truth. And if I believe you, Griff, I won't get into the details with Ernesto about our altercation here."

"You think I'm not telling the truth? Ernesto Tuchek hired me to protect his son. You think I'm lying?"

"No, I think you're withholding part of the truth."

"And why's that?" His smug look reappeared.

"Because there are three of you, and I don't believe you need three grown men to protect Stanley Tuchek. Plus, I heard your conversation with them." I waved at the two men standing directly behind him. "That speech was all about finding out what I know and imploring me not to get involved. That's a little more than protection, wouldn't you say?"

He was about to open his mouth for a rebuttal. I held up my finger to stop him. "Lastly, there's this. The real kicker." I picked up the iPad. Griff didn't have a passcode set, so I simply had to tap the screen to bring it to life. When I'd declined the FaceTime call, that app shut down and I quickly saw the open app behind it.

I thrust the iPad out the window. Pride welled inside me when Griff glanced at the app and his smug look evaporated. The open app was a live camera feed. And the feed showed Stanley's living room and small kitchen.

I stated the obvious. "You know very well that I didn't lay a solitary finger on Stanley when I was in his house. You were watching our interaction on this feed. Did the attorney general give approval for this type of surveillance? That I'd like to know."

Griff's Adam's apple bobbed. He thought for a moment, no doubt giving serious consideration to my proposition. While he backed away to confer with his men, I thought about Stanley. Recently he called me out of the blue and asked if I could help him out. When I asked about what, he said he didn't want to talk about it over the phone, only in person. I didn't like his vagueness, so I politely declined. He was then slightly more forthcoming, telling me he was the chief investigator for the nation's number one true-crime podcast, hosted by a man named Rogan Ross, and that they were working an international murder case and desperately needed my expertise.

That piqued my curiosity. And since I didn't live far from Lompoc, I agreed to meet. In person, however, Stanley remained cagey with details, even though I pressed him. All I learned was that Rogan Ross was in trouble, and the expertise Stanley needed from me was traveling to Mexico to bring his boss home. I berated Stanley for not asking me this over the phone and saving us both time. And since I had no plans of being a chauffeur, I told him no and pretty much stormed out of there.

I refocused on Griff, who was approaching the back passenger window. "I'll tell you everything I know," he said, "but I'm warning you now, it's not that much."

"Humor me. What are you really doing with Stanley?"

"Keeping him out of trouble."

That sounded closer to the truth. "And what kind of trouble is he in?"

Griff thought for a second. "I should've said making sure he doesn't get *into* trouble. Apparently, he's barking up the wrong tree. He's in way over his head."

"Any more clichés? You forgot, 'Out of his league.' Give me some specifics."

"You know he's working for that famous podcaster Rogan Ross, right?"

I nodded.

"His father told me that Ross was involved in some international murder investigation that was garnering way too much attention. And not the good kind of attention for a podcaster. Know what I mean?"

"I don't."

Griff sighed. "Attention that could get Ross killed."

I looked away. *Which is why Stanley wants me to save Ross.* I turned back to Griff. "What international murder investigation are we talking about?"

"That I don't know."

I narrowed my eyes.

"I'm serious. I don't. No clue."

"You know nothing?"

"I mean, I know it has something to do with Ross's latest podcast season, but I don't listen or pay attention to podcasts."

I did. I'd recently gotten hooked on podcasts, in fact. But I waited until full seasons had been released before starting a new one. And it was my understanding that Rogan Ross's latest season had released only four episodes, so I'd paid it no attention for the time being.

"Anyway," Griff continued, "the AG hired me to sit on Stanley. Apparently, Rogan Ross is pushing Stanley to help with the investigation, and the AG wants no part of that for his son. I'm supposed to keep the kid safe, report to his dad daily, and make sure the kid isn't working the case. Ernesto Tuchek doesn't want Stanley getting death threats like Ross has been getting."

Griff motioned at me. "You, of all people, should understand that. Am I right? Didn't go too well last time the kid had death threats, did it?"

"You know who I am, even though I showed up with no warning tonight?"

He nodded.

"You recognized me when I arrived at Stanley's then?"

When Griff hesitated on his response, I knew there was more to it. I thought about the hidden security camera in Stanley's house.

"Wait, are you monitoring his cell, too?"

Griff gave a dismissive wave of his hand. "Mr. Chase, it doesn't matter how we know. We're aware you and Stanley have a history, and as I said, the AG hired me to make sure his son drops the case. So . . ."

I held up the iPad. "So, you must not have audio on your illegal video feed inside Stanley's house. Because if you had audio, you would've heard our conversation and wouldn't have felt the need to come after me."

"There was a hiccup with the audio feed," Griff said. "Certainly, there was, I can admit that. It was spotty at best. But I do know Stanley was telling you, albeit vaguely, about the investigation, and I wasn't sure why you left so quickly."

"Why'd you come after me so intensely?"

He thought for a moment. "I've been hired—and paid handsomely, mind you—to make sure Stanley drops this whole thing. It appeared you might get involved, and I'm somewhat aware of your skills as an investigator, so I wanted to put a scare into you. Run you off the road, you know. Maybe put a gun in your face and implore you to drop it. Just being honest here. Promise it wouldn't have gone further than that."

"You said you know who I am, so probably not wise to come after me."

He bobbled his head. "In retrospect, obviously not. I underestimated you, for sure."

"And overestimated your abilities," I added.

Griff reluctantly nodded. "Sure."

"I'm calling Ernesto."

"Wait," he said, holding up his hand.

Before he continued, I addressed his concern. "I believe you're telling the truth, for the most part. And since I'm a man of my word, I won't mention anything to Ernesto about you trying to run me off the road. I have one question for him, that's all."

"Which is?"

"Not your concern." I motioned at his men. Mr. Average had pulled out his piece. They were clearly annoyed that I was still in the car, and still in control. "Keep your dogs at bay while I make the call."

Griff eyed me and didn't move.

I gently laid my hand on the Savage Stance. "You don't want me getting loose lips with the attorney general, do you? And you certainly don't want me to use this." I patted the handgun.

He sighed and turned back to diffuse the situation with his men. While he did that, I opened the FaceTime app and dialed Ernesto Tuchek back.

The AG answered quickly. There must've been a slight camera delay on his end because he immediately said, "Griff, what's going on? I know you've been calling. What's the urgency? You know how late it is on the East Coast?"

I stayed silent and gave the camera my best smile.

"Wait," Ernesto said, "is that . . ."

I gave a courteous wave.

He remained silent for a moment, clearly in disbelief. Ernesto Tuchek was a hairy, mythical beast of a creature. Permanent five o'clock shadow. Thicker and darker eyebrows than Martin Scorsese. And deep lines on his brow from a constant scowl. His face filled most of the screen. It was so fat and all-encompassing I couldn't see much background.

Eventually, he recovered. "Garrison Chase, well I'll be damned. What on earth are you doing answering Griff Murphy's call?" Before I could respond, he said, "And where the hell is Griff anyway?"

I couldn't resist. Turning the screen and pointing the camera out the car, I said, "Wave to the Attorney General, boys. Step in close, lighting is nonexistent out there and I want Mr. Tuchek to see your smiling faces."

The men didn't budge.

"Garrison," Ernesto boomed, "seriously, what on earth."

"Sir," I replied, turning the iPad back. "What's Stanley working on? What's this big international murder investigation he's doing with Rogan Ross?"

"Of course," he said, "I get it. Stanley hasn't dropped the case, has he? He's trying to bring you in to help. Damnit. I knew it."

"What case, sir?"

"My boy's going to be next, for sure. I'm surprised the Mexicans haven't killed Ross yet. That damn Ross is manipulating my son. For all the—"

"With all due respect, sir," I interrupted, "exactly what case are they working on?"

Ernesto finally tuned in to my question. "Stanley obviously didn't recruit you for help if you don't know what case I'm talking about. And you certainly haven't listened to Ross's latest season, I guess."

I refrained from saying, *duh.* It took a lot not to be sarcastic. Through slightly clenched teeth I repeated myself. "Tell me what case you're referring to, sir."

He blasted on, however. "According to Stanley, Rogan Ross has broken the case wide open. And from what I've gathered that's partly due to Stanley's help. Unbelievable. My son, a mathematician, for crying out loud, and that knucklehead podcaster, Rogan Ross, of all people. Those two solved an international murder investigation involving a serial killer, maybe even serial killers? I mean, come on. I can hardly believe it."

Serial killers?

"I wouldn't have believed it—couldn't, in fact—if it weren't for the death threats on Ross. And they must be serious if he went into hiding in Mexico. How's that safe, anyway? It's—"

"Sir!" I snapped. "What case are—"

"The Night Night Killer, Chase. Geez, calm down."

Night Night Killer? I was at a momentary loss for words. Everyone knew of those serial murders since they'd garnered international media attention the past few months. When I found my voice, I said, "Sir, are you telling me they know the identity of the killer?"

"Not they," Ernesto said, "just Ross knows. Want to know what infuriates me the most? What really chaps my ass?"

I played along. "I do, sir."

"That yahoo Rogan Ross won't share any information with the authorities, Mexican or American. Not a single piece of intel. He's gonna reveal the identity of the serial killer in the season finale of his stupid podcast. On a podcast! Can you believe that?"

Honestly, I couldn't. Revealing a killer's identity on a podcast would send the killer into hiding and make it hard for authorities to capture the person. It was a terrible idea that could pervert the course of justice.

"Can't your son stop this?" I asked. "Can't Stanley talk some sense into Ross?"

"I've been trying to convince my son to intervene, but he's not listening to me. And he's no longer taking my calls."

"Have you leaned on him, sir?"

"*Leaned?* What do you mean by that exactly?"

I rephrased. "Have you stressed or implored him to persuade Ross?"

"I have. I've implored him to release any evidence they have to me and my office. I've been incredibly vocal about that, in fact, maybe losing my temper about it once or twice, if I'm being honest. I imagine that's why he's upset with me and has stopped communicating."

"If that's the case then, sir, do you give me permission to take a crack at Stanley?"

A brief pause. "As long as we're clear there's no physicality involved."

"Promise, sir."

He nodded his giant melon of a head, then pointed a chunky finger at the screen. "Stop this, Chase. My office needs to step in and apprehend this murderer or murderers, not some true-crime podcaster. We can't have a serial killer's identity being outed on a podcast. Think you can get Stanley to convince Ross to drop this?"

"I think I can, sir. On one condition."

"What's that?"

"Call off your goons, take them off this case. They don't need to be tracking me or Stanley. The men look like they need a rest, anyway."

Ernesto thought for a moment, then said, "Hand Griff the iPad."

I smiled and handed it over, then Ranger and I headed to the Caprice.

THREE

The fifteen-minute drive back to Stanley Tuchek's took me eleven minutes.

Along the way, I recounted what I knew about the serial killings. About eight months ago a string of murdered Mexican men, ranging in ages from around sixteen to forty-five, were discovered in the triangular border area where California, Arizona, and Mexico intersected.

So far, thirteen bodies had been found. All the victims were discovered on the Mexican side of the border, and all the bodies were posed in the exact same way: curled up in the fetal position with the man's hands clasped together and placed underneath his right cheek. The killer left a calling card in the victim's shirt pocket. It was cream-colored, business-sized, and had two words on it: *Night Night.*

Hence the moniker, Night Night Killer.

The interesting thing is that none of the bodies were harmed. Not a wound, scratch, or broken bone on any victim. They all died via lethal injection of pentobarbital. Since they weren't violently killed, there was little evidence left at the scene or on the bodies. And all the victims were found on the outskirts of desert towns, so there were no eyewitnesses to the placing of the bodies.

Without concrete evidence, or even a stitch of circumstantial evidence, the intervening months had produced tons of wild theories. One I could remember was that a deranged veterinarian was on the loose. That theory stemmed from the fact that pentobarbital was a common medication used for euthanizing animals. Obviously, a psychotic, murdering vet must be the killer since he or she would have access to pentobarbital.

Like I said, *wild theories*.

Now to find out Rogan Ross may have solved the case was mind-boggling. To go from no good theories to a potential outing of the killer's identity on a podcast was quite the swing.

Walking toward Stanley's house, I said to myself, "You're gonna have to fill in the gaps here, kid."

I stood at his front door and debated barging in. Stanley was a night owl, so I knew

he'd still be up. Since I needed to play this cool and get some answers, I went with a hard knock instead.

Everything Stanley Tuchek did was fast, so he answered within eight seconds. The kid whipped open the front door, pushed up his thick-rimmed glasses—as was customary—and said, "What are you doing back, Agent Chase? Especially after storming out of here like you did."

"Stanley, I haven't been a federal agent in years. I've told you that—"

"Right right," he said, nodding fast.

Stanley Tuchek looked like a human ferret; that was the best way to describe him. His head and facial features were narrow and pointed. His hair was slick-backed and dark. Of note was his hairline: it started from—no lie—an inch above his eyebrows. Having barely a forehead contributed to his ferrety-looking face. The kid was petite framed with a long torso. Since his stature was in such stark contrast to his father, I figured Stanley must've been adopted.

I pushed past him, walking straight into his living room without being invited. "For the last time, Stanley, just call me Chase."

Stanley spun and matched my steps. "Whatcha doing?"

I was staring at the ceiling. There was only one thing up there that could hide a camera. Grabbing a chair, I stood on it and pried off the cover from the smoke detector. After yanking out a pin-head camera with a two-inch-long cable, I tossed it at Stanley.

"Looking out for you," I replied. "That's what I'm doing."

Stanley cradled the hidden camera, in awe. He managed, "What's this?"

"You had a brief stint with the NSA, you should know what that is."

It was true. Stanley Tuchek was a mathematical genius who finished college at a young age and was recruited by the National Security Agency. The agency wanted him to be a cryptologist, or something along those lines, but Stanley had a pipe dream of being a field spy, which was never going to happen. To prove his worth, however, Stanley broke into the NSA's mainframe and stole some highly classified information. That stupid and illegal move set off a chain reaction of events, including Stanley receiving death threats and me being employed to protect him.

Stanley pushed up his glasses and met my gaze. "I meant, how'd it get there, and how'd you know about it?"

"Please tell me you're aware your dad hired Griff Murphy to keep an eye on you, and to keep you out of trouble."

"I do. In fact, you know what?" He pounded his fist on his leg. "I bet he planted this a few days back when I invited him in for coffee. My dad had said he was gonna keep an eye on me, and I'd noticed a strange car lurking around, so I put two and two together and confronted Griff in his car. But then I felt bad about it and invited him in to make amends."

"You shouldn't feel bad. That's some sophisticated equipment, and it's illegal."

He didn't respond to that comment. "I went to the bathroom when he was here. That must've been when he connected this."

"Stanley, what's your story? I want to hear your side of things, especially why your dad feels the need to hire a PI to covertly monitor you."

He snorted, another trait he did too often. "If you hadn't rushed off, you'd know."

"If you'd been forthcoming with details, I might not have."

He thought about that. "You're right, my bad. Ross was adamant I keep the details secret, and I wanted to honor that. But I guess it backfired."

"It did. But I'm here now, and I'm ready to listen."

Stanley waved me into a leather Barcalounger, then plopped down a few feet away into a mismatched loveseat. Since I wanted to start at the beginning, I said, "And why am I here in Lompoc, of all cities? When did you move here?"

"A few months after . . ." He swallowed.

"The debacle you put me through?"

He gave a subtle nod, then moved on. "I got a job with Musk's SpaceX company after the NSA mishap. They launch rockets from Vandenburg, and I was involved with several of their projects. Making pretty good money with them, I must admit. But it wasn't a great fit. You know—since I've told you this before—I've always wanted to be in law enforcement, or somehow involved in solving crimes."

"Sure, I remember. So, after SpaceX you got a job with Rogan Ross and his podcast? That's quite the transition. What happened there?"

"2018 happened. April twenty-fourth, to be precise."

I thought about that date, but I couldn't place anything of importance happening then. "And what happened that day?"

"The Golden State Killer was arrested."

He paused. Obviously, I knew about that infamous case, so I gave Stanley a nod, which seemed to move things along.

"At first," he continued, "it was just sheer interest. I mean, how did they capture Joseph James DeAngelo after all those years? He'd remained unknown for four decades, now suddenly the Golden State Killer aka the East Area Rapist aka the Original Night Stalker is arrested on his front lawn just a few hundred miles from here. Crazy, right?"

"They found a DNA match, isn't that what happened?"

Stanley snorted. "Sort of, it was way more involved than that, though. Authorities had genetic material from DeAngelo for decades, but there was no match in CODIS, which was why the case stumped the cops for decades. You're familiar with CODIS obviously?"

I nodded again. CODIS was the FBI's DNA database. It stood for Combined DNA Index System. It took all the criminal DNA from local, state, and federal cases and combined it into one massive database. When a crime happened, and genetic material could be collected from the scene, authorities would run the material through their extensive database. If the perpetrator had previously committed a crime, he'd easily be identified in CODIS.

"CODIS has obvious limitations," Stanley said. "It's great to ID repeat offenders, but what if the perpetrator of a crime had never been caught and convicted before, or what if it was the perp's first offense?"

This was obviously a rhetorical question since Stanley blasted on. "That's where investigative genetic genealogy can really help."

"And by that you mean, 23andMe, Ancestry.com, and the like?"

"Again, sort of. Those are companies that work in the broad field of genetic genealogy. They take your genetic material and develop a DNA profile, which can then tell you all sorts of things about yourself."

"Like your heritage and your relatives."

"Exactly. The cops had some of the Golden State Killer's genetic material from a rape kit that had been well preserved. They sent the material to one of those companies, I believe it was FamilyTreeDNA, and they received a DNA profile of the Golden State Killer. Using that profile, they then set up a fake account to find matching relatives in a public DNA database known as GEDmatch. At first, it only matched some very distant relatives, so it wasn't helpful. But they kept at it. Soon, another genealogy company, I believe it was MyHeritage, found a much closer relative, one who ultimately helped break the case."

When he paused, I jumped in. "Got it, at least the gist. What does any of this have to do with you getting a job with Rogan Ross?"

"The fascination turned into a hobby, then an obsession. Not with the Golden State Killer himself, but with how he was apprehended. Specifically, how they used old DNA like that to reverse engineer a family tree. You know my strengths and skills lie in mathematics. And since DNA is all about sequencing, it's basically math, at least it is to me. In the end, I fell in love with the field and learned everything I could about DNA profiling and investigative genetic genealogy."

Wanting to speed the kid along, I said, "Rogan Ross, Stanley."

"Right. So, I'd been a huge follower of Ross's podcast for years. A couple of years ago he was developing his investigative team and looking for a DNA specialist. Of course, I wasn't a specialist and had no formal training in the field, but I landed a job with him because I told him I'd work a case for free and prove my worth as a DNA investigator. Ross was a penny-pincher and had nothing to lose, so he took me up on the offer. I helped him with season three, the case of that missing college girl from thirty years ago, the one from the Central Coast. When we helped authorities solve that case, he took me on full-time."

I had listened to season three. To be honest, I was interested in how the kid helped with finding the girl's body, but it was after one in the morning, and I just wanted to understand how all this connected to the serial killings.

"Okay, so Ross takes you on and now you're working for him on the latest season. How—"

"I actually don't work for Ross anymore."

"Geez," I said, sighing. "Really?"

"We're more like colleagues now. We're co-owners together in this company." Stanley pointed to some red letters stitched onto his plain white shirt, on the left side directly above a wrinkled pocket. I hadn't paid attention to the T-shirt.

It read, Futurum.

"That's Latin for the future," Stanley explained. He sensed my frustration with another rabbit trail, so he got to the point. "Ross uses our company to do his DNA research. He—"

"No offense," I interrupted, "but Ross is a podcaster and not a cop, and he certainly isn't a crime scene investigator, so how and what type of DNA research would he possibly do?"

"My guess, Chase, is that you haven't listened to the first four episodes of his latest season?" Before I could answer, he blurted, "I get it. You're not the podcast type."

He had that wrong. However, I didn't go into details with Stanley about my current obsession. I'd gotten into podcasts after breaking up with my long-time girlfriend, Karla Dickerson. We'd had a long-distance relationship for years. It got to the point where it was either me moving back to LA where she was from or asking her to leave her career and move to the

Central Coast. I couldn't commit either way and we broke up instead. Anyway, listening to hours of podcast episodes while I was alone kept my mind distracted. It helped me not focus on what an idiot I was.

"I have not listened to Ross's current season, you're correct."

"Where to start?" Stanley tapped his fingers on the loveseat's arm rest. "As soon as Ross learned that these male victims were found near Palmera, he jumped on the story and headed to Mexico to investigate. He'd been interested in Palmera for some time, long before the murders. Are you familiar with that Mexican town?"

I shook my head.

"It's essentially an industrial border town in Mexico, but it was created by American companies."

Furrowing my brow, I asked, "What do you mean?"

"Big American manufacturing companies, ones like General Electric, built factories there to produce American goods. The companies chose that location to capitalize on low-cost land and dirt-cheap labor. More and more American companies moved their production facilities to Palmera over the past decade. By 2020, it had grown to a massive size. But the area was just a bunch of ugly factory-type buildings and super unattractive. To try to spruce up the area, the companies got together and littered the place with palm trees. They transplanted full-grown palm trees everywhere, all around the buildings, around the entire industrial perimeter, up and down the connecting roads. Like I said, everywhere. And that's how it got its name, Palmera."

"Right, that's Spanish for palm tree."

"Correct. These factories produce a ton of electronic and medical equipment for Southwestern United States. Palmera's located an hour from Mexicali and close to Yuma. Interstate 8 is directly north, just across the border. If you head east on I-8, you're in Phoenix or Tucson in no time. And if you head west, within hours you're in San Diego. Palmera draws thousands of workers from the southern Mexican city of San Luis Rio Colorado and even more workers from Mexicali. Something like five buses leave Mexicali every morning and head to Palmera.

"When news hit that the victims worked in Palmera, Ross headed to

Mexico to investigate. He pumped out those four podcast episodes and had plans for more because he believed he was on to something."

"On to what?"

"You really have to listen to the episodes, Chase."

To appease him, I said, "Sure, kid, will do. Next time I have a few hours to myself I'll listen. For the time being, give me the CliffsNotes."

He eyed me, then began. "One of the things Ross investigated were the American CEOs of these companies. Apparently, several times a year they held their upper management meetings in Palmera. They catered wild after-parties, too. Quite unruly stuff, from what I understand. Tons of booze, drugs, and large-scale abuse of local women. I mean, extremely bad abuse. Like holding these women against their will, binding, torturing, basically complete sexual degradation."

I found myself clenching my fists.

Stanley continued. "Ross had a theory that perhaps the male victims were employees who were fed up with their American bosses abusing their local Mexican women, so the employees made that known and paid the price for doing so. When Ross went live with that theory in episode three of his podcast, you wouldn't believe what happened."

Stanley waited for me to say something. When I didn't, he inched forward on the loveseat and leaned toward me with an excited look on his face, but he still didn't say anything.

"What, Stanley?"

He looked around, then back to me. "Mexican authorities approached Ross and gave him some crime scene evidence. They knew about Futurum and wanted us to process some DNA evidence from the murder scenes, which they believed would back up Ross's theory concerning the American CEOs' involvement. The Mexican authorities believed, and I think they're right about this, that using a third-party American company would hold more weight."

"Did it? Did the evidence back up Ross's theory?"

Stanley smiled. "It did."

I took a moment and pushed out a breath. "So, you know the identity of the killer or killers?"

He shook his head. "Only Ross does. He has the evidence under lock and key. He's very careful not to say anything to me over the phone, text, or in writing. Ever since the fourth podcast episode dropped, he's received death threats and is now hiding in Mexico. He's terrified to leave the country with the evidence. And—"

"And that's why you need me to get him."

"Exactly, I need you to bring Ross and his evidence safely back to the States. You must. Please, I need you. I don't know anyone else with your set of skills, and I certainly don't trust anyone to do this job except you."

"What's he going to do with the evidence?"

I knew the answer, of course. But I wanted to see how forthcoming Stanley would be. Plus, at this hour, I didn't want to go into detail about my FaceTime call with his dad.

He didn't answer my question right away.

"Stanley."

"You probably won't like this, Chase, but Ross has plans to out the killer publicly on his podcast."

"That's crazy," I stated flatly. "Why would he do that?"

"Ross doesn't trust the authorities, on either side of the border."

"And why's that?"

He shrugged. "Honestly, I don't know. I agree it's not an ideal plan. I've tried to convince Ross otherwise, or at least find out why he's so determined on this course of action, but he's been either stubborn about it or simply unresponsive to my request. I'll try again, though."

"Do your best, Stanley. The best course of action is to feed credible leads to law enforcement, who can then vet the evidence, keep it under wraps, and hopefully pounce on the unsuspecting perp or perps. Ross ruins that if he goes public naming the killer."

"You sound like my dad."

Standing, I said, "If you want my help, that's the cost. Convince Ross to abandon the idea of outing the killer or killers on the podcast. Got it?"

He nodded. I walked toward the front door, stopping at the bay window and pulling the blinds down a touch.

Stanley asked, "What are you looking at?"

I was making sure Ernesto had kept his end of the bargain. Sure enough, Griff's sedan was nowhere to be seen. Instead of answering his question, I said, "I'll be back in the morning to check in. Hopefully you've convinced him by then."

"What if I can't?" Stanley said. "What if I fail?"

"This is important, right? It's crucial we catch this killer and bring Ross back safely."

"Of course, yes."

"And we agree it's best the authorities handle this, correct?"

"Naturally."

"Then there's no room for failure, kid. None."

With that, I turned and left.

FOUR

IN THE EARLY MORNING, I packed up a few things and headed south to Mexico with Ranger at my side.

Heading south wasn't a huge inconvenience for me. I was supposed to drive to Mexico three days from now to pick up Simon anyway. So, I'd simply leave a few days early and find Rogan Ross and make an assessment from there on what to do. As promised, I stopped at Stanley's house on my way down. I woke him by pounding on the door.

"What'd Ross say?" I asked, pushing past him after he opened the door.

When he didn't answer, I turned around. The kid was still standing by the door. Typically, he'd have already shut the door, spun, and been on my six. I hadn't seen him move so slowly before.

"You okay, Stanley?"

He blinked a few times. "Haven't had my coffee yet. And I'm not a morning person."

"I see that."

He proceeded to the loveseat. He wore the same white, pocketed T-shirt as last night. Only a pair of striped boxer shorts covered his lower body. Stanley's legs were skinny and hairy. The only skin I could see on his legs came from his protruding, knobby knees.

After collapsing onto the loveseat, he said, "No news yet. I reached out but Ross hasn't responded."

I remained standing and crossed my arms.

"Don't worry, Chase, he'll respond. I promise. Probably this morning some time. Have a seat, you're making me nervous."

I didn't sit.

"Please," he said.

Since I had something else to speak with him about, I obliged and sat in the Barcalounger. I eyed the kid. "The evidence given to Ross by the Mexican authorities; can you trust it?"

He furrowed his brow. "What do you mean?"

"I mean, the theory that some high-powered corporate muckety-mucks are doing illegal activity in Mexico and then killing men, either by themselves or more likely a hired hand, to keep the men silent about said abuses, is believable. If Mexican authorities caught wind of this and had evidence of it, I can see how hiring a third-party from America to validate the evidence makes sense. But there's also one big problem."

"And that is?"

"A chain of custody issue, as it relates to evidence."

Since Stanley looked like a lost puppy dog, I explained. "You must maintain integrity of the evidence at any crime scene. Items are bagged and tagged and sent to secure evidence lockers. Anyone who processes the evidence or takes it out for evaluation signs their name on a dotted line. All to make sure everyone knows exactly where the evidence has come from, where it's been, and who's handled it. Chain of custody is crucial. But here you have Mexican authorities handing Ross crime scene evidence, who then sends it to you in a different country. There's tons of problems and skepticism that will arise because of that."

Stanley sighed.

"And it's not like Mexico—and I love the country, by the way—has a sterling reputation when it comes to their police force."

"What's that supposed to mean?"

"Think about this: What if the Federales have been investigating this string of killings and they learn they have a serial killer in their midst?

What if they know that person or persons is from Mexico? But then along comes Rogan Ross with this very public theory that it could be American CEOs trying to cover up their sins. Mexico wants to cast dispersion away from themselves, since they don't want to admit they have a serial killer on their hands, so they use Ross and your company as a patsy. They feed you guys some fake evidence that they know will point to some American or Americans."

He snorted. "Boy, you're skeptical, Chase, and awfully paranoid."

"Any good investigator is, Stanley. Tell me everything you know about this evidence."

He thought for a moment. "I was responsible, along with a colleague at Futurum, to develop DNA profiles from the samples sent to me by Ross. Most of the crime scene evidence was secondary transfer DNA and very hard to work with, but we have a small, sophisticated lab here in Lompoc and we managed to do the job. Once we developed profiles, we did the same thing the cops did with the Golden State Killer case."

"You sent the profiles to one of the genetic genealogy companies to find relatives using a dummy account."

"Yup. If we found a match with, say, one hundred or more centimorgans, we could reverse engineer a decent family tree with limited suspects. We did that with several of these profiles. I have a person who performs that service in-house. Anyway, those family tree results we then FedExed to Yuma where Ross was staying at the time, before he crossed the border and went into hiding. Ross would use our proprietary software to search databases to limit the suspect pool even more. Mexican authorities also gave him access to some of their databases, and from what I understand that really helped Ross with this case."

I didn't know what centimorgans were, or what it meant to reverse engineer a family tree, but I did get the gist of what he was saying. "You're saying only Ross knows what's going on then? Only he knows who's really responsible?"

"Essentially, yes. It's a complicated process and there's so much more you need to know. Especially what our company and software does, and why we're perfect for this case."

"I disagree, Stanley."

"With what?"

"With having to understand your company." I glanced at my watch. "You have the next eight hours to contact Ross and convince him to abandon this notion of outing the perps on his podcast. Now, how do I find Ross's location? Where's he hiding?"

"I actually don't know."

I scrunched my brow.

"But I'll find out, he'll text me and I'll forward it to you. But it will be in code, and you must use WhatsApp. It's end-to-end encryption, and the safest."

I'd heard that before. WhatsApp was a favorite communication system between criminals because it was near impossible to crack. "If you text me an address via WhatsApp, why would it also need to be in code?"

He snorted. "Come on, really? Let me see your phone."

I reluctantly obliged.

As soon as he saw it, he exclaimed, "Ah! An iPhone SE. Even easier for someone to crack."

He sensed my frustration and explained. "Sure, WhatsApp is end-to-end encrypted and impossible to crack remotely. But all someone needs to do is knock you out, Chase, and use your thumbprint to open this phone and access the app. Heck, they could cut off your thumb, take your severed digit and phone with them, which would give them unlimited access to your phone. It's harder with facial recognition, of course." He chuckled. "You'd have to cut off their—"

I interrupted him. "Who's the paranoid and skeptical one now?" Before he could remark, I continued. "Just tell me the code, Stanley."

His eyes lit up. "It'll be a nonsensical sentence. A bunch of real words strung together in no coherent order. What you do is start at the final word of the sentence. Take the last letter of that final word and the first letter of that same word and write it down. Last letter is written down first, followed by the first letter. Do the same thing with the second last word, and so forth, all the way to the first word that starts the garbled sentence. Ignore any two- or three-letter words. They're not part of the code. Every word over three letters is in play, though. For the address, it always starts with the street number. But that number will be written out. So, an address of 2500, would start with t-w. As an example, the final word in the sentence might be 'what.' Then the second last word might be 'negative.' Then—"

"Got it," I said, holding up my hand and interrupting.

"You sure? Want me to send you a coded practice address?"

"Nope, I don't. What I want you to do is talk with Ross and convince him of what he needs convincing, then send me the address."

I made my way to the door.

Stanley stopped me by saying, "What if Ross is adamant and won't take another path?"

I shrugged. "Guess this will all be for naught then."

"But you'll be halfway or more to Mexico by the time you hear from me. And if I'm unsuccessful, you'll be pissed."

"True." I opened the door. Before closing it, I said, "And you'll owe me for time and expenses."

Once I was back in the car, I drove southeast toward Mexico. The approximately eight-hour drive flew by; my mind absorbed with the four episodes of Ross's latest podcast season, which was titled simply, *Palmera*. Each episode was nearly ninety minutes, so most of the drive was consumed by listening to Ross's deep, placating voice.

His eponymous hit series was called *Rogan's Roils*. I knew roil meant to stir up, to agitate, to bother, and that seemed fitting to me. Rogan Ross certainly liked to stir the pot. He easily picked sides, so he was far from a professional, objective journalist. He was not one to hide his motives or theories. On the contrary, Rogan Ross made his opinions and thoughts known, without question or reservation.

Perhaps that's his allure.

His latest season began with the first two episodes dedicated to the Mexican industrial town of Palmera. How it started, developed, and what it morphed into. Episode three was where things picked up steam. This was where he brought up his American CEO theory, which he then fleshed out in episode four.

One thing I liked about Ross's style was that he always used snippets of live interviews, and never shied away from tense interactions, even if the sound quality wasn't great. His podcasts were far from perfectly choreographed in the studio. That realness added to the gritty, believable element in his show.

The end of episode four was a great example of this. Ross played a sound bite where there was an intense thumping on a door. In a slightly panicked voice, which was rare for Ross, he revealed the cops were at his place. Then you heard the police barge in and shout in Spanish. I knew a little of the language, so the one command I could decipher was, "You're coming with us. Now."

Following that, you heard a fumbling with the recording device and then Ross whispered ominously, "I'll be back to report on this." A brief pause. "I hope."

That was the last episode in the season, and the final words listeners had heard from Rogan Ross in the past three weeks. Typically, in each of his previous seasons, episodes were always released one week apart. Always.

Of course, Stanley and I knew what was going on, but not the rest of the podcasting world. His sudden disappearance, combined with no new episodes being released, really stirred up his fans. There were all kinds of online chatter and theories and wild speculation about what was going on. In the true-crime podcasting world, there wasn't a greater story.

A few minutes after finishing the tense episode four, Stanley texted. At this point in the drive, I was by the Salton Sea and less than two hours from the border. I pulled off the 86 and onto a dusty, dry road that led to the slowly evaporating sea. It was summer in the desert and a million degrees outside. We'd been traveling for hours without a break, so Ranger and I hopped out for a quick tinkle. But then we piled right back into the vehicle and cranked the AC before roasting to death.

I read the text as the compressor strained to cool the cabin.

As promised, Stanley sent a gobbled phrase to my WhatsApp account. I tried reading it backward and deciphering the code without writing the letters down. It didn't work. Even after I'd written everything down, it still took me a while. Mainly because I was assuming the address would be in

English. When I realized *calle* was one of the words, which meant street in Spanish, I adjusted my expectation and deciphered the code.

Then I replied to Stanley's text with: *You succeed?*

In annoying fashion, he replied with poor punctuation: *yes everything good don't worry*

With Ross's hideout address in hand, Ranger and I were back on the road and headed straight south to the border. As usual, getting into Mexico proved to be a nonevent. For years I'd been a reluctant smart phone user. But now I had to admit I enjoyed the luxury of plugging a foreign address into my iPhone and having a lovely voice navigate me to the destination.

Except the destination was anything but lovely.

Ranger and I were in the state of Sonora, Mexico, in a small city called San Luis Rio Colorado. San Luis Rio Colorado was adjacent to the Colorado River, and directly south of the border. North of the town was Yuma, Arizona. From what I gathered, Palmera was maybe thirty clicks northwest of San Luis, situated along Mexican Route 8.

My dog whimpered and got my attention. He was sitting upright in the passenger seat, panting heavily, desperate to stick his head out the window and get some wind on his snout. I let him do that, but only for a minute since the stifling desert air rushed in and overwhelmed the air conditioner.

When Siri told me I was a few hundred feet from my destination, I pulled to the side of the dusty road and took survey. San Luis Rio Colorado was a typical-looking Mexican town. The roads were composed of powdery, dried red dirt. All the buildings were made of cinder blocks. From what I'd seen so far, there wasn't a home or business higher than two stories. The buildings, and some of their signs, were quite colorful. At least they were at one point in their existence. The reddish-brown dust that constantly swirled in the air seemed to coat everything in town, which muted the once bright colors.

I drove around the block to get a look at Ross's hideout, which was just ahead of my current position on the same side of the road. As I approached the building, I slowed and studied the structure. The street number I'd been given was 2684. On the front right side of the building hung most of the numbers. Though the four was missing, I could see from the sun's work that it had been there at one point. The number six was barely hanging on; it had pivoted down and now looked like a nine.

The building was two-story and painted a light salmon color. The ground floor had once been a *farmacia*, but it was now boarded up. There was a door opening, minus the door, on the bottom right side of the building. I could make out two steps on the left side of the opening, which I assumed was the beginning of a staircase that led to the second floor, and where I hoped Ross was cooped up. To the right of the building was a small parking lot that could maybe fit three or four cars. From my current vantage, the lot appeared to be empty.

As I turned the corner to view the building's other side, I studied the top floor. The front of the building contained only one window on the second story. It was cranked wide open. There were two small windows on the building's left side. One open, the other closed.

Driving past, I confirmed there were four parking spaces behind the building, and all the spaces were available. After circling the block, I parked three buildings down from Ross's hideout on the same side of the street. There were a couple of small shrubs on the front lawn of the home I'd parked in front of. Between those shrubs I had a view of the staircase's first steps.

I was eager to speak with Rogan Ross, to find out what he'd discovered over the last few weeks. But if his life was truly in danger, then I wanted to sit back, wait, and observe from a distance. Look for any imminent threats. See if I could spot anything or anyone unusual in the area. I was also curious about Ross's behavior and recent decisions.

Has he been holed up for weeks in this building, or does he freely come and go? Just how scared is this guy? And why is he hiding in Mexico, anyway? Why not make a run for the border and get to safety in Yuma?

Since it was six in the evening, my plan was to wait a couple of hours until after sunset. Then I'd use darkness to hide my approach. Earlier, Stanley had texted to inform me of a secret code phrase: deoxyribonucleic acid. DNA, in other words. To prove I was sent by Stanley, I was to use that phrase with Rogan Ross. Hopefully, I'd glean some answers from Ross, then load him and any of his equipment and evidence into the Caprice and make a beeline to the border.

I hadn't brought much firepower with me, just one piece. Years ago, I'd found the perfect concealed spot to hold a gun within the Caprice's doorframe. I stored the Savage there in the rare case I was stopped at the border. Or if I was stopped by the Federales at one of the many checkpoints.

While surveying the area, I slowly pried off the interior doorframe until the metal skeleton was exposed. Where the left armrest was located was now an open three-by-twelve-inch-long rectangle. It was a deep pocket, and the Savage Stance was tucked away at the bottom of that pocket.

Since the opening was so narrow, you couldn't fish your hand into the rectangle to extract the gun, which was why I'd placed it there. It was near impossible to see, and equally as challenging to get out. You simply needed the right tool, which was a neodymium magnet I'd bought off Amazon for twenty bucks.

Grabbing the thick, round magnet from the glovebox, I placed it against the metal frame at the bottom of the pocket. The small gun sucked toward the powerful magnet, then I slowly dragged it upward to the opening.

With the gun in hand, I spent the next ninety minutes watching Ross's hideout, along with its surroundings. It was a mixed residential/commercial area, so homes and businesses were intermingled. I saw nothing out of the ordinary. Across the street from the hideout was a closed tire shop with a homeless man lying motionless on a piece of dirty cardboard. Since most of the businesses were boarded up, a large population of transients shuffled up and down the street.

Ross's building was quiet and uneventful during the ninety-minute surveillance session. I confirmed that there was a small light glowing from the second-story window. But I hadn't seen any movement by the window, nor had I seen that light flicker from any movement inside. Not until I was about to head to the hideout, when near darkness had descended, did I see anyone approach the building.

It was a shoeless kid, maybe eight or nine years old, passing by the Caprice's passenger side. I couldn't make out many details, other than he had a brown paper lunch sack in his hand. The kid approached the opening and placed the sack on the first step.

After watching the kid round the corner, my eyes flicked back to the sack. They never left that brown paper bag. Probably six or so minutes later, I saw a hand reach down and grab the bag, providing confirmation that someone was indeed inside the building.

I fired up the Caprice and slowly drove into the parking lot behind the hideout. Once parked, I let Ranger out, but I kept seated and eyed the Savage Stance. After a moment, I decided to leave the gun since the area looked safe. In my mind, there was no need to make things uncomfortable with Ross if he happened to spot my piece.

Ranger and I walked into the opening and saw that it was indeed a staircase to the second story. I waited at the bottom, figuring Ross had heard the Caprice pull in back, so he'd come to the top of the stairwell to meet me.

But he didn't. After a few silent minutes of waiting, I stroked behind Ranger's right ear and patted him on the head.

"Come on, buddy," I said. "Let's go meet a famous podcaster."

FIVE

THE STAIRWELL to the second floor was pretty dark. Turning on my iPhone light, I confirmed there were no lightbulbs or even a light socket in the stairwell. And there was no door at the top either.

There were glass fragments on every step. The closer I got to the top of the stairs, the more pieces of broken glass I found. It was like someone had shattered bottles against the staircase wall, and the carnage had rained down on the steps.

As I cleared a path with the toe of my boot, I commanded Ranger behind me to protect his paws. At first, I thought the broken shards were likely a product of wild parties and neglect. But when I reached the top of the stairs, I knew I was wrong.

A six-foot-wide hallway ran down the left side of the second story. Scanning the concrete floor with my light, I saw thousands of shattered glass pieces. They covered nearly every square inch of the hallway. There was also a broom leaning against the far wall. I could see brush marks on the dirty floor, heading out from a door located straight ahead. I pictured Ross sweeping a clear path coming out that door, then reversing and putting the shards back in place as he retreated to the room with the paper bag. This was clearly an early warning detection system.

I guess Ross is taking the death threats seriously.

To my right was another closed door. While clearing a path with my boot, I proceeded to that door. As soon as I was inside, I scanned the room with my light.

The place was small and barren. One window was in the room, and it was shut tight. The stagnant, hot air overwhelmed me as I stepped in and surveyed everything. No closet, no bathroom, just a low-lying twin bed with a soiled mattress and a small wooden desk in the far corner.

With Ranger close behind, panting heavily from the heat, I slowly made my way to the other door. Before I made it there, I heard a loud voice coming from the room. It was muffled, so I couldn't exactly make out the words, but I was pretty sure it was Rogan Ross's voice.

The door to the room was wooden and old and cracked in several places. With the dry heat, the cracks had widened a lot, so I could easily see into the room. After a quick peek, I confirmed it was Ross inside. He had on over-the-ear headphones and was speaking into a microphone while sitting at a desk in front of a computer.

I knocked, then stepped back and waited. When he didn't come, I knocked louder. When he still didn't come, I thought, *so much for his early warning detection system.*

Finally, I tried pounding on the door. That worked.

Ten seconds later, I heard, "Who's there?"

"It's Garrison Chase, Ross."

"Who sent you?"

"Stanley Tuchek."

"And what's the—"

"Deoxyribonucleic acid," I said before he could finish the question.

The door unlocked and next thing I knew I was face-to-face with a sweaty Rogan Ross. If it hadn't been for his voice, I wouldn't have recognized the man.

"Hell, am I glad to see you," he said.

"With all due respect, Ross, or maybe it's Rogan. Sorry, which do you prefer?"

"Ross is fine."

"With all due respect, Ross, you don't know me."

"But I know Stanley, and I trust my colleague." He ushered me in and pointed at my dog. "Who's this?"

"Ranger," I said.

As he bent over to pet Ranger, I studied him. I'd only seen a thumbnail picture of Ross on my phone before. That photo was a handsome, professional picture of Ross that he used for his podcast page. The man before me looked nothing like that photo. Currently, Rogan Ross looked like an overworked fry cook.

His dishwater brown hair was stringy and wet and pulled behind his large ears by a green headband. The sweatband was soaked and contained an irregular line of dried sweat stretching temple to temple. His face was bearded, with scraggly brown strands going every which direction. I noted he wore the same white, pocketed T-shirt as Stanley. Ross's shirt, however, had large brown stains creeping out from the pit areas. His brown cargo shorts weren't sweaty like his shirt, but they were badly soiled. It looked like he'd been wiping his hands on them for weeks.

Rogan Ross straightened and immediately apologized. "Sorry, not just for how I look, but how I smell."

"All I smell is carne asada." Which was true. The air, though stifling, smelled like wonderful Mexican food. "The kid drop off a burrito for you?"

"Yes, but it was al pastor, not carne asada. I've been surviving off burritos the past while. One a day. You easily spotted the boy, huh?"

I nodded.

"You see anything else?"

As my eyes darted around the L-shaped room, I shook my head.

Noting my prying eyes, he said, "Welcome to Ross's Refuge." He pointed to the far corner where a seatless toilet was located. A laundry basin with a rusted tap was to its left. "That's where I freshen up." He waved his hand toward a twin mattress on the floor with two colorful Mexican blankets spread on top. "And that's the boudoir."

Walking to the desk area, he said, "And this is where the magic happens. Your timing is impeccable. I'm halfway through recording an important episode."

Everything in the room was old and crumbling and faded. But Ross's workstation was a thing of modern beauty, so it stood in stark contrast to its surroundings. There wasn't a lot of equipment on the desk, but what was there looked top of the line, from the laptop to microphone to recording devices. Thousands of dollars in technology. And a thousand yellow sticky notes, too.

"Oh, and I can't forget the air conditioner."

I looked up, confused, since I was now sweatier than Ross. Ranger was overheating as well. He'd collapsed on his side, probably to feel the somewhat colder concrete on his body and get below the suffocating heat layer.

Ross pointed to the two open windows on opposite walls. "Cross breeze is amazing. Can you feel it? Really conditions the air."

I smiled, appreciating his sarcasm. *I like this guy.*

"You been in this penthouse the whole three weeks?" I asked. "Ever since you dropped episode four?"

He returned the smile. "Penthouse, I like that. No, I haven't been here that long, just ten days. Before that, I was at a chain motel in Mexicali. Local cops put me up there."

"And you left because?"

"Not safe."

When he didn't elaborate, I prodded. "Not safe how?"

Sighing, he said, "That's a long story."

"I got time."

He shot back, "I don't."

I scowled.

Ross tried to clarify. "I mean, like right now I don't have time."

Still not liking that answer, my scowl deepened.

"Listen," he said. "I'm probably two hours out from wrapping part one of the best podcast season of my life. I'm biased here, so maybe it's the best true-crime podcast season ever, or at least will be. When I'm recording like this, I'm in a zone. It's bad, I'll admit it. Didn't even hear you drive in or come up the stairs. But I need to get this done, then you need to get me out of here in the morning."

I remained calm. "Part one, Ross? I had a lot of questions before, now I have even more."

"I'm sure you do. What I was thinking . . ." He hustled over to the bed. Picking up a small square silver device with earbuds attached, he continued. "I have episodes five through seven downloaded on this old Apple Nano mp3 player. Figure it's probably safest on this device since who would steal an old, obsolete Nano, am I right?"

I didn't respond.

"While I finish, listen to these episodes, Garrison. Or is it Chase? Sorry, which do you prefer?"

"Chase is fine."

"You'll be the first to hear these episodes, Chase. And, of course, most of your questions will be answered. In fact, it will be great to have someone else know what I know. A relief actually. What do you think?"

Honestly, it was a decent idea. But I needed some answers from him right now. "What I think, Ross, is that we need to cover some basics before I listen to your podcasts."

"Like what?"

"Like, why you're here in Mexico still, and why you need *me* to bring you back. Sounds like the Mexican authorities turned on you in Mexicali, so why not break for the border yourself and hide out in Yuma?"

"Because I don't trust anyone, not the Mexican authorities or the Americans. Both parties are looking for me at the border, so I don't stand a chance of getting across. If the Mexicans don't nab me before I cross, the Americans will get me at the border checkpoint."

Before I could respond, he continued. "Stanley told me you're skilled and trustworthy, and I need somebody like that right now. Plus, it's my understanding you have a sedan with a trunk."

Suddenly it dawned on me. "So, you want me to smuggle you across the border? That's quite the ask, Ross, and quite the risk."

He nodded. "It is, no doubt. The way I see it, you and I have zero connection, so nobody is looking for you. You're on no one's radar, so you can freely and easily cross the border. And besides, when was the last time a border agent popped your trunk and looked inside?"

I didn't particularly like his plan, but at least I knew what it was. And since I had more important questions to ask, I moved on. "I'm doing this because of what you uncovered, and to protect the evidence you have. Just as long as we're in agreement about what to do with the intel you've gathered."

"What do you mean? Not sure I'm following."

I sighed. "The agreement Stanley and you discussed."

Rogan Ross tilted his head, genuinely confused.

"About my involvement," I continued. "The cost for me helping out and seeing this through."

"No idea what you're talking about."

"Stanley didn't discuss my terms with you?"

"Nope," he replied, shaking his head. "Stanley didn't say a word about that. Not a word."

SIX

I DIDN'T THINK it was physically possible to feel any hotter.

Apparently, I was wrong.

Rogan Ross knew something was up with me. I imagined it had to do with the steam emanating from my ears. To try to diffuse the situation, he thrust the Nano toward me. "Please, Chase, give this a listen. I promise it will help. You'll know what I've been going through the past three weeks, and what I've uncovered."

When he thrust it at me again, I intercepted his hand. I didn't smack it away in anger. Instead, I grabbed his wrist and held it firmly.

"What Stanley didn't tell you were my terms of agreement. And they're important, wouldn't you say?"

"I'm sorry, Chase. The kid is . . ."

I let go of his wrist. "Forget Stanley. The situation is straightforward here. I agreed to get you and the evidence to safety if you turned over your findings to the authorities. None of this outing the killer on your podcast business."

"Well, that's gonna prove to be complicated, Chase. And here's why."

He started to hand the Nano back, but I waved both hands at him to stop, then I ordered him to sit on the bed as I walked toward the desk to get his chair.

Over my shoulder, I said, "I'll listen to the episodes, Ross, absolutely I will. But we're gonna talk about some things and set the record straight before that happens."

I took pause at his desk since I saw something familiar poking out from under a manila folder. Pushing the folder aside revealed a black handgun. A Beretta 92 FS. It was a reliable 9mm pistol, one of the most reliable pistols in the world, in fact.

Holding it up, I asked, "You know how to use this?"

He was about to respond with yes, then stopped himself. "Uh, not really."

Since there was a healthy black market for guns in Mexico, and Ross reasonably feared for his life, it wouldn't be terribly difficult for him to acquire a gun like this. I put it down on his desk and wheeled the screechy chair toward the bed.

"I can get details," I said, "from your podcast. For now, I need to know broadly what's going on, and why you don't trust anyone. Most importantly, why you feel the need to out the killer publicly."

He scooted back on the bed until his spine touched the wall. The window was immediately to his left. "How much do you know? That will give me a place to start."

After sitting in the chair, I said, "I listened to the first four episodes of the season, so I know the backstory. I also know the Federales or local police gave you some crime scene evidence to process, which you sent to Stanley. Ultimately, that evidence confirmed the American CEO involvement, maybe even the killer or killers themselves, then you went into hiding."

He nodded along but didn't say anything. Instead, he stared out the window.

I interrupted his thinking. "That about right, Ross?"

"So much more has happened," he said, shaking his head. "So much you and Stanley don't know."

"Like I said, give me the condensed version."

He refocused and looked at me. "Alright, I was at a motel in Palmera putting the finishing touches on episode four when the local police came knocking. They took me to their station. There I met a detective who said that I was onto something with my podcast, and that they needed my help. Long story short, I was given evidence to process since they didn't have the type of equipment we had in the States. Something like that would never happen in America, but we were in Mexico, after all, so I didn't question it. Anyway, I was given various fibers, semen and hair samples, pieces of broken glass with touch DNA on them, pieces that looked like they were from stemware like a wine glass, and what looked to be napkins, too."

"Stemware and napkins, why? Those items weren't found at the crime scenes, were they?"

"I never got a solid answer to whether they were found directly at the crime scenes or not. At first, it confused me, but my developing theory helped to explain it."

When he didn't elaborate, I said, "I suppose I'll find that out in a later podcast, right?"

He nodded. "You will. The Mexican authorities also gave me blood."

"Blood? I thought the victims were all drugged and there was no blood at the scenes?"

"The blood was extracted from the deceased victims. Not only did the cops want us to process any perp DNA that we could isolate from the evidence, but they also wanted us to use our software to identify the victims since they couldn't do it. It was a great test for our company, so I was all in favor of that part of the investigation. Mexican authorities gave me access to some crucial foreign databases and our software was able to find matches. Stanley doesn't even know the results because I was doing this all in hiding while in Mexicali."

He paused, probably because of the confused look on my face. He pointed to the logo above his shirt pocket. "You don't know what we do, do you?"

I shook my head. "Not exactly."

"I'll fill you in on that later. Back to the story: So, I was ecstatic to identify all these victims and the connection they shared, which you can hear about in episode six. I was also, of course, thrilled we isolated American CEO DNA from some of the evidence provided. But just as I'm putting this all together, I'm approached by one of the local cops at the Mexicali motel, one of the men who originally took me to the station. This cop tells me the detective leading the Night Night Killer investigation is full of shit. That I'd been given false evidence to implicate the CEOs. And, in reality, the Night Night Killer is actually Mexican, and the local authorities are using me and Futurum to get back at America for their exploitation of local Mexican workers."

"Geez," I said, standing and pushing the chair back. "I told Stanley there was a chance you and your company were a patsy in all this."

Ross nodded. "I mean, that was in the back of my head before the cop told me this. So, when he admitted to it, I was crushed. And I didn't think he had any motive for lying. Until . . ."

"Until what?"

"Until I confronted the lead detective," Ross said, shaking his head in frustration. Droplets of sweat rained down on the bed. "And that set off a witch hunt in his local police station."

"How so?"

"Apparently, this detective went nuts and shook down all the cops involved in bringing me to the station and watching me at the motel. He came back to me with a story about a corrupt cop on his team. Told me that a week prior, the FBI field office in Phoenix had been in Palmera poking around and asking questions. And one of those FBI agents approached this Mexican cop. The agent threatened the cop, told him to feed me the story about the evidence being fake, obviously to cast dispersion away from the American CEOs."

"Threatened him with what? His life? No way. I can't believe that."

Ross shook his head. "No, not his life, his family. This Mexican cop has some close relatives living in Arizona, and two of those relatives were of somewhat questionable character. The agent said they'd spend some considerable time in the American prison system if the cop didn't come through and push the false narrative."

By this point, I was pacing and thinking.

Ross continued. "At first, I thought the detective may be feeding me some serious BS. But then I confirmed that the Phoenix field office had visited Palmera, and that this local cop indeed had some relatives in the States with spotty criminal activity. So, it was plausible the FBI, or at least a rogue agent in the Phoenix office, was shaking down the cop."

I think Ross paused to let me say something, but I was still too entrenched in my thoughts.

"Now I have a huge problem, Chase, because I don't know who's lying and who's telling the truth. If this detective is telling the truth, then we have a cover-up by the FBI, but if he's lying, then he's covering up the truth about a Mexican serial killer. And who knows how far up the chain his orders go. My plan, once I was safely back in America and secured the evidence I had, was to visit the Phoenix field office and ask some questions and try to figure this out. I even called them today and set up a meeting for tomorrow, hoping you'd get me across the border safely in the morning."

I stopped pacing and looked at Ross. A woman I knew had recently been promoted to the top job at the Phoenix field office. "With whom?"

"Believe it or not, one of the top dogs there, a woman."

"Which woman?"

"What's her name?" He tapped his fingers on the bed. "It's written on a sticky note on my desk."

I hurried over. There were at least thirty yellow sticky notes in view, most were stuck on top of the desk or on one of the many manila folders. A few were stuck on a monitor that was attached to the laptop, which acted as a second screen.

"Where?" I asked as my eyes darted from note to note.

"Top left corner of the desk."

My eyes tracked there. At the top of a sticky note I read her name: Ramona Sanchez. Below that was a location and time.

I asked, "Did you speak with her directly?"

He nodded. "Yes, but not at first. Once I told them who I was, they reluctantly patched me through to her. What does it matter, anyway?"

I didn't answer since I was back in my head. I knew and trusted this woman, enough to know she wouldn't be involved in a conspiracy to protect American CEOs.

Boy, will she be surprised if I show up to the meeting with Rogan Ross.

"Chase, what's going on? Talk to me."

I refocused. It wasn't time to inform Ross that I knew the Special Agent in Charge of the Phoenix field office. Besides, something else chewed at the back of my mind.

I said, "I get why you don't trust anyone and don't want to give evidence to the feds. However, the evidence is in question now, right? That must mean you don't know the Night Night Killer's identity, which means you can't be revealing the identity in your podcast finale."

"Yes and no," he replied.

Before I could question him, he said, "Remember I told you I was currently wrapping part one of the finale? My plan is to let listeners in on these two conspiracy theories, which is going to generate a lot of buzz. Meanwhile, I'll investigate this rogue agent and the FBI's involvement in part two of the season, see if that story holds up. It's incredibly important to figure out if this detective is telling the truth or not. Because . . ." Ross stood and walked to his desk. He sorted through some files and held up a folder. "I believe I've isolated the killer's identity."

"How'd you do that? Broadly speaking, no need for a science lecture."

"Episode six goes into the details. But basically, I isolated a single male profile that wasn't an actual victim, nor was it a match with any American CEOs that have a company in Palmera. So, it's good evidence, and it could be our man. But if the detective is lying and has given me false evidence to throw me off, then I can't trust anything the Mexicans gave me, certainly not this profile." He waved the folder.

I couldn't stand it any longer. "Okay, so who? Who do you believe is the Night Night Killer?"

"Don't know," he stated.

I deflated. "You don't know. I'm confused. Didn't you just say you knew his identity?"

"Sorry, let me clarify: I've identified his DNA profile, Chase, not his actual identity. Those are two different things. I haven't been able to figure out his name and whereabouts. With our software, along with Stanley's expertise, I think we'll figure it out, though. I just need the kid to do his magic. He's much better and faster at using our software since he created it."

"What about the CEOs then? I thought you connected one or more of them to the scenes?"

"Right, I did. But there's also a plausible reason for why their DNA is attached to some of the victims, especially since much of the evidence is touch DNA. At any rate, it doesn't necessarily make any of them the killer. You'll find out that connection in episodes five and six."

I nodded. "But they still could be involved, right? The CEOs simply hired a hitman to do the job and you have that hitman's DNA profile in your hand."

"Absolutely." He waved the folder again. "Stanley needs to identify this person, then we need to figure out who he's connected to, or who he's been hired by."

"Right," I said. "But we first need to confront the Phoenix field office. If we can conclude this agent in their office is indeed trying to throw us off, then we'll know the detective is telling the truth, and we can reasonably trust the evidence he gave you."

"That's the plan."

"And I'll go along and help with this plan if you agree to my original terms."

Ross hesitated on his response.

"Listen," I said, "I know plenty of people in law enforcement on the other side of the border. A few people I trust with my life, a few that will properly handle this. I promise you."

He thought about it, then pointed at me. "As long as it's not Stanley's father."

I nodded. "Agreed."

"Now, I have a part one finale to wrap, and you . . ." he said as he handed me the Nano, "have some listening to do."

I took the mp3 player and earbuds.

"When I'm finished," Ross continued, "which should be before first light, I'll pack everything in your car and then hopefully we can cross the border without incident."

"I'll give you some privacy and listen in the other room, but I'm going to leave Ranger in here with you. He'll be on the alert while you're recording."

"Sounds good. Very good, since I'll be distracted."

"Oh, and since you don't really know how to use this, I'll take it with me." I swept up the Beretta 92 FS. Ross didn't argue.

Instead, he walked over to his bed and said, "Take this blanket for the bed in there. You're liable to get some skin disease if you lay on that mattress without protection."

After ordering Ranger to stay, I went to the other room. I laid the blanket on the mattress and got into the same position Ross was in the other room: directly beside the window with my spine pressed against the concrete wall.

I pushed the earbuds in, which blocked out most of the ambient noise, and began listening to episode five. About a half hour in, I couldn't stand the heat and got off the bed. The backs of my legs were saturated with sweat from sitting on top of the blanket. I moved onto the cold concrete floor to find some relief. Not caring it was dirty, I laid on my back with my knees up and my bare feet flat on the floor. The Nano was on my chest and the Beretta was on the ground to my immediate left.

I kept listening. So far, episode five detailed what had happened with Ross after the cops pounded on his door. Just as the podcast moved into new territory, I felt my eyes grow heavy. I knew the tiredness was a combination of the intense heat and a long day. Plus, I'd been trying to slow my breathing and remain still for fear of sweating even more. All that made me sleepy.

I turned up the volume on the Nano and settled back into position, hoping Ross's loud voice would keep me awake. Minutes later, while listening with my eyes closed, a smell wafted into the room. It was sharp and pungent, and I immediately opened my eyes and sat up.

And saw thick, white smoke pouring through the open door.

Ripping out the earbuds, I heard a hissing sound. I knew it was gas pouring from some canister that I couldn't see. I swept up the Beretta and stayed low, crawling fast toward the door to close it.

The smoke overwhelmed me, however. As I grabbed the bottom edge of the door to swing it shut, I collapsed onto my chest in a coughing fit. Once the coughing stopped, I inhaled the smoke. Just a little. I had to. I desperately needed a breath.

As I sucked in air, my lungs caught on fire.

Before I knew it, as I lay on my back clutching my throat, darkness descended.

SEVEN

MY EYES FLICKERED OPEN, first the left then the right.

It was dark. *Where am I?*

Sitting up, it took a few seconds for my eyes to adjust, then to remember where I was. *Mexico, that's right. At Ross's hideout. Wait, Ross and Ranger. Are they OK?*

I stood on a shaky pair of legs and stumbled to Ross's room. Busting in, I immediately saw my dog lying on his side in front of the desk. Which, by the way, was barren. No laptop, screens, folders, or sticky notes. Nothing.

Ranger craned his neck in my direction and whimpered, so I knew he was okay. My eyes flashed to the corner, to the area Ross had referred to as the boudoir. The podcaster was laying on his side in the middle of the bed. For a moment, I thought he was asleep.

Then, because of his body's placement—in the fetal position with his hands clasped and tucked under his right cheek—I panicked and ran over, shouting, "Ross! Ross!"

He didn't move.

Fearing the worst, I reached him and shook his shoulder. Rogan Ross didn't stir. I felt for his pulse. Nothing.

"No, no, no." I frantically poked at his neck. I knew it wasn't that hard to find the carotid artery, but I kept trying anyway, desperate to feel a pulse. After searching both sides of his neck and placing my hand over his mouth and nose to feel a breath, I staggered back, as dejected as I had been in recent memory. Suddenly I moved forward, reaching my hands toward the pocket of his dirty white T-shirt.

I fished out the infamous calling card.

As I looked over the cream-colored business card with the words Night Night emboldened on the front, I slithered to a sitting position.

Rogan Ross is dead. The latest victim of the Night Night Killer.

With my back against the bed, I flicked the business card away and pounded my fists on the concrete floor, pissed that I failed to protect him. Pissed at my mistakes.

Why did I put those stupid earbuds in and turn the podcast up so loud?

I kept thinking about that. If I hadn't put in the earbuds, or at least had the volume low, I might've heard the killer sneaking up the stairs. At the very least I would've heard the hissing gas a lot sooner, and I could've acted right away. Maybe not passed out so quickly.

My thoughts kept spiraling on all the things I could've done differently. I could've sat at the top of the stairwell, or maybe on the landing, and listened to the podcasts there. That would've probably kept me awake and helped me spot the killer.

Suddenly I was pulled back to reality as Ranger licked my left elbow. My dog teetered on shaky legs, so I knew he still felt the effects of the gas. As I rubbed behind his ear, I thought about Rogan Ross's loved ones and his millions of fans, and the shock that would follow. Then I looked around—at the near desolate room—and thought about all the evidence he'd given his life to collect.

Now gone.

After wallowing a moment longer, I stood and went to the desk. Not one thing was on that desk. Searching the rest of the room, I found nothing. No folders or files or even a single sticky note.

The Night Night Killer had taken Ross's life, and everything else of investigative value.

My mind flashed to the Nano, and the incredibly important episodes that were downloaded onto the mp3 player. I rushed to the other room. The first place I looked was on the ground where I'd succumbed to the gas.

No sign of the Nano.

I searched the bed, whipping off the blanket from the mattress, then scraping the mattress of its frame. Nothing. In fact, the only thing left in the small room was the Beretta 92 FS.

The killer had placed it directly in the center of the small wooden desk.

I collapsed into the chair, thinking about why the killer had left the gun and placed it on the desk. The killer was known for maintaining a clean crime scene. To date, he hadn't used any weapon other than a syringe, so it made some sense why he didn't use the gun or take it with him.

Why spare me, though?

Just then, I noted a sliver of light filtering into the room. Dawn was breaking. I had to move. Immediately I started thinking about a plan, about how to handle the dead body. About how to handle the murder in general.

Do I do the logical thing and call the police? The more I mulled that over, however, the more uneasy I felt about that move. Mainly because Rogan Ross was clearly onto something big. Obviously, his death threats and conspiracy suspicions were now validated by his murder. Completely.

But who's responsible exactly?

That proved to be a complex problem in my mind. I debated over and over about calling in the homicide. In the end, I came to the same conclusion as Ross: I didn't trust anyone, certainly not the local authorities. If I called this in, no doubt the Mexican detective would question me. And who knows how he'd respond to my presence at the murder scene. Who knows if he'd suspect me as the killer. And if that were the case, would he haul me off to jail? Worse, prison?

The more I thought about that, the more I leaned toward not calling it in. Besides, I didn't have that much to tell the police about the crime scene, anyway. Of course, I did know broadly what Ross had been up to, and about what he'd discovered. But, ultimately, I didn't feel comfortable telling any of those details to the detective. Not until I found out if he was corrupt or not. So, I decided I was out of there. I'd head across the border and meet Ramona Sanchez at eleven, then decide how much I should tell her.

With my mind made up, I went back to Ross's room. Ranger was up and doing much better. The paper sack that had contained Ross's burrito was on the floor, and a couple of napkins had spilled out. Using those napkins, I methodically wiped down any surface I'd touched, or thought I'd touched, including the calling card, which I tucked back into his shirt pocket.

Then I went to the other room and did the same.

Before I left the building, I stood over the desk and contemplated what to do about the Beretta. Since it was the one thing I knew the killer had moved, I decided to take it with me. Though I doubted the killer would've left prints on the gun, you never knew, so it was worth a shot to get it checked. Plus, in my mind, leaving the gun behind unnecessarily complicated the crime scene.

To preserve any potential evidence, I gingerly placed the Beretta into the brown paper sack, which was the best storage bag I could find. Following that, Ranger and I proceeded down the stairs.

Early sunlight was in full effect now, so I had to be careful not to be spotted leaving the crime scene. At the stairwell landing, I glanced left and right. Aside from the homeless man across the street sleeping on his side— still not moving—nobody was in sight. I hurried around the corner toward the Caprice.

Ranger hopped in through the driver's side door. I followed. After firing up the car, I put the Beretta and Savage Stance into the hidden door compartment, then I backed out and slowly left the parking lot. The temperature was probably at its lowest for the day, maybe around ninety degrees, so I rolled down the window for Ranger.

He popped his head out as I steered north, headed to the nearest border crossing, then on to Phoenix. I pictured that sticky note with Ramona Sanchez's name on it, along with the location and time for today's meeting.

Addressing Ranger, I said, "We need to figure out who's telling the truth, pal. More importantly, we need to catch this killer." My mind drifted to my son and the fact that I'd be back in Mexico to pick him up soon. I patted my dog. "And we only have two days to do it, buddy."

EIGHT

To MAKE sure the tall man didn't circle back, Leon waited five minutes before moving.

When he felt confident the coast was clear, he reached from under his blanket and grabbed his phone, which he'd perched against the back wheel of the shopping cart. The cell was pointed directly at the building across the street. The video camera was on, so he pressed the button to stop recording, then replayed the video and smiled.

Gotcha, he thought.

Leon still didn't move, though, for close to an hour. He waited and watched, all the while listening to Rogan Ross's final episode on the mp3 player. At the hour mark, he knew the tall man hadn't alerted the police to the murder. Nobody had shown up to the salmon-colored building, certainly not the police, so Leon suspected no one was coming.

Sitting up, he stopped the mp3 player, then pulled out the earbuds and breathed a sigh of relief. His impromptu plan had worked; it'd been worth the risk returning to the scene.

After taking care of Rogan Ross, Leon debated taking out the tall man, too. But he didn't want to use the gun for fear of noise, not to mention the mess it would make. And, unfortunately, he didn't have a backup dose for his syringe. The tall man showed up unexpectedly, so he wasn't prepared to deal with an extra man and his dog.

Leon spent hours going through all of Rogan Ross's files. After reading everything and listening to some podcasts, he felt confident that Rogan Ross had not learned his identity. Therefore, the tall man didn't know either.

Therefore, he could live.

With the tall man and dog still unconscious, Leon took two trips to load his shopping cart, which he'd kept at the bottom of the staircase. He placed every important item of Ross's into the cart, then covered the equipment and files with his ragged blankets. He pushed the cart a mile and a half to his vehicle, which he'd parked at the local bus depot. At his car, he emptied the shopping cart into the trunk and headed back to the scene. He took his same position across the street from the building, then set up the video recording.

For the second time in a few minutes, Leon replayed that video. This time he zoomed in when the footage was playing. Though it was quite early in the morning, there was enough light to ensure a clear, grain-free record-ing. The tall man's identity could easily be determined.

Phase two is underway, he thought. Though it wasn't how he planned for this phase to start, it would work, nonetheless. In fact, it would cause even greater confusion. And the more confusion he could generate, the more chance what was really going on would stay buried.

Leon packed his few belongings and headed back to his vehicle.

Got work to do, he thought. *First a video to edit, then a decision on whom to send it to.*

By the time he reached his car, Leon had made up his mind. Since both the Americans and Mexicans would love to know the Night Night Killer's identity, he'd send it to both parties.

You may get to live, tall man, but you're about to get a rude awakening.

NINE

I drove straight to Phoenix, stopping just once for gas after crossing the border.

Along the way, I did my best to remember my conversation with Ross. Unfortunately, I hadn't learned anything from the podcasts since I passed out before reaching new territory.

But I couldn't continue dwelling on what I hadn't learned, or what I hadn't asked. I tried that for about an hour. All it did was send my mind into a flurry of self-deprecating thoughts, which was certainly not productive.

Instead, I nailed down the details of what I did know, of what I could remember. Following that, I thought about Ramona Sanchez. We'd met a few years back on a job I was doing for a buddy who runs an investigative firm out of Washington, DC. At that time, my pal's firm had been hired by a senator who'd received death threats from another senator. To make a long story short, I discovered the bodies of both senators, in what initially appeared to be a murder-suicide. I met Agent Ramona Sanchez when the feds were called in.

I quickly realized there was a third person involved in the senators' deaths, but only Agent Sanchez believed me. She and I worked the case, and together we uncovered a massive cover-up among some of the top politicians in our country. And then Ramona and I took those men down.

For that, she was rewarded with a promotion, first taking a senior agent position in Washington, then taking the top job in Phoenix. The fact that she didn't hesitate to take down these powerful politicians told me it was near impossible she'd be involved with a conspiracy to protect American CEOs, especially when it involved a mass killing situation.

I arrived in Phoenix an hour before the planned meeting. Ross and Ramona were set to meet at a Mexican restaurant at 11:00 a.m. After locating the place, a spot called Pepe's, which was slightly west of downtown, I parked the Caprice a block away on the other side of the street.

Once parked, I pulled out my phone to text Stanley. He needed to know that his partner was dead. Plus, I wanted him to get on the road to Phoenix so we could communicate in person. I needed to tell him what Ross had been working on, and to see if he could possibly make sense of the DNA evidence he'd processed for Ross. Plus, I wanted to give him the Beretta to scan for fingerprints or touch DNA.

Playing Stanley's code game, I fired off a text to him through Whats-App, which amounted to this garbled sentence: *dada earned sushi snakes other.*

Translation: *Ross is dead.*

Since that text took far too long to compose, and too many brain cells, I sent the next text in plain language: *Drive to Phoenix now. Will text address later.*

Then I waited for Ramona Sanchez.

She arrived a few minutes before eleven, sweeping out of a compact, nondescript white car, which I guessed was an Uber. At first, I didn't recognize her. During the case we worked in Washington, she always wore a professional knee-length skirt and tweed jacket. But today she wore dark black jeans and a white, cotton button-up shirt. Her sleeves were haphazardly rolled up to her elbows, and it appeared she had some type of cowboy boot on her feet.

When in the southwest, dress the part, I guess.

Ramona strode purposefully past the restaurant, then darted between

Pepe's and the business next door to it, which was a photocopying store.

"Back soon, pal," I said to Ranger. "Hopefully it won't get too hot for you." I turned off the Caprice, rolled down all four windows, then made my way to the restaurant.

Looking down the alley, I saw a small patio at the back of the restaurant. I assumed Ramona was waiting for Ross there, or that she entered the restaurant through the back door. I proceeded in through the front door. A kind-looking, perhaps thirty-year-old waitress was bussing a table to my right. When she glanced my way, I told her I was meeting Ramona Sanchez. She ushered me to a small room at the back of the restaurant.

The room was filled with oversized dark-stained wood furniture with plenty of colorful tapestries on the wall. I imagined it was usually reserved for a small dinner party. Fifteen to twenty people could probably fit in the room.

In the far corner, at a chunky wood table meant for four, sat Ramona Sanchez. She was facing the room's entrance, so her mouth dropped a little when I breezed into the room. It'd been a while since I'd laid eyes on Ramona, but she still looked as striking as ever. Her silky, jet-black hair hung to her shoulders, as straight as a ruler. Ramona's skin was smooth and flawless. It had a deep olive hue and seemed to glow in the room's somewhat dim lighting. I always thought Ramona Sanchez could be Sofia Vergara's sister or close cousin. At the very least, she looked related to the Vergara bloodline. If my father were alive, he'd say, "She's easy on the eyes, son. Very easy on the eyes."

That was one thing my father and I could agree upon.

"Garrison Chase?" Ramona said with a sheepish grin, which quickly turned to a confused look. "What on earth are you doing here?"

As the wheels in her head spun, I returned the smile and took a seat across from her.

Suddenly she nodded and said, "I get it. You know Stanley Tuchek, of course. And Ross and Stanley work together, so he wanted you to join the meeting since you have a history working for the feds. Didn't know you were all in this together. Where is Rogan Ross, by the way? Parking the car?"

Before I could respond, she reached out and touched my left hand. "So good to see you, Garrison, it's been too long."

I momentarily got lost in her vibrant green eyes and warm touch. I wanted to respond with something witty, but my mind was blank. Also, it didn't seem appropriate considering how I'd have to answer her question about Ross.

Taking a direct approach, I said, "He won't be coming. Ross is dead."

She pulled her hand back and looked straight down at the table. Blinked a couple of times. Just then the waitress interrupted us by placing a basket of glistening tortilla chips on the table and a small bowl of cranberry-red salsa next to it. The waitress asked if we'd like to hear the lunch specials.

Ramona looked up from the table. "I'm afraid we won't be eating. I just lost my appetite." She glanced my way. "But if you'd like to eat, by all means."

I rarely lost my appetite, so I was ready to go. But again, that didn't seem appropriate in the moment. "No, I'm good, thanks."

When the waitress left, Ramona leaned forward. "Rogan Ross is dead. Dead how?"

I looked around. "We okay to talk here?"

"This is a safe place. My dad used to take me here as a kid. He's a friend of the owner. Any time I need a quiet place to meet a source, or speak with someone off the record, I take them here."

I hadn't known she grew up in the Phoenix area, which may be one of the reasons she relocated here from DC. But that was a conversation for another time.

"Dead like murdered," I responded.

"You're kidding?"

Ramona slumped back. Her side of the table was against the wall, so her head rested against the large red cushion behind her. "Murdered, Garrison? Really?"

"Take a moment," I said, "because it gets worse."

She remained still, with her head tilted slightly toward the ceiling. "How so?"

"He was murdered by the Night Night Killer."

She slid forward. For a moment, Ramona didn't speak. Instead, she leaned on her forearms and glared. An outsider watching might think she was pissed at me. I knew better. Since Ramona was a deep thinker, I knew her mind was reeling at that piece of intel, which caused a scowl on her face.

Finally, she spoke. "But Rogan Ross is midthirties and white. And American. None of those traits fit the Night Night Killer's victim profile or his MO."

"Understood. But this isn't about the killer's MO. This is about silencing Ross because he was onto the killer."

"He was? I mean, for real he was? I know he proposed some theories in his podcast. And there's been some wild rumors in the halls of the DOJ that he might out the killer's identity on his podcast. But I didn't really give him, or those theories, any credence."

"Well, you should've, because now we know they were credible. He actually had the killer's DNA profile in his possession, just hadn't identified the man yet."

"Tell me you have that DNA profile."

"I can't. I'm sorry. The killer took Ross's life, and all his evidence."

She leaned back again. Moments later, she brought the conversation around to me. "So, how'd you get tangled up in this? What's your story?"

"Stanley Tuchek. He approached me and asked for help with Ross. Told me Ross was in hiding in Mexico with important information, too scared to make a move. Since I found the whole story fascinating, yesterday I drove to Mexico with the intention of grabbing Ross and bringing him—along with his evidence—safely back to the States."

"When was he murdered exactly?"

"This morning, early hours."

"In Mexico?"

I nodded. "Just across the border from Yuma."

She glanced at her watch, then opened her phone. "If this murder happened over eight hours ago, why haven't I heard about it yet? My phone should be lighting up."

I braced for the scorn. "Because I'm the only one that knows, and you're the first person I've told. My guess, since Ross was in hiding and not exactly entertaining guests, is that his body hasn't been found yet. It could be a while, in fact."

Ramona put both palms on the table. "You didn't call it in?"

"Nope."

"Seriously?"

"Seriously."

She leaned onto her palms. "And why not?"

"Well, for one, because of this very meeting."

"What's that mean?"

"Like I said, Ross believed he had the killer's DNA profile in hand, but he also had conflicting reports in his head. He had multiple stories about who was trying to cover up for the responsible party. In his mind, either the Americans were trying to cover up the CEO involvement via a rogue agent in your office, or the Mexicans were trying to cover up a Mexican serial killer by using their lead detective on the case. Out of due diligence, Ross made this meeting with you to see if he could clear your office of wrongdoing."

Ramona narrowed her eyes, clearly not happy.

I tried to smooth things over. "I trust you, Ramona, implicitly, which is why I'm telling you everything. It's not out of the realm of possibility that you have a rogue agent on your hands who's in the back pocket of some wealthy CEOs. It's also very plausible that the Mexican detective leading the case is outright lying. Point is, I'm with Ross on this one: I don't trust any party at this point, certainly not the local authorities in Mexico. Which is why I didn't call them. If they're deep into a cover-up, who knows what they might've done with me, or tried to pin on me, right? Especially if they know the killer is Mexican and just murdered an American citizen. They'll double down on the cover-up."

"My field office?" she said. "My office? You and Ross think that someone in my office is corrupt? Is what, covering up for a mass murderer of innocent Mexican men? That's what you think?"

"Maybe I should start at the beginning. I jumped right to the conspiracy without providing context and details."

She huffed. "Maybe you should. Go ahead, start at the beginning."

So, I did.

As I progressed through the story, Ramona slinked back and calmed down. Near the end of my story, she was relaxed and asking appropriate follow-up questions. At the end of my tale, I paused to allow Ramona some time to process everything. I was also hungry and could no longer sit and stare at the bowl of chips and salsa.

As I partook, Ramona shook her head and said, "You're unbelievable."

I crunched a chip. "How so?"

"Let me get this straight: You drive to Mexico to bring a famous podcaster and his damning evidence safely back to the States. Instead, the podcaster winds up murdered, all the evidence he collected is taken, you're somehow spared, then you sneak away from an international murder scene because you're unsure who you can trust—which may have some steep repercussions for you—and now you're crunching away on chips and salsa like you might never eat again."

I shrugged. "Not sure what my appetite has to do with any of this."

"Just that you have one is impressive. You do realize that the Night Night Killer might have you next in his sight. His MO is a death blow via injection. Since you showed up unexpectedly yesterday, maybe the killer didn't have enough pentobarbital. Right? Which means you could be his next target."

She had a point, for sure. I could be next on the hit list. However, since the killer could've taken me out with the Beretta, I wasn't entirely convinced of that. At any rate, I didn't want to bring up the Beretta with Ramona until Stanley processed the weapon, or until I had confidence that nobody on her team was on the take.

"First of all, I appreciate your concern, Ramona, but I can take care of myself. Second, I crossed the border. And to our knowledge the killer hasn't crossed the border and been active in the States."

"That's an assumption, Garrison. An awfully big one."

"It is," I agreed. "But a valid one, right?"

She didn't answer. "It seems you and Ross are giving a lot of credit to the story about one of my agents being corrupt. How come? What makes you think it isn't all a lie to cast dispersion away from a Mexican serial killer?"

"I mean, it could be a lie, absolutely. What gave Ross pause was the fact that some important details from the Mexican cop's story checked out."

"Like what?"

"Like your office visited Palmera with a few agents at the time the Mexican cop said you did, so there was opportunity."

"True, but that's fairly common knowledge and doesn't mean much. What else?"

"It also checked out that this Mexican cop had close relatives in Arizona with a criminal past, which is a decent pressure point that someone could push."

"Again true, but not that hard to find out, and still a stretch. I'm skeptical, Garrison."

"And you should be. How well do you know your agents that visited Palmera?"

"Pretty well, but I haven't been in Phoenix long. So . . ."

"So, it's worth looking into."

She reluctantly nodded. "It is, and to be honest, not that hard to do."

"Right. I'm sure you can find out if any of the agents who visited Palmera ran a check on the cop's Arizona relatives."

"I'll dig, absolutely." Right then her cell buzzed, but she didn't look at it. "In the meantime, what to do about Ross's body? We must report it."

I thought about that. She was right. One thing that concerned me was the young kid finding the dead body. I could see the kid leaving a burrito on the steps tonight, then returning the following night to see it still sitting there. The kid might venture up the stairs to check on Ross. And in that heat, with forty-eight hours of rigor mortis doing its thing, I couldn't imagine the sight and smell.

"You're right, Ramona. I debated making an anonymous call after crossing the border. But you can't find a pay phone these days, which meant I had to use my cell. And a so-called anonymous tip could easily be traced back to me, and therefore not so anonymous."

Ramona frowned. "Which is problematic for you since you're guilty of fleeing a murder scene."

"Exactly."

Her cell buzzed again.

As she went to grab it, I interrupted her. "What if your office calls it in? You can tell local authorities you received a tip about Ross's hideout location. They'll storm in there to apprehend him, only to find him dead."

While looking at her phone and punching in the security code, she said, "That could work."

I took the moment to open my phone. Since I kept the phone in perpetual silent mode, I had no idea if Stanley had responded to my last text. Sure enough, he had. He'd sent two texts via WhatsApp. Both were in code. It took me a little bit to decipher the first text.

It read: *Freaking out about Ross*. Before deciphering the next text, I looked up. Ramona was staring at me. She had that same scowl on her face as earlier. This time, however, I couldn't tell if she was deep in thought about something or actually pissed at me.

She glanced at her cell, then back to me.

"What's up?" I asked. "Are you going to call it in?"

"Nope. I'm not."

"Why not?"

"No need."

"They already found the body?"

"They did."

"Good," I said.

"Great even," she replied. "It gets better."

"How so?"

"They also have a picture of the killer fleeing the complex."

"No way." I thought about that for a second. "But the killer left in the dead of night. It would've been pitch-dark. Yet they have a clear picture?"

"They do. It's a decent shot of the man's face." Ramona pinched her fingers against the screen, expanded them, then slowly turned the phone so I could see the picture she'd zoomed in on.

All I could do was gulp.

TEN

I RARELY FELT PANIC. In fact, I can't remember the last time I panicked.

But as I sat there staring at my mug, which filled Ramona's cell phone screen, I was pretty sure panic was the feeling in my body. My face started to flush, and I felt my heart and blood pressure increasing.

"Garrison," I heard Ramona say in the background. "Garrison."

When she waved her hand in front of the phone, I snapped out of it. I was still in a stupor, though, and said something dumb. "That's me."

"Uh, yeah," Ramona replied.

I grabbed her phone. "How'd someone get a picture of me?" I used my fingers to zoom out. Immediately I understood. The picture originated from across the street, and there was a sidewalk in the bottom half of the picture frame.

"The homeless man!" I exclaimed. "It was him."

"Sorry," Ramona said.

"There was a homeless dude curled up directly across the street from Ross's building, in the alcove of an abandoned tire shop. He must've taken this picture, unbelievable. I wonder . . ."

"Wonder what?"

I didn't answer right away since I was thinking about what this meant.

"Garrison, wonder what?"

"I wonder if the killer was the street person, or if . . ."

Ramona was annoyed at me trailing off again, so she rolled her hand. "Finish your sentence, please."

"The killer might not be the dude sleeping at the tire shop. Maybe the killer approached him and offered him money to take the picture. That's a possibility, right?"

"It is, but you're off on a tangent. This is huge, they're suggesting you might be the Night Night Killer. You!" She pointed at me. "A BOLO and APB have already been issued. This is beyond bad, Garrison."

"Believe me, I know, I get it."

Her phone beeped a couple of times, and she took it back from me.

I continued. "If the homeless man was paid off by the killer, then he might still be in the same location, or at least relative vicinity. And if we found him and got confirmation that someone paid him for that picture, that would give credibility to my story. Plus, he could describe the real killer."

Ramona didn't respond. She was glued to her phone.

Now I was the one waving my hand to snap her out of it. "What, Ramona. What is it?"

"That picture is a screen grab from a video. There's actual time-stamped footage of you leaving the building, and it's not good." She turned the phone again so I could see the video.

Sure enough, Ramona was right. It looked bad. You could see me cautiously looking around the corner before a quick retreat toward the Caprice with Ranger at my side.

"You have to come back with me, Garrison."

Being a former FBI agent, my mind instantly went to how this would look from an investigator's perspective.

She stood. "We have to get out in front of this now, before it blows up even further."

"I can't. I can't go with you, not now at least."

"Yes, you can. You will, in fact."

I stood and shook my head.

"Don't do this," Ramona said. "Please, it's bad enough for you."

"It's worse than you think."

"How so? Your story makes sense. It's explainable. And besides, you can't be the Night Night Killer. You just visited Mexico like yesterday, right?"

"I've been to Mexico three times in less than a year. The latest just a few weeks back."

"What?"

"My mother recently remarried, to a Mexican citizen. She's living in northeastern Mexico. I dropped off Simon there a few weeks back so he could visit his grandma."

Ramona looked away and didn't say anything.

I kept thinking from an agent's perspective. "The FBI will consult with Border Patrol, if they haven't already, and see that I've returned from Mexico a few times this year already. And you know what it's like getting into Mexico. In Tijuana, it's a cattle call. American cars filter into Mexico with no stopping. Which means there'll be no official record of when I actually entered the country."

She remained silent.

I kept at it. "You and I have history, and it's public. You're going to be pulled from the case. Since it's a conflict of interest, you'll have to be recused—"

"It's already happened," she said, breaking her silence. "Just got the text. In fact, my entire field office has been taken off the case. Tucson is taking over."

I sighed.

"That's a little win, though," she said.

"How so?"

"Less scrutiny on me, and less scrutiny on our ties. I can advocate for your innocence better than if my office was handling your case."

I thought about it. "Agreed."

"Still best if you come with me now."

"Still disagree. With a case of this magnitude, and my initial guilty look, you know what's in store for me. I'll have to lawyer up and fight this. The best thing I can do for myself is figure out the killer's true identity. And I need Stanley's help with that. But if you take me in now, there's no way I'll be able to speak with him and get out in front of this."

"Why do you need him so bad?"

"I need to tell him everything Ross told me. I need the kid to relook at the evidence he has to see if he can discover what Ross had figured out. Ross had made some important connections between the victims. Hopefully Stanley can figure out that connection and isolate the lone male profile Ross had discovered. First, though, you need to find out if you have a mole on your team."

"And if I find out my team is clean, that'll mean any evidence Stanley has is untrustworthy."

"Correct, but the reverse is also true. Anyway, we must start somewhere." My mind started listing off things for her to do. "You can also send a team to San Luis Rio Colorado, or get Tucson to do so, and try to find that man by the tire shop. Plus, you or Tucson needs to get a warrant for my cell records, if that isn't already in the works. You need to triangulate my movements in Mexico. Since I'm not the killer, I imagine there'll be some large holes and serious doubt about me being the killer once they coincide my movements inside Mexico with when and where the men were actually murdered."

"Maybe," Ramona said. "But I still think I can do all this with you in custody. It looks even worse if you don't turn yourself in."

"I agree with you. But I just need time, a day, maybe twelve hours. Get some things in order before I'm locked up."

"A day? Twelve hours? You said it yourself; a case of this magnitude means every law enforcement agency in the southwest will be gunning for you."

"Come on," I said, grinning. "You know me. I can stay off the grid for twelve hours. Maybe I don't even need that long." I opened my phone and deciphered Stanley's second text. It read: *On my way.*

Glancing at my watch, I did the math. "I'll meet with Stanley in about seven hours from now. I might need only eight to ten hours on the lam. I'll even turn myself in to you. How's that?"

She didn't respond.

I asked, "You have a pen?"

She nodded and handed me one.

With my phone still open, I wrote down a few numbers on my palm.

"What are you doing?" she asked.

"Updating my palm pilot."

Ramona scowled. "Seriously, Garrison."

"Going off the grid starting now."

I powered down my iPhone, pulled out the battery, and used the pen's tip to eject the SIM card. Holding out my palm, I said, "I wrote down your number and a couple of others. We need to communicate, so I'll buy a burner phone with cash."

She shook her head. "Can't believe we're doing this."

"You have a WhatsApp account?"

"Hell no."

"Get one and use your number for the account."

I started to walk away, but she grabbed my hand and pulled me close. Taken back, I stood there dumbfounded as she cradled my hand in hers.

Then she flipped my hand over. After pulling out a small notepad, she copied down the numbers on my palm, ripped off the paper, and handed it to me. "All it takes is a clammy palm and those numbers are illegible."

I nodded and took the paper.

"For the record," she continued, "I'm totally opposed to this plan."

"Understood, you should be. Which is why I'm going to do this."

"Do what?"

I shouted, "Not a chance I'm going with you. No way!"

Then I turned and ran, making a scene as I bashed my way through the kitchen and out a rear door. Ramona and I had been seen in the restaurant together, so me dramatically fleeing the scene protected her.

After weaving through the back patio furniture, I launched off a picnic table and grabbed the top of a cinder block wall. I fought my way over the top and landed in the alley, then sprinted away.

And like that, I was literally on the run.

ELEVEN

When I reached the Caprice, the first thing I did was set a timer on my watch. I gave myself one hour to get everything in order before going fully dark.

With the clock ticking, I drove toward Sky Harbor International Airport. Before arriving, I cruised the hotel strip until I found what I was looking for: a sketchy motel with no large lobby and parking directly in front of each room. It was the kind of motel that wouldn't require a credit card security deposit, so it wouldn't be unusual to pay in cash.

In the Caprice's trunk, I kept a bag of beach stuff since I often took Simon there. Putting on a navy-blue bucket hat and sunglasses, I checked in and made sure to get a room that faced the motel's backside. I brought Ranger and my duffel bag inside the musty-smelling room. I'd also extracted both guns from their hidden compartment and stashed them in the bag.

Inside, I quickly changed out of my clothes since I'd been caught on camera wearing that outfit. The picture of my face making rounds through law enforcement agencies showed me with about five days of whiskers. So, I stepped into the tiny bathroom and shaved as quickly, and as closely, as I could. Wearing a stupid bucket hat, sporting large sunglasses, and now a fresh shave, I felt incognito enough to step into public.

I left Ranger behind and headed to the airport and parked in the long-range lot. I went inside the Departures terminal and found a bank machine and took out as much cash as it would allow. Looking at my timer, I noted I'd been on the move for fifty-three minutes. The bank withdrawal would be my final tie to the electronic world.

And it would throw off investigators.

Shortly, if not already, the feds would be monitoring my financial transactions. They'd see I'd pulled money from a machine at Sky Harbor. No doubt they'd be here in less than an hour. Hopefully they'd also locate the Caprice.

Federal agents would know I was a former government operative, so they'd probably assume I'd left Sky Harbor on a flight under an old alias. However, my intentions were to lay low until Stanley was in town. At any rate, it would keep the feds busy trying to figure out what alias I'd used, and where I'd jetted off to.

I made my way to the Arrivals terminal and hopped onto a crowded shuttle bus. My motel certainly didn't offer a shuttle bus service, but I noticed a fancy Marriott down the street about a quarter mile, so I rode their bus to the hotel. Just down from the Marriott, closer to where I was staying, was a run-down liquor and convenience store. I popped in there and found what I needed: a pay-as-you-go cell.

Back at my motel room, I felt confident everything went well. I barely spoke to anyone, was lost in crowds most of the time, and easily avoided eye contact with people. Of course, the latter was easy since I wore sunglasses and a bucket hat the whole time.

I plugged in my new cell and got it up and running. I stored three numbers in the phone: Stanley's, Ramona's, and my buddy Slim's. I used the room's Wi-Fi to install WhatsApp, then sent Stanley two coded texts.

The first one read: *Chase's new cell.* The second said the name of the motel followed by the room number.

After that, I sat at the small table and collected my thoughts. There was a notepad and pen on the table, so I used that to write down a few points. The notes amounted to a list of four things I needed Stanley to do.

One, I needed him to process the Beretta for any fingerprints or touch DNA. Two, I needed him to reexamine the evidence he'd given Ross and make the connection between the victims. Three, I needed him to find the single source male profile located on two of the victims. And finally, I needed him to take that profile and, as Ross had said, work his magic with the software he'd developed.

I paced the room for a while. Ranger was on the bed watching me, occasionally whimpering. I knew he was attuned to my emotions, and that he just wanted me to relax.

But I couldn't.

It was hard for me to rely on others; to wait on Ramona's investigation into whether she found a mole on her team; to give important research to Stanley and then wait on him for results. I wanted to do something, anything, at least make some progress on my own. What I most wanted to do was drive back to San Luis Rio Colorado and see if I could find that street person. If he was nowhere to be found, that meant he was the killer, which was valuable intel. And if I did find him, he could be shaken down for important information.

Heading to San Luis was a win-win.

But I couldn't do that since they'd be on the lookout for me at local border crossings. Plus, I didn't have use of a vehicle, nor could I rent one. I was destined to stay put and practice patience. Not exactly my strong suit.

Continuing to pace, I suddenly thought about the media. I flipped on the TV and rifled through the news channels, sort of expecting to see my face plastered everywhere.

I didn't.

However, soon enough—when the feds didn't quickly scoop me up—they'd appeal to the public for help locating me. Instead of dwelling on that inevitable fact, I decided to do some proactive learning. From my stint as a federal agent, I knew the ins and outs of DNA and how law enforcement used profiles to hunt down suspects, but I didn't know much about what Stanley had told me. About investigative genetic genealogy and reverse-engineering a family tree. That technology exploded just after I quit my job as a federal agent, so I never got a crash course in it.

Using my new pay-as-you go cell and free Wi-Fi, I spent the next two hours researching and reading articles about the basics of investigative genetic genealogy. To me, it was a fascinating topic. I learned that historically most DNA testing used what was called STR analysis, which stood for short tandem repeat analysis. It basically meant a person's DNA profile was determined by the number of times a small section of DNA was repeated at a specific chromosomal location. During my time with the feds, there were thirteen core locations that were analyzed using the FBI's CODIS system. Apparently, that has now expanded to twenty core locations.

New DNA technology, however, uses what is called SNP analysis. It's pronounced *snip* and stands for single nucleotide polymorphisms. My understanding is that there are mutations in a person's genetic code that have been passed down for generations. These shared mutations between individuals—and there are literally hundreds of thousands of them—help genealogists locate relatives much further back in time. STR analysis is valuable to identify recent, close relatives. In contrast, SNP or snip analysis is great at going back in time and finding distant relatives from hundreds of years ago.

Where STR falls short, snip analysis picks up the slack. And that's very helpful when it comes to solving crimes with DNA profiles that haven't been identified in CODIS. With this new technology, genetic genealogists can use a DNA snip profile from a suspect to find a distant relative, let's say a cousin. From there, they can go back further in time to find their common ancestor. From that point, genealogists build out a family tree until it gets to the timeframe for when the crime had occurred. The family tree then provides law enforcement with a list of potential suspects. From there, investigators use good, old-fashioned detective work to narrow down the suspect list. When they have a suspect in their crosshairs, the next step is to get a DNA sample from that individual to confirm whether he or she is the right person.

That was exactly what had happened in the Golden State Killer case.

They'd established a profile, then uploaded it to some public DNA databases. Eventually, they built out a family tree and narrowed down the potential suspects to six male cousins. The DNA profile they'd built also suggested the killer had blue eyes. Since only one of the male cousins had blue eyes, investigators zeroed in on that man, Joseph DeAngelo.

After lengthy surveillance, and some help from a garbage truck driver to grab some DNA-bearing items from Joseph DeAngelo's trash, the cops had their man.

I smiled at the genius of it all. Without investigative genetic genealogy, the Golden State Killer would still be living his comfortable life in Citrus Heights, California. I just hoped Stanley could use his expertise and proprietary software to do something similar with the Night Night Killer.

Glancing at my watch, I had two more hours to burn before the kid arrived. Since I had a drug-induced, half-assed sleep last night, I decided the best course of action was getting some shut-eye. As a former operative who'd been on countless missions, I was taught to eat and sleep whenever I could.

So, with the cell on my chest, and Ranger at my side, I tried to sleep. But it didn't come easy. I knew I'd be face-to-face with Stanley soon. He'd once again ticked me off by lying about talking with Ross concerning my terms of engagement. But now I really needed Stanley to help solve this case and clear my name.

Do I berate him, or let it go?

With that thought in mind, I eventually drifted off to sleep. Only to be woken an hour and a half later by the buzz of my cell phone, alerting me to a text. It was from Stanley. The text caused me to bolt upright. It wasn't in code, so I knew the kid was panicking and had rushed to send it.

It read: *bein followed*

I responded: *You sure?*

yes what do I do

How long till you're in Phoenix?

20 min

Don't come here.

where

I thought for a moment, eventually deciding on: *Marriott, just down the same street.*

k

Use the valet, don't park. Meet me in lobby bar.

see u in 20

I put on the bucket hat and sunglasses and headed out the door. But I stopped before closing it and rushed back into the room. After shuffling through my duffel bag, I found what I was looking for: the Savage Stance.

With the gun tucked into my belt, I made my way to the Marriott hotel.

TWELVE

I tipped the bartender, then took my Old-Fashioned cocktail to the front of the lobby bar.

With a drink in hand, I blended in with the evening crowd. Plus, bourbon soothed me and helped clear my mind. I didn't like the idea of Stanley Tuchek being tailed. Not one bit. I wondered if the tail was Griff and his henchmen.

Had Ernesto gone back on his word and sent his men into action?

In the end, what I really hoped was that Stanley Tuchek was mistaken. That he was simply being overly paranoid.

I chose to sit at an empty corner booth that faced some large floor-to-ceiling windows. From that vantage, I had a clear view of the lobby entrance and the valet stand. I didn't have to wait long. In fact, I'd only had two sips of my cocktail when Stanley rolled in. He drove a silver, midsized Audi SUV. After reluctantly handing his keys to a valet, Stanley glanced over his shoulder a few times as he made his way inside the hotel and toward the bar.

Standing, I waved him over since I didn't think he'd recognize me with the bucket hat on. As he approached, I didn't watch him. Instead, I watched where the valet was taking his car, which was on the west side of the hotel complex.

"Chase!" he said, rushing over. "Is that you in the silly hat? Am I ever—"

"Are they here, Stanley? Your tail."

"Yup. Pulled in just after me."

"Where?"

He pointed out the window, toward a small parking lot of five spaces. It's where you parked to check in if you didn't want to use the valet.

"Black sedan," he said. "Arizona plates. Tinted side windows."

"Got it. I see them. You're positive they were following you?"

He snorted and pushed up his glasses. "I am, Chase. I'm not stupid."

"When did you spot them?"

"As soon as I crossed into Arizona."

"Did you recognize them? Is it your dad's PI team that he hired?"

Shrugging, he said, "Too far away to see their faces."

I kept my eye on the vehicle.

Stanley said, "Those are in style now, did you know? Except I'm not sure if that applies to someone your age."

Without looking at him, I said, "What?"

"The bucket hat. All the young kids are wearing them. You look a little weird, little out of place, if I'm being honest."

I paid the comment no attention since a large man wearing a cowboy hat got out of the sedan's passenger side and headed toward the entrance. It wasn't Griff, or Mr. Average, and it certainly wasn't Mr. Gangly. I'd never seen this man before.

"Come on," I said, grabbing Stanley's arm. "We gotta move."

"But you've barely touched your drink. And we're safe here in a public bar, aren't we?"

I didn't respond since I was focused on the closest exit. There was an outdoor patio on the west side of the lobby bar. I ushered Stanley onto the patio, then motioned for him to hop over the waist-high wall.

"What are we doing?" Stanley asked.

I jumped over. "Just come on, we'll talk when we're out of view." Once he'd hopped over, and we were safely in the parking lot, I looked around for the valet driver.

"Can you please tell me what's going on, Chase."

"We're losing your tail. Think about it: Coming to a hotel and giving your keys to a valet means you're staying put, at least for a little while. The men following you won't think you'll be fleeing out the back door. No way."

He thought about that, then said, "Smart, I like it. There he is. The valet." Stanley pointed to my right.

"Get your keys back. Give him your ticket and some cash."

"Cash? Can't remember the last time I carried cash."

I sighed and fished out ten dollars and handed it to him.

"Sorry," Stanley said as the valet approached. "Forgot I reserved at the Double Tree not the Marriott. I apologize."

Stanley handed the valet the ticket and bill.

"No problem," the valet said, happily handing over the keys and eyeing the ten bucks. "Double Tree is a mile that direction."

Stanley and I hustled to where the valet had parked the Audi. He drove, and I navigated.

"Go out this side street," I said, "not back onto the main street. The cowboy might get suspicious when he doesn't find you at the check-in desk or in the bar."

Stanley chirped his tires as he turned onto the side street.

"Be a little more discreet, kid."

He huffed. "You know I'm twenty-three, right?"

I shrugged. "Okay, so what? I figured you were somewhere around that age."

"Why do you keep calling me 'kid' then? You're probably not that much older than me. Ten years maybe? It's hard to tell with your . . ." He pointed to my head.

"With my what?"

He cleared his throat. "With your bald head."

"What's that supposed to mean?"

"I mean, having no hair makes you look older, but maybe you're just

81

one of those guys that unfortunately lost his hair early, like in college. Is that what happened?"

I didn't respond.

"Fine, it's a sensitive area. I get it. Just don't call me kid anymore."

"Fair enough. You look young, Stanley. Calling you kid is a force of habit I'll try to break. If I fail, take it as a compliment. Now turn left here."

For a few moments, as we navigated a circuitous route back to my motel, we sat in silence.

Finally, Stanley glanced over and swallowed. "He's really dead, is he?"

I nodded.

"What happened? Were you with him when he was killed, or did you find the body?"

I thought for a second. "Both."

"Haven't heard anything on the news about his death. Was listening to the radio most of the way here, too. Is Mexico keeping it under wraps?"

"Don't think so. I imagine news will be out soon about his death." I paused, then followed up with, "And my involvement."

"You're involvement. What's that mean?"

"It means I was involved, or apparently involved."

When I didn't elaborate, he said, "That's all you're gonna say? That's all you're giving me?"

"Nope, we have lots to talk about, Stanley. A ton, in fact. And you have work to do as well. Motel is just up here on the left. We'll talk there."

I directed Stanley around the back. We'd entered the motel's lot from the opposite direction of the Marriott. So far, no sign of the black sedan.

Getting out of the car, I asked him, "You a dog person?"

"A dog person? Um, maybe. Why?"

Ranger greeted us at the door, and Stanley immediately backed away.

"Okay, kid—sorry, I mean Stanley—you're not a dog person, for the record."

"You brought your dog to Mexico?"

"He pretty much goes everywhere with me these days."

Stanley tiptoed around Ranger and sat at the small table. Ranger followed him and started sniffing his leg.

"Come on, boy," I said. "You haven't been out for a tinkle in a while. I'd offer you something from the mini-bar, Stanley, but as you can see this is not that type of place."

"I can see."

"Be right back." Before closing the door, I noticed Stanley glancing at the notepad on the table. "Feel free to read that. I listed out what I need your help with."

With Stanley's bug eyes glued to the notepad, I closed the door and proceeded toward a small, grassy area to the left of the room. Not even a minute in, while waiting for Ranger to find a suitable pee spot, I heard the low rumble of a vehicle approaching.

Glancing casually to my right, I witnessed a car backing into a parking spot at the motel next door.

It was a black sedan. With tinted side windows.

THIRTEEN

I KEPT my attention on Ranger while eyeing the vehicle from the corner of my eye.

Since the car was a few hundred feet away, and I only had a side view of the vehicle, I couldn't see the license plates. So, I couldn't say for sure it was Stanley's tail.

Still, I was not a believer in coincidence. Assuming it was the tail vehicle, I immediately suspected Stanley's Audi had a hidden GPS tracker. That was the only explanation for them finding us here. No way had they seen us leaving the Marriott out the back. And they had no clue where I was staying.

"Come on, Range, just go already." My dog was twisting around and making me dizzy watching him.

For a moment, my mind entertained the idea that these guys could be at the motel coincidentally. Assuming they lost their tail, and since it was getting dark, maybe the motel next door just happened to be the one these men chose for the night.

Could that be?

After Ranger finally relieved himself, I went back to the motel room, fighting the urge to stare at the sedan. As soon as I entered, Stanley held up the notepad.

"There's good news and bad news. Definitely bad news. The problem—"

"Black sedan is here," I said, cutting him off.

"Wait, what? It is? How?"

I gingerly pulled back the curtains on the window and eyed the vehicle. The fact that nobody had gotten out yet was troubling. What I wanted to see were the men leaving the car with bags in hand.

But I didn't.

"I think your Audi has a tracker. You said you picked up the tail when you crossed the border. Did you stop for gas or food or something?"

"No, I didn't. What does this mean? What do we do?"

While eyeing the sedan, I said, "We find out for sure. We get in the car and leave the lot, but not in a rush. Light on the gas pedal and no squealing tires. We'll see if they follow."

"Got it," Stanley said, rushing to the door.

"Slowly. I know that's hard for you. Everything you do is fast, but let's leave here like we're just going out to dinner. Okay?"

He nodded quickly.

A minute later, we pulled out of the parking lot and turned left. As we made the slow turn, I glanced left. The sedan hadn't moved. I turned around in the seat and kept my eyes glued to the front of the motel for the next thirty seconds. Still no sign of the sedan leaving the lot.

"What do I do now?" Stanley asked.

I looked ahead. "Get on I-10 and head south."

Stanley did as directed. For five minutes we rode in silence. I had my neck craned and was looking backward, seeing if I could spot the black sedan.

"What now, Chase?"

We'd just crossed over Highway 202 and were entering a barren landscape. Cars were thinning out, too. "Let's keep going another ten minutes. Should have an easier time spotting them if they're trying to catch up with us."

"Got it. That gives you time to talk about Ross and your involvement in his death. What did you mean by that? What exactly happened?"

Stanley deserved an explanation, so I gave him the whole story.

He didn't say a word until I finished. "So, what, I'm driving a fugitive around now? Great, Chase, just great. What's that make me?"

I couldn't help myself. "An accomplice, Stanley. Not to mention a liar as well."

"Liar? What are you talking about?"

"What did your text say? The response you gave me yesterday when I asked if you had success with Ross?"

I waited for an answer. Stanley swallowed and remained silent.

"Right," I continued. "You said everything's fine, don't worry. That's exactly what your text said. You didn't even speak with Ross about my terms, did you?"

Stanley was about to rebut, but I held up my left hand. "Ross told me you never mentioned it, so I don't want to hear any excuses, kid. And, yes, you deserve to be called kid because you lied like a teenager. The good news for you is that we need to move past this. I need your help to identify the killer and clear my name, and you need my protection since you may be next on the killer's list."

"You think so? You think I'm in that type of danger?"

"Maybe, maybe not. I don't know who's tailing you. It could be a different PI team hired by your dad, or it could be some men hired by the Night Night Killer. All I know is that it's not good. The main point is that we need each other from now on, and that means we need to be truthful."

He sighed. "I'm sorry, Chase. I—"

"Like I said, let's move beyond this." While I kept my eyes on the side-view mirror, checking for a tail, I said, "Now talk to me about the good and bad news. You said something about that after reading my notes, when I walked into the motel room and cut you off."

"Right, one of the things you wanted me to do is retest the evidence. There's good and bad news when it comes to that."

"What's the bad news?"

"It's something we call consumed DNA."

86

"What's that mean exactly?"

"Ideally, you want to hold back some of the evidence from a crime scene. But sometimes you need to consume an entire sample to meet the minimum sensitivity requirements of DNA testing. The evidence we received from the Mexican authorities was scant, unfortunately, so . . ."

"You used it all up?"

He nodded. "Our testing consumed everything."

"That's not bad news, Stanley, that's terrible news."

"Well, yes and no."

"How so?"

"I can't recreate the evidence or reprocess anything because we have nothing left to test, which is the bad news. But the good news is that I have backups of the results I sent to Ross in Yuma."

Suddenly a light went on inside my head. I smacked Stanley's knee. "Of course you do." I smiled broadly. "You may not have any of the evidence left but you have the important part: the results. Which means you may be able to pinpoint the single source male profile and hopefully identify the Night Night Killer."

"Backups are industry standard, Chase. I mean, I didn't even have to physically do anything since our software automatically backs up any results we have to a secure cloud."

I mulled that over, suddenly thinking about Ross and whether he had a backup of his podcast episodes. I said out loud to myself, "Why didn't I think of that earlier?"

"Think of what?"

"The killer took all of Ross's files and his Nano and his computer. But just like you, he would've made backups of his podcasts and files, right?"

He immediately shook his head. "No, not Ross. You'd think so, but he was an extreme security fanatic."

I furrowed my brow. "If he was extreme, he'd use a backup then. Maybe multiple backups. What am I missing?"

"He was so extreme, Chase, he didn't even trust the cloud. He was an air-gapper."

"Air-gapper?"

"He uses an air-gapped computer, which means it's physically isolated from unsecured networks like the internet."

"Wait, he's not connected to the internet when he's working or using his computer, not at all?"

"Nope, not the internet or any system that's connected to the internet. Totally isolated so he can't be hacked. It's virtually un-hackable."

"Virtually?"

"The only way to infiltrate an air-gapped computer is via a USB device, or some sort of removable media, or a firewire connection with another machine."

I thought for a moment. "The fact that his laptop was taken means any results or podcasts he had on there are gone, correct?"

"Yup, which is more bad news, but maybe we can glean something from the results I kept in the cloud."

"Hopefully."

After about a minute of silence, I pointed straight ahead. "Take this upcoming exit. It's the rest stop ahead."

"But it's closed. A sign just said that."

"I know, just do it, take the exit."

Stanley took the ramp but stopped abruptly. There was a small wooden barricade across the road, though it didn't extend all the way across. On either side of the barricade were some orange traffic cones that stopped cars from getting around the barricade and entering the closed rest area.

I got out and pushed the cones on the right side away with my foot. Then I picked up one end of the barricade's easel and angled it backward, just enough for the SUV to get by.

Waving Stanley on, I said, "Squeeze through."

He did.

I put the barricade and cones back in place and hopped into the Audi.

"What are we doing exactly?" Stanley asked.

"We're seeing if you really do have a tracker on this vehicle. If you do, and these men show up here and remove the barricade, we'll know they want a piece of you. And what better place for a nice conversation about that. Am I right?"

"Not in the mood for that conversation, or confrontation, Chase, if I'm being honest. Seriously, what's your plan?"

"Drive around, do a full loop. I want to see the complex in its entirety."

He did. The rest area was circular in shape and contained two distinct buildings. On one side of the circle was the entrance to the rest area, along with the women's bathroom and the main parking area. On the opposite side of the circle was the men's bathroom, along with a secondary parking lot.

When we arrived back at our starting position, I said, "You wait up there." I pointed to my right, to the edge of where the headlights faded. "Behind that collection of large boulders up the incline. I'll take the Audi to the other side of the rest area, to the men's complex. I'll park right near the bathroom building and find some shadows to hide in. Your tail, if they do show up, will be drawn to the Audi's location, so you'll be safe. Your job is to keep an eye out for their arrival, and to text me if they show up. I'll handle them from there."

"You'll handle them?"

"I will."

"That's all you're going to say?"

"It is." I showed him my concealed weapon. "Now get out."

As we passed each other in front of the SUV, Stanley stopped in his tracks and pointed at a sign to his left. The Audi's headlights lit up a small blue billboard.

It read: *Poisonous snakes and insects inhabit the area.* Below that warning was a picture of a scorpion and a rattlesnake.

"You're kidding," he said. "It's pitch-dark out there. I don't want to go into the wilderness and get bit and die."

"You'll be fine."

"But I'm terrified of snakes, probably scorpions, too. Don't know for sure since I've never come across one."

Just then we were faintly backlit.

We both glanced backward at the same time. The exit ramp was a few hundred feet behind us, and at a lower elevation, so we couldn't see an actual vehicle or the source of the light.

"A car's here," Stanley said. "Those must be headlights. They're here, Chase. They're at the barricade."

I rushed toward the open driver's door. "Get in position now. Up the hill. Go, go!"

Stanley took off toward the boulders, and I stepped on the gas before the Audi's driver's door had closed.

FOURTEEN

I FLOORED it to the other side of the rest area.

Since nobody was around, I parked in the handicap spot closest to the men's bathroom complex. The women's bathroom was positioned by the entrance to the rest stop where the main parking area was located. That complex completely obscured my view of any approaching cars, which was good since it allowed me to get in position undetected, but bad in the sense that I'd have to rely on Stanley for intel about the approaching vehicle.

Though I suspected the men's bathroom door would be locked, I tried to push it open anyway. No luck. An internal deadbolt was engaged, and the steel door didn't budge. Looking around, there was only one spot to conceal myself: a bank of vending machines to my right.

Above the vending machines was a large yellow light. It lit up the entire side of the building. The glowing bulb had a wire cage around it.

I grabbed a few nearby stones—ones small enough to fit through the openings in the wire cage—and flung them at the light. On my fourth attempt, I broke the bulb, which immediately plunged the area into near darkness. It wasn't completely dark since it was a cloudless night, and the moon was full and bright.

Just as I was deciding which end of the vending machines to hide behind, my cell buzzed.

Stanley texted: *theyre here, black sedan*

Since I knew for sure they were tracking the Audi, my assumption was that the sedan would swing around and park near Stanley's SUV. With that in mind, I proceeded to the far end of the vending machines, furthest from where I'd parked the Audi. I tucked myself beside the last machine in the row and pressed my back against the concrete block wall. I pulled out the Savage Stance gun, released the safety, and listened. But I didn't hear anything, certainly not an approaching car. And I should have by now.

Using one hand, I texted: *where are they*. It pained me to not use capitalization and punctuation, but one-handed texting was hard. Plus, time was of the essence.

Stanley responded: *parked by womens*

Makes sense, I thought. Probably not smart for them to roll up directly beside the Audi. Better to approach from a distance.

Stanley texted: *getting out of car*

I asked: *they armed, can you see any weapons*

not they, just one guy got out, its cowboy dude

does he have a gun, you see one

no

Before I could respond, Stanley texted: *wait, yes, he opened trunk, has a machine gun!*

A machine gun? No way. Stanley was mistaken. The guy probably pulled out an AR-15, which is a style of semi-automatic rifle, not a fully automatic machine gun like in the military. People get them confused often, and it wouldn't be unusual for a cowboy from Arizona to have one. At any rate, an Armalite rifle was serious business. The fact that he was carrying an AR-15 changed everything in my mind. More than likely, these men were hired by the serial killer to either kill or capture the kid, most likely the former.

Stanley texted: *he's walking your way, be ready, your little gun is no match*

stay put. let me know if other guy gets out

I tucked the cell away. Immediately I thought about the path Mr. Cowboy would take. The bathroom complex was shaped like a rectangle, and the entrance into the men's bathroom faced the secondary parking lot where the Audi was parked. The backside of the bathroom faced the direction the man was coming. That meant he'd have to come around one corner or the other.

Currently, I stood beside the vending machines at the closest end of the rectangle to the direction he would probably approach from. Not liking that position, I moved to the other end of the vending machines. Now I was closer to the Audi.

What if he heads to the SUV first, and he comes around the side I'm now facing? I thought about that. It was a possibility he'd want to clear the vehicle first. *What would I do in his situation?*

After some internal dialogue, I decided to stay put. If it was me approaching, I'd want to clear this side of the building before checking out the vehicle. In case I was mistaken, though, I stretched out my arm and pointed the Savage toward the exposed corner. If Mr. Cowboy checked the SUV first, then came around this side where I was easily visible, I'd be ready to fire. Since I had the element of surprise on my side, I was confident I could shoot first before the AR-15 mowed me down.

I waited and breathed and listened. Within moments, I heard footsteps. They were surprisingly loud. That made sense since the man wore hard-soled cowboy boots and the area between the bathroom complexes was concrete. Plus, he probably didn't feel like he needed to tiptoe while carrying a semi-automatic rifle. No doubt that weapon gave him an air of confidence.

Footsteps grew louder, but I couldn't quite tell which direction they were coming from. If I had to use my gun, I didn't want to kill Mr. Cowboy, so I crouched as low as I could and prepared to fire at his lower body.

With my gun arm outstretched, I waited and listened. His footsteps would trail off if he moved along the backside of the bathroom toward the Audi, so when the steps gained volume, I knew he was approaching from the other end.

Since I didn't need to cover the open corner anymore, I brought my gun arm tight to my side. My body was already pressed against the vending machine, but I leaned further into it anyway.

The footsteps stopped.

I held my breath.

No doubt Mr. Cowboy had just come around the opposite corner and seen the bank of vending machines. If it were daylight, he could stoop over and look along the ground to see if he could spot feet underneath the farthest machine. But it was too dark for that.

Still silence.

The man had two choices: One, proceed slowly and closely in front of the machines. Or two, move away from the building and take a wide approach; see if he could spot someone tucked behind this end of the machines.

Two slow, cautious steps followed. Their sound wasn't trailing off, so I knew Mr. Cowboy was taking the direct approach, not the wide one.

Still holding my breath, I kept thinking about the rifle. *He means serious business. He wants Stanley dead.*

Two more steps.

There were six machines in a row. Since Mr. Cowboy was tall like me, I figured it would take him two steps to cross each machine. By now, he'd cleared two machines and was by the fourth one.

More steps. Still slow, but this time he took four steps.

Now he was just one machine away from my position.

I kept envisioning the AR-15. The thought of that weapon blitzing this end of the machines felt real, and inevitable. Suddenly I knew I had to be the aggressor.

Switching the Savage into my left hand, I turned the gun on its side and brought it parallel with the ground. It hovered just above the concrete, and hopefully just below the bottom of the vending machine. It would've been best to lay prone and glance under the machine to confirm the gun was in the right position. But Mr. Cowboy was close, he was right there, and I didn't dare move. Not even a breath. The only move I made was tightening my trigger finger.

Another step.

I pulled the trigger, fast and smooth. Twice.

FIFTEEN

IN BETWEEN FIRING, I moved the gun a few inches. A piercing scream followed the second shot.

I sprang from my position with the gun outstretched. Immediately I saw Mr. Cowboy hopping on his left foot while cursing in the process. He'd been shot in the right foot. His hopping had caused him to pivot to his left, so his back was to me.

I sprinted toward him. He heard me coming and pivoted his head, saying incredulously, "You shot me!" Then his brow furrowed, and he swung his upper body to the right.

When I reached him, I batted the muzzle up and away with my right hand.

Tat-tat-tat! Three rounds blasted into the night air.

Sliding my right hand down the hot barrel, I grabbed the handguard and yanked the rifle toward me.

"*No, you don't!*" he yelled, keeping a firm grip on the AR. To gain leverage, he'd stopped hopping and planted his bloody right foot.

I stepped on it.

"Bastard!"

Immediately the rifle came free. I dropped the Savage and latched on to the handguard with my left hand, then swung the rifle in a wide arc toward his head. Mr. Cowboy raised his hands to protect his head. At the last moment, I adjusted and swung the rifle lower, clobbering him just under his armpit with a solid baseball swing. A ferocious blow.

Mr. Cowboy couldn't cry out in pain since the wind had been knocked from him.

As he fell, crumpling under his injured foot, I tossed the rifle away since I didn't need it anymore. For about eight seconds, I left him alone and listened for approaching footsteps from the other man.

Nothing, and no text from Stanley either, so I turned my attention back to Mr. Cowboy.

He writhed on his side, holding the top of his right cowboy boot. Blood dripped from the toe of the boot.

I waited until he sucked in a few breaths, then asked, "Who sent you? Who do you work for?"

Another breath, then he seethed, "My foot, you'll pay."

"Let's not make this more painful for you. Just answer the question: Who hired you? I want a name. And tell me who the Night Night Killer is."

He repeated himself. "You'll pay."

"For the record," I said, "I don't want to do this." I stepped on the side of his boot, right by the bloody toe. I eased off after two seconds, and one short scream.

"You rat frickin' bastard," he said, breathing hard.

I leaned over to repeat my question. Just as I did, I saw what he'd been doing while writhing around holding his lower leg. He'd pulled out a short-blade knife from inside his boot. So, I was prepared for the sudden slash.

I straightened in time to avoid a facial laceration. But the blade sliced my right kneecap. It wasn't a deep cut, but it was painful and stung like hell. I didn't show any pain, though.

Now I was the one seething. "A name. Now. Last time I ask, partner." I'd backed up a few steps to avoid another cut. This gave Mr. Cowboy the opportunity to get on his feet, or foot, I should say.

Instead of responding, he carved his knife in the open air and motioned at my knee. "You feeling that? It's only gonna get worse. Like I said, you'll pay."

Since I was listening for his pal's footsteps, I didn't say a word. Instead, I debated making a move toward the Savage, which had skidded away when I'd dropped it. It was approximately five feet to my right and closer than the rifle.

Mr. Cowboy read my mind. "Go for it," he said, "I dare you. It'll be your last move."

I stood still and watched him work the knife. He wasn't an amateur with it. I could tell by his short stabbing motions, and the fact that he moved the knife with small arcs. An inexperienced person with a knife usually made large arcing swipes, which were easily intercepted and blocked. It made it much harder to block a knife when a person repeatedly jabbed with the tip and didn't swing it side to side.

"Before I take that knife from you," I said, "tell me why you're after Stanley? You gonna kill the kid or deliver him to Mexico?"

"You're a cocky SOB, aren't ya?"

Mr. Cowboy's bloody right foot led him forward, but he was sliding his boot forward using the heel. His weight was too far back on the leading foot, so he didn't have much forward momentum or power.

When he got within striking range, I kept my eyes on the jabbing knife and said, "I am."

Then I dropped to the ground, simultaneously kicking out his front heel and clamping onto his wrist with my two hands. As he fell, I twisted his wrist until I heard a pop and the knife clank onto the concrete.

"My wrist!" he yelled. "You broke my wrist."

After kicking the knife away, I grabbed my handgun and again listened for his partner.

No footsteps, so I tucked the Savage away and approached him. "Listen, Captain Obvious, I'm gonna keep breaking body parts until you talk. For your sake, maybe we skip all that and go straight to you telling me the name of the man who hired you."

He got to his feet and scoffed. To his credit, the man was a tough, obstinate fella. When I was a few feet away, I stopped and motioned at his cowboy hat. "Let me fix that, it's a little skewed."

I reached for his hat with my left hand. He tried to stop me with his noninjured hand, which was his left. I knocked that hand away with my right, then quickly batted the brim of his cowboy hat with the fingertips of my left hand. With the hat covering his face, I buried a monstrous right-handed punch into the middle of it.

I felt cartilage smush. He squawked.

I saved him the words and exclaimed, "I broke your nose!" Then I planted another solid right, this one aimed slightly lower than the previous one. "And now your teeth!"

He staggered back, stopping when his spine touched the middle vending machine. He tilted his hat up with his left hand. Seething and bloody, he stepped forward and jabbed a weak left at my face.

I caught his fist with the palm of my right hand, then used the flat of my left hand in the middle of his chest to throw him backward. He smashed into the vending machine with tremendous velocity, his cowboy hat fluttering to the ground in the process.

Since the glass didn't break, just wobbled on impact, I knew it was Plexiglas. I spun Mr. Cowboy around. He had stringy, long brown hair, which I grabbed a handful of, then smashed his face straight into the Plexiglas.

I spun him to face me. "Ready to talk now?"

He said something, but his mouth was full of blood so I couldn't understand it. Since he smiled, I knew it wasn't the answer I was looking for.

"Fine then," I said. "Your choice."

Spinning him to the right, I grabbed the back of his head and smashed his face into the next machine, then faced him forward again. "How about now?"

He sprayed blood into my face.

"Not the answer I'm looking for."

Suddenly I heard footsteps to my left, from the area where I'd parked the Audi. I pulled out the Savage and aimed it that direction. Footsteps grew closer, and I tightened the trigger.

"Chase! Chase!"

I eased off the trigger. It was Stanley's voice. Seconds later, he exploded around the corner. I turned back to Mr. Cowboy. He was still dazed.

Over my shoulder, I said, "You okay, Stanley?"

"I am."

"Where's the other guy?"

"No other guy. It's just him."

I looked back. Stanley was pointing at Mr. Cowboy. I didn't like that piece of intel, not at all.

Turning back to Mr. Cowboy, I said, "Where's your partner?"

He grinned.

I spun him to the right. Now he was in the middle of the next machine, which was last in the line. I pulled his head back and gave him a face full of Plexiglas.

He laughed after the blow. I figured all his facial nerves were shot, so the blows didn't hurt anymore. But I gave him another mouthful of machine anyway.

The final blow was heavy, so heavy it caused the entire machine to shake. Two items inside dropped into the collection chamber. Spinning him around, I leaned him against the concrete block wall since there were no more machines. He slithered to a sitting position. I waited for a few seconds as his eyes fluttered open and closed. When they didn't remain open, I smacked his cheeks a few times, which woke him up.

"Ready to talk now? Where's your partner? Talk to me."

Before he could respond, from behind I heard, "Step aside, Chase."

Turning, I saw Stanley approaching with the AR-15 and yelled, "No. Stop!"

He didn't listen. Stanley had turned the rifle around, and the stock's butt end sailed over my right shoulder. The end connected squarely with Mr. Cowboy's forehead, who passed out on impact.

As the man's head slumped forward, I glared at Stanley.

"Kid, what the hell are you doing?"

SIXTEEN

"What am *I* doing?" Stanley scoffed. "I'm taking this guy out of commission, that's what I'm doing!"

I turned and drew my weapon. Squinting, I aimed the gun toward the darkened parking lot, then addressed Stanley over my shoulder. "I don't want him out of commission. I want him talking, not unconscious."

"You can lower your weapon, Chase, we're alone."

I sighed.

"Wait, you're mad at me?" he said. "Really? After I just witnessed you smashing his face on these machines, you're upset with me for cracking his forehead? I mean, you bloody shot him!"

Still not looking at him, I said, "You went to their car, right? And cleared it, I assume."

He snorted. "Of course."

"Ever think that the second man got out at the barricade? That he's now lurking out there, ready to take us out."

I finally turned in his direction. Stanley's eyes went wide. He was still holding the rifle by the barrel, so he flipped it around and pointed it toward the secondary lot.

"You were supposed to stay put," I seethed. "Feed me intel from a safe spot."

"But I heard shots," he fired back. "Multiple shots. And there was no one in the car, so I had to come check on you."

There was no time to argue. I turned back to Mr. Cowboy and kneeled beside him. While taking off my belt, I said, "If the second man's out there, he probably doesn't have a rifle. Otherwise, we'd both be dead by now."

Stanley had no response to that.

I tightened my belt around Mr. Cowboy's right calf, then used the loose end of the belt to fasten it around his other leg. "This will hopefully stop him from bleeding to death, and from hopping away."

"What's next?" Stanley asked, swinging the rifle left and right. "What's the plan?"

"First, you're giving me that." I wiggled my fingers at the rifle. Stanley reluctantly handed it over, and I reluctantly handed him my Savage Stance.

"Go to the Audi," I said. "Wait in there until I get back."

"What are you going to do?"

"Lock the doors and don't get out of the vehicle, and use that gun as a last resort. Understood?"

He nodded quickly.

Before he could ask again, I said, "I'm gonna walk a wide perimeter and see if the other man is out there. I have no idea if he is, or if he stayed behind at the motel. Now go." I motioned him away.

WITH AN AR-15 LEADING ME FORWARD, I didn't feel the need to be stealthy, so I walked a big circle in record time. Since I didn't spot the cowboy's partner, I headed back to the main parking lot. Along the way, I thought about the man staying behind at the motel. The only reason to stay behind would be to search my motel room. Sure, there was a handgun I didn't want messed with, but Ranger was my main concern. My dog wouldn't let some stranger break in and snoop around. Which meant the other man would either be scared off by Ranger, or he'd silence the dog. And since these men meant business, I feared the latter.

At the main parking lot, I used Mr. Cowboy's keys and drove the sedan around the circle, hopping over the curb when I reached the men's bathroom. Then I backed the sedan until the rear bumper was two feet from Mr. Cowboy, who was still knocked out.

Stanley had left the Audi and was scampering over.

When he reached the sedan, I got out and handed him Mr. Cowboy's cell. "Unlock it. I don't know if you need a thumbprint or code or face ID."

"Probably facial," Stanley said, eyeing the phone. He positioned the cell in front of the cowboy. He picked up the man's slumped head and within seconds had the phone unlocked.

"Let me see it," I said.

Since it was an iPhone, I knew how to check for open apps. Sure enough, the first open app was a tracking program. The map was of the rest area, and the pulsating circle on the screen was right where the Audi was parked.

I showed the screen to Stanley. "Proof your car has a tracking device."

He glanced at it. "How and when was placed it there?"

"We'd know if you hadn't conked this guy out."

"You're assuming he'll easily talk." Before I could respond, Stanley continued. "I'm gonna find and rip that tracker off the Audi. And this guy" —he thumbed over his shoulder—"will be awake sometime soon. And we'll see how chatty he really is."

"Don't touch the tracker, Stanley."

"Really?"

"Really," I said, not looking at him. My face was buried in the iPhone, scanning the recent text messages Mr. Cowboy had been exchanging with his partner. "The last message from this guy to his partner was, 'Securing the target.'"

"There's no follow-up text from that?"

"Nope, there's been no time."

I kept scanning messages further back, not just for intel, but for how they communicated to one another, and in what format. For instance, did they typically use punctuation and capitalization, and was communication in plain language or code?

After a thorough scan, I noted they used plain language, very short phrases, and that Mr. Cowboy employed proper grammar. The other guy not so much. I also learned that they referred to me as the bucket hat dude.

I texted back: *Target secured.*

By this point, Stanley had clued in on my plan. "Very nice, I got you. We pretend to be Mr. Cowboy and use his car, but then what?"

I didn't answer. Instead, I waited for those three pulsating dots to tell me his partner was preparing a reply. When the dots didn't materialize, I turned my attention to Stanley.

"Let's get the cowboy into the trunk."

It took some finagling, but we managed to do it after a few minutes. I put the AR-15 in the trunk, too, though I'd extracted the magazine first. There was a set of jumper cables in the trunk, so I used the cables to secure his hands behind his back. Since there was some leftover slack from one end of the cable, I tied that loose end to the belt around his calves. That way Mr. Cowboy couldn't move his legs and kick the interior.

Stanley stood beside me as we gazed inside the trunk.

He said what I was thinking. "Geez, we better not get pulled over. Imagine the cops saw this."

"Give me your belt."

Stanley hesitated.

"Just give it to me, Stanley."

After taking the belt from him, I leaned into the trunk and pulled off the man's right boot and sock. My quick assessment was that Mr. Cowboy wasn't going to bleed to death, so I balled up the sock and shoved it in his mouth, then used the belt around his head to secure the sock in place.

"Little excessive," Stanley said, "don't you think?"

"If by chance we do get pulled over, we don't want him shouting or making noise, right?"

"Definitely not. But why don't we just leave him in my Audi?"

"He's no use to us in the Audi. Since he's gonna wake up soon, I'd like to get him talking. The back seat is split in two, so each side folds down. We can check in on him without pulling over."

"Got it," Stanley said.

I picked up the man's cowboy hat and exchanged it for my bucket hat, stuffing the flimsy, cotton hat into my back pocket. Then I ordered Stanley into the back seat. I also told Stanley to keep active on the iPhone, so it didn't lock. Before getting into the sedan, I trotted to the vending machine and extracted the snacks I'd knocked loose.

Inside the sedan, Stanley asked, "Snack time? Really?"

"I've learned to eat when you can, and these two items were free. M&M's or SunChips?"

"Regular M&M's or peanut?"

"Peanut."

"I'll take the chips."

After handing him the SunChips, I exited the rest area. I didn't stop at the barricade. Instead, I swerved to the right and took out a few orange cones. Since we were headed away from the motel, which was where I planned to return, I proceeded to the next freeway exit and circled back. While entering the northbound on ramp, we heard the first sounds from Mr. Cowboy. I was going to have Stanley check in on the man, but the iPhone buzzed.

"What's the text say?" I asked Stanley.

"Bucket hat dude followed by a question mark."

I thought for a second. "Say, 'Taken care of. Not a problem.' You have use to capitals, Stanley, and periods. You know how to do that?"

A snort, followed by, "Yes."

A reply came within a minute. "What's it say?"

"He asked where bucket hat dude is at. What's our response?"

"Say he's secured in the Audi."

A buzz came three seconds after Stanley sent that text. "Now he's asking for an ETA. Are we headed back to the motel?"

"We are."

"You sure that's where this guy is?"

I thought for a moment. "Pretty sure, can't think of anywhere else he could be. I don't think they could've stopped and dropped him off somewhere along the way. Don't think they had enough time."

"Why don't I just ask and clarify our meeting spot?"

"Hell no."

"Why not?"

"Mr. Cowboy was what, ten minutes behind us?"

"Sounds about right."

"They would've formulated a clear plan in those first ten minutes, then separated. Asking

for clarification of that plan would be a dead giveaway that it isn't Mr. Cowboy responding."

"You're right, sorry. I'm not very good at this."

"Tell him we'll be there in fifteen minutes. Actually, say twenty. I should be cautious and drive the speed limit."

A brief pause. "Okay, done. What happens at the motel?"

"Let me think."

We rode without talking for a few minutes. Mr. Cowboy's muffled cry interrupted the silence.

"Check on him, see if he's willing to talk. The belt isn't very tight around his mouth, so you can pull it down without releasing it."

Stanley unlatched the left side and folded the back seat down. Immediately the cowboy's cry jumped an octave.

Stanley hesitated.

"He's harmless," I encouraged him. "He can barely move."

A few seconds later, I heard, "Damn you two." Some heavy breathing followed, then the cowboy said, "You'll both pay, you'll pay dearly."

"Speaking of paying," Stanley said, "who's paying you? Who hired you guys?"

He scoffed. "Wouldn't you like to know."

Stanley asked a few more times with no response.

I said, "Forget it, he's not ready."

After securing the gag, Stanley latched the seat closed. The cowboy, however, carried on with his muffled cries. "Knock him out again, Stanley. Just like you did the first time."

"Really?"

"Yeah, we can't have him making this much noise."

"Sure thing."

Through the rearview mirror, I watched Stanley reach into the trunk and slide the AR-15 out. Stanley wasted no time cracking the man on the forehead with the rifle's butt end.

Silence ensued for the next five minutes. While I was formulating next steps in my mind, Stanley was scouring the man's iPhone.

After five minutes, I glanced at him in the rearview mirror. "Find any useful intel?"

"Nothing. It's clear this phone is used strictly for business communication."

"Nothing interesting at all? Any name or names?"

He shook his head.

"Any texts about their employer, anything at all?"

"Nope."

"Okay, here's the plan: I'll drop you off at the Marriott. I want you to stay put at the lobby bar until I come back for you." He started to say something, but I cut him off. "Nonnegotiable. These men are after you, Stanley, they mean business. They either want you dead, or they want to take you to Mexico. You need to take refuge in a public place like the hotel bar."

When he didn't respond, I said, "Got it?"

I glared at him in the rearview until he nodded, then continued. "From there, I'll head to the motel next door to mine, find the darkest area to park, then text cowboy's partner that I'm here. With tinted windows, bad lighting, and wearing this cowboy hat, I'm fairly confident he won't be suspicious. All I need, anyway, is for him to get close to the vehicle. I can go after him, if need be. It would be great if he hopped into the passenger seat, and I was waiting for him with my gun drawn. But I'll be ready to go after him if I have to."

"Not to be overly simplistic, Chase, but what if we just report these two to the police? Let them handle it. I know you're currently wanted by them, but I could call it in and meet the cops at the motel, tell them the truth: that these men put a tracker on my car and have been following and harassing me."

I scoffed. "And explain that you wrestled an AR-15 out of a man's hands twice your size, knocked him out, and stuffed him in the trunk of his own car?"

"Well, when you put it that way."

"Plus," I continued, "we get no intel from the men that way. Do we? And we really need to know their employer's identity. If we got a name, we could stop a serial murderer and clear me as the chief suspect."

"You're right, it was a stupid idea."

I thought for a second. "Not totally."

"Really?"

"If things go as planned and I get intel from cowboy's partner, I could knock him out and tie him up, too. Then we could park the car near a police station and call it in. If we find out they were hired by the Night Night Killer, we could tip the cops off to that fact, which would ultimately get the Tucson FBI field office involved."

He mulled it over. "Okay, sounds good. We'll circle back after everything and pick up the Audi, right? We can use your car, which is where, by the way? I didn't see any vehicle parked out front of your motel room."

"One step at a time, Stanley."

"Can I at least take your handgun with me? You know, for protection, just in case."

"Nope, you can't."

He sighed and sat back in his seat. When we arrived at the Marriott, I took the cell from him. Before he exited the vehicle, he said, "Be safe, Chase."

"Will do."

When I approached the two motels, I decided to drive past them to see if I could spot some man lurking around. Since I didn't see anyone suspicious, I circled back and entered the parking lot of the motel next door to mine. After a quick scan, I backed into a parking space in the same area the men had first parked, three spots down from their original location.

After shutting off the sedan and pulling out the Savage, I used Mr. Cowboy's cell and sent a simple text: *Here.*

Then I waited and watched, my eyes scanning left and right. Every time they passed my motel room I thought about Ranger. When approximately eight minutes had past, I figured I had it wrong; that the motel wasn't the planned rendezvous point. But then I heard a sound and saw movement from the corner of my eye.

Glancing back at my motel room, I drew a quick breath and held it.

A man had just stepped outside, and he was gingerly closing the door behind him.

SEVENTEEN

I DIDN'T LOOK at the man.

At least I didn't at first. My eyes were glued to the room's front window. I'd grown stupidly attached to Ranger, so I was hoping to see his snout push back the curtains.

But I didn't see that.

Eventually, I refocused on the dude striding toward the sedan. Like his partner, he also wore a cowboy hat and boots. His royal-blue Wranglers were tight, and his plaid snap-button shirt was tightly tucked into those jeans. With such poor lighting, I couldn't make out any facial details other than a bushy, dark mustache.

The stocky man had my duffel bag slung over his shoulder.

I slinked down in the seat. To play it cool—and hide my face—I put Mr. Cowboy's cell in my left hand and turned my head to the left, pretending to be fixated with whatever was on the screen. Though my right arm was casually at my side, my right hand gripped the Savage and pointed it low along the seat line.

From my periphery, I estimated the man to be less than thirty feet away. He was purposeful in his walk, not being cautious upon approach. I felt confident that he was going to pop open the door and have an impromptu meeting with the Savage Stance.

I was wrong.

Mr. Cowboy in the trunk suddenly let out a muffled cry. Since it was late and eerily quiet outside, the approaching man stopped, about ten or twelve feet away.

Damn!

"Virg," he said, "that the target making noise? He in the trunk?"

I didn't answer since I was contemplating my course of action.

"Virgil!" he shouted.

I scrambled from the vehicle as fast as I could; my compact handgun stretched out front. By that point, the man had pulled out a gun, too. We stood on either side of the vehicle, both leaning across the hood. He jabbed his gun first, then I followed with my own jab. It was a tense, five-second standoff.

Neither of us fired our weapons or said a word.

Realizing our luck, we both ducked and took cover by our respective front wheel. Though I couldn't see the man, he said, "Well played, nicely done. Wouldn't have thought you'd get the one-up on Virg, then pretend to be him."

Not sure what else to say, I kept it cordial. "Appreciate your respect of a job well done."

He didn't respond.

I continued. "Your partner—"

"Partner?" he interrupted. "I don't like that word, not at all."

"Colleague better? Or is he a friend, maybe a brother?"

"Not a brother per se, but a brother from another mother."

Perfect, I thought, *exactly what I wanted to hear.* "Listen, you two are obviously close. He's going to live, but he needs medical attention quickly."

"What'd you do to him?"

"Shot him."

"So, he's bleeding to death in my car?"

"He likely won't bleed to death. But if you don't get him to a hospital fast, he's probably gonna lose his foot, may be crippled for life."

"You're cold, man."

"You two are the ones chasing a twenty-three-year-old computer geek, using an AR-15 and a tracker and who knows what else for the job. Who put you up to this?"

No response.

I kept at it. "Who sent you after Stanley Tuchek?"

"Brother, you're skilled, so I'm assuming you're smart. You should know that neither I nor Virgil would ever reveal who hires our services. Think about the repercussions for my clients."

"Think about the repercussions of not getting your brother some help."

A moment of silence, then, "What are you proposing?"

"Tell me who hired you and I'll diffuse this situation by walking away. Then you can take the car and get Virgil help. Easy breezy."

He scoffed. "Yeah, easy breezy lemon squeezy. As if I can trust you."

"And I you."

"What's that mean?"

"You could tell me Vladimir Putin hired you. My point is, we both must go out on a limb here."

He kept quiet. I hoped he was considering my proposition. When he didn't respond after twenty seconds, I said, "Or we simply have a shootout here in the parking lot. And I'll be honest, I like my chances."

"Why? Cuz you got the best of Virg? You have no idea of my talents. I could be way more skilled than him."

"Don't think so."

"Man, you're cocky."

"Here's my first gesture of trust: I won't shoot you right now."

"Cocky isn't the word for you, son."

"Pal, I could've already planted a round into your left ankle, right through that snakeskin boot of yours. You should've tucked your whole body behind the tire."

I heard him scrape his boot behind the wheel. "There you go," I said. "That's better. You almost suffered the same fate as ole Virg."

There was an uncomfortable moment of silence. I broke it. "Second gesture is this." I took the sedan's keys and tossed them onto his side of the hood. I poked my head up to see if he would grab the keys.

He did.

"Deal?" I said.

"Not enough," he replied.

"How about this then?" I smacked my gun onto the hood so he could hear the noise. "That was my piece. It's out of my hands. Why don't you do the same?"

I popped my head up to see if he would. At first, he didn't, though he did pop his head up to confirm my gun was on the hood. For twenty seconds, we played an awkward game of what looked like whack-a-mole. I'd poke my head up, he would as well, then one of us would quickly duck again.

Eventually, he put his gun on the hood.

"Alright," I said, "we're making progress. Now I'm going to stand. Slowly."

As I did, he got to his feet quicker and said, "Why? To get an elevated position on me? No way, not going to happen."

"Don't be so paranoid," I replied. "I'm standing so we can have a gentlemanly conversation face-to-face."

Instead of responding, we had a mini stare down for ten long seconds. Both of us had our palms flat on the hood. Our guns were about six inches from our fingertips. I was fast on the draw and confident I'd beat him in a shootout, but that wasn't my intention.

"We have a deal now?" I asked.

"One more thing."

"And what's that?"

"Stanley's location."

I scoffed.

"You tell me where the kid is, then I'll be able to finish my job. Then I won't care if you know my employer's identity."

"What's your plan with the kid?"

He didn't bite. All he said was, "Location."

"You know I can't do that."

"Then neither can I. Which means we're at an impasse."

I conceded. "Suppose you're right." Just as I was thinking about my next strategy to employ, a distant pounding interrupted my thoughts. The noise came from behind the stocky cowboy. To his credit, he didn't pivot. He was at least savvy enough not to turn and look.

I stared over his right shoulder. A man was pounding on my motel room door. The man yelled, "I told you to leave, mister. Dogs are not allowed. You're supposed to be gone. I just got another noise complaint."

Under my breath, I seethed, "What'd you do to my dog?"

"The dog's making noise, isn't he? He's alive. I'm not some monster, you know."

"Yeah, but is he barking, or is he whimpering in pain?"

The man pounding on the door saw us standing by the sedan and started moving in our direction. As he got closer, I saw it was the motel's check-in clerk.

My eyes flicked back to the cowboy. We both stood ramrod still, debating what to do. The clerk approaching us headed straight for the cowboy. Since the cowboy was short and wide, I figured the clerk couldn't see the weapons laying on the hood. All he could see was the man's expansive back.

"Excuse me," the clerk said upon approach. "You guys seen a tall man out here wearing a bucket hat? Actually, he's about as tall as you, sir." The clerk proceeded closer, eyeing me with every step. "Wait a minute . . ."

The cowboy made a move toward his gun.

So did I. But the cowboy faked grabbing his gun and spun to his left instead. He grabbed the clerk and slipped his beefy forearm across the clerk's neck. Before I knew it, I had the Savage in my hand, ready to fire, except the gun was leveled at the clerk's chest.

The clerk started to scream but was cut off by a tightening forearm.

"Put the gun on the hood," the cowboy said, shuffling closer to the car. He picked up his piece. "Or I break this guy's neck."

"You wouldn't," I replied.

"Try me."

My mind came to the quick conclusion that I truly didn't know what this man was capable of.

"On the hood," he repeated.

I complied.

"Open the driver's door." After I did that, he said, "Throw Virg's hat in there, along with his phone, which I know you have, then back up."

I did as I was told.

"Farther," he said.

Once I was a safe distance from the vehicle, he proceeded toward the driver's door, prodding the clerk forward with his gun. I scrutinized every step, looking for any opportunity to make a move.

None came.

The cowboy was slow and methodical and never took his eyes off me or made a mistake. After opening the driver's door, he turned the clerk to face me and slipped inside the car. "You make a move toward this vehicle," he said. "This man gets a round in the middle of his back."

The clerk's eyes were wide, and his chest heaved.

I mouthed to the clerk, "Relax, I won't move."

The cowboy fired up the sedan. While the engine purred, he addressed me. "Now where's Stanley?"

"Like you, I have professional standards. I can't tell you that."

He jabbed his gun at the clerk. "Even with this guy's life on the line?"

The clerk swallowed, then screeched, "Just tell him. Please. *Please!*"

I eyed the cowboy. "You won't shoot an unarmed man in the back, will you?" The clerk's chest heaved uncontrollably.

"You're willing to bet this man's life over that?" the cowboy asked. "Over your assumption?"

We had our third stand-off; this one the shortest, but the most intense. I caved. "Fine, he's at the DoubleTree, a mile that way." I pointed in the opposite direction of the Marriott.

As soon as he squealed off, the clerk fainted. By the time I reached him, he was already coming to. "You okay?" I asked.

After a few deep breaths, he tried to speak but couldn't, so he nodded instead. When he got to his feet, he found his voice.

"You're that man, aren't you?"

I nodded. "Yup, that's my dog in the room."

He quickly shook his head, then started backing up. "No, the man from TV." He pointed at me. "The man the cops are looking for."

I deflated, knowing the story had finally broke.

Just when I thought things couldn't get worse, I heard what I believed was Stanley Tuchek's voice in the distance.

"Wait, Chase, wait for me!"

Squinting toward the front of the motel complex, I saw Stanley at the street corner waving desperately after the sedan. The car had turned left, away from the Marriott.

What is Stanley doing? Does he have something to tell me? Does he think I'm driving and leaving him behind?

As the sedan's brakes squeaked, I ran toward the scene, yelling as loud as I could, "*No, kid. No!*"

The cowboy spilled from the vehicle. Stanley stared at me, then flashed a look at the cowboy. Before he could turn and run, the man flashed his gun and commanded Stanley into the back seat.

I tore after the sedan.

But it accelerated just out of my grasp. All I could do was bang the rear quarter panel with an outstretched left arm as the vehicle raced away. I stood in the middle of the road staring at the license plate and taking a mental picture, then my eyes flicked to the rear window. Stanley Tuchek's little weasel head spun and faced me.

The glasses he wore seemed to magnify the terror in his eyes.

EIGHTEEN

A CAR HORN HONKED, then some driver had a few choice words for me.

I'd been standing in the road, worrying about Stanley, and wondering what my next move was. Snapping out of it, I moved from the middle of the road, making sure not to look directly at the driver since the story about me had hit the news. Once I was on the side of the road, and the car behind me had roared off, I kicked the curb.

Stupid kid. Twice I told him to stay put, and twice he didn't listen. Why did he leave the Marriott anyway?

After a moment of wallowing, I knew I had to refocus, so I bee-lined it to where the sedan had been parked. The Savage had skidded off the sedan's hood and was underneath another car. I grabbed the gun and put it in my duffel bag, which was right where the stocky cowboy had dropped it. I hustled to the small motel lobby.

And made it just in time. The check-in clerk was on his cell and about to talk.

"Hang up," I ordered him, while pushing open the lobby door. Cornering the man, I shouted, "Now!"

Instead of hanging up, the clerk dropped his phone. He pleaded, "Please don't kill me, please!"

I picked up the cell, ended the call, then sighed. "Man, I'm not going to kill you. I'm not that guy."

"That's not, that's not," he stammered, "that's not what the cops are saying."

"Get in that room." I pointed behind him. There was a small office directly behind the check-in desk. The clerk backed into the room, holding his hands up high.

I didn't even have my gun out.

Once inside the office, I closed the door behind me and said, "Did I kill you earlier when I had the chance? I made sure not to move. I saved your life, actually. Right?"

He shut his eyes, nodding in the process.

I continued. "I have to borrow your car. Where's your keys?"

The clerk pointed a shaky finger toward a small desk in the corner of the room. I hustled over and grabbed a keychain that had Jeep written on it.

"Take whatever you need," he said, cowering in the opposite corner. "Just leave me alone. I beg you."

Another sigh. "Dude, you're going to be fine. And you'll get your car and this other stuff back, too."

"What other stuff?"

"Have to take your cell with me, sorry. Don't want you calling the cops as soon as I leave. I need to clear my name first. You can at least keep these." I took the battery and SIM card from the cell and placed those two things on the desk. There was an older stationary phone to my right, so I ripped the cord from the wall, then stuffed the old phone and the clerk's cell into my duffel bag and headed to the door.

"Sorry, but I also have to lock you in." Holding up his keys, I said, "Which one locks this door?"

"The smallest one on there."

Nodding, I apologized once again, then locked him in.

His two-door Jeep Wrangler was parked just left of the lobby. I fired up the vehicle and headed to the back of the motel complex. My heart was firing on all cylinders as I unlocked my motel room door and stepped inside.

Fortunately, I heard a strong bark from Ranger.

He was in the bathroom, unharmed, and incredibly pleased to see me.

I ordered him into the Jeep, and before long, I was once again headed south on the freeway. The only safe, quiet place I could think of to regroup was the closed rest stop area.

While driving for the next ten minutes, my mind moved a million miles per hour, thinking about what I needed to do, and how I was going to do it. Who to call first, and how to handle Stanley's abduction. I also wondered why Stanley hadn't stayed put. It seemed like he needed to tell me something.

As I took the exit ramp to the rest stop, I turned off my headlights and eased the vehicle to a stop just in front of the barrier. Then I got out and moved on foot toward Stanley's Audi. I highly doubted the cowboys would be here. My guess was that they were halfway to Mexico by now. But I had a thought that maybe they'd come back to this location if they intended to kill Stanley. Maybe they'd staged a suicide with Stanley inside his car.

Geez, I hope not.

Once I was near the Audi, I could see that the area was abandoned, so I headed back to the Jeep. Moving the orange cones out of the way, I proceeded to the blue warning sign. Since I wanted to hide the Jeep, I put it in four-wheel-drive and veered right of the sign and climbed the sandy hill, concealing the Jeep behind the large outcropping of boulders.

With the Jeep turned off, the first thing I did was send Ramona a text through WhatsApp. I told her it was an emergency and that we had to meet ASAP. While waiting on her response, I got out and used the light on my burner cell to make sure there was no LoJack or some other anti-theft device on the Jeep. It was easy to check the undercarriage since the Jeep was lifted. I found no tracking device.

Next, I used a quarter and removed the Jeep's Arizona license plates. With Ranger by my side, I took those plates and my duffel bag to Stanley's car, but I left the clerk's cell and old phone on the Jeep's driver's seat. When I reached the Audi, I put the Arizona plates on his car. I found that the screws were long enough, so I didn't even have to remove the California plates. I just put Arizona right over top.

After that, I found the cowboys' tracking device and pried it off the metal frame. Ranger and I loaded into the Audi, then I checked my phone in case I'd missed a text from Ramona.

I hadn't.

I resent her the same text. Following that, I texted my friend and colleague, Hans Schlimmergaard, aka Slim, and told him to find a secure line and call me ASAP at the burner cell number.

Then I waited. My chief concern, of course, was Stanley. His father had to be informed of the developing situation, and I thought it best to come from Ramona. No doubt Ramona would get the Tucson office to reach out immediately. Plus, I had the license plate number in my head and the feds could run the plates right away and issue an APB on that vehicle.

I also wanted to get in touch with Mick Cranston, a good friend of mine who lived in California. I wanted Mick to lean on Griff Murphy, double-check that he or his subcontractors weren't involved with Stanley's capture. I highly doubted that they were. Since the Night Night Killer took out Rogan Ross, it made sense that he'd be after Stanley, too. And considering the killer likely resided in Mexico, it stands to reason that he'd hired some morally ambiguous American cowboys to snatch the kid and deliver him somewhere. No doubt the serial killer paid the men handsomely. I bet that the cowboys didn't know they were delivering the kid to meet his demise.

The cell in my hand buzzed. It was a text from Ramona in my WhatsApp account. It was a number followed by, *call me.*

I did.

She answered with, "I can't believe I bought a pay-as-you-go cell, and we're talking like this. What's the emergency?"

"Stanley's been taken. He's in trouble, serious trouble."

A deep breath into the phone, then she said, "Is that enough to make you come to your senses and turn yourself in? This is even further out of hand, Garrison."

I hesitated to respond.

"You know," she went on, "the story's gone public. That fact alone should cause you to come in."

"Actually, it's the opposite."

"How so?"

"Now that it's public I'll be scrutinized even more. And if I turn myself in, then I what, have to rely on a lawyer or the Tucson office to clear my name? No way, now I absolutely must clear my name on my own terms."

"Boy, you're stubborn. And you don't trust many people, do you?"

When I didn't reply, she said, "Tell me about Stanley. Just how serious is his situation? In the restaurant, you told me he was on his way to Phoenix, and that you were going to have him recreate the evidence. Did he?"

"Nope."

"What happened?"

"No details over the phone, let's meet and discuss. Write this down, though." I gave her the sedan's license plate number and told her that Stanley had been swept off in that car.

"Got it," she said. "I'll call the AG myself, and I'll leave you out of the story for the time being at least."

"Appreciate it."

"Where are you?"

"I'll send a pin of my location through WhatsApp."

"I'll be there." Then she hung up.

Before I'd put the cell down, it started ringing. It was an unknown number, and I assumed it was my pal.

"That you, Slim?"

My buddy's deep voice boomed, "What the hell have you gotten yourself into?"

"I take it you watched the late-night news?"

"Just before turning in, I flicked it on and saw your ugly face."

"How bad is it?"

"The picture they used, that what you mean? Pretty bad, for the record."

"No, how bad was the report? I haven't heard what they're saying."

"Not as bad as it could be, I guess."

That brightened me a little. "How so?"

"They're calling you a person of interest in the Night Night killings."

"Least I'm not the chief suspect, that's what I assumed they'd reported."

"This ain't good. Terrible, in fact. Obviously, you're not some serial killer, I think." He gave a hearty laugh, then continued, "But we have some work to do."

"We do. How quick can you get to Phoenix? I need your help here."

"Saving your ass again. You owe me. And our company."

"*Our* company? Am I a co-owner now?"

"Hell no, being a serial killer and all, you wouldn't pass the background check. Anyway, I meant my company—of which you work for—is gonna take a serious PR hit here."

"I'm glad you're chiefly concerned with the bottom line. At least I know I'm talking with the real Hans Schlimmergaard and not some impostor from a burner number."

"Ouch."

A momentary pause. "You're right, that was low, sorry."

"No worries, I'm only partly concerned about the bottom line. I, unfortunately, care about you."

Awkward silence. "A little," he added. "Just a little. I'll catch the first flight out this morning."

"Appreciate it, Slim."

"Anything you need me to do in the time being? I take it you'll fill me in on all the details and the plan in person."

"We definitely need to talk face-to-face about that. I forgot to write down Cranston's number, so I don't have it stored in this burner. Can you contact him for me? Give him this number."

"Sure, what do you want to tell him?"

I quickly looped Slim in on my plan to have Mick Cranston shake down Griff Murphy.

After I finished, he said, "I take it you still know how to stay off the grid?"

"You know I do."

"How will I find you?"

"I'll text you an address using this number through WhatsApp. Download that app if you don't already have it."

"10-4. I'll buy a plane ticket and travel under an alias. Since we work together, no doubt the feds are already monitoring your friends and associates." Slim had a near identical past as mine. We both kept some aliases from our covert operative days.

"Which won't be too much work for them," he continued. "Am I right?" He laughed. Before I could react, he explained his own joke. "Since you don't have many friends or associates. Get it?"

"Look forward to seeing you, pal. I mean, if my eyes can take you in all at once." Slim was a behemoth of a man, and I frequently chided him about his size.

"Took you long enough to crack a fat joke. You're slipping."

"See you soon, pal."

He hung up without saying goodbye.

I used the controls on the side of the seat and slipped the top part of the seat backward until it was near horizontal. Ranger stood over me and licked my face. "Thanks, Range, now sit. Be a good boy. I have some thinking to do."

Instead of dwelling on what was happening to Stanley, I focused on his company, Futurum. My recall from our conversation was that a colleague had helped him process the evidence given to Ross. Which meant somebody else, beside Stanley and Ross, would have access to their results via their backup system.

I must find out who that was. But how?

My thoughts revolved on that for about fifteen minutes, and by the end of that time I felt like I had some solid ideas for moving forward. Just as I started thinking about how to find the homeless man in San Luis, lights straight ahead distracted me. They were headlights coming up the entrance ramp.

Glancing at my watch, I figured it was too soon for Ramona to be here. It'd been just a half hour since I communicated with her. And she would've had to first contact the AG, run the plates through her system, and liaise with the Tucson field office. Not enough time to also then drive here.

I grabbed the handgun from the duffel bag and left the Audi, taking Ranger with me. I sprinted toward the bank of vending machines. Standing in front of them, I listened to the vehicle's engine. This time the car didn't stop at the women's bathroom area. I could hear the revving engine getting closer to the men's area, where I'd parked the Audi, so I put Ranger at the far end of the vending machines and commanded him to stay. Then I tucked myself behind the end of the vending machines closest to the Audi.

And waited.

The car shut off. Unfortunately, I had no view, so I kept listening.

A car door opened, then I heard footsteps. There was only one set. The person sounded light on their feet. *Was it Ramona? Or was it one of the cowboys tiptoeing?*

I peeked out from the machines but saw nothing.

Pressing my back against the concrete wall, I disengaged the safety and breathed steadily through my nose. The footsteps were like whispers. After one more slow breath, I stepped out and prepared to engage.

But a woman was already in a firing stance, and she was locked onto my position.

NINETEEN

"YOU'RE LIKE A CAT," I said. "Actually, more like a panther, so quiet and sneaky."

Ramona relaxed her stance. Immediately Ranger trotted out from his position. He could tell from my voice that things were fine. He wagged his tail incessantly as he approached Ramona.

"Who's this beauty?" she asked while tucking her firearm away and giving Ranger a good scratch behind his ears.

"Ranger's his name."

"Didn't know you had a dog and apparently travel with him."

"A story for another time."

She nodded. "You're lucky I didn't fire, with the way you popped out like that. Reminded me of a jack-in-the-box."

I said, "You got here way quicker than I imagined. Didn't you have some calls to make?"

"I *can* multitask, Chase. I spoke with the AG and the Tucson field assistant director on the drive."

"Sorry, I forgot people do that."

"Exactly how old are you?"

I smiled. "So, how'd Ernesto take the news?"

"Better than I imagined."

We started walking toward the cars with Ranger trotting behind. "How so?" I asked.

"He wasn't very emotional, and that surprised me a bit. What didn't surprise me was how analytical he was. He fired off tons of questions about what exactly happened, and, of course, I couldn't answer. I wanted to tell him to call you for details." She slugged my shoulder. "But since you insist on being on the lam, I had to leave you out of it."

"Did he ask how you or your office found out about the abduction?"

"Of course. I told him an eyewitness saw Stanley being thrown into a car at gunpoint, and that person immediately called in to the local feds, which was my office."

"How'd the eyewitness know it was Stanley Tuchek?"

"Stanley shouted out for help and said that his dad was the Attorney General."

"You're quick on your feet."

"I guess so. And it's the last lie I'm gonna tell for you, so you know."

"It was somewhat true, right? I mean, I'm the eyewitness, Stanley was forced into a car by gunpoint, and I called and told you about it."

She shook her head and didn't say anything. When we made it to the vehicles, I motioned for her to get into the Audi.

"Whose car?"

"Stanley's."

"But it has Arizona plates."

"Again, another story for another time. Get in. I want to know what Tucson is thinking. I was surprised to hear that I was a person of interest and not the chief suspect."

She settled in the passenger seat while Ranger hopped in back.

"So, Tucson immediately started pulling your cell and financial records," she said, "which wasn't a surprise. It quickly became clear that you were in Mexico a few times during the killing spree, but that you were also in the States during the bulk of the murders."

As she paused, I jumped in. "Okay, so why go public with the story if I can be exonerated by the evidence?"

"That's just it," she replied, "you can't yet."

"Why not?"

"Because they're entertaining the theory that you're the mastermind behind this, but that you've had help. That you traveled a few times to Mexico to subcontract these murders, and that you could've been orchestrating much of this from home."

I shook my head and looked out the window. "And what would my motive be for killing young and middle-aged Mexican men? It's outrageous."

"Exactly, they're nowhere near a motive, Chase. But you're a former investigator, you know at this point they don't have to prove motive. Anyway, that's why you're a person of interest and not the chief suspect. And that's why you need to turn yourself in and explain everything. I mean, your mother lives in Mexico and you've dropped off and picked up your son how many times this past year? You were on your way to get him, weren't you?"

She was right, of course. I ought to listen to her and turn myself in. When I didn't respond, she said, "What are you gonna do, Chase? Talk to me."

I deflected. "What about your agents? Did you clear them or find a mole?"

She hesitated to respond.

I said, "Not answering my question, I see."

"Yeah, wonder where I learned that."

"Fair enough. I'll answer your question first, then you fill me in on what you learned. I know you're right about everything, and I will turn myself in, but . . ."

She sighed. "But what?"

"But I need more time." I held up my hand. "Hear me out: I just need to set a few things up first, then I'll turn myself in tomorrow evening. If I don't have these things in place while dealing with the legal ramifications, then they might not happen. And I want to give myself the best chance to catch this killer and clear my name."

"Set up what exactly?"

"Slim's on his way to Phoenix. I'm gonna send him to Mexico and see what he can find out about the street person. I think that's my best use for him. Unless, of course, Tucson is on it and has already sent someone. Have they?"

She shook her head.

I continued. "My other buddy, Mick Cranston, is shaking down a PI team that the AG had hired to protect Stanley."

"This shouldn't preclude you from turning yourself in. And they sound like they're in motion, anyway."

"True, I have one more thing to find out, and I need your help with it."

"You're gonna ask me to do something that could get me in trouble, aren't you?"

"Don't think so. Maybe. I'm not sure." I batted my eyes in a playful manner.

She rolled hers. "What is it?"

"I'd like you to pull the records for Stanley's company, Futurum, which is based out of California. Find out who's also employed by them. I know it's only a few people. It would be great to know their details, including phone numbers, not to mention the address of the Futurum lab in Lompoc. I have no means or resources to do so right now. One of the Futurum employees helped Stanley process the crime scene evidence sent to them by the Mexican authorities. There's a backup of the results. With Stanley in the wind, we need this person to get the results. It could help us break the case and catch the killer. I may get my pal, Mick Cranston, to help on this, too."

She bobbed her head side to side, thinking about it. After a few moments, she said, "Okay, I'll do it. You or Cranston contact this person, get the results sent to the Tucson office, then turn yourself in." She glanced at her watch. "Twelve to sixteen hours from now. Deal?"

I nodded. "Now what did you learn about your team?"

"Still running down a few things. I'm not prepared to say just yet."

"You're kidding?"

"I'm not. I've been a little preoccupied trying to find out what Tucson has on you. I'm trying to clear your name, you know."

"And I appreciate it. But—"

"I get it," she interrupted. "It's important to find out if I have a corrupt agent in my office. Trust me, I realize that."

I said it, anyway, because it was so important. "If your team is clean, then it means the detective is lying, and we can't trust any evidence the Mexican authorities gave Ross."

Perturbed, she narrowed her eyes. "Like I said, I know. You realize that if I do confirm there's a mole on my team trying to sabotage this investigation, it's a huge problem for the agency. And me."

"I know, I'm sorry. I'm just impatient."

"That's an understatement, but I'll cut you some slack since you're being unfairly targeted as a serial killer. Anyhow, I'll get there with my team. Just need to be absolutely sure of the lead I'm running down."

"I'll give you twelve to sixteen hours to do so. Deal?"

She slugged me, which was becoming a habit for her.

"Oh," I said. "One more thing."

"One more? Really? You already said that."

"Sorry, I forgot about him." I thumbed over my shoulder at Ranger. "You seem to be a dog person, right?"

"Now I'm a dog sitter for you, too?"

"I mean, I'll probably be in jail soon. And this guy needs some love."

On cue, Ranger stuck his long snout into the front seat and nuzzled under Ramona's left arm.

She melted. Ramona turned in her seat and grabbed Ranger from behind the ears and started rubbing. "How could I say no to this face. So cute!"

"You're definitely a dog person," I said.

And I liked dog people. A lot.

TWENTY

I SAT in Stanley's Audi for thirty minutes debating what to do.

In the end, I made a decision that would piss Ramona Sanchez off: I put my bucket hat on, eased low in the driver's seat, and drove back to California.

Slim would also be perturbed that I had bailed on him. But my plan was to immediately send him to San Luis Rio Colorado to find the homeless dude, so I didn't exactly need to meet with him in person to let him know that.

My reasoning for bailing to California was two-fold: One, Stanley said Futurum had a small lab located in Lompoc. That was where I assumed his employee worked, and I needed to get in touch with that employee so I could get access to their backup system.

Two, since Ramona hadn't cleared her team of wrongdoing, I didn't exactly trust the Arizona feds, so I wanted to deliver the Beretta 92 FS to Stanley's employee. That way the lab in Lompoc could process the weapon for fingerprints or touch DNA and then compare anything they discovered to the backup results they had on file.

I knew I could get my buddy Mick to help with this task. But he didn't have the Beretta in his possession, of course. Also, he'd be busy shaking down Griff Murphy, and time was of the essence. Since I was a wanted man, everything had to happen quickly.

My guess was that Ramona would contact me late morning with the names of Stanley's employees, along with phone numbers, and the lab's address. By that time, I wanted to be in Central California so I could get a jumpstart with whomever Stanley had been working with.

Though Ramona would be ticked I didn't turn myself in to her office, or the Tucson field office, I felt like being in California would also protect her. The more distance between us, the less likely anyone would find out she'd been helping me behind the scenes.

Once everything was in motion by mid to late afternoon, my plan was to turn myself into either the Long Beach resident agency, where I once worked, or the FBI field office in Los Angeles. I'd figure that out later.

To get through a long night of driving, when I stopped to fill up for gas, I also purchased a twelve-pack of Mountain Dew, which I believed had the highest amount of caffeine for a soda. To avoid frequent stops and being seen, I urinated in the empty Mountain Dew bottles while driving. By the end of my trip, with twelve Dews in my system, my urine was as fluorescent as the soda itself.

After eight and a half hours of being on the road, I was back on the Central Coast, at ten in the morning. Since I wanted to be close to Lompoc, I headed a few miles west of town and parked at Surf Beach. I craned the seat back, opened the windows to let fresh sea air into the vehicle, placed the burner cell on my chest, tilted the bucket hat down to cover my face, and fell immediately to sleep.

I woke one hour later after a quick buzz from the burner.

Slim texted: *Just landed. Where are you?*

Change of plans, I replied. *Call me from your burner.*

A minute later my cell rang. I said, "Sorry, pal, but I had to leave Phoenix."

In the background I heard airport sounds. "Okay, smart guy," he said, "and you wanted me here because?"

"You're gonna help catch the killer."

"And how's that?"

131

"Have you seen the video of me leaving the building where Rogan Ross was killed?"

"Yup, I'm one of the millions that've seen it. Count me down for like five of those views."

"Good." I went on to explain the who, what, where, and why of the video. The whole time I was telling him the story, I could hear lots of talking in the background, including from Slim himself. Apparently, he was checking in at a rental car counter.

After I told him everything, I asked, "Did you follow all that while securing your car?"

"Sure did. And for once, I'm tracking with your logic. If I can find this homeless dude, I can lean on him for information about who paid him to film the building. And if I can't, then we know for sure the serial killer himself was there and that he did the deed, not you. Either way it should help your case."

"Whatever you find out, you may need to tell the Tucson field office."

"Why's that?"

"Because I may be incarcerated by then."

"They onto you? I thought you knew how to stay off the grid."

"No, they're not onto me. I'm turning myself in by day's end."

"Hmm. Think that's best?"

"I do. With you and Mick working these different angles, I'll be okay. In fact, I think we can even nail this killer."

"Want me to send Jimmy your way? Or at least give him this number?"

Jimmy Schuberman was Slim's lawyer. I'd used his services before. He was quite the East Coast character. Incredibly annoying, but effective, nonetheless.

"That can't hurt, I guess." I thought for a second. "Send me his number, and I'll reach out if I need to. I'll also drop a pin of the San Luis Rio Colorado location in WhatsApp. I drove around the town a little when I was there, so I know a decent portion of the transient population hangs out at the local bus depot." I also gave him a broad description of the man and his possessions as best I could remember.

"If he's still in the town, I'll find him."

"I know you will."

"Good luck, pal." Then Slim hung up.

Following the catnap and conversation with Slim, I felt reinvigorated, so I drove into Lompoc to check out Stanley's house. With him missing, and his father pulling out all the stops, I wondered if the police or feds would be at his house looking for clues. When I approached Stanley's place, I stopped at the curb about two blocks away and surveilled straight ahead.

His driveway was empty, and there were only a few cars parked on the street. None were cop cars, and I guessed none were unmarked fed cars either. All the vehicles were empty of people, so Griff and his men appeared to be still off duty.

Feeling confident no one was on surveillance, I did a quick drive-by to confirm my suspicion. Just after passing Stanley's place, my cell buzzed, alerting me to a text.

It was from Ramona, and it was long.

Once I was out of Stanley's neighborhood, I pulled over to the side of the road and read the text. Ramona had sent the names of Stanley's three employees, their job titles, contact information, and the lab address.

Futurum employed a geneticist, forensic scientist, and a genealogist. After checking a maps app on my phone, I learned the lab was located just outside of town. Since it was working hours, I figured I'd start there. On my way to the lab, I wondered if the feds or cops would be there. But it turned out they weren't.

The address was a one-story industrial complex at the edge of town, on the east side. The complex was comprised of several individual steel buildings with high, peaked roofs. Along the road was a sign outlining the companies residing in the complex. It was the type of place you'd pass by on car or on foot and have zero interest. I mean, hardly even worth a glance.

Pulling into the parking lot, I drove around until I found building D. There was one car, a silver Toyota Corolla, parked out front. There was also just one door, a heavy steel one, at the front of the nondescript gray-and-black building. A small red-and-white sign saying Futurum was fixed to the right of the door. On the building's front side, there were no windows to peek in to see if anyone was working. There was also no open sign or an hours sign hanging anywhere, so I rapped on the door.

After a minute, I knocked again. This time louder. When nobody came, I proceeded around the back of the building. Before turning the corner, I heard the steel door screech open.

Turning back, I realized I still wore the bucket hat and sunglasses, so I took them off. My plan was to be straightforward and tell the truth. If an employee had been watching the news and freaked out at my presence and called the police, it was a chance I had to take. Since I was turning myself in anyway, it wasn't a big concern or risk for me if that happened.

A Black woman, probably midthirties, with curly hair and bright aqua-blue eyes popped her head out from the door and asked what I was doing. It wasn't accusatory. She seemed generally perplexed at what I was doing there.

"I've been working with your boss, Stanley," I said. "I understand this is his company."

Before I could continue, she said, "He's not here."

"I know. It's you or one of your colleagues I need to speak with." I remembered the names Ramona had sent in her text. There were two women's names and one male name. "Are you Sage or Victoria?"

She scowled, ever so slightly, and didn't answer. Instead, she said, "Who are you?"

"Garrison Chase."

Eyeing me, she said, "I heard of you."

Uh-oh, this can't be good. But she didn't slam the door on my face, and she said nothing about me being a wanted man.

"Let me see some ID," she said, wiggling her fingers.

I obliged, handing over my California driver's license.

While scrutinizing my picture, I gave her the once-over. The woman had beautiful skin and a youthful glow. She wore black Adidas three-stripe jogging pants and a green half-zip sweatshirt. She also sported some big, cushiony running shoes.

She looked more like a long-distance runner than a scientist.

After about fifteen seconds, the woman let out a breath and opened the door. The initial scowl, and the tenseness in her body, were gone. She looked relaxed, relieved almost.

"Come in." She motioned with her hand.

As I started to, she continued, "I've been expecting you, Mr. Chase."

That stopped me in my tracks. Now I had the scowl. "Expecting me? What do you mean?"

"I mean what I said. I've been expecting you."

In shock, I managed, "How?"

"Stanley, of course. He said you'd likely be in touch, and if you were, I was to give you everything we had on the Night Night Killer. I thought he meant sending you the results, not you coming here in person to get them." She shrugged. "But, oh well. Here you are."

When I didn't move, she said, "Well don't just stand there, come in, let me show you what we have."

I cleared my throat. "When? When did Stanley tell you this?"

Since I still didn't move, she literally grabbed my arm and pulled me inside, then shut the door.

Looking at her watch, she said, "Three hours ago. That's when I last heard from the boss."

TWENTY-ONE

LEON GLANCED at himself in the rearview mirror.

As far as he could tell, he looked very much like the gardener whose truck he was driving. He was fresh shaven, wore a curled-brim baseball cap pulled low on his head, and sported wraparound sunglasses that he'd taken from Raoul, the gardener.

While nearing the front gate of the opulent villa, he breathed slow and steady. He was reminded of a story he'd read about Jeffrey Dahmer. Apparently, Dahmer was stopped by the police when he had his very first victim in the car. The body had been dismembered and placed in doubled-up garbage bags. When the police glanced into the back seat and saw the trash bags, Dahmer coolly responded that he was taking yard clippings to the dump.

Dahmer had been so calm and collected with the cops that they didn't think twice about the garbage bags. Leon hoped he'd keep his cool like that as he approached the check-in gate.

As he pulled in front of the gates and stopped, Leon noticed the extra security. Which made sense considering everything that had happened to this family. For protection, the surviving brothers had rallied at their eldest brother's mansion. Naturally, they'd doubled their security efforts at the sprawling estate.

When one of the guards stepped out of the shack, Leon rolled down his window.

In flawless Spanish, he said, "Raoul Montalban. Here for the monthly weed and pest control." Leon jacked his thumb over his shoulder toward the truck bed.

Inside the bed were an array of gardening tools, a weed eater, a lawn-mower, a rake and shovel, along with two large garbage bins with lids. The metal bins were fastened by a rope and held tight to the back of the cab. There was also a small hibachi bar-b-q and a weed sprayer attached to a back harness.

The guard glanced into the truck bed and gave everything a thorough check, then he briefly looked at Raoul. With complete indifference, he made a note in what Leon assumed was a logbook, then waved at the guards by the gate to step aside.

Driving through, Leon tried to contain himself. By the time the gates had closed behind him, a huge grin had spread across his face. He parked the beat-up white truck around back of the mansion where all the service members were required to park.

Hopping into the truck bed, Leon eyed the two garbage cans. He honestly couldn't remember which one held the chemicals. He rattled the bins, but they were both heavy and hard to move, so he pried off the lid from the can on the left.

"Not that one," he said to himself while looking down.

There, curled up in the can, was the corpse of Raoul the gardener.

TWENTY-TWO

THE WOMAN STARTED WALKING into a vast, open room, looking over her shoulder after a few steps. "I'm Sage, by the way, not Victoria."

All the neurons in my brain were focused and firing, attempting to comprehend how exactly she'd heard from Stanley a few hours ago. As a result, my muscles weren't working, so I stood there like a statue.

"Are you coming or what?" She stopped walking and put her hands on her hips. "What am I missing here. You look incredibly confused."

I snapped out of it. "Sage, are you positive you heard from him three hours ago?"

"What kind of question is that? Yes, I got a text from him at about eight this morning. What's exactly going on? Because Stanley texted from a different number, which was strange for him."

"A dozen hours ago I watched him get abducted at gunpoint."

She walked fast toward me, saying, "No, you're kidding. You're kidding! Really?"

"Didn't he mention that in his text?"

She stood to my left, chewing on her lower lip. "No, nothing, nothing at all."

"What did the text say?"

She dug out her phone, unlocked it, scroll around, then handed me the phone.

The text was from a 623 area code. It said: *its stanley, not my phone, don't DO NOT text this number back explain later. garrison chase may contact you if he does, give him everything on the night night killer. in meantime work on this*

Below his text was a grainy picture of a piece of paper. It took me a second to realize what it was: the notes I wrote while in the motel.

I looked at Sage.

She said, "It's a list of four things he wants me to do. I've been pulling all the data and organizing the results."

Nodding, I said, "That's the note I gave him in Arizona. Those are the things I needed him to work on. And that's why I'm here."

Sage scooped under my left arm and pulled me into motion. "Let me hear everything over a cup of coffee. I'll make you one."

While walking, all I could think about was Stanley. "The good thing is he's alive, at least he was early this morning. I would've thought for sure he was dead by now. Has nobody reached out to you about his whereabouts?"

She shook her head. "Not a soul. He left the other day; said he was going to Arizona on business and would be gone a day or two. Said he'd stay in touch via text."

"I bet he got hold of his captor's cell, then fired off that text and sent the pic."

She nodded. "Then he would've deleted the text and put the phone back without anyone the wiser. He's a furtive fellow."

I laughed. "That's a polite choice of words. I would've gone with sneaky son of a bitch, but he is your boss after all."

She smiled, which was radiant and lit up the dim kitchen. "That's why he was so adamant to not text back. I mean, he's never used a capital letter before in his life, so I knew he was serious, and I didn't dare respond."

"Yeah, I think you're right. That's exactly what's happened. He lifted the cell."

"Not surprising, is it? You ever notice how fast he moves?"

"Have I? No, not at all." I grinned.

"If Futurum fails, he could make a living pick-pocketing people." She gestured to a state-of-the-art coffee maker and then an Italian espresso machine to its right. "Cup of coffee or shot?"

"Double shot would be great."

"Tell me what happened in Arizona."

While she flipped some switches, ground some beans, and pulled two double shots, I told her what had happened with Stanley and his pursuing cowboys. I also brought her up to speed on my visit with Rogan Ross and what I'd learned there. She hadn't heard of Ross's murder. She'd never actually met the podcaster since he was a silent investor in Futurum.

As she sat across from me with a concerned look on her face, sipping on a frothy head of espresso, I asked, "I take it you haven't been watching the news lately." Which, obviously, bode well for me.

"Never," she said, shaking her head. "I don't have time. If I'm not working here, I'm training for an IronMan. There's one coming up in a few months in Morro Bay that I've entered. Don't have time for television or news or social media. Even if I did, I wouldn't indulge."

I was instantly fond of Ms. Sage.

She was silent for a moment, a deep crease coming across her forehead. I asked, "What's wrong?"

She kept her head down. "If Rogan Ross was killed for investigating this, whether for a theory he was advocating or for whatever evidence he had on him, or both, and now Stanley was abducted for his involvement, I'm next." Looking up, she said, "Right? I'm in trouble, too. That only follows."

Sage had a point, but I wasn't going to let her worry. "You'll be fine. Nobody knows you're working on this except me and Stanley."

"You don't know that. You can't be sure of that."

She was too smart to be placated, so I proposed something. "How about this: You turn everything over to me, and I in turn give it to the feds. I'll head to the LA field office this afternoon. Once I give them the evidence, I request WITSEC for you. Shouldn't be a problem since we're giving them crucial evidence in an international serial murder."

"WITSEC?"

NIGHT NIGHT KILLER

"Witness security. Until we resolve all this and hopefully bring the Night Night Killer to justice. What do you say?"

"What about you? WITSEC for you, too?"

"I've got my own federal issues to deal with."

"Like what? What's that mean?"

I deflected. "Never mind, you watch the news one day and you'll understand. Now let's get to the evidence."

She stood. "You're not going to tell me, are you?"

"Nope, I'm not."

Reluctantly, she waved me on. "Let's go to the lab then."

I followed Sage out of the kitchen. We proceeded across a large, open floor. The area was sparsely furnished with only a few cubicles set up in the middle of the room. Vast amounts of polished concrete surrounded the small triangle of desks. The place looked like some sort of starter business that was waiting for its first infusion of capital.

We walked to the far corner of the office—if you could call it that—and stopped in front of a wide door. After opening it, we stepped into what was clearly a receiving room. Most of the back wall was a large roll-up steel door. To the right of the door was an eight-by-ten-foot metal platform. Sage stood on the platform and punched a code into a keypad mounted on the wall.

"Come on," she said.

As I hopped on, the platform started lowering. She sensed my confusion. "Originally this building was a start-up winery. We're headed underground to where they stored the wine. This platform is how they got the barrels down to the cellar. Stanley converted the area into a lab, and this is the only way to access the underground. Stanley thought it was the perfect place to conceal a laboratory."

I motioned upward. "So that's basically a front then?"

"Yup, all the work happens down here. It may be overkill, but Stanley's superprotective concerning his company. It's a competitive industry and he's paranoid about outside entities. He talks way too much of corporate espionage, trade secrets, things of that like. Personally, I think he watches

141

too much television, but considering the possibilities for Futurum, I also understand his paranoia."

I wanted to ask about that, but we suddenly stopped, and lights flicked on, exposing a short hallway. We'd descended about fifteen or twenty feet. It smelled slightly mildewy, and there was some dampness in the air.

As soon as we stepped off the platform, I heard a compressor kick on and fresh air immediately started pumping through a wide ceiling vent. At the end of the stark bright hall was a solid door with no window. Sage punched in a code and the door sucked off its rubber seal and cracked open.

Pushing the door, she said, "Welcome to Futurum, Garrison Chase."

The first thing I noticed was how small the room was. I'd say it was roughly thirty feet by forty feet. And it was all open, no walls or dividers or cubicles. The concrete ceiling and four walls were painted bright white. The feeling in the room was dry, and there wasn't the faintest smell of mildew like there was in the hallway. I figured that had to do with several high-tech air purifiers and dehumidifiers pumping away in each corner of the room.

If you liked white noise while working, this place was nirvana.

Along three of the walls were various scientific instruments. Everything looked new and state-of-the-art. The only items I could identify were a centrifuge and an electron microscope. I had no clue what the other pieces of equipment were.

Sage caught me looking at them. "That's where we do the forensic lab work, Victoria and Fred's stations. Stanley and I work over here." She gestured to the wall on my right where there were a bank of computer monitors and two desks.

"What do you think?" she asked.

I joked, "If this is the future, it looks pretty small."

She plopped into her desk chair. "All we really need are these," she said, motioning toward the computers.

"That's good," I replied, "because there's no room to expand this lab. Is there?"

"You don't know what we do. Do you?"

I shook my head. "Not really."

"Would you like to know?"

"Eventually. For now, I'm curious about the results you and Stanley sent to Ross. In particular about the Night Night Killer. Ross had told me he isolated a single source male profile from the evidence, and he was pretty sure that profile was the killer. Do you know what he was talking about?"

"Sort of."

"Sort of?"

"I think I know how he came up with it."

"How?"

She pointed to the far monitor, which was the only one turned on. "These are the suspect profiles we pulled from the forensic evidence the Mexican authorities sent us. You can see a few have been identified, and a few haven't." Sage pointed to a list on the bottom part of the screen. There were some men's names listed, followed by their titles. Those identified were CEOs of American corporations. Of course, I didn't recognize their names. And I was only familiar with one of the companies listed, General Electric.

"These three suspect profiles," she continued, "I haven't been able to identify, but they probably were by Ross since he was using our software."

I nodded. "That's exactly what happened. That's what Ross told me in Mexico." I pointed to the three suspects on the screen. "One of those profiles is likely the killer, someone who wasn't a CEO and didn't share the familial connection with the victims. Can't you use the software and help identify these three profiles?"

She hung her head. "I can't."

My countenance dropped as well. "You can't?" I motioned to Stanley's desk. "Your boss's computer is right there."

"Understood, but it doesn't work that way. At least we haven't set things up that way."

At this point, she was looking down and to her left. Again, she chewed on her lower lip. Without looking up, she said, "I can't even access Stanley's computer to try to run the software. They're both so security conscious."

"How exactly have you set things up? Tell me about that."

"We're compartmentalized. Considering what's happened, it's dawning on me just how stupid that is."

"Compartmentalized how?" I asked.

"Well, Fred and Victoria stay in their lane, I stay in mine, and Stanley and Ross have access to the software. I haven't had the need or desire to learn or run the software. I've been solely focused on reverse engineering family trees. Which"—she held up her hand—"I know is a big problem now since Ross is dead and Stanley is missing."

"Huge problem."

Sage's frustration was palpable. She stood and began pacing the small room.

To snap her out of it, I tried to be positive. "We have the profile, Sage, it's one of those three, so it's still a win. Huge, in fact, since we're not at ground zero anymore. I'll turn the information over to the feds, and they may be able to identify the suspects. Plus, Stanley's still alive, right? Pardon the pun but he may weasel his way out of his situation, and then he could help."

She stopped pacing and nodded.

I motioned to her desk. "Now tell me what else you know."

She rushed over. "Grab Stanley's chair." The twinkle in her eye was back. "I'll show you."

After pulling the chair beside hers, Sage clicked away on her keyboard, entering a variety of passwords until the other two monitors flickered on, which were already alive with information.

"We were sent two lines of evidence from the Mexican authorities," she said. "One batch related to potential suspects. This was a lot of secondary transfer DNA from broken glass and what appeared to be napkins. There were some hair and saliva and small amounts of semen on those pieces. We were also sent blood from the victims. Fred and Victoria worked their magic and provided me with DNA profiles for both victims and suspects. With that in hand, I started my job."

I jumped in. "Taking those profiles and comparing them with any public DNA database you could get a hold of. In hopes of finding a familial relation, then tracing that back to a common ancestor. Right?"

She looked mildly impressed but didn't say so. "Exactly."

"Tell me about the victims first. It's my understanding there wasn't much known about them." I thought back to my meeting with Rogan Ross. "But Ross did say he'd uncovered a connection between the victims."

"Connection?" She scoffed. "That's an understatement if ever I heard one. Did Ross not tell you about the connection?"

"He didn't."

"But you met and talked about this stuff, didn't you? Before he, um . . ."

"We did. Why do you sound so surprised?"

"Because the connection is huge news. Just surprised he wouldn't have told you."

I didn't want to get into the weeds about how I was supposed to listen to the episodes on an mp3 player while Ross was putting the finishing touches on the final episode. Trying to contain my excitement, I prodded her. "What is it? What's the big news?"

Her eyes lit up as she pointed at the middle monitor. "Take a look at this family tree. You seem to know about this stuff. Incredible, right? Check out the victim profiles, they're the ones highlighted in red."

I scooted forward in the chair and looked at the screen. All I could tell was that it was a large family tree. Nothing more.

"Well?" she said. "What do you think?"

I looked at her. "Sorry, Sage, I overplayed my hand. I understand the basics of reverse engineering a family tree, but I don't really know what I'm looking at."

"They're related!" she exclaimed.

"What do you mean? Like a few are?"

"No," she said, shaking her head. "Every single victim of the Night Night Killer is related. They're either brothers or cousins."

I sat back in the chair, feeling my head start to spin.

TWENTY-THREE

"Brothers and cousins," I said under my breath, "brothers and cousins. Unbelievable." I looked at Sage. "And this hasn't been reported by anyone, right? I mean, I've never heard it mentioned on the news."

"Whether the Mexican authorities truly don't know the victim's identities and connection, or they do know and are keeping it under wraps, is anyone's guess."

"Think it's really fifty-fifty like that?"

"Probably not. Building this tree has been difficult, there's lots of holes as you can see"—she pointed at the monitor with the family tree—"which is mainly because the family is massive, and there's not much information about them. My guess is that Mexico hasn't put it together yet."

"And why do you guess they haven't?"

"Because the family resides partly in Mexico and partly in America. I was only able to put this together because the patriarch here," she said as she pointed to the top of the family tree, "is American and has a criminal history, which enabled me to identify him. The authorities in Mexico, if they have an expert doing what I'm doing, wouldn't have discovered this because of the patriarch's American origin. They wouldn't have access to the type of databases that we do. That's why this case is absolutely perfect for our software. This case was supposed to put our company on the map, but now I don't think it will. Not with . . ."

As she trailed off, I kept her focused. "Explain that, Sage. Why is this case perfect for your software?"

She eyed me. "So, you do want to know what we do?"

"I want to know everything. I need to know. I need to understand it."

Sage pushed back from her chair, thought a moment. "It's my understanding you're an investigator and formerly a federal agent?"

I nodded.

"Then you know that for a crime scene, or identifying an unknown dead person, it all begins with getting a DNA profile."

"Sure."

"For a suspect profile, if that person had previously committed a crime, authorities could quickly find a match in a database like CODIS and identify the person. You know about the limitations with CODIS, I assume?"

"I do."

"That's the bad news, but the good news is that companies like 23andMe and Ancestry.com have become incredibly popular over the past decade. Suddenly investigators have these large databases to cross-check a profile if there is no match in CODIS. On top of that, while we were seeing an explosion of people submitting their DNA to these databases, advances in forensics led scientists to extract a DNA profile from the tiniest of samples. Of course, with these advances comes concerns with privacy issues."

She paused.

To move her along, I nodded. "Understood, it's a thorny problem."

"Our company, however"—Sage gestured to our surroundings—"isn't about the forensics. Not at all, in fact. That's why there's no plan to expand this lab."

"What do you mean?"

"Well, there's already amazing forensic companies out there doing incredible work. Labs with vast budgets that we can't compete with, nor do we want to. There's a company out there called Parabon NanoLabs, for instance, that is doing mind-blowing stuff with phenotyping. They offer a

DNA snapshot service that can take a suspect's profile and predict eye color, hair color, ancestry, even face shape."

"Phenotyping, huh? Isn't that just a fancy name for predicting physical characteristics from a DNA profile?"

"See, you do know your stuff."

"I've actually heard of Parabon. I've listened to quite a few true-crime podcasts over the past year, and Parabon has been mentioned multiple times for helping to solve cases. It makes sense that you couldn't compete with a big lab like Parabon. Which begs the question: Why even have one?"

"I'll get there," she said, "hold on. So, all these forensic labs are competing to evaluate evidence and quickly extract a DNA profile. From there, my industry jumps in. Using the DNA profile created by a lab, we try to find distant cousins through various databases and then find common ancestors and build family trees out from there, though Futurum isn't about the investigative genetic genealogy side of things either."

Before I could ask why they existed then, she continued. "Genealogists give investigative agencies a basic pool of suspects that we glean from a family tree. From there, detectives, cops, federal agents, and the like, perform detective work to examine the potential suspects from a family tree. There's no way around that fact. Sometimes the tree won't be large, or it's quick to eliminate suspects from the list because people are dead, so often it's not a time-consuming process. Other times, though, there's a huge pool of suspects, and it takes investigators a long time to track down these people and find out where they live, if they're alive, et cetera.

"Enter Futurum." Her aqua-blue eyes were wide and alive with excitement. "Stanley saw an opportunity in a post–Golden State Killer world. In the GSK case, for instance, investigators had been given several suspects developed from a reverse-engineered family tree. Moreover, some phenotyping work had been done with the GSK's profile, and it had been determined the killer had blue eyes. Within the GSK's family tree, there were only two males currently alive with blue eyes, so that narrowed the suspect pool down and helped them quickly nab Joseph DeAngelo."

"I knew about the blue eyes, didn't know there were only two suspects. Very interesting."

She nodded and carried on. "Once investigators are given a pool of suspects, how they quickly narrow down the list is by cross-checking a profile with a multitude of databases. In GSK's case, once you know the suspect has blue eyes, you get access to the California DMV database because height, weight, and eye color are all listed there. Solving crimes comes down to having access to information in databases and cross-checking that data with what you know about a suspect. And that is essentially a mathematical problem, one that Stanley's an expert in. Specifically, in writing code and developing advanced algorithms. You tracking?"

"I am."

"Good. Instead of an investigator first checking this database, then that database, then another, eliminating suspects one by one, crossing people off a list, that sort of thing, investigators would use the Futurum software. And that's as simple as entering a suspect's name into a search string. Then Futurum cross-checks all the databases it has access to, which is done on the backend. Literally minutes later there's a spit-out of whether the person is dead or alive, where they live, height and weight, known relatives, all their offspring, current job, last ATM purchase. Possibilities are limitless. It comes down to speed and convenience for a detective or investigator. Using our software dramatically speeds up their work. It eliminates a lot of manual steps."

I digested it all for a moment, then said, "So it amalgamates all the data from a variety of databases then."

She nodded. "Within minutes, seconds sometimes."

"I get it. The power of a software package like that makes sense. Couple of questions, though."

"Fire away."

"What's the economic model? How do you make money? By selling the software to agencies, I gather."

"We have two streams of income. Yes, the idea is to sell access to the software to all local, state, and federal investigative agencies. A onetime cost that isn't much at all. A fraction—"

"Really?" I said, cutting her off. "Like how little?"

"We're not entirely sure yet. But little enough that an agency would never balk at using the software because of cost. We want it to be a no-brainer decision. Also, by having it at a low cost, it eliminates competition from other companies doing the same thing. Fortunately, we aren't in this to be Jeff Bezos or Bill Gates, and we don't want to be salespeople. Selling at a marginal cost to the many thousands of investigative agencies in the US nets us plenty of money, especially since we're a private company and profit is split between the five of us." She paused and swallowed. "Four now, I guess."

An awkward silence followed. I asked, "What's the second source of income?"

"Updates. Again, at a marginal cost. As time marches on, we trust more and more databases and information will be added to the backend of the software. Clients with the existing software would pay a yearly mainte-nance fee, which means updating algorithms to speed things up as well as incorporating new databases into the search string."

"All this assumes access to databases. And a lot of companies will fight hard to protect the privacy of their clients. Many will refuse to play ball."

"You're absolutely right. One of the reasons we named the company Futurum pertains to the fact that we're betting on the future, that in the next decade this will all change."

"You sure about that?"

"We've already seen certain public databases initially be open to law enforcement, then individuals complained about privacy issues, so the information was then inaccessible, only to recently reopen again. With major breaking stories like the GSK case, and more to come, we're confi-dent public opinion will change."

"Okay, so you're gambling the value of your software will basically outweigh the public's privacy concern."

"Yup. The GSK case helped move the needle in our favor. Plus, forensic companies are routinely solving cold cases these days. It's all gaining momentum. We believe companies will give access to their data in the future if it means pinpointing violent crime offenders. We're also betting on state and federal laws to change in our favor, too."

I thought about that for a moment; the big picture had become clear.

"Basically," Sage continued, "we want to be the Google of search engines for violent crime suspects. That's our company mission. It boils down to that."

I repeated the mission: "The Google of search engines for violent perps. I like that, and it's quite a big vision."

"It is. And I think it's doable. Has Stanley ever given you the spiel on Google?"

I shook my head.

"You ever use Bing or the Yahoo! search engine?"

I laughed. "Nope."

"I'll spare you the details, but Google's success amounts to speed and relevancy of search terms, which is all about the algorithm it uses. Simply put, Google has a better algorithm than its competitors. And Stanley thinks he can build the best algorithm for our particular software, and I'm betting that he can."

Stanley Tuchek was indeed a mathematical genius, so I imagined it was a safe bet, but I didn't mention that to Sage. Instead, I said, "So Fred and Victoria are betting on that, too, I imagine."

She nodded. "Stanley is forty percent owner in the company. Ross had a thirty percent share, which I guess will go to his widow since he put up most of the seed money for this place. And Fred, Victoria, and I each have a ten percent stake."

"So, this"—I gestured to the lab area—"is a necessary first step to help Futurum solve some crimes?"

"Right. We need some of the basic forensic equipment to extract profiles to develop trees so that we can demonstrate how effective and fast the software is that Stanley developed."

"Which is why revealing the Night Night Killer's identity would put Futurum on the map. Launch your company in other words. And maybe why Ross was so determined to reveal the killer's identity on his podcast."

She nodded.

I didn't say anything since this newfound information started my mind in a conspiratorial direction.

Sage interrupted my thoughts. "What are you thinking? Your face is getting red, and I think I could slot a quarter in that crease on your forehead."

I'd been thinking about a new theory concerning Ross's murder, one based on corporate espionage and malfeasance. What if it wasn't the Night Night Killer that wanted Ross and Stanley to stop? What if it was a competitor of theirs that didn't want Futurum to succeed? Could they have hired someone to kill Ross and conveniently frame the Night Night Killer as the culprit? *Then I show up and they decide to muddy the waters even more.*

"Chase!" Sage snapped her fingers.

"Sorry."

"Seriously, where did you just drift off to?"

It was a bit of a wild theory, so I didn't want to mention it. "Just thinking about the Night Night Killer, hoping the feds can do something with those profiles to help identify him."

"Me too. Hope they can find Stanley as well. On that list you gave him there was mention about a gun and doing some testing."

"Right. I'll leave it with you for processing. It was left at Ross's murder scene. If there's any DNA evidence found on the weapon, you can cross-check it with those three profiles."

"I'll call in Victoria to work on that. We might get lucky."

Thinking about the list, I said, "That just about covers the things I needed from you. Giving you the gun for processing, trying to locate the single source male profile, and establishing the connection between victims. Hopefully the feds can run with the three profiles and at least narrow it down."

Sage furrowed her brow. "You know, I've been at this since early this morning. I have more to offer than just that."

"Like what?"

She put her hands on her hips. "Like a theory as to what the hell's going on, about what I think Ross had ultimately discovered."

Eyeing her, I said, "Really?"

"Really."

I perked up in the chair. "Do tell, Sage, do tell."

TWENTY-FOUR

"The victims share more than just a blood connection," she said, "more than a family tie. And I believe that connection helps explain what's going on."

When she paused to gauge my reaction, I rolled my hand. "You have my attention."

"From what I gathered on the internet, this man here"—Sage pointed to the top of the family tree on the middle monitor—"is named Humberto Salazar Senior and he's the long-dead patriarch of an infamous polygamous cult called the Salazar Family Line. They go by the nickname of The Family, or *La Familia*."

"Never heard of them."

"You wouldn't unless you lived in that triangular border area where the murders have taken place. The Salazars are a huge family in that region, and Humberto's successor, his firstborn son, took the family legitimate decades ago. He stopped all the criminal ways of his father, so they've been operating under the radar for some time. Though they keep to themselves as a large family, they do play a prominent role in the community."

"How so?"

"Commerce. They own several successful companies in the area. And get this," she said as she leaned toward me, "one of those companies is a high-end catering business that works on both sides of the border."

Catering? Immediately I thought about the parties that the American CEOs hosted in Palmera. What if these male victims weren't company employees but were the caterers at these wild parties the corporations threw? What if they saw firsthand the terrible abuse and corruption?

Sage interrupted my thoughts. "The authorities sent us what we believe is fabric from napkins and pieces of glass from broken stemware, and that has always puzzled us as to why. But if we reason that these victims worked in the catering industry, then it kind of makes sense, right? This is what I think Ross found out." She pointed to the family tree of victims. "He found out these men's identities, and he learned that not only were they closely related, but they all worked for the same catering company."

"I think you're onto something. Perhaps these caterers worked the wild parties and saw the terrible abuse of their local women and paid the price for doing so. Stanley said it was real bad, like binding them against their will, sexual torture, and the like."

"Perhaps? I think it's more than a perhaps, don't you?"

I bobbled my head. "The authorities in Mexico must know the connections between these victims, otherwise why send Futurum catering items like napkins and pieces of stemware? They know a lot more about what's happening than they're letting on, which makes me not trust them."

"Agreed," she said. "The victims were all found in the middle of nowhere, and I believe the reigning theory is that they were killed elsewhere. Maybe the Mexican authorities knew the original crime scenes were at these parties, and the evidence they sent us was found at the actual murder scenes?"

She waited for me to respond, but I didn't stay anything. She finally asked, "Why do you look so skeptical?"

"Rogan Ross was skeptical about the evidence, and I am still. Giving Ross this type of evidence could be for the sole purpose of substantiating his claim that the serial murders were commissioned by the CEOs. And, ultimately, to cast dispersion away from a Mexican serial killer."

"All that to save face, though? Just because they don't want to admit to a serial killer being from their country?"

I shrugged. "Maybe, I don't know. But they may double-down on that since the latest victim was a prominent American."

She chewed on her lower lip. "Maybe."

I kept thinking, this time out loud. "Maybe The Family isn't so legitimate. You said they work on both sides of the border, so it stands to reason that they could be into drug smuggling or human trafficking or both. Not out of the question, right? Maybe there's a rival gang or cartel that doesn't like that fact, so they're wiping out the family. And maybe the Mexican authorities know this and don't want to admit they have another big drug cartel problem on their hands. And they've conveniently found a scapegoat in Ross's theory about CEO involvement."

She pointed at me. "That sounds better. And it explains why they sent us some common evidence that you could easily get from a catered party. The narrative is already in place via Ross's podcast, and they're sending us fake evidence to substantiate said narrative. They're playing us, Chase, aren't they?"

"Could be." The whole situation was even trickier if you considered the conflicting stories from the Mexican lead detective and local cop. But I didn't want to get further into the weeds with Sage about that.

So, I moved on. "All this good work you've done"—I pointed at her computer monitors—"I'll give to the feds to figure out. It will be their responsibility moving forward. How can I share this data and results with them?"

"I've got just the thing." She reached into a drawer and pulled out what appeared to be a thumb drive, except it was slightly bigger and wider than most thumb drives I'd seen. "A Stanley Tuchek invention," she said, holding it up. "This is the latest prototype."

I smirked. "You both know that thumb drives have already been invented, right?"

"This isn't your typical thumb drive, Chase."

"I see that, it's bigger and wider."

"Okay, smartass, enough. It's bigger and wider to fit your full thumb on the body of the drive, and that's so it can scan the user's unique thumbprint for access."

"Interesting," I said.

"Since Stanley and Ross were so security paranoid, and they both despised sending important information via the internet, Stanly made his own real thumb drive."

"Gotcha. So how does it exactly work?"

"I'll show you." She plugged the drive into her computer and pulled up a basic software program. "Let me see your thumb, put it on this flat part of the drive."

I did.

Within twenty seconds, she said, "Okay, I scanned your thumb, you're good. You're the sole user for this drive. Now let me copy all the results I have onto the drive. When you deliver this to the feds, you'll have to be physically present to allow them access to the drive's contents."

There was some silence as she finished copying all the files.

After it was over, I said, "Nifty."

She made a face. "Nifty? How old are you exactly?"

I grinned. "This is a lot better than carrying around a file full of papers or a regular thumb drive that anyone could access."

"Exactly. And by its look, you can't tell that the body has a built-in fingerprint scanner. And that was on purpose. Somebody steals it, they could never access it because there's no code or password to be broken. You physically need your thumb to retrieve the files, and you wouldn't know that from looking at the device."

She handed me the drive. "Just don't let anyone cut off your thumb. Now let's head above ground. You can get me the gun, and I need to call Victoria to have her process it. No cell signal down here. Another precaution that's turned into quite the annoyance."

I pulled out my phone. Sure enough, not one bar of reception. Since I'd been below ground for some time, I wondered if I'd missed any texts or calls.

"Topside it is," I said.

"Topside?" Sage screwed up her face. "You work in the Navy or something? This isn't a boat, you know."

I really did like Ms. Sage.

Once above ground, we headed across the vast office floor toward the front door. A few steps in, my phone started chirping. I had two messages. Since one of the texts was from an unknown number, while walking, I clicked on that one first. It read:

Aug, it's Gabe. Couldn't find Griff. He's not in Cal.

Gabe or Gabriel was Mick Cranston's codename. Mine was Augustine. Back in our operative days—which seemed like eons ago—that was how we referred to each other on missions. I quickly shot him a text:

He on vacation? Visiting family?

Then I read the next text, which was from Ramona. It made me stop in my tracks. Sage, who was a few steps ahead of me, stopped and turned. "You coming?"

But I didn't look up since my eyes were glued to Ramona's text. It said:

Mole in my office.

TWENTY-FIVE

Leon had spent the better part of the last hour with the weed sprayer attached to his back. He'd walked the perimeter of the vast estate, occasionally spraying the odd dandelion or weed that had sprouted up in the lush grass. All the while, however, what he was really doing was getting the lay of the land. Studying the entrance and exit points and noting where security ran their patrols.

The place was buttoned up tight, just as he suspected. Most of the security men were protecting the estate's perimeter. There was nobody near the house itself.

Currently, he was inside the flower beds that snaked around the perimeter of the mansion. The first floor was elevated approximately eight feet above ground. As you approached the double front doors, you ascended about ten steps. Upon first glance of the property, the estate seemed to hover slightly above the surrounding landscape.

As a result, the first-floor windows were well above Leon's height, so he operated under the radar in the bushes below. For precautionary measures, though, in his right hand he held a large box filled with what looked like fine sand. The box had a picture of a spider and a scorpion, each with a red circle and a strikethrough around the respective nuisances. With the scoop in his left hand, Leon dug it into the box and then troweled a thick line of the sand along the base of the mansion.

Except it wasn't sand or bug deterrent. It was ammonium nitrate powder.

It took him an hour and a half to lay down the powder. The only part of the estate that he didn't cover was the front doors. Next, he grabbed the rake from the truck and got to work.

At this point, Leon was visible, and he felt the guards' eyes on him from time to time. However, he was working just like any gardener would, so no eyes lingered longer than they should.

The flower beds around the mansion contained different trees and bushes of various sizes. Within the beds were lots of dead leaves and broken branches, which Leon raked into small piles about every ten feet or so. After he finished that project, Leon went back to his work truck. On the tailgate, he setup the small hibachi. He dumped a huge pile of charcoal briquettes into the grill and then doused them with an excessive amount of lighter fluid.

He lit the briquettes and jumped into the truck bed. Leon swapped out the canister of weed spray with a backup canister from one of the garbage cans. Inside that canister was gallons of lighter fluid.

Working quickly, Leon used the sprayer wand and doused the edge of the grass that butt against the flowerbeds. He also soaked the small piles of debris he'd raked up and the base of the two wooden front doors.

Since the estate was on lockdown and sealed up tight, he didn't have to worry about the smell wafting through an open window or door. If the perimeter guards questioned the lighter fluid smell, Leon would point to the hibachi and let them know he'd just lit the briquettes, and that he was going to cook some meat for his lunch.

Once he'd circled the property, he stopped spraying the lighter fluid about ten feet from his truck. Now came the most physically demanding part of the job: He shimmied the garbage can with Raoul's body to the edge of the tailgate. Bearhugging the can, he slowly lowered it onto the ground with a huff.

Following that, he angled the can slightly and rolled it into the middle of the grass. Once there, he popped off the lid and pulled out a calling card. Except this calling card was slightly different.

It's time to take credit for my work.

He perched the new calling card on Raoul's forehead. Leon reasoned the metal garbage can would preserve Raoul's corpse and the calling card from the impending inferno.

After putting the lid back on, his final step was to spray the lighter fluid from where he'd stopped earlier to the truck's gas tank. Then Leon traced a line of fluid from the tank to the lit hibachi.

Dropping the canister at the base of the tailgate, he casually strode toward the grove of trees at the back of the property near the river. Behind him, the flames shot along the grass in record speed.

Leon didn't turn back to watch. Only when he made it to the tree line did he glance over his shoulder. At that moment, the nitrate powder was sizzling and erupting and sending immense flames up the mansion walls.

Boom! Leon flinched as the white pickup suddenly blew.

Creeping deeper into the trees, Leon waited. The property was in a desert climate, so a landscaped area such as this took an immense amount of water. To properly feed the estate, decades ago the family had begun diverting water from the medium-sized river at the rear of the large lot. That river flowed into the Colorado River a few miles away.

Along the river, the family had built a boat dock with an accompanying boathouse.

Within a minute of the explosion, two security guards from the boathouse came racing down a dirt path on ATVs. That was Leon's cue. His escape plan was in motion. Before proceeding to the dock to commandeer a boat, he studied the scene.

The mansion, and its surrounding landscape, was engulfed in flames. The fire raged, crackling and popping and sizzling and shooting yellow and red bolts into the air. Black smoke was filling the blue sky and choking out the sunlight. It was apocalyptic.

Four security guards from the gate ran frantically around the estate, keeping their distance but looking for any point of entry for help. There weren't any.

Satisfied with the conclusion to phase two, Leon ran toward the river. He knew this would set war in motion. Without a doubt.

TWENTY-SIX

I ROLLED south down Highway 101 in Sage's silver Toyota Corolla.

She had one of those cell phone holders that attached to an air vent, and my burner was clipped into it. I eagerly waited on a call from Ramona. I'd told her to call me as soon as she could get free from work.

After giving Sage the brown paper bag with the Beretta 92 FS, I swapped vehicles with her. She had no problem using Stanley's SUV since it was quite an upgrade from the Toyota.

It was midday. Once again, I wore the bucket hat and sunglasses combo. I was headed to the FBI's Los Angeles field office. During my stint with the feds, I worked out of the Long Beach resident agency, and my boss at the time, Frank Lemming, was someone I could trust with my life. Recently he'd moved to the LA office, so I was headed there to give him the evidence, and turn myself in.

To be honest, I felt good about everything. I probably should've been more concerned or upset about the corrupt agent in Ramona's office. But the fact that one of her agents leaned on a Mexican cop, and then that cop lied to Ross about the evidence, meant there was a better chance the Mexican detective was on the up-and-up. Which meant I could somewhat trust the evidence given to Ross. Therefore, the information stored on the thumb drive in my pocket might actually lead somewhere.

Considering the current turmoil in the Phoenix and Tucson offices, I also felt good about my decision to leave Arizona. Though I hoped it was only a rogue agent bought by one or more of the American CEOs, I wouldn't have felt comfortable turning over evidence, especially to the Tucson office.

The cell buzzed, and I stabbed the answer button before looking at the number. "Talk to me, Ramona."

"Ramona? Ramona Sanchez?"

It was Slim.

"Yeah, pal, Ramona Sanchez," I replied. "I'm waiting on a call from her." Slim had helped on the case that Ramona and I worked, the one with the dead senators in Washington.

"About what?" he asked. "Is this personal or professional? Does Karla know?"

"Professional. Ramona's not in DC anymore. She's heading the Phoenix office now and I'm having her work an angle." To avoid talking about my ex, I got right to it. "What do you have for me, buddy?"

"Lots."

"Let's hear it."

He cleared his throat. "When I rolled into San Luis, I first checked the alcove across the street from Ross's hideout. Surprise, surprise, there was a dude sleeping there."

"Really? Was it—"

"Of course not," he said, cutting me off.

"And how do you know?"

"For one, the man was in a wheelchair."

"Could be fake," I said.

"Both legs were amputated above the knee, pal."

"Oh, probably hard to fake then."

"A little. Anyway, the man lost them in a car bomb planted by a local drug cartel. He wasn't the target. Talk about wrong time, wrong place. This guy borrowed his friend's car to get milk, and bam! Anyway, though his life was spared, he lost both lower legs and an eye. Now he's addicted to smack to deal with the pain and trauma. And that was five years ago. He's had the alcove spot for the better part of three years."

"Except for lately."

"Exactly. He was approached by another street person who offered him three days of heroin for the spot. This wheelchair dude said hell yes and spent a few days at the bus terminal shooting up. Even confirmed that fact with some less than reliable people at said bus terminal."

"What'd the guy look like? The man who offered him heroin?"

"That's the thing, the wheelchair dude is not a great eyewitness. Not just because he has one eye, but also because he was tripping when I met him, and his memory of the other guy is hazy. Been hanging with him and feeding him and making sure he gets lots of water. I'm trying to stop him from doing heroin so I can get him lucid enough to recall the dude who offered him smack for his spot."

"Has it worked?"

"Not yet, but I'm going to keep at it."

"Good, because we're close to isolating the killer's profile. And if we could get any description of him, even the smallest bit of intel, that could eventually help with identifying him."

I didn't want to explain investigative genetic genealogy and phenotyping to Slim, and thankfully he didn't ask. "Once you hopefully get a description, I have another job for you."

"And that is?"

"Find out everything you can about a local cult called The Family."

"Never heard of them. How do they fit in with the big picture?"

I spent the next five minutes outlining what I'd learned from Sage. After bringing Slim up to speed, he told me he was on it. I told him to feed any intel he discovered to Ramona since I'd be incarcerated in a matter of hours. Before ending the call, I gave him Ramona's burner number, then told him that any communication from me would have to come through Jimmy Schuberman, our lawyer.

To my surprise, Ramona didn't call back for a couple of hours, and

Mick never responded to my text. When Ramona's number popped up on the burner, I was already driving through Los Angeles.

"What'd you find out?" I asked.

She blew a big breath into the phone. "Still having a hard time believing this, Garrison. I knew in the back of my mind it was a possibility, but I honestly thought I'd prove my team was clean. Which I obviously didn't."

"Are you in a place you can talk about details?"

"Yeah, I'm in my car, and using the burner phone."

"Aren't you glad you have one now?"

"Glad isn't an emotion I'm exactly feeling."

"Fair enough. So, who was it?"

"Richie Balboa, a junior agent of mine. Richie wouldn't have been my pick for this, not at all."

"How come?"

"He's reliable, very dependable, so I wouldn't have thought he could be bought. From a performance perspective, though, he's average. Not smart, not dumb, mainly flies under the radar. He's plain, you know, totally vanilla. The only thing that sets him apart is his mouth. He's a talker, and that's an understatement. His nickname in the office is Richie Blaboa or Richie Blabs."

"Doesn't shut up, huh?"

"Nope, never. Which is why when I confronted him with some evidence, he immediately clammed up, so I knew he was on the take. Never seen him quiet before."

"He lawyer up?"

"Nope, not yet. Hasn't mentioned it."

"And he hasn't said a word to you or anybody? Not one word?"

"Nothing, totally closed down."

"What's he been doing? What's his demeanor?"

"Scared. He's wringing his hands so hard I think the skin's going to peel off."

I thought for a moment. "Wonder if he's scared for losing his job and doing time, or if he's scared of whomever put him up to this. Whichever CEO is involved."

"Could be all of them, they could be in cahoots."

"Could be. Have you verified a recent healthy deposit in his bank account?"

"Not yet, there are some issues with that."

"What kind of issues?"

"Well, I guess it's just one issue."

When she didn't elaborate, I said, "What issue?"

"Me. I'm the issue."

"Uh-oh, what happened?"

After a brief pause, she said, "It was a six-person team from my office that traveled to Palmera, three guys and three gals. From what you told me, the agent that approached the Mexican cop was a man, so I only had three suspects to investigate. The thing is, any computer or federal email address that my agents use are fair game, so I don't need permission from a higher authority or a warrant to access a federally owned computer or email address. With the help of an IT person, I can do some digging. And digging I did."

"And what'd you find?"

"Richie Blabs sent an inquiry about an inmate to the Arizona Department of Corrections via his federal email address. Suspicious, right? But not exactly incriminating. One of my IT gurus did a search on his computer for the name of the inmate. Up pops an email Richie sent to an American family member of the Mexican cop. In the email he was asking verification of this family tie with the prisoner."

"Perfect, so you nailed him then."

"I did. It's weird, though. Richie uses an iMac at work. In the Mail app on his iMac, he has his personal gmail account on there as well. Legal freaked out a little because the email to this family member came from his gmail account, not his federal account, which we shouldn't have access to. Except, of course, Richie chose to put his gmail on his work computer. It's sort of a gray area. Anyway, Legal is going to work through the issue. Doesn't appear that it will be a problem. In the meantime, though, they've asked me to step aside."

"Step aside? What's that mean?"

"They're not too happy that I went full steam ahead on this investigation. Probably should've run my ideas through Internal Affairs first. But you know how much I love red tape."

"About as much as I do."

"IA has it now and they're working on a warrant to get access to Richie's finances. And I'm sure they'll have no problem getting a judge to sign off on it. But I'll be on the outside looking in for now."

"How far outside?"

"I had a few weeks of vacation begging to be used up."

"Nothing forced, right?"

"Nope, I proposed using vacation time."

"So, you still have your badge, right?"

"I do. Why?"

"Because I have a job for you. Unless, of course, you want to put all this behind you and spend some time in Maui."

"And miss the opportunity to be bossed around by you, a suspected serial killer? Hell no. Whatcha got for me?"

"A visit across the border to Mexicali. It's no Maui, that's for sure."

"Who and what is in Mexicali?"

"The Mexican detective." I let the statement hang for a moment.

She broke the silence. "I get it. Now that I confirmed we have a corrupt federal agent in the Phoenix office, I assume you think we can trust this detective?"

"That's a little far. He could have an angle, for sure. I'm not denying that. From what I understand, though, he went nuts trying to ferret out the mole on his team, so I think it's worth you two having a conversation."

"About what?"

"Their investigation, of course. I think this detective knows a lot more about the victims and the crime scenes than he's letting on."

"No doubt, Garrison. But do you really think he'll spill the beans to an American law enforcement agent?"

CRAIG N. HOOPER

"I think you have a badge, not to mention your looks."

"What do my looks have to do with anything?"

"You're an attractive woman with a badge. Some men would find you persuasive and hard to say no to."

Ramona huffed into the phone. "Not sure, Garrison, if I should be flattered or offended."

"Not sure why you wouldn't be flattered."

"You're something else."

"Just the facts, ma'am."

"Alright, I'm not the type to lay on the beach, more a desert girl anyway. I'll head to Mexicali pronto."

"And you can hook up with Slim in San Luis Rio Colorado maybe. He's gathering some information for me as well."

"About what?"

I told her about the Salazar Family Line and everything I gleaned from Sage.

After my story, she said, "So you have the evidence on you now, and you're turning yourself in like you promised?"

"I am."

"You should probably avoid my office, Tucson is best."

"Or neither office."

"What's that mean? My guess is that Richie is working solo on this. This isn't some big conspiracy, Garrison."

I came clean. "I'm in Los Angeles, Ramona. Gonna turn myself in to my old boss." Before she could jump in, I said, "I actually visited Stanley's lab in person and spoke face-to-face with Sage. Thought it was best for you if I was out of the state."

There were a few seconds of silence, then Ramona said, "I understand."

To keep the conversation moving, I brought up the kid. "What's up with Stanley? Have you heard anything? Any progress on finding him or the car or the cowboys?"

"You know, it's interesting. Before leaving the office, I checked on the situation. Couldn't find anything about the abduction. No internal memo

168

alerting the Arizona field offices to the kidnapping. No APB or even a BOLO from what I could find."

I thought about that. "That's beyond strange. You know, Sage hadn't been contacted about Stanley, and there weren't any agents at his office or home. You'd think Ernesto would be pulling out all the stops to find his son."

"You're right, you'd think so. Wonder what the hell's going on?"

"Maybe he went straight to the marshals."

"Probably, that's probably what he did."

I mulled that over some more. The US Marshals were experts in fugitive hunting, so they knew how to find people. It would make sense for Ernesto to put them on the task of hunting Stanley's abductors. "I could see him contacting them first. Just is odd that he hasn't also reached out to federal offices in your state. I mean, you contacted the AG late last night, and his son was taken in Arizona."

"Agreed. Not sure what to make of it, and I can't really find out either, not now."

I'd arrived at the LA office on Wilshire Boulevard. While parking in the far corner of the lot, I relayed to Ramona that any future communication would have to happen via my lawyer, Jimmy Schuberman.

I said to her, "He's got a heavy Boston accent. You might think he's playing you, but it's for real. He's a character but a damn good lawyer, just don't tell him I said that."

After hanging up, I took some quiet moments before heading inside the federal office. I thought about my former boss, Frank Lemming. He was a no-nonsense kind of guy, so I needed to present one coherent theory. He wouldn't want to waste time hearing several alternate theories. So, I went through the evidence in my mind of how I would present the case to him. My best theory, based on the evidence I had, amounted to this:

High-powered corporate American CEOs were partying out of control in Palmera. It was well known they were doing horrible, illegal things to local women. The catering company employed at these lavish, wild parties was The Family. The male members working these parties banded together in frustration over what they were witnessing. As a coherent family unit that was powerful in the area, perhaps they felt emboldened to confront the American CEOs. In turn, the CEOs silenced this group of men by hiring a *sicario*, which was Spanish for hitman. It could be there were multiple sicarios involved, too.

When the CEOs caught wind of Ross and Stanley's podcast, they sent a sicario to deal with Rogan Ross. They also had problems stateside with Stanley Tuchek, not to mention the FBI was also investigating the murders. As a result, they paid off a local FBI agent to cast dispersion away from them, and they hired some local cowboys to kidnap Stanley Tuchek, either to kill him or to simply stop him from investigating.

There were obvious holes, and some unanswered questions, too. For instance, I could see Frank asking why this Spanish hitman or hitmen were posing their victims the way they were. I'd have to be honest with him and admit I had no idea. In the end, I'd have to convince him that my theory was sound, and that it could be backed up by the evidence I had on the thumb drive.

Feeling good about my decision, I prepared to call Jimmy Schuberman. After thinking about that a moment longer, I decided against it. All my lawyer would say was to shut my mouth, not breathe a word, but I had no intention of playing that game. I wanted to clear my name and send the feds after the real suspects, as fast as I could.

So, instead of doing the wise thing and calling my lawyer, I looked up the number to the

LA office and dialed.

As it rung in my ear, I said to myself, "Here goes nothing."

TWENTY-SEVEN

FRANK LEMMING WAS TYPING an email when his office phone buzzed.

Without looking at the phone, he pressed the blinking light with his right hand while his left kept typing. "What it is, Brenda?"

"A call for you, Frank. It's . . ." A slight pause, then she continued, "Garrison Chase."

He stopped typing. "You're kidding."

"That's who he says he is. You know, he's wanted in connection—"

"More than aware, Brenda."

"Shall I put him through?"

"Yes but give me thirty seconds."

"Will do. He'll be on line two when you're ready."

Frank pulled out his handkerchief and dabbed at his glistening fore-head. *Garrison Chase? What the hell?* He loosened his necktie, blew out a big breath, and wondered what Chase wanted from him.

He stabbed the line two button.

"Chase, I see not much has changed with you, still getting in trouble. I thought some of your previous messes were bad, but this, pal, this takes the cake."

"I see a lot has changed for you, Frank. Moving to the big city and taking Phil Hornsby's job. The assistant director, huh?" Chase laughed. "Remember what we use to say?"

Frank huffed into the phone. His official title was Assistant Director in Charge, which was an unfortunate and unflattering acronym. His predecessor was indeed a dick, so it was fitting. Not so much for him he hoped.

"I took this job, pal," he said, "just to redeem that title."

"Let's hope you can."

"Where are you?" he asked.

"Close."

"How close?"

"Close, close. I'm turning myself in to you but want a reassurance first."

"What kind of reassurance?"

"That it's quiet. Don't need or want a ton of fanfare when I enter the building."

"Probably doable," Frank said.

"I've got some evidence with me, so I'm hoping you and I can go someplace quiet to look at it first, then discuss."

He paused.

"Please, Frank, you know I'm innocent."

"For damn sure you are. You're not smart enough to pull this off, not that many murders. But you know how it is, right? We have to show we're taking this situation serious. You can't just waltz in here, we shake hands like we're old friends, then go and have a chat over whiskeys. You're a person of interest in an international serial murder case, and you've been on the lam."

"I get it, I do. Of course, I'm innocent, but the damage to my name is already out there. Just don't need to make it worse. I have a son to think of, Frank, and you know there's a dozen or more eyewitnesses in that lobby right now and everyone has a phone these days. I don't need a video of me being handcuffed circulating the internet."

After a long sigh into the phone, Frank said, "Okay, I'll keep it on the down low."

"Just you, Frank. Come to the lobby window. When I see you, I'll come in. Thing is, I'll be wearing a beach hat and sunglasses, so people won't recognize me. Shouldn't be a problem for you then. Once we're behind closed doors and out of the public eye, bring in whomever you like to hear my story and evaluate the evidence."

"Got it. I'll be down in five."

"Thanks, Frank, I appreciate it."

"Another one you owe me, pal." Then he hung up.

Frank stood, then immediately plopped down into his chair. He trusted Garrison Chase. He knew Chase was a straight shooter, so he highly doubted the man was playing any sort of game. To cover his butt, though, Frank wanted someone else to know about the plan, just in case things went sideways. Just as a precaution.

So, he picked up his office phone and made a quick call.

TWENTY-EIGHT

It took Frank ten minutes to arrive at the lobby, not five.

Since I was in the far corner of the parking lot, I couldn't see well, so I used the cell and zoomed in as close as I could with the camera feature. Frank's sweaty face appeared to the left of the main lobby doors. He was dabbing at his forehead and swiveling his big head left and right.

I exited Sage's Corolla, taking the cell, wallet, keys, and thumb drive with me. In the trunk, I left behind my duffel bag with the Savage Stance. While proceeding to the front doors, the burner in my back left pocket chirped. Continuing to walk, I dug it out and glanced at the number.

At first, I didn't recognize the number, though something about it was familiar. It started with 623, and I knew that was the area code for southern Phoenix. As I studied the rest of the number, I realized it was the same number that Stanley used to send a text to Sage earlier.

I was nearly positive.

After clicking on the message, I read the two short sentences and abruptly stopped walking. By this point, I was thirty yards from the front of the FBI building. In front of me were about ten steps that ascended to a large concrete area where many people milled about.

I didn't take those steps.

Time stood still. I know that's cliché to say, but it was the only way to describe the next few moments. As I stood there, my mind slowly and concisely processed what was going on, every single detail.

While I stared at the cell, another text popped up. It was from Mick, and it said:

Just confirmed. Griff is in Arizona on business.

Suddenly it all came together. My eyes flicked toward Frank. He stared directly at me, continuously dabbing at his forehead. My former boss was always sweating, so it wasn't unusual to see him blotting the dew on his brow. It was his other hand that caught my attention. He jiggled the change in his pocket.

That's a rare habit for Frank. It only happens when he's incredibly nervous.

My eyes flashed back to the cell. I closed Mick's text thread. Behind it was the text from the new number Stanley had been using.

It read: *it was my dad. he kidnapped me*

The text was downright shocking, to say the least. But I wasn't frozen in place thinking about why Ernesto Tuchek kidnapped his own son, how he did it, or where Stanley currently was. I was thinking about *who* Stanley's father was, the attorney general of the United States.

The AG was the head of the Department of Justice. Ernesto Tuchek oversaw the FBI, the DEA, the US Marshals, the ATF, the National Security Division, INTERPOL, all the prisons, the list goes on.

This same man, one of the most powerful men in America, kidnapped his own son. No doubt to keep him quiet, to keep him from investigating the Night Night Killer and the American CEOs. And he hadn't pulled Griff off the case. He'd sent his hired man to Arizona to deal with his son.

The AG is involved!

I looked at Frank. With his handkerchief arm, he waved me in. Aggressively, I might add. All the while his other hand was still in his pocket jiggling change. Then, for a millisecond, I saw his eyes glance left. My eyes followed that direction.

The LA field office also shared space with Veteran's Affairs and the

Passport Agency. So, there were lots of people lined up outside the building, as well as strolling around the concrete area.

I saw the two men whom Frank was probably looking for. They were agents dressed in casual clothes. It was their posture that gave them away, not to mention they both held small walkie-talkies in their hand. These men were too rigid and alert, staring out toward the parking lot. Not exactly looking at me, but in the general vicinity.

Frank is betraying me.

Frank's ultimate boss was the AG. No doubt Ernesto Tuchek reached out to Frank and probably other directors with a contingency plan in case our paths crossed.

After a quick fist clench and scowl at my former boss, I slowly backed away. Frank's face went from a light red to a deep purple. He lifted a walkie-talkie to his mouth and said something. Immediately I saw the two agents start hustling through the crowd.

I shook my head at Frank, then spun and raced to the Corolla.

TWENTY-NINE

SQUEALING out of the parking lot, I bashed the steering wheel while looking through the rearview mirror.

The two agents were standing in the road, staring at the Corolla as it raced away. I knew they were memorizing Sage's license plate. The feds didn't keep any vehicles in the public parking lot, so the agents wouldn't be in hot pursuit, but they would immediately issue an APB, an all-points bulletin, and BOLO, be on the lookout.

That sent me into emergency mode. Right away I wanted to text Stanley back and find out what happened, and ask if he was safe, but I had more pressing concerns. I dialed Mick Cranston's number. He picked up on the third ring.

"Chase, shouldn't you be talking with your lawyer right now and not me?"

"Probably," I replied. "I'm in trouble, Mick."

"That's the understatement of the year."

"Beyond what you know from the news or Slim. I have no time to explain, but I do want to say thanks for that intel on Griff. It helped."

"No problem. What do you need?"

"A vehicle. Can I steal your FJ55?"

"How about borrow? I'd prefer that."

"Stealing is better. Don't want you to be an accessory or involved in any way. Leave it in your driveway, maybe put the keys in the visor or gas cap. All I ask is that you give me five or six hours before reporting it."

Silence on his end.

Just as I was about to say something, he said, "I have a better plan. The Land Cruiser is in storage, in a place off the 5 in San Juan Cap. I'll head there now. I'll cut the lock on the rolling door and leave the keys in the FJ's visor, which will make it look like you broke into the unit."

"Good, I like it. Plus, you won't need to report the theft right away."

"Exactly. And you can hide whatever vehicle you're currently driving in the unit."

"Thanks, Mick, I owe you. Can you leave a burner in the FJ, too? As soon as I'm finished with this conversation, I'm retiring this one."

"I'll leave one in the glovebox."

I was about to say thanks, but Mick cut me off. "If your cell is potentially comprised, we're ending this conversation now. I'll send a text with the storage location address." He hung up before I could respond.

I pulled over when his text came through. There was a white napkin in my armrest compartment, so I used that to write down the address and unit number. After looking up the address with the cell, I also wrote down the other phone numbers I had stored on the burner. Then I shut off the phone, took out the battery and SIM card, and got back on the road.

I proceeded south to San Juan Capistrano; except I didn't take the logical route. The direct route would require me to hop onto the main freeways as I weaved through Los Angeles and into Orange County. Freeways that would have lots of traffic cameras and electronic billboards that would no doubt be blasting a silver Toyota Corolla alert.

Since I didn't want to use my phone, I couldn't find out more information from Stanley, so I focused on navigating a clandestine route along back roads and small highways.

It took me twice as long to get to San Juan Capistrano, so I arrived at the storage facility in two hours instead of one. As promised, Mick had closed the roll-up door and put a broken lock back into place. Since nobody was around, I quickly exchanged places with the vehicles and rolled the door shut.

Inside the unit, I sat in the passenger seat with the Corolla's door open so there was some light to see. I turned on the burner Mick left for me, then transferred numbers from the napkin to this new cell. After that, the first number I texted was the 623 area code from Stanley. I asked if he was safe. I wrote the text in code so Stanley would know it was from me. Plus, if his abductors had taken the phone back, I felt confident they wouldn't understand the garbled sentence.

While waiting on his response, I thought about my next steps.

I was only two hours from Tijuana, so I debated heading across the Mexican border and rendezvousing with Slim and Ramona in the Mexicali area. But that was risky. Sure, it was easy to enter Mexico via Tijuana, but leaving Mexico would be problematic. And I wouldn't want to be caught by authorities south of the border and face imprisonment there.

I chose to stay in the States.

Since the authorities would be on the lookout for a silver Corolla, and Sage's car wouldn't be discovered anytime soon, I felt confident driving down major freeways in the FJ. So, I headed south on the 5 until I connected with the 8 in northern San Diego.

Heading east, I continued driving. My plan was to stop at Calexico, which was an American city directly north of Mexicali. The whole time I drove I stared at the cell, willing for it to ring or chirp and alert me to a text from Stanley.

Along the way, I wondered about the AG and his involvement. No wonder Sage hadn't been contacted about Stanley's disappearance, why there were no agents at Stanley's house, and why Ramona hadn't heard of an APB issued for Stanley's kidnapping.

The AG wants to keep everything under wraps.

I kept thinking. Had the attorney general recruited and leaned on Richie Blabs to cast dispersion away from the CEOs? That would explain why Richie was so nervous and hadn't contacted a lawyer. Anyone in their right mind would be terrified to go against the most powerful lawyer in the country.

My thoughts grew darker. Was Ernesto Tuchek a frequenter and participant in these wild parties, and thus as guilty as the CEOs for hiring a sicario to suppress their debauchery? Or was he perhaps not involved in the parties per se, but was covering for the CEOs because of their status as powerful and influential businessmen?

Could his silence be bought?

A text interrupted my thoughts. It came when I was just outside of Calexico. Immediately I knew the text was from Stanley since it was a long, garbled sentence.

I pulled off the 8 at the next exit, which was a spot humorously called Plaster City. Idling on the side of the road, I tried to decipher the coded message in my head. When that didn't work, I grabbed the napkin and wrote out the letters, starting with the last word in the sentence and moving backward to the beginning.

Stanley wrote (punctuation mine): *I'm safe, can't talk. Meet at rest stop.*

After looking at my watch and doing the calculation in my head, I responded in code. *Sure. Four hours.*

Pulling back onto the freeway, I thought about Stanley and how he'd escaped. That

thought consumed me. Where my mind eventually circled back to was his father. How deep was Ernesto Tuchek involved in this mess?

I mulled over different theories for most of the journey to Phoenix. When I was less than an hour from the city, my thoughts stopped, and my feelings took over. I was amped. The closer I got to the rest stop, the more excited I became. Stanley Tuchek could very well hold the key to everything that was going on.

Very soon I might unravel this mystery. And it may be the conspiracy of a generation.

THIRTY

THROUGH THE LOCAL GRAPEVINE, Leon had heard there was a large American asking questions in San Luis Rio Colorado. Questions he shouldn't be asking, which didn't sit well with Leon.

It wasn't just the questions that bothered him, it also pertained to the timing of them. Phase two was underway, and he had a lot going on at the moment. Ever since he'd boated away from the raging mansion fire, he'd been trying to get an accurate report of the brothers' deaths.

So far, he'd received conflicting news reports over the lives taken in the fire. Ideally, he wanted to terminate that particular line of brothers. But if there was a survivor, it wasn't the end of the world. Currently, this unexpected problem interrupted his next steps, so he'd have to go to San Luis Rio Colorado to figure out what to do.

Since Leon had recently shaved and showered, he didn't look the part of a street person anymore. Instead, he planned to take on the role of a successful businessman. That made sense since he looked clean-cut, and it also reflected the clothes he was currently wearing.

The problem was his vehicle. If Leon played a businessman, he'd have to drive a decent car, and a decent car definitely stood out in San Luis. But standing out was the last thing he wanted to do.

In fact, it went entirely against his motto.

After some debate, he put his street clothes back on and hopped into the beat-up vehicle he'd taken to San Luis earlier in the week. He figured this was the best way to blend into the background. His fresh-shaven look, however, would stand in stark contrast with his attire, vehicle choice, and smell from his clothes. His solution was to stay in the car and keep his distance, that way no one would get a close look at his face.

Good thing observation was one of his main strengths.

He drove the old sedan into town. It didn't take him long to find the Yankee. The behemoth of a man had short-cropped strawberry-blond hair and was built like a dump truck. Nobody in the small town, or country for that matter, looked like this particular American.

Leon discovered the man at a local taco stand, stuffing his face and chatting up anyone in his vicinity. Considering the large man was currently distracted, Leon leapt into action. His plan was to tail the man, but there was no point these days in following a person closely with a vehicle. Not when you could buy a magnetic GPS tracker on Amazon for next to nothing. Following someone closely could easily get you spotted, so it was much better to use a tracker.

When Leon approached the man's rental car, he swayed and shuffled his feet to appear drunk. After a slow collapse to the ground, right by the vehicle's front passenger tire, Leon stuck the GPS magnet onto the metal frame, easily out of sight. Then he got up and stumbled his way back to his car.

In the driver's seat, Leon fired up his cell and opened the tracking app. For the next few hours, from a distance, he tailed the man between places in town. Everywhere the big man went, he questioned people. The good news was that locals were tight-lipped. Nobody was truly engaging in any prolonged conversation, which gave Leon some comfort.

That is, until the red-haired Yank headed toward a part of town Leon was familiar with. Leon had the app opened on his lap while idling in a grocery store parking lot. He followed the blue dot on the screen, thinking, *no, he can't be going there.*

Sure enough, the blue dot stopped near a house Leon knew well.

Taking a circuitous route to that location, he parked out of sight and proceeded on foot toward the run-down bungalow on the east side of town. The rental car was parked out front, and the big man sat in the driver's seat. Leon knew exactly who lived in the bungalow.

Leon watched the large man extract himself from the car and amble to the front door. He hoped the owner wasn't home or wouldn't give the outsider the time of day. But when the screen door opened, almost falling off its rusty hinges, and the big man stepped inside, Leon knew he was in potential trouble. While circling back toward his car, he focused on a solution instead of wallowing in anger.

By the time he was in the driver's seat, Leon was deep in thought. In fact, he was so deep in thought about his next steps that he didn't see the two men get into the rental car and drive directly toward his position.

Slinking down in his seat, Leon watched as the big man and the bungalow's owner drove by. Suddenly Leon had a thought. An incredible thought. The more he pondered that thought, the more he felt this newfound development was exactly what he needed.

And the bonus: the plan would set a slew of angry men after the occupants of the rental.

THIRTY-ONE

I'D BEEN so focused on Stanley and his father that I hadn't reached out to Slim or Ramona and let them know my new burner number. Of course, they both assumed I was in custody by now and weren't expecting me to reach out.

So, just before crossing over the 202 and heading south toward the rest stop, I pulled into a gas station. I quickly sent them both a text, saying I was back on the run and had a new cell. Then I topped up the Land Cruiser and proceeded to the rest area.

By the time I made it to the exit ramp about ten minutes later, my heart was racing as fast as the FJ's engine. The anticipation of hearing Stanley's story had wound me up. Right as I stopped in front of the barricades, Slim texted my new number. He said: *big news to share.*

After putting the FJ in Park and flipping off the lights, I responded: *Me too.*

Following that, we exchanged several texts. Slim asked where I was. When I told him in Arizona, he informed me he was also on his way back to the States via Arizona with an important "package" in tote. Of course, I wanted to press him more about that, but Stanley was my chief concern at the moment, so I didn't push it. Instead, I sent Slim a pin of my location. He responded that he'd meet me at the rest stop in a little over an hour.

To play it safe, I ran on foot up the exit ramp until I could see the rest area in its entirety. The cowboys' sedan was parked near the sign alerting people to the desert's dangerous creatures. Seeing the vehicle gave me pause.

I crouched and eyed the area. But it was the middle of the night, so I couldn't see any occupants in the car. I texted Stanley at the 623 number and asked what he was driving. He immediately responded that he'd taken the cowboys' sedan.

I hustled back to the FJ, then drove up the exit ramp.

Stanley got out before I reached his location. I rolled down my window. When I was close, I asked, "You check that car for a tracker?"

"Shoot, no," he responded quickly, shaking his head. "Didn't think about that." He dropped to the ground beside the car.

"I'll do it," I said. "Hop into the passenger seat."

"One second. I need to get something from the car."

While Stanley did that, I gave the undercarriage of the cowboy's sedan a thorough check,

which took a few minutes.

"It's clean," I said to Stanley, who was holding a laptop and a cell and standing by the

FJ's passenger door. "Climb in."

Once we were seated, I asked, "You doing okay? You look uninjured."

As he nodded, I fired up the vehicle and made a sharp right-hand turn. The FJ bounced over the curb and raced up the sandy hill.

Stanley braced himself. "Where are we going?"

"Let's stay out of sight." I gestured at the phone on the seat next to his leg. "I'm assuming that's the cowboy's iPhone. It could have its location turned on."

Stanley snorted. "Like I didn't turn that off right away. I'm not a rookie here, you know."

"Obviously not since you escaped your abductors unharmed. What happened?" By this point, I was maneuvering behind the large boulder outcropping. The Jeep was still there, and its presence distracted Stanley.

He tensed. "Why's there another vehicle up here?"

"Don't worry, I left it here. Nobody's around. Trust me." I held up my hand since Stanley was about to respond. "It's a story for another time. Yours is more important." I parked beside the Jeep and shut off the FJ. "Now tell me what happened. And start at the beginning. Why on earth do you never stay put? Why'd you rush back to the motel, anyway?"

"Griff," he said.

"Griff?"

"Yup, after you dropped me off, I went into the bar. I took a seat in the corner farthest from the main door, right by the exit door; the one by the patio. Griff had been in the bathroom when I arrived. I instantly spotted him as he headed back to his table."

"Did he see you?"

Stanley shook his head. "At the time, his presence confused me. I wasn't sure if he was there because my dad hired him to keep tabs on me, or if he was there because he was working with the cowboys. The more I thought about it, the more I realized he must've been connected with the cowboys. Otherwise, how would Griff know I'd been to the Marriott bar before? That freaked me out, so I slipped out the patio unnoticed and ran back to the motel. I wasn't thinking straight, so when I saw the sedan, which you'd been driving last, I shouted and waved after it. Just had to tell you about Griff."

I nodded and said, "I assume Griff subcontracted the kidnapping job to these Arizona cowboys."

"Actually, I confirmed that fact."

"You did? How? Wait, I'm getting ahead of myself. Back up. What happened after the cowboy ordered you into the car?"

"We headed northwest. At least I think it was northwest. When we were out of the city, he pulled off the freeway and took an abandoned back road. He ordered me into the trunk after getting the injured cowboy out.

"We drove for a while, really not sure how long it was. Soon enough, I started whining about the bathroom, and I didn't stop until they pulled over. By gunpoint, they put a gag around my mouth, then ordered me out of the vehicle and into an end unit of some run-down motel complex, which, from what I could tell, was smack-dab in the middle of nowhere.

"I was handcuffed to a bedframe for the night. The guy you shot was in the queen bed next to mine. There was a nightstand in between our beds. He kept checking his phone throughout the night. He'd place it down on the stand, then drift in and out. The man was in pretty bad shape. He was either drifting in and out of sleep or consciousness, I couldn't tell. Anyway, the next morning, the other guy went into the bathroom for a decent stretch. So, I watched the injured cowboy intently and waited for my opportunity."

"You could reach the phone?"

He nodded. "I could with my free hand."

"That's risky, Stanley."

"Yes and no."

"How so?"

"From the get-go, these guys didn't harm me or threaten harm. Couple that with the fact that my dad had hired Griff, and I had reason to belief that Griff hired these men, I didn't think they'd hurt me."

"I take it you got the phone and reached out to Sage in the morning then?"

He tilted his head at me. "You got in touch with her?"

"I did. How'd you exactly get the text off?"

"The cowboy had just put the phone down and drifted off, and the other dude was now taking a shower, so I snatched the cell and contacted Sage. It was the only number I remembered off the top of my head. Plus, I had that note from you in my pocket and snapped a picture of it. I wanted her to access the backup results and try to answer the questions you had." He narrowed his eyes at me. "You and Sage spoke in detail?"

"We did, and I learned a lot from her. She's sharp. But first, how'd you escape?"

"I was inside the texting app on his phone, of course. After I sent the text to Sage, I went back and deleted it. The cowboy was still asleep, so I looked at his other messages. While doing that, a new text came through. And it was from Griff." He paused and blew out a big breath.

"What'd it say?"

"Griff asked if the package was still okay. He reminded the cowboys that the client paying the bills wanted the situation handled with extreme care. That the package had to be delivered unharmed to Vegas."

"Sorry, Stanley."

He looked at me with misty eyes. "Well, at least my dad wasn't trying to . . ." He swallowed, then finished the sentence, "kill me or send me to Mexico like you thought."

Not sure what to say, I simply nodded.

Stanley continued. "The driver went outside and fired up the sedan and popped open the trunk. He'd backed the vehicle up close to the door, so I assumed they planned a quick exit after stuffing me into the trunk. Before leaving, the driver took a quick bathroom break and told the injured cowboy to unlock the cuffs, handing him the gun prior to taking his pee.

"Since I now knew they wouldn't harm me, as soon as I was uncuffed, I stomped on the dude's injured foot. Then grabbed his phone and broke for the door. I was in the vehicle and burning out of the parking lot before Mr. Pee-er or Mr. Hobbler had made it out of the motel room."

"Then you drove straight here?"

"That's right."

I thought for a few seconds. "So, what's your dad's involvement with the CEOs? What do you know about that?"

He hesitated for a moment, then shook his head slowly and said, "Nothing."

"Really?"

Again, he hesitated, then shook his head.

It felt like he was lying, so I said, "What are you holding back, Stanley?"

"Nothing," he snapped. "I told you."

He clearly was, but I'd give him a minute, then circle back to the topic. "Since you still have the cowboy's phone, did you happen to respond to Griff's text?"

That question calmed him a little. "I did. In fact, I took a move from your playbook and responded, saying the package is 'secure.' Played the part of the cowboys and pretended that everything was status quo."

Thinking about that, I said, "Good job. That was probably wise."

"Thanks. I did one more thing I think was smart."

"What's that?"

"I figured out where I was, then called 911 and asked that an ambulance be sent to the motel because there was a gunshot victim there."

I smiled. "Nice."

"I figured that would really cramp their style and ensure they didn't grab some other vehicle in the motel lot and come after me. Plus, I think that cowboy needed medical attention."

"You're getting better at this, kid."

He shot me a look.

"Sorry, Stanley."

I circled back to his dad. "Did you maybe pull over at some point and contact your dad, confront him about the kidnapping?"

He looked away and said, "No, I haven't confronted him yet."

Before I could ask another question, he added, "I'm scared, Chase. Scared of what he's doing, what he's involved in. But I'm also pissed at him." A brief pause, then he continued, "Enraged is more like it. It's one thing to protect me, another thing entirely to abduct me. Honestly, I don't know how to handle this."

"Understandable, Stanley. We'll handle it together."

"What did you get from Sage? You said you learned a lot."

"I did." I spent the next ten minutes telling him what Sage had found out about the workers being related and being part of a local family cult. And about the corrupt agent on Ramona's team.

After Stanley digested that story, he asked, "What's your theory?"

"I think the CEOs are in damage control and are trying to hide their crimes. I think they have the money and resources to hire a skilled hitman, who's cleaning everything up. These men are powerful and have reach, enough reach to turn a federal agent."

He narrowed his eyes. "Enough to get my father involved as well. Is that what you think?"

I shrugged. "You tell me; he's your father. Could he be involved, either directly or indirectly?"

"Not directly, no way." He vigorously shook his head.

"Do you know if he's been frequently flying to Phoenix or Tucson this past year?"

"You think he's that involved, do you? That he's in on these parties with the CEOs?"

"Just being thorough, Stanley, that's what good investigative work entails."

"For the record, no, I don't know his schedule. Have no clue of the last time he was in Arizona. He's the attorney general and travels a lot. And we live on opposite coasts and haven't been on great speaking terms since Christmas."

"That's just it, Stanley, your father is the attorney general, which . . ."

He sighed. "Which what?"

"Which makes me think he's definitely involved. Otherwise, why go to these lengths? I mean, he hired some questionable characters to first illegally monitor you then kidnap you."

Stanley shot me a look. "Could be just for my protection, so I wouldn't get involved. Have you not considered that?"

"Sure, could be, I'll give you that. Could also be for *his* protection. Right?"

Stanley looked out the open window and wrung his hands.

"He knows the law," I continued, "theoretically better than anyone. Yet he hired a team that was covertly monitoring your private home. Maybe he didn't know the team was doing that, but maybe he did. My guess is he did since his next step was to have Griff subcontract a kidnapping job." I paused, then followed up with, "At gunpoint."

Stanley remained silent, still gazing outside.

"And maybe your dad got to that federal agent, not the CEOs. Remember, he's technically in charge of the FBI. He's—"

"Stop!" Stanley shouted, turning my way. The look on his face shut me up. He was misty-eyed again. His face looked red and strained, like he was wrestling with something big.

A few seconds later, he spoke. All he said was, "Indirectly."

"Indirectly?"

He nodded. "My dad's not directly involved, but indirectly."

When he paused, I swallowed.

"And I have proof," Stanley said, lowering his head. "I have proof."

THIRTY-TWO

I WAITED for Stanley to elaborate, but he didn't. Instead, he whipped open the laptop and searched for something on the computer.

"Where'd you get that?" I asked, pointing at the computer. "Is it the cowboys'?"

He shook his head. "There was two grand in cash in their glovebox. I stopped in Phoenix at a Mac store and bought this MacBook Pro." He kept working on the laptop, pulling up some files.

Finally, he turned the screen toward me and pointed at it. "There's my proof."

I glanced at the computer. It appeared to be a screenshot of some company profile. Filling the screen were several corporate figures with their pictures and short blurbs about who they were.

Before I could ask why I was looking at this, Stanley said, "Let me explain. The last time my father and I were together was at Christmas. He wasn't the attorney general at that point. The new president had been elected but wasn't installed until January twentieth. As I'm sure you know, the AG isn't an elected position."

"Of course. The president appoints the AG."

"My father wasn't officially the attorney general until mid-February of this year after Senate approval. Anyway, at Christmas last year my dad was unusually busy and very distracted. He was in a ton of closed-door meetings at our house. He told us there was something big brewing for him, but he didn't elaborate on what that was. On Christmas Eve day, my mother had finally had enough and ordered me to get my father for dinner.

"As I approached his office door, I could hear him shouting. You know my father has a deep, booming voice, right?"

I nodded.

"So, I could hear everything he was saying. If you ever listen to a one-sided phone conversation, you'll notice that the person you're listening to rarely, if ever, refers to the person he or she is speaking to."

"True, it's weird to use a name when you're in a one-on-one conversation with someone."

"Yup, though I didn't hear outright who he was talking to, in retrospect it now seems obvious it was someone big."

"Someone big?" I questioned.

"I don't know who exactly," he responded. "Maybe the president-elect, maybe a Senate member, perhaps the speaker of the house."

"Okay, understood. How'd you come to that conclusion, though?"

"I stood by the door because I wanted to wait until the conversation cooled down before entering. While I stood there, I couldn't help but try to piece together what they were talking about."

"And what can you remember?"

"That it had to do with a new job for my father. It seemed he had to do something to get that position, but he was hesitant and uncomfortable about it."

"You don't remember more details?"

"Not really. You have to understand, I've overheard many heated conversations from my father over the years because he's a hothead and speaks so loudly. I didn't pay much attention to this particular conversation. I was primarily focused on entering at the right time and getting Dad to come join us for Christmas Eve dinner before the food got cold. That way Mom wouldn't be even more pissed."

"Understandable," I said.

"Once he was appointed the attorney general a month and a half later, I realized that Christmas conversation likely had to do with the position, and that he was speaking with the president-elect or maybe a powerful member of the Senate, someone like that."

"Did you ask your dad about it?"

"Hell no! I really didn't want to know about any backdoor deal he'd made. I preferred not knowing, if that makes sense. The truth is, I didn't spend much more time thinking about the situation at all. Not until today, that is."

When he paused, I rolled my hand. "So, what's the connection between the Christmas conversation and the kidnapping?"

"During that conversation a lot of names were flying out of my dad's mouth. One of those names stuck in my head because it was funny."

"Funny? Funny how?"

"A few times my dad said 'barbacoa.' Which, as I'm sure you know, is a type of Mexican braised beef."

He paused again. To move him along, I said, "Sure, it's my third favorite protein next to carne asada and carnitas."

Stanley dabbed at his forehead with his sleeve. I could tell this story was stressful for him since I rarely saw the kid sweat. Plus, he didn't even smile at my comment.

A moment later, he continued. "By the second time he used the word, I realized he was referring to a person, pretty sure it was someone's last name. Like I said, it was funny to me, and that's why it stuck in my head. Since my father was known for mispronouncing names, I figured that was the case. Just my dad being my dad, you know." He jabbed his finger at the laptop screen. "Sure enough, he was mispronouncing."

I looked at the screen and tensed. One of the profile pictures and blurbs was of a man named Alvin Berbacoa. My mind immediately went back to the Futurum lab. I remember Sage pointing to the bottom of a computer screen where several CEO names were listed. Alvin Berbacoa was the one name I recalled.

"You okay?" Stanley asked, waving his hand in front of my face.

I didn't respond, too focused on the blurb below his picture. Apparently, Alvin Berbacoa was the Chief Financial Officer for the General Electric company, as well as the head of their foreign department. I stared at Stanley.

There was some tense silence. He said, "Well?"

Still somewhat shocked, I managed. "*Berb*-a-coa, not barb."

Stanley kept his focus on the screen. "Yup, Alvin Berbacoa lives in Phoenix. Travels to Palmera at least once a month. He heads up the Mexican division for GE, which is definitely the largest American company in Palmera. He's the most powerful player down there."

I added, "And his DNA profile was identified by Ross, from the evidence sent to your company."

Stanley looked up. "You're kidding me?"

I shook my head. "Nope, I'm not. Sage pointed it out to me in your lab."

Silence ensued as we processed this new intel. The dots connected easily. By Stanley's demeanor, he knew exactly what this all meant: that his father likely received the AG position if he covered up Berbacoa's foreign indiscretions.

I didn't say a word since this was awful, shattering news.

He spoke first. "Like you've said, the lengths my dad has been going to means it has to be more than just protecting me." Stanley sighed. "He's been protecting himself all along, that's what he's been doing. Damn him."

The kid's right hand gripped the door handle. It was shaking, and his knuckles were white. He kept going. "Protecting CEOs like Berbacoa, who I assume had hired a serial-killing hitman or hitmen to silence these workers, men who were ready to squeal about the horrors at these company parties." He shot me a look. "Chase, it's hard to believe, hard to take in. I don't know what to think or do."

I nodded my head and kept listening, unsure what to say. The kid was understandably in a state of raw emotion. He suddenly jabbed a finger at me. "If this is true, like we think it is, like the evidence suggests, I don't care whether he's my father or not, he can't get away with this. Neither can Berbacoa. They can't. And I'll help any way I can."

That gave me an idea, but I waited for him to calm a little before saying,

"What if we keep pretending to be the cowboys, just like you did earlier today?"

"Okay, go on."

"We pretend to be them and try to get Griff to confirm your father's involvement. Then we can bring Ramona in since we'll need someone of her clout to bring down your dad."

"Might work," Stanley said, pushing up his glasses. "Having a real fed involved." He shot a look at me. "No offence, Chase, but that could help."

"None taken. Griff probably won't admit to anything, or give any name, via text. Which means we'd need to meet in person. Which would be in Vegas since that's where you're supposed to be delivered to. What do you think?"

I glanced at Stanley. He was grinning ear to ear.

"What's with that look?" I asked.

"Forget Griff," he said.

"Forget Griff? What do you mean?"

Instead of answering, he tapped his laptop. "I needed this computer for several reasons. Primarily because I wanted to access our secure cloud backup system. Also, because I had my suspicion that Berbacoa could be a CEO in Palmera and wanted to confirm that. Lastly, since the cowboys had confiscated my cell when they stuffed me in the trunk, I wanted to check the Find My iPhone App and see if I could track my phone, and thus their location."

"Not sure what that has to do with anything, Stanley, and it certainly doesn't explain the goofy grin on your face. But don't leave me in suspense, were you able to track your phone?"

"Nope, they were smart enough to power it down. Here's the thing, though: The Tucheks still use a Family Sharing account with Apple. And on—"

I held up my hand to stop him. "Explain that, I'm lost. What's family sharing?"

"Basically, Chase, all the Apple devices in our family share the same Apple account. One person is usually in control, normally the mom or dad." Before he went on, he glanced at me and asked, "Why are you the one grinning now?"

"You get upset when I call you kid. Yet you're a twenty-three-year-old who still shares an account with Mommy and Daddy?"

"Funny, aren't you? For the record, it's something we did when I was still living at home with my parents, and it just never got turned off. I don't think my father even realizes that's still the case, or if he ever checks that app on his phone."

"I'm just messing with you, Stanley. Tell me what this all means. I'm still lost."

"Then stop interrupting me," he shot back. After clearing his throat, he continued. "My father typically carries two or three cells at any given time. He has one iPhone he uses for work, and another one for family. He also has a third phone, which is an Android, and he uses that one for discreet communications."

"Get to your point, Stanley."

"Okay, so, when I went onto the Find My iPhone website and logged in to our family account—to locate my phone—I saw the location of all the devices in our family. And I noticed at noon today that my father's family iPhone was at Reagan National in Virginia. Just before you arrived here, I checked again, and saw that he'd touched down in Vegas."

While he paused, my heart started beating fast. After a moment, I said, "You're right, forget meeting Griff. We'll surprise your dad instead."

"No, we won't."

"We won't?" I questioned.

"Nope. Not we, *I'll* confront him. And I'll wear a wire."

THIRTY-THREE

Leon tried his best to blend in with the jostling crowd.

The reporters and cameramen closest to the iron gates tussled for position. Everyone wanted to be up front so their camera lens could zoom in through the thick, black bars and show a clean image of the razed mansion.

Leon chose to stay in the middle of the pack. He didn't have a cameraman with him. Instead, he held a microphone attached to a hand-held recording device. Most of the reporters around him either wore badges stating their network news affiliation, or at least wore clothing with an embroidered news organization logo.

Since it was an impromptu trip to the mansion after his visit to San Luis Rio Colorado, Leon didn't have the time to perfect his disguise, so he sported no badge or logo. The good news was the pack of news people was in a state of disarray at this point. Nobody was paying attention to Leon's lack of affiliation. Even if he was questioned, Leon had already thought of the answer: He'd state that he worked for a small, independent news organization. The type of newspaper that wouldn't have the budget to brand their own clothing.

"*Bastante!*" shouted one of the guards on the other side of the gate. "*Bastante!*"

The crowd immediately settled. Leon listened as that same guard, who'd had enough, explained that everybody needed to push back and clear the area. Apparently, they were expecting a car to leave the property very soon.

This is what I've been waiting for, Leon thought.

Rumor had it that one of the brothers survived, the other two didn't. The surviving brother managed to take refuge in the estate's underground wine cellar. Not only was it hewn into solid bedrock, but the room was also climate controlled and self-contained, so it didn't succumb to the raging fire.

Leon hoped, as the other reporters did, that he could catch a glimpse of the surviving brother and confirm the speculation. What he really wanted the case to be, though, was three dead brothers. Three dead brothers in the primary tree of the Salazar line had vast implications. So, it reasoned that the rumor of a survivor could be fabricated, and that the men were truly dead. But they had every intention of concealing the fact by spreading a rumor to the news outlets.

"*Retirara, retirara,*" the guard said, asking the crowd to move back.

When the people didn't respond right away, two other guards behind him engaged their assault rifles and pointed the weapons at the complacent crowd. Everybody cleared a path as the gate screeched open and wheeled back on its track.

In the distance, Leon watched a silver sedan racing toward the gates. The sedan had tinted windows, which meant it would be hard to catch a glimpse of anyone in the back seat. However, Leon wasn't concerned about that.

He knew these men. He knew what fueled them was pride, not to mention unabashed arrogance. If any of those men had survived, if there was one sole survivor, that man would stop the vehicle in front of the crowds. Absolutely. He'd step out and give everyone a good look; let everyone know that he couldn't be beat, that he couldn't be taken down.

So, when that silver sedan barely slowed down as it approached the gates, then failed to stop in front of the crowd, Leon knew he was right. The rumor was a lie, a fabricated story.

The men were dead.

Phase three is now in motion, Leon thought, as he slinked from the crowd and headed to his vehicle.

THIRTY-FOUR

I ASKED STANLEY, "After you texted Griff that the package is secure, did he respond?"

He shook his head. "Nope. Nothing from him since."

"Did the other cowboy, the stocky one, reach out to his buddy's phone?" I gestured at the cell on the sedan's front seat.

"He didn't."

"Okay, good. There's a chance the cowboys haven't communicated with Griff because they're embarrassed you escaped and want to find you first."

"Or they're preoccupied at the hospital with the dude whose foot you shot."

"Maybe. We need to keep Griff on the hook, though. We need to text him from the cowboy's phone."

"And say what exactly?"

I thought for a moment. "Tell him we're delayed but the package is still safe."

Stanley picked up the phone and fired off a text. It amazed me how fast young people could text these days.

His eyes went wide a few seconds after the text was sent. "He's responding, I see three pulsating dots."

When the cell beeped, I immediately said, "What's it say?"

"He asked, how delayed?"

"Say five hours or so."

A moment later he looked up. "Okay, just did."

"When we're close to Vegas, say thirty minutes, we'll reach out to Griff again and tell him we're an hour out from delivering the package."

"Why an hour?"

"Griff hired the cowboys to deliver you to him, not your dad. Griff's smart enough to not let these cowboys know who the real client is, especially since he's the AG, or to see your dad's face. The cowboys are supposed to deliver you to Griff first, at one location, then Griff takes you to your dad at another location. While Griff is waiting for the delivery, we'll simply bypass him and go straight to your dad. And, of course, we'll know exactly where your dad is since you're monitoring his cell."

Stanley smiled. "I like it."

I kept thinking. "We definitely need Ramona in on this, especially if your dad gives up something incriminating."

"You're right, she should be there. Where is she now?"

"Not sure, probably Mexicali still, that's where she was today, trying to speak with a Mexican detective, but she may be headed back to Phoenix already depending on her success. She hasn't responded to an earlier text, so I'll reach out again and see where she is and if she can meet us here."

While I did that, Stanley fired off a bunch of questions about the detective and Mexicali. After sending the text, I brought him up to speed on what Ramona had been pursuing.

"We can trust the evidence sent to Ross then," Stanley said. Before I finished nodding, he went off. "I need to contact Sage right away, make sure the profiles and data she uncovered is uploaded to our secure cloud server, then I need to start running our software and see if I can make any identification of these three unknown profiles, try to narrow that down." He kept talking without looking at me. "Not sure if you're aware, Chase, but Sage can't access the software, maybe I should give her access and have her run things from the lab—"

I waved my hand in front of the screen to distract him. "We need to get in touch with Sage, I agree. See what, if any, progress she's made today and also see if Victoria found any prints on the Beretta. As for the results"—I reached into my left pocket and pulled out the thumb drive—"I have everything on here."

His big eyes grew wider. "What? Why didn't you say so earlier?" He was fast and snatched the drive from my hand before I knew it. He plugged it into a USB slot and tried to access the contents.

"You know," I said, "it needs my thumbprint to work."

"Sage set you up with this?"

"Yup."

"Then gimme your thumb, come on." He waved his hand at me.

"In a second, Stanley, just hold on. Let's talk about what you're going to say to your dad and how you're going to record it." I looked at my watch. We'd been sitting and talking for an hour. "Slim's gonna be here any second, with some sort of package in tote. No doubt we'll be distracted with that."

Stanley agreed and we began a short conversation. After a few minutes, just as we were feeling good about the Vegas plan, the back of our vehicle was lit up.

"Hopefully that's Slim," I said, exiting the driver's side. I proceeded to the side of the boulder closest to the entrance ramp. Moments later, I watched a newish Chevy Malibu roar up the ramp and park on the far side of the cowboy's sedan.

"Come on, Stanley, let's go."

On the way down the sandy hill, I watched my large friend struggle to get out of the vehicle. When I was closer, I said, "What, no Hummer at the airport to rent? Didn't know you could fit into a sedan, pal. Congrats."

"Good to see you, too," he replied. "I mean, I could see you from on top of the hill with the way the moon is shining off your chrome dome."

We embraced, doing the double-tab on each other's back with our fists, then quickly pulling away.

Slim smelled horribly. "Buddy, what type of cologne is that? Eau de gas?"

"Tell me about it," he replied. "Been smelling it the entire time since leaving Mexico, driving the whole way here with the windows down. The Malibu must have a gas leak."

"Doesn't quite smell like automobile fuel, though."

"Agreed," Slim said. "Could be transmission fluid mixed in. Who knows? I'll be rid of this vehicle soon, and it'll be the rental company's problem."

Stepping back, I said, "Stanley, meet Hans Schlimmergaard aka Slim. Slim, this is Stanley Tuchek."

Slim squeezed Stanley's hand so hard I thought the kid may buckle at the knees. Since Slim's hands were as thick and leathery as a catcher's mitt, most people squealed on impact from a handshake.

At least Stanley didn't squeal.

Slim bent down, looked through the Malibu's driver's side window and said, "Come on out, Silvio."

I'd been so distracted by my girthy friend with his strawberry-blond hair that I hadn't noticed he had an occupant in the passenger's seat.

"Your package is a human," I said.

"You're astute, buddy."

The Hispanic man exited the vehicle but stayed by the passenger door. Since he was pretty short, all I could see was his head hovering above the Chevy's roof. Silvio had dark, smooth skin and sported a thin black mustache. It was hard to tell his age, maybe between twenty-five and thirty-five. I was terrible at guessing a man's age.

"Silvio," Slim said, "this is Garrison Chase and Stanley Tuchek."

"Hola," said Stanley. "*Mucho gusto.*"

Slim interceded. "Silvio speaks very good English, by the way."

"Nice to meet you, Silvio," I said.

"Likewise," he replied.

I thumbed toward Slim. "This big brute didn't kidnap you, did he, Silvio?"

The smile on my face was suddenly wiped clean when Slim slugged me on the shoulder. Any other person's light punch wouldn't hurt, but Slim's meaty fist put a grimace on my face.

"Oh, Chase," Slim said, "always the jokester. Wait till you hear what Silvio has to say. He's an ex-communicated member of The Family."

"Really?" I said.

Silvio's floating head nodded. He corrected, "*La Familia.*"

"Would love to hear all about it." Since I didn't want to talk in the open, or in the stinky Malibu, I gestured to the sedan. "Let's talk in here. Slim you may fit, but you better take the driver's seat and crank the seat all the way back."

I dodged another one of his punches and climbed into the sedan's back seat with Silvio, who sat behind Slim. Stanley took shotgun position.

"Tell me about yourself, Silvio," I said, "and your family."

The quiet, mild-mannered Silvio didn't respond right away. Instead, he rubbed his palms on the front of his thighs. I noticed both his forearms were covered in tattoos, and his ears were pierced with dime-sized opal earrings. Silvio looked at Slim in the front seat.

My pal had turned his body and swiveled his neck so he could make eye contact with Silvio. Slim said, "It's okay, tell him what you told me. Tell him everything."

After a brief pause, he began. "I wasn't born here"—Silvio pointed down at the floor—"in America, but close, just across the border, into a very large family." Before he could start his next sentence, the sudden shattering of the rear window surprised us.

Shards of glass showered my upper body. At the same time, warm blood sprayed my face. All the while, the sub-sonic boom of a rifle shot vibrated in my ear drums, which temporarily deafened me. By the time I got my bearings, I felt something heavy in my lap.

Blinking away blood, I looked down.

What remained of Silvio's head rested on my left thigh.

THIRTY-FIVE

"*Down! Down!*" Slim shouted. "You okay, Chase?"

"Yes. Not hit. Shot came from the north. You okay, Stanley?"

He screeched, "Not hit either."

Since I was tall and had no room to slink down, I pushed Silvio's body back by his shoulders and folded at the waist. With my head between my knees, I felt as if I was preparing for a plane wreck.

I yelled to Slim, "We're open targets. We have to move."

Slim demanded the keys from Stanley.

It felt like an eternity waiting for the sedan to fire up. I expected more windows to be shattered, or at least to hear the rat-tat-tat of bullets striking metal.

But I heard nothing of the sort.

"Hang on," Slim said as the sedan roared to life. "In the footwell, kid, now."

"Straight back," I said. "Up the hill to the boulders. We'll have coverage there. Plus, there's a couple four-by-four vehicles, too."

"You sure?" he said. "I could book it to the other side of the rest area and exit onto the freeway."

"Let's get out of here," Stanley pleaded.

I thought about his laptop. He'd left it in the FJ with the thumb drive still in its slot. "I'm sure, Slim. There's important information in the vehicle we can't leave without. Plus, I have a gun in the Land Cruiser."

The gear shift dropped into reverse. "If you say so." Slim revved the engine.

I said, "You need to get a ton of speed to get through the sand."

Within seconds, the car rocketed backward, eventually slamming into the curb and bouncing over it. Beside me, Silvio's lifeless body went airborne for a moment, then flattened against the bloody seat and slipped into the footwell.

The sedan hit the sandy hillside with incredible velocity. Our momentum carried us almost all the way to the boulder outcropping. The engine whined as the tires dug deep into the sand. We slowly settled in place, even though the engine spun a million miles an hour. A cloud of sand and dust enveloped the sedan.

"That's as far as we go," Slim shouted, easing off the gas. "Out the right side."

I was first onto the ground; Stanley was next. I pulled him toward me to make room for Slim, who leopard crawled across the front seat, then tumbled head-first out of the vehicle.

Within moments, the three of us were crouched and huddled around the rear passenger tire. Our breathing was fast and deep. By their facial expressions, I knew I looked scary. I could feel bits of skin and skull and brains on my face and head. Looking down at my shirt, it looked unreal, like a Halloween costume.

"Sure you're okay, Chase?" Slim asked.

"Fortunately, the bullet missed me. Unfortunately, this is all Silvio. Let's focus." I gestured toward the back of the sedan. There was a three-foot gap between the rear bumper and first boulder. Three boulders comprised the outcropping. The huge rocks were overlapping and positioned in a north-south direction. Currently, we were by the south end.

We all stared and debated the distance in front of us, wondering if it was a wise move or not. The shooter was to the north, so the south side of the outcropping was the only place of refuge. But getting there was risky.

I motioned at the gap. "It's doable, right?" I looked at Slim.

He said, "Think so. No more shots fired, so we may be in the clear."

I nodded. "Silvio was likely the target, and hopefully the only target."

"I'll go first," Slim said, "since I'm the biggest and slowest. If I get plugged, you know it's not safe."

Stanley, who'd been quiet up until this point, spoke softly. "I'm the smallest and fastest, I'll go first."

In unison, Slim and I responded. "No way."

"No more discussion," I said, "go, Slim." For a big man, he moved quickly. Fortunately, no shots were fired.

"Go, Stanley," I said, tapping his shoulder. Still crouched, he retreated two steps, then exploded forward and dove, making it to safety without a shot being fired.

From across the gap, Slim motioned over his shoulder. "I'll go around the other side and see if I can make out his position, just in case he fires. Go in about twenty seconds."

I gave him the thumbs-up, then waited and counted off twenty seconds. They were the longest twenty seconds of my life, by the way. After that, I reared back like Stanley, eyed my spot, then went for it.

A thunderous crack filled the air.

The bullet missed me by inches. The large caliber round drove into the metal bumper and actually peeled it back a little. I scrambled to my feet and joined Stanley at the south end of the outcropping. A few moments later, Slim joined us.

"That was close," he said, patting me on the back as I doubled over and caught my breath. "Still whole?"

I nodded.

"I glimpsed the muzzle flash," Slim said, "and saw his approximate location."

Looking up, I asked, "Where?"

"Straight north, like you said. Probably 150 yards, no more."

I gritted my teeth. "But far enough back to cover both the east and west sides of the outcropping."

"Unfortunately, yes."

I thought about the Jeep and FJ parked on the west side. Either vehicle would perform well in the sand. The FJ had my duffel bag with the Savage Stance inside. A tiny handgun was useless against a sniper rifle, but firing some rounds in the sniper's direction could provide coverage so we could get away in one of the vehicles.

I looked at Slim. "Getting to the FJ is a potential death sentence, right?"

Slim nodded. "After that shot, I think so."

"But we have to get there. How though?"

"Why don't I go," Stanley offered.

"No," I responded quickly.

"But I'm small and fast, which makes me a hard target." He thumbed at Slim. "This guy definitely can't go."

Before Slim could respond, I said, "Out of the question, Stanley. I mean it."

He sighed. "Hear me out at least."

"Hear you out on what?"

"We both know my dad is somehow involved. Like with the cowboys, perhaps this shooter won't harm me. It's probably safest for me to go. I don't think they'll try to shoot me."

Slim interjected. "What the hell are you two talking about?"

"Fill you in later." Turning back to Stanley, I said, "We don't know what's going on right now. We have no clue who this shooter is or who sent him. Got it? Don't assume anything."

While Stanley sulked and leaned against the boulder, I pulled Slim aside. For a few tense moments, we discussed the problem. Slim thought that he should go since I was just shot at and was clearly a target. But I argued that he was too big and would be an easy target for the shooter. Eventually, I insisted on being the one to go to the FJ.

As soon as we broke our huddle, I noticed Stanley was gone.

Damnit, that kid. He never listens.

Slim called out, "Stanley! Get back here."

We could vaguely see him in the dark, crawling on his forearms toward the Jeep, which was the vehicle closest to the rocks. I was pissed, and that was an understatement. Standing beside Slim, my arms were straight at my side and my fists were clenched and shaking violently.

"Not much we can do now, Chase, but hope and pray. You gotta relax."

I dug the FJ keys out of my pocket and showed Slim. "Stupid kid doesn't even have the keys."

Slim's head dropped.

I said, "It's not like I locked the doors, so at least he can get inside and be somewhat safe. If he makes it there, that is."

"Yeah, but he can't drive the FJ and pick us up. What about the Jeep? Are the keys in it?"

"Not in the ignition. I left them under the visor, but Stanley doesn't know that."

Just then two shots cracked.

Immediately I looked in Stanley's direction. About a foot in front of his face two tufts of sand were obliterated. He scurried faster until he was underneath the Jeep's front end. He curled his small body beside the front driver's wheel.

"Geez," I said, "now I have to rescue him on my way to the FJ. Look at this kid." I pointed at his scrunched body. The front tire didn't exactly cover his appendages. "I'm surprised the shooter hasn't planted a couple of rounds in his legs or backside already."

"Me too," Slim said. "Why don't I go back to the sedan and create a diversion while you sneak up on the vehicles."

"Like what kind of diversion?"

"All I can do is fire it up and spin the wheels, create a lot of noise and a ton of dust."

"It's worth a shot."

With that, Slim was off. I stayed tight to the rock face and crept fifteen feet to the north. When I heard the sedan's engine revving, I made my move. Instead of crawling, I lunged head-first, then tucked and rolled.

No shots were fired. Moving quickly, I army crawled as fast as I could to the front of the Jeep.

"What are you doing?" Stanley screeched.

"Saving your ass. Straighten your body. Align yourself in front of the tire. Shooter is straight north of our position; you need to use that to your advantage."

Stanley did as he was told. My head was now just below his feet. However, I was far enough back from the Jeep's undercarriage that I was able to be picked off.

"What now?" Stanley asked.

"You stay put. I'm gonna roll left toward the other tire since I'm about to be shot." I suddenly rolled left, three fast turns until I was aligned with the other tire, then I scurried forward until I was directly behind the passenger side tire. No shots were fired, which surprised me.

I looked under the Jeep and toward the shooter's position. It was dark, and I couldn't see much, so I glanced at Stanley.

He stared at me with bug eyes and repeated himself. "What now?"

"You continue to stay put. I'm gonna keep rolling until I'm on the other side of the FJ. I'll have a safe angle to enter the FJ from there, as long as the shooter's not repositioning and moving west."

For a second, I remained motionless and envisioned how many rolls I'd need to do. I figured six would do. Just before moving, a light near the shooter's position distracted me.

It was a tiny beam, maybe from a mini keychain light, something small like that. At any rate, I froze in place and watched the light. It turned on and off, on and off. Seconds later, it registered: Morse code!

Somebody was trying to communicate with us.

THIRTY-SIX

THE SEDAN'S revving engine stopped. Stanley used the sudden quiet to hiss, "What are you waiting for? Go now. Go, go!"

He wasn't looking in the direction of the flashing light, and I didn't have time to explain Morse code and what was going on. So, I ignored him and continued to watch the light. Whomever was signaling repeated the signal. There were four letters.

I spelled the letters out in the sand: M-I-C-K

Mick Cranston was out there! What? Had he taken out the shooter? Or was he the shooter? No, that couldn't be. But if it was Mick, why hadn't he texted my burner?

Confused, I rolled toward the FJ. No shots were fired my direction, which confirmed to me it was my buddy out there. After five turns, I was underneath the front end of the FJ. Spitting out some sand, I checked my burner. No text from him. Maybe his phone was dead, or maybe he left it in whatever vehicle he'd driven. Suddenly I thought about his vehicle.

Nobody had followed me here; I was sure of it. I would've spotted a tail. As I kept thinking, I remembered how the cowboys had found Stanley and me at the motel. It was so easy and cheap these days to buy a GPS tracker. Perhaps that was what Mick had done. He loved that FJ so much I could see him installing Lo-Jack or some GPS tracker on the vehicle. Turning the cell's light on, I found the device after a minute of searching the undercarriage.

"Chase!" It was Slim's voice. He stood on the south side of the boulder and waved at me. "Is that Cranston flashing Morse code out there? My memory of the alphabet is a little rusty, but I think he spelled out Mick."

"Pretty sure it is." To prove my point, I slowly stood.

"What are you doing?" Stanley yelled. "You're gonna get yourself killed!"

"We're fine."

"Fine?" he shot back. "How the hell are we fine?"

Slim trudged through the sand when he saw that my head remained intact. Seeing him safely make it to the FJ also gave Stanley confidence to emerge from under the Jeep. Within moments, the three of us stood by the FJ's hood and watched the small beam of light approach our position.

"Who on earth is out there?" Stanley asked.

Just then, a text buzzed. I glanced at it. Mick texted, "Nixed the shooter. Wasn't positive it was you until you stood. You look terrible."

Stanley huffed. "Guys, I asked who's out there?"

"You'd never believe it," I said.

"Humor me."

Before I could respond, we heard multiple vehicles in the distance. Though my ears focused on the sound, my eyes watched Mick. He'd stopped his forward march. The light had been pointed at the ground, but it quickly turned off.

The throaty roar of at least two vehicles, maybe three, echoed off the rocks. Suddenly there was a crash. I peeled my eyes from Mick and saw two sets of bouncing headlights. Since we were at an elevated position, I could see down the entrance ramp, all the way to the freeway. A large, lifted truck had just crashed through the barricade. Another truck was hot on its tail. And neither showed signs of slowing.

Slim grabbed Stanley and hauled him toward the south end of the outcropping. I focused on my buddy instead. He'd turned the tiny light back on and was flashing Morse code again.

"Come on, Chase," Slim shouted after me, but I was locked onto Mick's position. He was walking backward while flashing Morse code. He gave me five one-second-long bursts of light, which was code for the number five.

He repeated the code, then followed up with a text: *give me 5 minutes. I have shooter's rifle and another one in my minivan.*

I heard vehicles screeching to a halt, followed by multiple car doors opening. That snapped me out of it. I hustled over to Slim.

He asked, "Cranston coming?"

"No, he retreated. He has a van stashed up the road. He told us to give him five minutes. He has the sniper's gun and another one."

"Still, you better get that gun you said you have. Hopefully that buys us five minutes."

"Will do. Might not need it, though. We're in the dark here, so they may not know we're here or be able to see the sedan."

"I doubt it," Slim said, motioning me over.

I knelt beside him. We both peered around the south end of the boulder outcropping. We could see pretty well since the lights from the women's bathroom complex lit up the parking lot. Parked on either side of Slim's rental were two massive 4WD trucks. I quickly counted ten men between the two vehicles. Everyone was armed to the teeth.

Slim pointed down the hill. "Won't take them long to spot those tracks."

Sure enough, Slim was right. Just near the edge of where the light started fading were deep, fresh tracks that the sedan had cut into the sand. I asked Slim, "Think we should pile into the FJ or Jeep and roar off into the desert?"

Thinking about that, he didn't answer right away.

I thought about it some more, too, then shared my concerns. "They'll hear us as soon as we fire up a vehicle. With the giant sand tires on those trucks, they'll catch up in no time."

"Exactly what I've been thinking," Slim said. "Plus, ten guys will light us up with rifles as soon as they're on our tail."

I was about to get the Savage Stance, but a noise stopped me. I looked down the hill. One of the men had a crowbar in his hand and was prying open the trunk on Slim's rental.

Once he was successful, the man started picking up and throwing white containers onto the pavement. I couldn't quite make out details, so I had no clue what the containers were. But whatever they were, they certainly fired up the men.

They huddled together for a moment, then quickly began fanning out. That got me moving. I raced toward the FJ, grabbed the handgun, and sprinted back to Slim's position.

"Where's the gun?" he asked.

Most of my hand covered the micro-compact weapon, so I opened my palm and turned it toward him.

"What the hell's that? Is that a toy? Are you for real?"

"No judgment, pal. It fits in my glovebox, so it's easy to lock in there."

"That barrel's so short we're gonna have to wait until the men get close to fire."

"I can keep them at bay until Mick arrives." I looked at my watch. "In four minutes or less, I hope. I don't necessarily need to take them out, Slim, just slow them down."

"Let's hope less than four minutes." He motioned toward the men.

They'd split up. Five headed east to the men's bathroom, and the other five headed west toward our position. Like the cowboys, the men carried Armalite rifles. We were in serious trouble if Mick didn't show up soon.

Slim sensed it, too. "Anything in the FJ or Jeep we could use as a distraction?"

"Nothing in Mick's FJ that I can think of. Didn't get a look around the Jeep, so there could be. I saw some trash and bottles in the back seat area."

"Come on, Stanley," Slim said. "Let's see if there's something we can use."

As they took off, I refocused my attention down the sandy incline. My hand squeezed the Savage when I witnessed two of the men standing by the deep grooves in the sand. One of them was drawing his arm up, following the tire tracks toward the sedan.

Damn, damn, damn.

The other man motioned toward the others, alerting them to the boulder outcropping.

At this point, I was laying prone on the sand. My arms were stretched out in front of me, pointing the Savage down the hill toward the impending doom. Just my arms and head protruded from the south side of the boulders. I practiced slow and steady breathing as I watched the five men spread out and start creeping up the hillside.

Soon enough, all five had moved from the dissipating light into the shadows. Squinting, I was able to make out only vague outlines of the men. My diaphragm pushed my chest into the sand as I tried to remain calm and control my breathing. At the same time, my mind calculated the two options I had in front of me: fire now or hold off and draw them close.

If I fired now, the shots would draw the other five to this location. Then I'd have to deal with ten men carrying semiautomatic rifles. But if I didn't fire now, five men would be on top of us in no time. I had the extended magazine in the Savage, which held ten rounds. With such poor visibility, and five men spread out maybe fifty yards from north to south, I'd have my work cut out for me with only ten shots.

Wiping the sweat from my brow, I used the same hand to pull out the burner cell. I perched the phone against the base of the rock and set a countdown for three minutes on the timer. I hoped Mick would be here in two.

My eyes locked onto the timer. I planned to wait forty-five more seconds until the countdown hit the two-minute mark. Then I'd spray five rounds toward the men. After that, I'd reposition at the north end of the outcropping and fire five more. Then hopefully Mick would be there. He was a talented former government operative who could be deadly with a sniper rifle.

With ten seconds before the two-minute mark, however, I noticed how quickly the men had advanced. Shadowy figures were now halfway to the sedan. Just as I prepared to fire early, Slim and Stanley were back.

"We got something, Chase." Slim was out of breath. In his right hand he held the square plastic gas can that was mounted to the back of the Jeep.

Stanley plopped four empty Coke bottles—the old-school glass ones—onto the ground. "Still don't know what we're doing with these."

I did. But neither Slim nor I had time to explain.

Slim pulled off his boots and socks and started shredded his socks into long pieces of fabric. I abandoned my position and grabbed the bottles, slightly corkscrewing them upright in the sand so they would stay steady. With a shaky hand, I unscrewed the gas cap and started dumping gas into the bottles.

It went everywhere.

"Steady, Chase," Slim snapped. "We need to conserve some gas."

"For what?"

"Last resort: We douse the Jeep and blow it."

Nodding, I said, "Gotcha."

While Slim threaded the sock strips into the bottles, Stanley finally clued in. "Ah, I get it, Molotov cocktails. Never seen one made before."

I crawled back into position. My eyes widened when I saw two men nearing the sedan. I glanced at the countdown. It read sixty seconds.

"Hurry, light 'em," I said over my shoulder. "Throw one at the sedan. Now!"

Moments later, I didn't see any flaming bottle flying overhead.

Looking back, I realized they didn't have a lighter. Stanley took off toward the vehicles, no doubt going back to one of them for a cigarette lighter. I looked at the countdown. The seconds took forever to tick down. I thought about the timing. A car lighter would require at least twenty seconds or so to warm up enough to light a sock wick. Right?

We have no time. No way.

I looked at Slim. He saw the fear in my eyes and said, "Break for the FJ and take our chances?"

I nodded.

"Fire two," he said. "Then we retreat."

My eyes locked onto to the farthest shadow on my right. The man was ten yards behind the passenger side of the sedan, hunched over and shuffling slowly through the sand, his weapon leading him forward. I squeezed off a low round.

He dropped, holding his leg and screaming.

My eyes flicked beyond him. The five figures down by the men's bathroom all pivoted in near unison. Refocusing, I fired another round through the sedan's windshield, just to scare anyone who was in that vicinity.

"Let's go," Slim shouted under his breath.

I scrambled back, picking up the cell on my way.

Timer read: thirty seconds.

Slim had two Coke bottles in each of his hands. He handed two to me, picked up the gas can, then we took off toward the vehicles. Seconds later, we could see the Jeep. The driver's side door was open, and Stanley sat in the seat.

He was yelling at the cigarette lighter. "Come on, you stupid thing, come on. Pop out!"

When we were thirty feet from the Jeep, two men suddenly sprang from the north end of the outcropping. Immediately the front man fired at me. The man behind him unloaded on the back of the Jeep and FJ. The window of the open Jeep's driver's door blasted to pieces, redirecting the bullet and saving my life.

Seeing clearly through the broken glass, I charged forward and raised the Savage and fired twice, dropping the front man. The man behind him retreated from view.

Stanley screamed, "It's bright red, it's ready!"

With the Savage outstretched toward the second man's approximate position, I said, "Give it to Slim. I'll cover you."

As soon as Stanley left the Jeep, I fired two rounds high over his head toward the boulder where I believed the second man had retreated to. When Stanley cleared the driver's door, Slim dropped the gas can and said, "Toss it, quick!"

Stanley did. I watched the lighter tumble through the air, end over end. Slim reached for it, but the hot end seared his palm, and it ricocheted off his hand.

No!

To make matters worse, the timer just ended, and a stupid musical chime started playing loudly. I scrambled in my pocket, trying to turn the cell's mute switch on. At that moment, the second man stepped out from where I thought he was.

He opened fire.

THIRTY-SEVEN

I DOVE face-first into the sand, by the front of the Jeep.

As the chime continued playing, the lower part of the driver's door took the brunt of a three-round blast. Looking to my right, Slim was on his knees reaching for the lighter. He picked it up, lit the frayed end of the sock protruding from the bottle, then sailed the Molotov cocktail in a high arc toward the furthest boulder.

Stanley covered his ears like he was ready for some type of explosion. Except that wasn't how Molotov cocktails actually worked. They don't explode like a bomb, they simply spread fire in all directions as the gas splatters everywhere.

Seconds later, we heard glass shatter, then a scream.

I looked up. Flaming gas had splashed off the rock, dousing the man. Standing, I drew the Savage and pointed it toward the blazing figure. The man stumbled about, then dropped to his knees. I put him out of his misery.

Since Slim's back was pressed against the boulder, he couldn't see. He asked, "Man down?"

I nodded.

"Bullets left?"

"Three."

"Two men up here still, with five more coming. I imagine the other five are at the base of the hill by now. And where the hell is Mick?"

"Now's not the time to be late," I muttered. "Come on, Mick!"

"Turn that damn thing off," Slim said, gesturing to my pocket.

After flipping on the mute button, I wiggled my fingers at Slim. "Gimme the lighter, I'll relight it."

He tossed it over, then I slowly moved around the Jeep's door while keeping the Savage pointed north. Since I couldn't see anyone else, I hopped inside and jammed the lighter into its holder. While waiting, I swiveled my head, wondering where the other two men were.

Which direction will they come from?

Slim had doused the Jeep's backend with gas, grabbed the rifle from the first man I shot, and circled back. He stopped by the driver's door. "Second man took out a rear tire in each vehicle. They're both useless now. But at least we got this." He held up the AR-15.

"What about the other one?"

"Charred pretty badly, not sure it's reliable. Plus, I think it's out of rounds. You want this?"

I shook it off. "You take it, I still have a few bullets left."

The lighter popped out. I handed it to Slim. "You cover our six, pal. Burn or shoot anyone behind us. I'll take lead and pop anything that moves in front of us. We'll head around to the north end. Flush out these last two men."

With Stanley between us, we slowly shuffled north. When we approached the curve in the farthest boulder, I paused because I thought I'd heard some movement ahead.

The tip of a rifle suddenly jutted from the around the boulder and fired. I leaned right and felt a short blast sail over my left shoulder. The rifle retreated behind the rock, so I didn't shoot and waste a bullet. Slim, though, reacted quickly and launched a Molotov cocktail.

The bottle smashed against the rock and sent a plume of flames around the corner. I heard the men retreat. Since I didn't want to lose ground, I charged forward with the Savage out front.

After side-stepping the flames, I continued until reaching the furthest point north of the outcropping. Nobody was in the immediate area. We'd pushed them around the east side.

Like I did at the south end, I dropped onto my stomach and surveyed down the hill, just in time to see the five other men dissolve into the shadows near the bottom of the incline.

I glanced down the entrance ramp. As soon as I wondered where Mick was, I found my answer. About fifty yards back from the barricade was a car. It had parked perpendicular across the entrance ramp. Two men, one by the front of the car and the other by the rear, were crouched over and pointing rifles toward the freeway.

At the freeway exit was a black minivan, dead center of the road. Mick was in the driver's seat, idling and waiting.

He has his own problems.

While I was watching this, Stanley took position behind me, on his knees directly by my feet. And Slim stood behind him, watching our backs. I heard some whispering ahead and refocused. I figured the two men were positioned just around the next bend.

Straining to listen, Slim interrupted the silence. "Lighter is dying."

I looked back at him and nodded. "Send one." I pointed toward the general direction of the whispering.

Slim struggled but finally got the sock wick to light. He sent it sailing on a forty-five-degree angle over the boulder. It crashed against the top of the rock and shot flames straight down.

Indeed, two men were around the bend. Both suddenly popped into view. The man farthest away was engulfed in flames; the other sprang from the rock so fast he avoided the ignited gas. But he jumped directly into my sight line, and I didn't hesitate to fire.

The man covered in flames crashed to the sand and started rolling down the hill. The giant pinwheel on fire temporarily lit up the hillside, which was an unexpected benefit. Now I could see most of the hillside, if only for a few seconds before the flames were smothered.

Slim rushed to my side.

"Five down, five to go," I said.

"Did you get a look at the hillside?" he asked.

"Yup, for a quick second, three were approaching near the sedan. The other two are right in front of us."

Stanley said, "Where the hell's your buddy anyway?"

I pointed left. "He's preoccupied."

Slim and Stanley glanced over. Within seconds, Slim looked back at me. "We're on our own, no backup. The farthest three will head around the south end. One of us needs to head them off."

"You go," I said. "You have more firepower for those three. I'll take out the two in front of us. Just leave me that last Molotov."

"But the lighter's out," Stanley said.

"I don't need it."

"And why's that?"

Slim grabbed Stanley. "No time for discussion. You come with me. I have a job for you, and you'll need the lighter."

"Be safe," Slim said over his shoulder while disappearing around the bend in the rock.

I turned my attention down the hill. The men must have been about halfway up since that was the darkest part of the hill and hardest for me to see. I debated making a move toward the last man I'd shot. His rifle would be nearby and useful. But after I plugged him, I know he staggered back a few feet before collapsing, so I thought it would be unwise to risk that type of exposure.

Besides, my current plan relied on stealth. And patience.

I held my position and squinted straight ahead, waiting for any changes in the darkness before me. It felt like thirty seconds before seeing the shadowy outlines, but I bet it was more like ten.

At the first sight of the men, about twenty yards in front of me, I grasped the narrow end of the Coke bottle and heaved it thirty yards down the hill. It flew in a high arc and landed with a thud behind the two men I could see. It didn't break since it landed in sand. As suspected, both men turned and froze for a second, then retreated down the hill to check out what they'd just heard.

Since sand was my friend, I was on my feet and rapidly approaching them in stealth mode; the Savage stretched out in front and ready to fire.

When the man farthest away bent over to inspect the ground, I fired a shot exactly where he was looking. The round shattered the bottle and flames leapt up. Unfortunately, the gas splashed downhill, which meant the fire didn't engulf him. But at least it lit up my surroundings.

I used my last bullet and shot the man by the bottle.

Dropping the Savage, I focused on the other dude. As he turned, wheeling the rifle in my direction, I tackled him like a professional line-backer, lifting him up and slamming his back against the ground. The man wheezed upon impact and the rifle flew back out of reach.

I bearhugged him and tried to squeeze any remaining air from his lungs. But the man was short and thick and wily, so he managed to drive a knee into my stomach. Not hard enough to hurt me, but I did lose my grip.

He scrambled from underneath me, rapidly throwing kicks at my face with his pointy boots. I managed to block one kick and grab hold of the boot. As I pulled it toward me, though, I found myself holding an empty boot.

A few feet beside us was a debris field of fire. The man had reached out and scooped under the sand. He flung a firebomb of sand and flames at my face. Luckily, I ducked in time and the shot sailed overhead.

I popped onto my knees. My right hand still held his boot. I quickly turned it around and put my fist inside, right down at the heel. With my left hand, I grabbed the man's pant leg and dragged him toward me. As he struggled to sit up, I leaned in with the right-handed punch of the ages, driving the heel of the man's own boot into his forehead. He flopped back.

Just then, an explosion occurred.

Glancing back, I saw flames pluming from behind the boulders. I knew right away that Slim and Stanley had blown the Jeep. Seconds later, I heard the familiar rat-tat-tat of a semiautomatic rifle. A quick screech of tires distracted me.

Mick raced the minivan down the entrance ramp, aiming it directly at the parked car, which was firing in his direction. In one hand, Mick held a rifle. In the other, he held a handgun. Quick flashes from both barrels were evident as Mick fired from inside the van, blowing out his own windshield.

He continued unleashing a barrage of bullets toward the two men standing behind the car. I imagined he was steering with his knees. Mesmerized, I watched the scene play out.

Mick's sudden blazing of bullets caused the two men to take cover. At the last second, Mick swerved the minivan to the left and bumped out the rear end of the sedan, spinning it and sending the two flying.

Suddenly I realized that my man was running down the hill. As I stood to take chase, another rifle crack went off. A whoosh buzzed my left ear as a bullet just missed taking off my head.

Dropping to my knees, I looked in the shot's direction and saw an eleventh man. He was in one of the truck beds with a rifle perched on top of the tailgate. And he could easily see me since there were still flames to my right from the Molotov cocktail.

I collapsed on my chest and rolled left, hard and fast. Just in time, too, as rounds kicked up the sand where I'd been. As I kept rolling, I heard the high-pitched screech of an engine. When I finally stopped spinning, I looked up and saw Mick's minivan cresting the top of the entrance ramp, actually getting some air under the tires.

The minivan landed hard, crashing and bouncing and sounding like it was about to fall apart. Mick's move saved my life since the sniper in the truck bed shifted his attention to the approaching van. But Mick was already on top of him and moments away from crashing into the truck.

Instead of shooting, the sniper did the smart thing and decided to bail. Even if he'd squeezed off a shot and hit Mick, the van's momentum would've crushed him.

Just before plowing into the truck, Mick hammered the brakes. Which was smart. I could see the puff from the airbag deploying. The reduction in speed caused quite the impact, but not enough to crush the minivan's front end.

The sniper hadn't made it out of the truck bed in time, but he had made to his feet. On impact, he catapulted into the air. Probably did two full revolutions before crashing to the pavement.

I was in motion, running toward the scene.

But first, I needed to get my man.

THIRTY-EIGHT

I CHARGED AFTER HIM. He had one boot on and one off, so I knew he couldn't have gotten far.

The sand was soft and deep, but it didn't slow me down since the hill was steep and my long legs gained a ton of momentum. In fact, I was moving so fast through the dark I came upon the dude at the last second.

He'd heard me coming and knelt on one knee, facing my direction. In front of him, he grasped a small switchblade with both hands. Fortunately, I'd been out of control on the rapid descent, so my arms were swinging wildly in circles; the way they do when you're running fast downhill. I saw the blade's glint and managed to knock the knife straight down with my left hand before our bodies collided.

Then my big frame steamrolled him. He was short and fast and beat me to his feet. As I stood, he suddenly dropped to the sand and tried to leg sweep me with his bare foot.

I hopped over the first sweep, then hopped over the next one; felt like I was jumping rope. When I sensed he'd try a third time, instead of hopping, I collapsed onto my knees and trapped his lower leg into the sand. I used the side of my right fist and clobbered straight down on the outside of his knee. It bent inward and I heard a snap.

"*Ahhhh!*" he shouted, a deep guttural cry.

I leaned over and braced myself on his face; my left palm smushing his cheek into the sand and muffling his cry. The wiggly fellow managed to free himself a moment later. I grabbed the back of his belt with my right hand just as he lunged toward the knife.

I hauled him back, and he plopped onto his butt. With his back to me, I threw a sweeping left hook at the side of his face, connecting squarely in front of his left ear. He timbered to the right. By the slackness in his body, I knew I'd knocked him out on impact.

Taking a moment to get my breath and look around, I saw Mick standing over the

sniper's body. That man lay motionless on the pavement. Suddenly the sound of an engine broke the temporary quiet. I looked left and saw the sedan Mick had spun racing up the entrance ramp. The car headed right at my buddy's position.

When I looked back at Mick, I watched him calmly draw a handgun from behind his back. With stillness and focus, he aimed the gun and fired, emptying a magazine into the approaching car's windshield. The sedan lost acceleration almost immediately, and the vehicle drifted to the right and bumped into the curb.

Thinking about Slim, I glanced up the hill. Flames still licked the tops of the boulders. Because of that, I could see the outcropping in its entirety. At the south end by the sedan, I witnessed Slim and Stanley hustling down the hill. Fortunately, I couldn't see anybody else on the hillside, so my buddy must've gotten the job done.

As Mick approached my position, I started taking off the dude's belt. When he was close, he said, "Not sure that will fit around your girth, Chase."

"It's for you, you skinny punk. This belt might be too big for you, in fact."

"I think you mean lean," Mick corrected. "And whose blood and guts are all over you? You look like Freddy from Halloween."

Mick was backlit from the parking lot lights. All I could see was his lanky frame and head. My buddy always had thick hair that he kept slicked back. With the current lighting, it appeared he had snow in his hair. The heavy gel seemed to be trapping some powdery substance throughout his manicured coif.

I asked, "Did you recently frost your tips or are you going prematurely gray?"

We fist bumped, then he bent over and shook his head, which sent snow fluttering down. Suddenly I understood. "I hear they use talcum powder in air bags, supposed to lube the bag as it deploys."

"Heard it was cornstarch."

"Neither seem to be good lubricants in my opinion."

We both chuckled. I had the man's belt off and used it to tie his hands behind his back. Mick spoke first. "What the hell went on here, anyway? Whose blood is on you? And who are all these men?"

"Honestly, I don't know."

"For real?"

I nodded. "At this point, I don't. I mean, I have a guess. Slim was in Mexico and brought back a guy who was an ex-communicated member of a local cult; a cult we believe is somehow involved with Palmera and the Night Night killings." I motioned at the blood on my shirt. "This is his blood and guts. Before we got his story, the sniper took him out. I was sitting beside him when he was shot. These other men might be current cult members that didn't want him to talk. That's my guess, anyway."

Mick took a moment to process that, then motioned to the passed-out dude. "At least there's one left alive to get some intel and confirm that theory."

"Exactly. Now tell me how you got here. I imagine you were tracking the FJ since I saw the GPS tracker. Were you worried about me or your precious vehicle?"

"Bit of both." He smiled.

"Seriously, what put you into action?"

"Well, when my good buddy was accused of some horrific crimes that I knew he couldn't possibly have committed, I jumped into action."

"That's the nicest thing you've ever said to me."

"Also, I really wanted to protect my baby."

"Sounds more like it."

He motioned to the outcropping. "Saw you standing by her earlier. Please tell me it's the Jeep burning up there."

"I think you might be lucky."

"Good. Seriously, though, when I was prepping the FJ for you, I thought it was a good opportunity to follow you from a distance since I'd already had a tracker on the vehicle. Plus, it's summer and my girls are at a camp for the week, so I had the time to figure out what you were doing and how I could help.

"I'd noticed the FJ had pulled off at this rest area, so I hung back. When I heard the first rifle crack, I ditched the van and slowly snuck up on the shooter and took him out. Using his scope, I could see the vehicles and knew people were behind the south end of the outcropping, but I didn't know for sure if it was you." He held up his keychain. There was a mini-Maglite on there. "Figured Morse code would be better and quieter to communicate than a text."

"Smart. You saved us. Thanks."

He motioned toward the crumpled truck. "Twice."

I nodded. "You're right."

"Listen, we need to call this in. It's gonna be a mess explaining everything to the authorities. It's going to tie us up for some time."

I had hesitations about that course of action, and I was about to share my concerns with Mick, but the dude I'd knocked out was stirring. Plus, Slim and Stanley were now in the parking lot looking around. Mick and I were out of the main lights and hard to see.

"You work on getting him to talk," Mick said. "I'll go to Slim."

I didn't have much success. I couldn't tell if the man wouldn't talk because he didn't speak English and couldn't understand me, or if he understood English but simply chose to be obstinate. The dude gave me the silent treatment.

Eventually, I hauled him to his feet and prodded him toward the parking lot where the other three were standing. It took us some time to get there since the man was limping badly from his busted knee. He also had a perfect triangle imprinted on his forehead from my punch with the boot.

229

Along the way, I stopped at the trunk of Slim's rental. It was still open. On the ground were a dozen rectangular plastic bottles. The labels were written in Spanish, but it was easy to tell the contents was lighter fluid since the label depicted a giant flame. Inside the trunk it reeked like lighter fluid. There was also a large white spray container, the type you use for big weed jobs. No idea why there were in the rental's trunk, I moved on and pushed the man forward.

When we got close to the group, I could hear the men arguing about next steps.

"What's this about the AG involvement," Slim said to me. "The kid here—"

"Stop calling me a kid!" Stanley demanded.

Slim huffed. "Stanley says his dad's involved somehow, really?"

I nodded and turned to Mick. "I understand your need to call the authorities, but I'm not sure that's the right move here until we figure out how deep this situation goes." I thought about Ramona.

While Slim, Stanley, and Mick kept arguing about next steps, I dug out my phone. It'd been in silent mode, so I might've missed a text from Ramona. She'd been planning on meeting at the rest area. If she showed up here, she'd be in a tough position. Sure enough, Ramona had texted back not long ago. She said she had news to share, and that she'd be at the rest area soon.

"What's up, Chase?" Slim asked. "Is this the appropriate time to check your Instagram feed?"

"Don't even have an account, pal." I didn't look up at him since I was firing off a text to Ramona, telling her plans had changed.

"What are you doing?" Mick said.

I deflected. "Anyone know why there were all those lighter fluid bottles in Slim's rental?"

"Is that what they were?" Slim asked. "Hadn't checked them out yet. And, no, no idea why they were in there. It at least explains the smell."

"Seriously, Chase," Mick interrupted. "Who are you texting right now?"

"I'm rerouting Ramona Sanchez."

"And who's that?"

"A federal agent on her way here."

"She runs the field office in Phoenix," Stanley added.

"You know her," Mick said, "a federal agent, and you don't want her here? Seems like she could help us, especially if you two are friendly."

"I get where you're coming from, Mick, but Ramona's presence here seriously complicates things and puts her in a hell of a position. Look at this scene," I said, waving my arm around. "There's AR-15s everywhere, and bodies, and a sniper rifle. These men came on a violent mission, and they met the wrong group of dudes. That's the truth, and this scene proves that. We can circle back and take responsibility for it later. Ramona will be pissed when she finds out, but ultimately, she'll have our backs. We first have to confront and nail the AG. Sorry, Stanley."

He sniffed and pushed up his glasses.

"Your dad really hired some goons to kidnap you?" Mick asked Stanley. Stanley nodded.

"And we have a plan to confront him about it," I said. "In Vegas."

"Just briefly," Mick said, "tell me what you think is going on here."

"Sure," I said. "I think the American CEOs were confronted by a catering company for the terrible way they were abusing local women. These catering employees are related and worked the notoriously wild parties. The CEOs hired a killer or killers to wipe 'em out. I also know Stanley's dad was indebted to one of these CEOs, and this CEO called in the favor with the AG."

Mick asked, "It's a huge cover-up, that's what you're saying?"

"That's my best theory, which is why I don't want to wait here for the feds since the ultimate federal boss appears to be involved. We need to clean the scene of our involvement and get on the road to Vegas, confront Stanley's dad and get some evidence before he gets suspicious. And, by the way, we're already behind schedule. We should be an hour closer to Vegas at this point."

"Okay, understood. But we're gonna clean the scene? Really?" Mick wasn't looking at me, he was looking at Slim. "You're okay with this?"

Slim shrugged.

Stanley said, "I think we have to. We have no choice."

"Afraid so, gents," I said. "Just of our involvement. And I'm going start right now." I started walking toward the hill.

"Where you going?" Mick said, sighing.

"To find my gun, then I'm gonna wipe down the sedan on the hillside. Why don't you get that man to talk. That's one of your specialties, isn't it? After that, you can change the rear tire on your FJ, so we can use it to get the hell out of here."

Mick asked after me, "Think this is the wisest move, Chase?"

"Nope," I said over my shoulder, "not the wisest. But it is a necessity."

THIRTY-NINE

STANLEY DROVE the FJ while I huddled low in the back seat.

In case anyone peered in through the window, I had the bucket hat and sunglasses covering my head and face. Fortunately, since I'd kept my duffel bag in the FJ, I had a change of clothes. At the first gas station off the freeway, Stanley pulled up tight to the restroom area. I hopped out and threw away my bloody shirt and pants and freshened up my face.

Now, Stanley looped around the arrivals area at Sky Harbor International, waiting for Slim to step outside. To remove evidence from the rest area, we had to deal with vehicles at the scene. Slim was currently turning in his car rental. Though the front end of Mick's minivan was beat up badly, the engine still ran.

After some deliberation, we agreed it would be best if he limped the minivan back to California and didn't come to Vegas. He took the lone survivor with him. His plan was to try to glean any intel from the dude before dumping him off at some random truck stop.

I'd rerouted Ramona to Kingman, Arizona. Our plan was to pick her up on our way to Vegas. Since there'd be four of us to help nail Ernesto Tuchek, we didn't think Mick was needed.

"He's taking a little long, isn't he?" I asked Stanley.

"I guess, but there he is anyway." Stanley weaved the FJ to the curb and Slim hopped in.

"Get this," Slim said, looking over his shoulder. He immediately laughed at my appearance. "Nice disguise. Hunched over like that, you look like some creepy old man at the beach."

"If you can, turn that big neck of yours around. No need to draw attention back here."

He faked like it was hard to turn his neck, then said, "Forgot you're a wanted serial killer."

"Correction, a person of interest in a serial murdering case."

"You two always banter like this?" Stanley interjected.

In unison, we said, "Pretty much."

I followed that up with, "Get what?"

"After I'd dropped off the rental," Slim continued, "I was walking back through the terminal. On one of the televisions a newscaster was talking about some arson case at the border. Apparently, some huge mansion was burned to the ground. I stopped to listen to the report because they mentioned one of the accelerants used was lighter fluid. I mean a huge quantity, and it was dispersed via a handheld weed sprayer."

"Really?" I said.

"Yup, and the mansion was home to prominent men in The Family."

As Stanley maneuvered his way out of the busy airport, Slim and I discussed what that meant. It seemed obvious that either Slim or Silvio was being framed as the arsonist.

But why exactly?

After discussing the timeframe of when the arson occurred and when he'd picked up Silvio, I asked him, "Did you stop somewhere and leave the rental unoccupied? Did you spot a tail at all?"

He thought for a moment. "No tail, but listen, I wasn't focused on that. I was in deep conversation with Silvio and listening to his story, so I wasn't paying close attention to my surroundings. After filling up with gas, I went into the station to get some snacks. Silvio followed and we both used the bathroom, so there would've been plenty of opportunity for someone to plant stuff in the trunk. I took the keys with me but didn't lock the door. All they had to do is pop the trunk latch and dump everything in there."

I thought about how the man at the rest area was so focused on prying open the trunk. "Those men were tipped off by whomever planted the bottles and sprayer. They were told you or Silvio or both of you were responsible for the arson, so they double-checked the trunk and found the evidence."

Slim nodded.

"Tell me Silvio's story since Stanley and I obviously didn't hear it. But first, now that we're out of the busy airport area, Stanley, can you pull over and let Slim drive? I want you to get on the laptop and communicate with Sage and look at the thumb drive results."

A few minutes later, after switching spots, our conversation resumed. I maintained my position, crouched low in the back seat. Stanley was in the front passenger seat furiously typing away while Slim drove. Stanley was sending instructions to Sage to show her how to access the Futurum software, which would help update the results she'd already uncovered. Apparently, Stanley didn't feel safe accessing the software remotely on his new laptop. Also, he was using internet via a hotspot from his phone, so the signal was less than reliable.

"So," Slim said, "the Salazar Family Line is a very strict, tightly knit circle of men. It's a strange cult, sort of a syncretistic blend of Judaism, Mormonism, and extreme Patriarchalism, maybe more like Monarchianism."

When he paused, I chided him. "Big words for you, my friend."

"I'm smarter than you look," he replied. "Anyway, Silvio was an outcast in the family, starting from his early teenage years. Eventually, he left the cult, which, like most cults, is extremely hard to do. For many years, Silvio feared for his life. He said the only reason he's still alive is that he kept his mouth shut. After years of remaining silent, The Family deemed him no longer a threat and left him alone."

"What changed?" I asked.

"Though it wasn't public knowledge at first, members of The Family, including Silvio, knew their family was being targeted by someone when the men started dying. Even the police were unaware."

"Really?" I said. "Family members didn't tell the cops what they knew?"

Slim nodded. "No way. From what Silvio said, they're incredibly private and keep to themselves. Plus, they have zero trust of the local authorities. Anyway, the men being killed were first-branch members—"

"Hold on," I interrupted. "What do you mean 'first branch'?"

"That's right, you don't know anything about them." Slim paused for a second. "Let me back up. The founder, a man named Humberto Salazar Senior, had three sons. Humberto was born in America but had Mexican parents. He was raised and schooled here. Ultimately, he was very well educated. He double majored in business and religious studies. He became an entrepreneur and an extremely successful businessman, on both sides of the border. He had an American wife but also many Mexican wives as well, like ten or twelve. By his late fifties, he'd amassed a fortune, and his sons had followed in his footsteps. They'd each taken multiple wives across the border and were working side by side in these business ventures. It's just that their roles were very stratified."

"Stratified how?" I asked.

"Basically, his firstborn was his right-hand man; that son was CEO of all the companies. He was Humberto's favorite and heir to the empire. The second born was sort of like the middle manager of all the companies, and the youngest son was the worker son. He was the one in charge of all the employees."

"Resentment between the brothers then?"

"From what Silvio said, absolutely, especially as time marched on and successive generations dug in and exacerbated the stratification. There became three clear branches of the family line, and in the contemporary Salazar family, the descendants of the firstborn son live like kings and the third born son like paupers. Descendants of the third born, like Silvio, are typically born and raised in Mexico, right by the border. They're mainly Mexican nationals and not American citizens. Third-branch members always refer to their family organization as *La Familia*. Whereas the first-branch members never use Spanish, they always refer to themselves as members of The Family.

"Anyway, when the firstborn descendants started being picked off some time ago, Silvio knew trouble was brewing. He figured this could cause a once-and-for-all rift between the family lines. There hadn't been a huge rift before because these pauper sons were at least being paid fifty percent more than the daily working rate of nonfamily members. For instance, if the daily working wage was ten bucks for the average Mexican, working class members of The Family made fifteen. So, sensing trouble and perhaps a renewed scrutiny on himself, Silvio applied for a Border Crossing Card, which he would need to travel to the States. He wanted to go there to start a new life, and because he'd thought he'd be safer there if fighting broke out within The Family.

"He'd just been issued the card but had no transportation into America. Along I come, asking questions about the family, so we strike a deal. He tells me everything he can if I get him to Phoenix."

Slim paused. I could see his Adam's apple bobbing.

I put my hand on his right shoulder. "Nobody could've known that you guys were being tailed and set up."

Eventually, he said, "I know, it's just hard."

There were a few moments of silence. To distract Slim, I asked him a question that I'd been wondering about. "In San Luis, did you ever get a description of the killer? You said you were trying to sober up that addict to see if he remembered anything."

"Right," Slim said. "The only thing he told me, when he was half lucid, was that he remembered the man being bowlegged. Nothing about facial appearance or scars or tattoos."

"Bowlegged? That's it?"

"That's it."

I half joked with Stanley. "Any of those phenotyping companies you know scan for bowlegged traits?"

Stanley didn't look up from his laptop. "That's a stretch, and a hard no. Fellas, for the record, Victoria found no prints on the Beretta. That's a dead end."

"This new situation confuses me," I said to no one in particular. "Totally throws a wrench into my theory."

"How so?" Slim asked.

"We have three players involved in whatever is going on. We have the CEOs, Stanley's dad, and The Family. My theory is that the CEOs were trying to get rid of these workers who catered their lavish and illegal parties, and the CEOs hired outside help for that. When the heat started pointing toward the CEOs, this Berbacoa fellow, who we can assume is head of the CEO cabal, called in a favor to the AG to deflect attention. Ernesto Tuchek felt indebted to Berbacoa, as Stanley overheard at Christmas, so Ernesto leaned on Richie Balboa, an agent under his control, to help throw off the investigation."

"Berbacoa?" Slim questioned. "Like Alvin Berbacoa of General Electric?"

Stanley finally looked up from the laptop and stared at Slim.

"How do you know that name?" I asked.

Slim sighed. "I know you're not into politics, Chase, but you're aware that our company deals in political investigations, right?"

"Yes, so what?"

"You really ought to pay more attention to political news." Slim turned to Stanley. "You know your father was an odd pick for AG. I mean, he isn't even in the same party as the president."

He snorted. "Of course."

"There were a lot of rumors and speculation," Slim said, "about your father getting the job and why. I can't remember the details, but I do remember Berbacoa's name being in the news quite regularly before the new president was installed, about some indictment he was involved in, but then nothing after that. The story simply faded."

"More confirmation," I said, "that Ernesto had some back-door deal with Berbacoa, which would be dropping an investigation against him. You don't remember any details?"

He shook his head. "No, but I can find out. Back to your theory: what throws a wrench into it?"

"My theory assumes the caterers were being picked off by this sicario hired by Berbacoa and his colleagues. Except you're saying that the worker bees in The Family are all third-branch members, but the victims are first-branch members."

"Right," Slim said, "I see what you're saying. It doesn't add up."

I kept thinking. "Unless . . ."

"Unless what?" Slim prodded.

"Unless the workers have a clear chain of command. For instance, they report the CEOs' behavior to their ultimate bosses, the members in the first branch."

"Gotcha. And the first-branch members confront the CEOs and are taken out because of that."

"Or," Stanley interjected, "it's more devious than that."

"What do you mean?" I asked.

"CEOs, like Berbacoa, are no dummies, obviously. Perhaps they're well aware of how The Family operates, so they know about the different branches and the rift that exists between them, and they use that to their advantage."

"You really are learning," I said, tapping Stanley on his shoulder. "That's a better theory, I think. We have an internal war raging here within The Family. It stands to reason that the CEOs knocked off members of the first branch, thinking that the blame could then be placed on the working third-class branch."

We all thought about that for a few minutes. Eventually, I added, "Manufacturing a war within The Family helps the CEOs get rid of the eyewitnesses to their past crimes, and casts dispersion away from them. A win-win, though one thing still bothers me."

"What's that?" Stanley asked.

"Why the Night Night Killer poses the bodies the way he does?"

Again, more silence. Slim hadn't said a word for a few minutes, so I asked him his thoughts.

He replied, "I have something even bigger that bothers me about Stanley's theory."

"Go ahead," I said, "what is it?"

"It presupposes the men in The Family are deeply concerned about the CEOs' horrible treatment of local women."

"It does," I said.

"The problem is that according to Silvio, women were of no value in The Family. They were a means to an end. They existed for pleasure and to give birth to sons."

I thought about that. "Maybe that's true for the first-branch members but not the third. Maybe the third-branch men, those who were relatively poor, didn't share that same view of women within The Family."

Slim shook his head. "Not according to Silvio. In fact, one of the major reasons he left the cult pertained to how they treated women. He was one of the rare men, even within the third branch, that despised how women were viewed and treated."

I sank back into the seat. "Just when I thought we were getting somewhere."

For the next while, we bounced some more theories off each other. But no one theory could reasonably account for all the details. Further investigation was clearly needed. I was also hopeful about Ramona. She'd said she had some news to share, and we were about to hear it since we'd just entered the city limits for Kingman, Arizona.

"There's a travel center coming up in a quarter mile, Slim. Ramona's waiting for us there."

Stanley turned to face me. "Do we tell her about the rest area fiasco?"

"Absolutely not, not now at least. She has news to share, maybe that helps us. Who knows? Rather not bring it up."

"Agreed," Slim said, pulling off the freeway. "Did she at least hint at what she found out?"

"Nope."

"Is she going to follow us to Vegas? Or are we going to take her on board? Cuz if we're carpooling, I'm not leaving the FJ here in the middle of nowhere."

"I think we carpool, that way we can hear her news and bring her up to speed about how we're gonna nail Ernesto. Sorry, Stanley."

"You don't have to apologize," he said.

"There she is," I said, pointing. "Third car from the end."

Ramona was out of her vehicle as soon as she recognized us. I'd taken off my old man's beach disguise and rolled down my window. "Good to see you," I said. "Hop in."

She looked around for a bit, then shrugged. "This is a much cooler ride than mine."

Ramona sat behind Slim. She'd never met Stanley before, so I introduced them. Stanley stayed turned around as Slim got back onto the road. His bug eyes were buggier than usual. Which didn't surprise me. As I've said before, Ms. Sanchez was easy on the eyes.

I didn't waste any time. "So, Mexicali was successful? You texted that you have news?"

She smiled. "Sure do. Gleaned one big piece of intel and one small one."

"What's the big piece?"

"The Mexican detective has been holding back something, and it's pretty shocking."

When she didn't reveal it right away, I prodded her. "Like what?"

She cleared her throat. "Like the identity of the Night Night Killer."

FORTY

"Before you get too excited," Ramona continued, "they don't know his exact identity."

My shock turned to confusion.

Ramona sensed it. "The killer goes by *El Cameleon*," she said. "That's what they know so far."

That didn't necessarily help my confusion. "The Chameleon?" I questioned.

She nodded. "The killer left a new calling card. He left it with a victim at the mansion that was burned down. That's the big news I have to share."

"What do you mean by new calling card?" I asked.

"I'll show you instead." She pulled out her phone. "Naturally, the detective wouldn't let me have or handle the card, but he did allow me to take a picture of it. As long as I didn't go public with it." She handed me the cell. "There are two pictures."

The first picture was the front of the business card, and it looked the same: nothing but the words Night Night written on it. The second picture was the back of the card. There was a faint watermark image that stretched from edge to edge. It was the outline of a chameleon.

I looked at Ramona. "I take it this *El Cameleon* is known in Mexico?"

She shook her head. "Not throughout Mexico. Locally, yes, and The Family knows the name."

"How so?"

"About a year before the killings started an exposé in a local paper outlined a number of

atrocities credited to the seemingly innocuous family cult. The source was unnamed but went by the moniker, *El Cameleon*. Since some evidence in that story checked out, many speculated *El Cameleon* was an insider."

"Like inside The Family?" I said.

"Yup," Ramona replied. "The story didn't gain much traction and, ultimately, went nowhere. But then The Chameleon pops up taking credit for these latest murders. The detective thinks *El Cameleon*'s been biding their time, then stepped it up."

I thought about that. "Or the CEOs knew about this story, and they hired *El Cameleon* to do their dirty work. Or they hired some random sicario to pretend he's *El Cameleon*. All for the intention of casting dispersion away from themselves. To make it appear that The Family is turning on itself."

Silence ensued.

After a few moments, I said, "The revelation that the serial killer is *El Cameleon* hasn't gone public, obviously. Why's the detective keeping it under wraps?"

"Good question," Ramona said. "And the answer is he doesn't want the killer controlling the narrative. Doesn't want this murderer getting any glory, calling the shots, or renaming himself. He believes the killer now wants credit for his work, but the detective won't give him the satisfaction."

Slim said, "And the detective didn't hesitate to tell you all this? Sorry, just trying to understand. I know you're a federal agent and your office had been working the case. Seems strange they'd be willing to talk with you."

She looked at me. "Earlier, Chase suggested my looks could open some doors. Isn't that right? Isn't that why you sent me down there?" She batted her eyes playfully.

"See," I said, "I was right. Wasn't I?"

She slugged me on the shoulder. "No, you're not. You're dead wrong. The detective and I struck a deal."

"Sounds more like it," Slim said.

"What kind of deal," I asked.

"The other thing I learned, the small detail, was that the evidence sent to Futurum was just a fraction of what they collected. From what I can tell, this local detective ran a smart investigation. He knew any evidence sent to a third-party company in another country had chain of evidence problems and could never be used in court. That wasn't his intention, though. He never sent Futurum the totality of evidence, just samples. He wanted Futurum to do what they're supposed to be good at, which is quickly narrowing the list of suspects down, then the Mexican detective would take it from there once they had a name.

"Before Ross went in hiding, the detective had given him access to several Mexican databases. And, as we all know, because of that, Ross had made significant headway and ultimately had the killer's profile in hand. But Ross had two problems: One, he didn't exactly trust this detective, and two, he was a security freak and kept everything on a local, air-gapped computer. Which ultimately destroyed the results and any progress he'd made when he was murdered."

Stanley nodded along. "He was ten times worse than me. Maybe twenty times."

"Still a little confused," Slim said. "What's the deal you struck?"

Ramona reached out and touched Stanley's shoulder. "Deal was for Stanley."

Stanley looked back and blinked rapidly.

She continued. "Even though the detective now believes it's an inside job, which has narrowed the search field, the fact is: The Family is massive. With the Mexican authorities' limited resources and expertise, they haven't gotten very far. The deal was I get the intel if I promise to deliver Stanley to Mexicali. The detective wants Stanley to do what Ross was doing, use the Futurum software. He believes Stanley can recreate the results that Ross had uncovered after being given access to these Mexican databases. The detective even has additional database access, databases that Ross didn't use. He believes that may aid Stanley in getting an actual name of *El Cameleon*, and not just the killer's DNA profile. Except he needs Stanley to be there in person to do all this, insists on it, in fact."

For once, Stanley was at a loss for words.

"Seems like a no-brainer," I said. "Right, Stanley?" When he didn't respond, I pushed it. "You can prove your software's worth and identify this killer, and whoever hired him, if that's the case. Put your company on the map, which is what Ross wanted as well." A pause, then, "What's the problem? You seem hesitant."

He pushed up his glasses. "I agree this is a great opportunity. Just hesitant about going to Mexico, especially considering what happened to Ross. Would rather stay here."

"Not sure that's an option," Ramona said. "Don't think this detective is going to give you carte blanche remote access to certain Mexican databases, like he did with Ross. But don't worry, I'll accompany you to Mexicali, after this meeting with your dad, of course. Tell me about that, and what we're doing in Vegas."

Stanley spent a while detailing what had happened with him and the kidnapping.

After his story, she turned to me. "How does the AG fit into all this?"

"I think he's helping to cover up CEO involvement, or at least thwart any investigation into the matter. What about this detective? I know he believes this is an internal family matter, but does he have any thoughts about CEO involvement? I mean, he sent Futurum evidence that Ross ultimately identified as belonging to CEOs like Alvin Berbacoa."

"He admitted that part was pretty baffling at first."

"How so?"

"Initially, the male victims weren't identified by the Mexican police force. They had no idea who these men were. That was why the detective also sent Futurum DNA evidence from the victims. He reasoned Ross could identify the men if they were American. Sure enough, he did. The detective learned the victims belonged to The Family, which, of course, ran a huge catering company, so he initially assumed the victims were caterers working the American parties." She looked at me. "Which is exactly what you thought, right?"

I nodded.

Ramona continued. "But the more the detective thought about it, it didn't add up."

"Why?" I asked.

"The detective had evidence like fingerprints on broken glass and semen on napkins, not to mention some indirect evidence. In his mind, it all seemed too convenient, too contrived."

I said, "The detective thinks the CEOs were being framed then? Is that it?"

She nodded. "That's his current theory."

"If you know what you're doing," Stanley interjected, "it's quite easy to plant DNA evidence at crime scenes these days. Not only direct evidence but also secondary transfer DNA. It's easily detected these days, and it can totally throw off an investigation."

Slim looked at Stanley. "Y'all know a lot more about these things than I do. Explain secondary transfer DNA."

"Sure," Stanley said. "DNA detection these days is a lot more sensitive, which means we can identify a DNA profile from the tiniest of samples. But this also creates a double-edged sword since DNA is so easily transferred from common surfaces. Cross contamination happens, mix-ups in labs that process samples can be common if strict protocols aren't in place. All this makes it easier to identify the wrong suspect, or to frame a suspect. Journalists and the media refer to this as touch DNA, but scientists use the term secondary transfer DNA, which can either be direct or indirect transfer."

"Got it," Slim said.

"For me," I said, "it's incredibly important to know the origin of the catering evidence."

"What does that matter?" Stanley asked.

I turned to Ramona. "Were the napkins and broken glass found at the murder scenes? We have to know that."

"Huh," Ramona said, thinking hard. "You're right, we do need to know that, and I didn't think to ask that question to the detective."

"Did you get the inclination the napkins and stemware were found on or around the men's bodies?"

"No, unfortunately, I didn't get any sort of inclination."

Stanley asked, "Why are you so concerned about where this evidence came from?"

"Because," I said, "if the napkins and stemware and broken glass were found at the murder scenes, then it likely absolves the CEOs of any wrong-doing. Right?"

Stanley turned. "How so?"

"The CEOs wouldn't hire *El Cameleon*, or someone to pose as *El Cameleon*, to kill these men to cover up their crimes, then have the same hitman leave evidence behind that frames or implicates the CEOs."

"Oh, right," Stanley said. "Of course."

"You're onto something," Ramona said, "it's really important to find out where this line of evidence originated. I should've asked the detective. Damn. I guess we're for sure going back to Mexicali. I have his cell number, too, so I'll fire off a text and ask, see if he responds."

I nodded, excited at that prospect.

"Still, though," Slim said, "it feels like the CEOs and AG are deeply involved in this. Doesn't it? Or am I the only one not fully buying this theory?"

"It does feel like they must be involved," I said. "What if . . ."

Ramona prodded. "What if what, Chase?"

"As I've said before, what if these caterers had a strict chain of command they must follow. The workers would never approach or confront American CEOs directly, so they let their big bosses know instead. Those men, the first-branch members who were picked off, brought the situation to light and pay the price for doing so. Then, when the workers realized what was happening, perhaps they gathered this evidence from the wild parties and sent it directly to the local Mexican police force. What if it wasn't a frame job like the detective thinks? What if it was the workers corroborating their story of CEO involvement to the authorities? And that the CEOs had hired this sicario to silence these men."

"Could be," Slim said. "It makes sense since caterers would have direct access to the sorts of evidence sent to the police."

"Agreed," Ramona said. She pointed out the window at a road sign that said Vegas was forty miles out. "Gentlemen, not to change topics here, but we only have a half hour before Vegas. What's the plan?"

I nodded my agreement. "Stanley, keep Griff on the hook. Send him a text that we're on track to meet in one hour. Then start closely monitoring your dad's iPhone to see where he goes."

Moments later, he said, "Text sent. Monitoring starting."

We spent the next twenty-five minutes discussing the plan.

Five minutes from the location, I got Slim to pull over and said, "Let's review the plan to make sure we're in sync. Slim, you first."

"I'll hang in the hotel's lobby and make some calls," he said. "Find out everything I can on Berbacoa and the former indictment against him, and why it went away."

"Good. Ramona?"

"I'm driving to Ernesto's final location while Stanley and you hide in the back seat. The AG has no idea what I look like, so I'll do a drive-by, get the lay of the land. I need to make sure it's safe, that no one's around, before dropping off Stanley to approach his dad."

I was concerned that in the past few hours the cowboys had swallowed their pride and contacted Griff. And that now Griff and/or the cowboys were onto us, and they'd be hiding in the wings, waiting to pounce on Stanley.

"Great," I said. "After the drop-off, Ramona and I will hang back at a safe distance and continue to look for Griff and the cowboys. If I can sneak up for protection, I will. Stanley, if we're in an open area and have a line of sight, you scratch behind your right ear when you have the necessary recording and want Ramona to sweep in and arrest your pops. If there is no sight line, text Ramona when you have the intel." I eyed him. "You have the cell ready?"

"Yup, I'll record everything."

"Let's get into place then."

We got into our respective positions. Slim headed into one of Vegas's many huge hotel lobbies. I got as low as I could in the back seat. Stanley, now submerged in the rear footwell, had the laptop open on the seat. "Meeting place should be just around back of this hotel."

Ramona drove and followed Stanley's directions.

Within two minutes, he said, "Okay, we're here, should be straight ahead."

Immediately, she responded, "You're kidding, I hope?"

"Nope," Stanley said, "my dad should be directly ahead, no more than fifty yards."

She sighed.

"What's wrong?" I said.

"Look for yourself."

"Sure it's safe?" I asked. "Don't want him spotting me."

"I'm sure."

I slowly peaked over the back seat. My heart sank.

"Abandon plan," I said. "We have a big problem."

FORTY-ONE

"What do we do?" Stanley said, pointing straight ahead. "What the hell are we going to do?"

We all stared at the towering concrete parking structure through the windshield. The building was rectangular shaped. On either end were two huge, round turrets where vehicles wound up or down the structure. The massive parking garage stretched high into the air, maybe fifteen to twenty levels in all.

I looked at Stanley. "I take it the tracking app doesn't account for elevation?"

He glared at me. "It does not. He could be on any level. At least we know he's near this end of the structure, by the entrance ramp."

After some quick thinking, I said, "I'll wait in the FJ and monitor the exit. Ramona, why don't you take the elevator to the top, start winding your way down, level by level, looking for Ernesto. He's obviously sitting in some rental car near this end of the structure. Stanley, you start at the bottom and work upward."

"But it'll be weird if my dad sees me, right? Because I'm supposed to be dropped off by Griff."

"It will," I said. "But he's your father and won't get spooked at the sight of you, so he won't take off. He's here to get you, anyway. Right?"

Stanley nodded, and I said, "Go find him. Start your cell recording now. Whoever spots him first, send a quick group text."

I got into the driver's seat while Ramona headed to the elevator and Stanley scurried inside the first level. I repositioned the FJ so that I was near the exit and could see cars approaching the gate. Even though it was large, it wasn't an unusually busy parking garage. There were maybe two to three cars leaving every couple of minutes.

I sat and watched the exit for approximately ten long minutes. That was when Stanley texted that he'd found his dad on Level E in a black Lincoln Navigator. He was approaching the vehicle and signed off.

Thinking the first ten minutes were long, the next ten were torture. My mind flipped and flopped between all the things that could go right with Stanley's deception, and all the things that could go wrong. What distracted me was Ramona. I watched her approach the FJ. When she was close, I waved her over to the driver's side and crawled into the passenger seat.

She hopped in. "Are we back to the original plan then?"

"Think so," I said. "While you wait here, I'll walk up to the fifth level. From below, I can peek and assess the Lincoln's location and orientation, see whether it's safe to sneak up on it or not. Still got my silly disguise, too." I held up the bucket hat and sunglasses.

"Might as well," she said. "I can cover the exit."

Minutes later, as I neared Level E, I'd learned exactly how the parking spots on each level were laid out. There was a certain point on the incline, right before reaching the next level, where I could pop up and look the length of the structure and see most of the cars parked on that particular level.

Since the SUV was a large, black Lincoln Navigator, I spotted it not long after scoping out Level E. The Lincoln was approximately ten spots around the curve on the left-hand side. Parked at the third spot around the turn was a large truck. It looked like it barely fit inside the parking structure, like one of those vehicles that scratched the concrete ceiling at certain low points.

To view the Lincoln, I actually had to look around this big truck, which worked out well since I didn't want to walk around the bend and be spotted. So, I backed down the incline and weaved in between the last two cars on Level D. When the coast was clear, I hopped up and grasped the concrete ledge above me, to the right of the big truck, then hauled myself up. My movements were blocked by the truck's massive front end.

There was about a foot and half between the front bumper and the concrete wall. I kneeled and slowly shuffled forward until I was at the midway point of the truck. Then I focused my attention on the Navigator.

Stanley and his dad were in the front seat talking. Of course, I couldn't hear anything, and I was too far away to read lips. I waited and watched for a few minutes. After that, the conversation started getting heated. Within moments, it escalated, and the men started putting their hands on each other.

I needed to see better, so I got to my feet, though I stayed crouched over. It looked like Stanley and his dad were wrestling over something. It appeared to be the cowboy's phone. I couldn't confirm, though, because the moment I made myself more visible, I heard an engine start. Glancing to my right, I saw a boxy cargo van, parked directly across from the truck, suddenly lurch forward.

Griff was driving. He gunned the accelerator and aimed it at the rear of the truck.

I was about to be crushed against the concrete wall. I had no time to go left or right and get out of the way. It was either jump onto the hood or duck flat underneath the car.

I chose to duck.

Metal on metal crunched as the cargo van made impact. Following that, the truck's front end smashed against the concrete wall. It all happened so fast I had no time to think or be scared. All I could do was breathe a sigh of relief. The truck was lifted high, so I remained unscathed.

For a moment, I lay there and took stock of my surroundings. The security alarm from one of the cars beside the truck was in full effect. There were honking noises and flashing lights. I could also hear a hissing sound, which I figured was from the van's engine.

To my left, I saw feet rapidly moving alongside the truck, so I shimmied away from the concrete wall. While Griff ran to the front end to see if he'd smushed me, I popped out from behind the front passenger tire.

Griff heard me and spun around. "Damn," he said, right before I filled his mouth with my fist.

He staggered back against the concrete wall, dabbing at his bloody mouth.

I ran at him, bent at the waist, then torpedoed my head into his stomach. He slithered to the ground. I was going to pull him up by his messy hair, but I heard the Lincoln backing out, so I took off after it instead.

The big SUV whined in reverse as it emerged from its parking spot, then the vehicle abruptly stopped. I heard the gears grind as Ernesto dropped it into Drive. Just before it rocketed forward, Stanley dumped out the passenger door, landing on his butt and rolling.

I sprinted to his location. "You okay?"

Ernesto screeched the brakes, and I looked up. For a second, our eyes met as he glared at me through the rearview mirror. Then just as quickly he gunned the Lincoln and took off.

While I was helping Stanley up, he said, "I'm good. I'm fine. It wasn't moving fast." Since he looked okay, I pulled out my phone to alert Ramona since I wanted her to tail Ernesto.

Just as I was unlocking the phone, Stanley yelled, "Behind, Chase!"

It was too late. Griff had given me a taste of my own medicine, ramming me in my back with his head. I staggered forward a few steps, clenching my teeth at the pain. The burner cell flew out of my hand and skidded underneath a nearby car.

Pissed, I spun around and took three steps toward Griff. Just as he managed to straighten, I snapped his head back with a right-handed punch. As his head returned to its normal position, I stepped into a harder punch, which flattened all the cartilage in his nose.

"No!" he screeched, putting his hands to his face to stem the flow of blood.

I stepped toward him again. This time, since his face was covered, I sent a quick left jab to his throat, which crumpled him to his knees. I turned to Stanley. "Call Ramona. Tell her about the Lincoln and have her tail it."

Then I turned and faced Griff. He was clutching at his throat, searching for air.

"Since you can't talk, you'll have to listen. It's over for the attorney general, pal, which means it's over for you. So, you better get on the right side of things. Understood?"

He wheezed and shook his head.

"You're in a world of trouble, Griff, but your client is even worse off. I have a federal agent with me. I'm sure she can help broker some sort of deal. Get reduced time if you turn against Ernesto. Understand now?"

Griff got to his feet. He swallowed a few times, then managed, "I'll take my chances with the AG."

"Not wise," I said, moving toward him.

He pulled out a gun and pointed it at me.

That gave me pause. I knew he wouldn't harm Stanley, but me, I wasn't so sure. He almost cut my midsection in half by ramming the truck.

I stopped my advance. "Don't be stupid here. You're not going to shoot me."

He wiped blood from his mouth. "Try me."

I motioned behind him. A car had come around the entrance ramp and stopped dead when it saw our standoff. There was an elderly couple with wide eyes sitting in the front seat. "You gonna shoot me in front of an audience?"

He eyed me, probably not believing that someone was behind him. After a few seconds, he glanced over his shoulder, then just as quickly looked back. "You're right, I'm not going to shoot you." Then he turned and ran at the car, pointing the gun and screaming at the old folks to get out. When I saw them comply, I turned and pointed at the stairs beside the elevator.

"Let's move, Stanley," I yelled. "We have to get out of here." The elderly couple had originally been stunned, but now I witnessed the man pulling out a cellphone. He was either gonna call the cops, or video the scene, or both.

As we ran toward the stairs, Griff raced toward the exit in the hijacked car.

While winding down the stairs, I asked Stanley, "Get a hold of Ramona?"

"Yup, she's tailing my dad."

"Good, let's head back to the lobby and get Slim."

"What about Griff?" he asked.

"That's why I'm hustling. I want to see if he takes off, or if he waits for us at the bottom."

Once we hit Level A, we had to move quickly toward the other end of the parking structure since that's where the exit was. About halfway there, we saw Griff gunning it out of the garage. He wheeled right at the next cross street and headed toward the front of the hotel.

I stopped running and looked at Stanley. "He's getting the hell out of here."

Stanley nodded. While we caught our breath, he dug out my burner from his front pocket and handed it to me.

"Thanks," I said. "Forgot about this. Tell me what happened with your pops. Let's not run since the cops might be on their way, but we can walk fast."

We picked up the pace while moving in the hotel lobby direction.

"Well," Stanley said, "he obviously wasn't surprised to see me. To make a long conversation short, he acted like a seasoned politician. He did his best to turn the tables on me and deflect most of my questions."

"Can I listen to the recording and hear for myself?"

Stanley hung his head.

"Oh, you're kidding, you didn't record it?"

Immediately he looked up. "No, I did, of course I did. But I guess I wasn't that smooth when questioning him, probably too nervous. He rightly assumed that I was recording everything and grabbed the cell and deleted the recording. I had to wrestle him to get it back."

"So, you have the cell but there's no recording?"

He nodded. Now I was the one hanging my head. Eventually, I took a deep breath. "Go ahead then, tell me what he said, what he did or did not admit to."

"He admitted to hiring Griff to abduct me. He wasn't aware Griff had employed extra help. Anyway, he said it was all for my protection, that was what he repeatedly said. I mean, over and over, Chase, like a broken record. From the beginning he didn't want me involved, that he was prepared to do whatever it takes. Griff was supposed to deliver me here, then he was taking me home to the East Coast. Even bought a plane ticket for me."

"So, he's headed to the airport?"

"Most likely."

I texted Ramona, telling her that Ernesto was headed to the airport, in case she loses him.

"Okay," I said, "please tell me you confronted him about his involvement with Berbacoa and the murders."

"Of course I did. The only concrete thing he said there was that he was not involved with the murders, and neither were the CEOs. He assured me of that, bet his life on it, in fact. He even guilted me about thinking that he'd be involved in something like that."

"You pushed him, right?"

He nodded. "I did. All he'd say is that there were things far over my head that I couldn't possibly understand. He said, yes, he had a deal with Berbacoa, but for my protection he wasn't going to say what it was."

I scoffed. "More like his protection."

"Maybe, maybe not," Stanley said.

"You don't believe him, do you?"

"I believe he has nothing to do with these killings." Stanley narrowed his eyes. "Yes, that's what I believe. I really do, Chase. He's my father. As far as anything else, though, I don't know."

I leaned my head back and thought. Stanley was already feeling terrible about the situation, so I didn't add more fuel. What I wanted to do was utter how useless this operation was, that it got us absolutely nowhere, but I kept that to myself.

I stayed silent for the remainder of our walk to the main lobby. We found Slim on a couch in a cell conversation with someone. When he saw us, he hung up and said, "How'd it go? Did we nail him?"

Stanley and I both shook our heads. I think the way we collapsed onto the couch spoke volumes to Slim because he didn't push it by asking a follow-up question.

So, I asked, "What'd you find out?"

"A bit of everything, a bit of nothing."

Stanley screwed up his face. "What does that mean? Why don't you just talk normal?"

Slim laughed. "Because that's exactly what I learned. Something big went on with your father and the General Electric company, that's for sure. The indictment was sealed, so none of my contacts were willing to talk about it, especially not over the phone."

Stanley sighed. "You struck out, too, then?"

"Yes, but I have some favors out there and believe I can find out the details, just have to fly back to the East Coast and speak with some contacts in person."

That gave me a sudden idea. I turned to Stanley. "Can you order an Uber or Lyft or whatever to take us to the airport?"

He snorted. "Uh, yeah. Of course, I can."

"Do it." Turning to Slim, I said, "Maybe we can get you on the same flight the AG is on. You can keep an eye on him."

Slim nodded while I stepped away and called Ramona.

She answered with, "You're right, he's at the airport."

"Okay, park and go inside the terminal, see if there are any flights to Reagan National soon. If there is, my guess is that the Ernesto is on that flight. Also, if there is a flight, buy a ticket for Slim. He needs to head back East and speak with some contacts in person to get the unadulterated scoop on Ernesto. Slim's worked with heads of judicial Senate committees, so he has the leverage to find out the details of a sealed indictment, one that mysteriously went away."

"Okay," she said. "Maybe I should go as well, especially if Stanley has solid evidence against his dad. Slim may have the contacts, but he can't arrest someone."

"Stanley got nothing."

"Really? What happened?"

"Basically, his dad got wise to the recording and deleted their conversation."

A brief silence. "Maybe I still go," she said. "Once Slim works his contacts and we have proof of the AG's involvement, I can sweep in and nail him."

"That's your boss you're talking about. The ultimate head of the FBI."

"I know. Crazy, right? I'll head to the East Coast and keep an eye on him. Slim will be busy meeting people anyway."

"Sounds good, but you're also needed to accompany Stanley to Mexicali. Right?"

"I'll contact the detective and tell him I'm not coming with Stanley. That you'll accompany him. Take the FJ, it's parked in the short-term lot, area H."

"A wanted suspect in an international serial murder case waltzes across the border and into a Mexican police station. Great."

She scoffed. "The detective doesn't buy the theory that you're involved, in any shape or form."

"It's a risk, though."

"So's arresting the Attorney General of the United States."

"Fair enough," I said after a moment. "Okay, so that's the plan. Let's do it."

As soon as I hung up, Stanley said, "Lyft's out front."

"Really? That quickly?"

The kid shook his head at me. "You're so old."

FORTY-TWO

Still being cautious, I hunkered down in the back seat while Stanley drove the FJ south to Mexico. To my left was Stanley's laptop. I was waiting on the latest email and results from Sage. In the meantime, I was busy texting with Ramona. Ernesto's flight was overbooked, so she and Slim didn't get a seat. They had, however, secured a flight to Virginia on a different airline that left twenty minutes later.

I knew when Ramona was in the air, she wouldn't be able to communicate, so I wanted to get as much information I could about this Mexican detective. Not only his name, but also cell details, what he looked like, and where he worked, etc.

"Anything come through from Sage yet?" Stanley asked.

"Not yet," I said.

"You might have to refresh, you know. We're not in great cell reception area, and we're using a hotspot, so internet is patchy at best. She should've emailed by now."

I refreshed the laptop screen. Sure enough, Stanley was right. An email from Sage came in a few minutes ago. "There's something here."

"What's it say?"

"Let me read it, will ya?"

He looked at me in the rearview mirror. "You probably need glasses, don't you?"

"Watch it, kid."

After a minute of reading, I lit up and said, "We're one step closer."

"You're kidding. How?"

"Sage used your software and analyzed the three single source male profiles we've yet to identify. Remember how it was thought that these single source profiles weren't a victim or a CEO?"

"I do."

"That was wrong. Futurum found a match with an American citizen, who just so happens to be a major CEO in Palmera. Sage said she matched one of the profiles to a CEO of a massive solar company."

"So obviously not the killer but could be connected."

"Exactly. Now we only have two unidentified suspects left." I thought out loud. "We have confirmed DNA evidence from four top executives. Four of the largest American corporations in Palmera. We have GE, this solar company, there's a medical device provider, and an aerospace corporation. They're all involved in whatever's going on."

"I like what you said earlier, you called it a CEO cabal. That's exactly what this is. What else did Sage find out?"

I glanced over the email again. "That's about it. According to her, she's exhausted all the American databases and has filled in the genealogy tree as much as she can."

Stanley slammed his palm on the steering wheel. At first, I thought he was upset for Sage not making further progress, but then I realized he was thrilled.

"What's up?" I asked.

"So jazzed on this, Chase. I'm so excited. We're almost exactly where Ross had left off. He'd been given additional foreign database access that helped him pinpoint the killer's profile. I'll get access to those same databases and be able to narrow it down, just like he did. Even better, you heard Ramona say that the detective would give us some additional access that Ross didn't have, right?"

"She said that, for sure."

"We're going to identify the killer, which is gonna put Futurum on the map." He looked at me in the mirror. "Oh, sorry, and also clear your name."

"That's why you're so excited, is it?"

"This Mexican detective, what's his name by the way?"

"Gerardo Diaz."

"Diaz is going to be blown away by how fast I solve this. Just one issue, though." He drummed his fingers on the wheel.

"What issue?"

"They can't force me to use their computers. I don't want them playing funny business and insist I use their computers and make me download the software onto one of their machines. No way. You must back me up on that, Chase."

I shrugged. "I'll try. I mean, Diaz may see my face and cuff me before I get a word out. You might be on your own."

"He tries that, he won't get my help, he won't get access to Futurum. I have your back, you have mine."

"Agreed."

We drove in silence for a while. With the computer on my lap, I plugged in the thumb drive and updated all the latest information onto it, then pocketed the drive. After, I stared at the screen for a long time. Eventually, Stanley asked me what I was doing.

"If I'm going to have your back, I want to make sure I understand everything. I need to know exactly what you'll be doing in Mexicali with your software. I've been looking at this complicated genealogy tree that Sage has put together, for far too long now."

When I didn't continue, he said, "And?"

"And I'm trying to understand how it all fits together. Let me see if I have everything straight."

"Fire away, we have nothing else to do."

"Your company was sent multiple sources of DNA evidence. Ross and Sage were then able to produce a DNA profile from every piece of evidence sent to Futurum. Right?"

He nodded.

CRAIG N. HOOPER

I continued. "All but two of those profiles remain unknown, and they're from the suspect side. The victims' profiles, which you established from the blood evidence, were cross-checked with known public DNA databases in the States as well as loaded into the Futurum software. Since the victims were first-branch members of The Family and born in America, we identified the victims and their common ancestors, then reverse engineered this huge family tree."

I paused. He said, "That's right so far."

"For the suspects, Futurum was sent direct and indirect DNA evidence. Of the suspect evidence, all but two of the samples were linked to CEOs of these major American corporations."

"Again, correct."

"So, we have two suspect profiles that are still unknown. But we do know something very important about them, right?"

"What do you mean by that?"

"I mean, they aren't part of this bloodline." I pointed at the family tree on the screen. "They can't be, it's impossible. We have these two profiles, and they share no genetic characteristics with members of The Family."

"You got it," he said.

"So, it's unlikely the main culprit, this *El Cameleon*, is part of the Salazar Family Line, like Diaz thinks he is. He's outside the cult, not an internal member, and thereby a hired man. We just don't know by whom."

"Impossible to be part of The Family," Stanley corrected. "Not unlikely."

"Okay, so your hope is to add some Mexican national databases to your software, then run these two profiles through these new databases and hopefully get a hit."

"I will get a hit, Chase. Because that's what happened with Ross. That was why he was so confident he had the killer's profile in hand."

"Gotcha, that makes sense."

"Ross didn't share any of these results with Detective Diaz or members of Diaz's team. Not only because he was so security conscious, but also because he didn't trust Diaz. I'm guessing this police department we're

262

about to visit has none of the profiles or results that we currently have, even though they have the same evidence. Why I'm so excited is how fast we could see results."

I eyed him in the rearview. "Explain that."

"Ross never told me what databases he was given access to. Mexico doesn't have the type of exhaustive criminal DNA database like our American CODIS system, but our country has been working with them for years to develop something similar. All to help stop criminals involved with drug smuggling and human trafficking. So, Ross may have never run one of these profiles through their version of CODIS. If this detective gives me access to some type of database like that, we could identify the killer in minutes."

"Provided The Chameleon's a former criminal and been arrested before."

"Sure. I'm just trying to point out how quick this could potentially go."

"I get it, just don't get too excited."

"Such a downer, Chase," he said, eyeing me in the rearview mirror.

"Just realistic, Stanley. You could identify this killer, and Diaz could sweep in and arrest him. The killer may give up his employer, but what if he doesn't? What if he's as tight-lipped as that surviving cult member with Mick?" I suddenly thought about my buddy and what, if any, progress he'd made with the man he'd taken.

"Like I said, you're always thinking of the negatives, Chase."

I fired off a text to Mick, then turned sideways in the seat and laid on my back. I put the burner cell on my chest.

"You taking a nap?" Stanley asked.

"Maybe. Just resting for now."

"You're something else."

"I was taught to eat and sleep whenever you can. All I'm doing is waiting on a text from Mick or Diaz, or from Ramona or Slim after they land, so I might as well get some shut-eye in the meantime."

"Diaz knows your burner number?"

"Yup, Ramona gave it to him. Would like to know if Diaz answered Ramona's question about where the catering evidence originated."

"That's right, that's important."

Waiting on the cell to buzz, I closed my eyes. Eventually, my mind slowed down, just enough for me to drift off.

FORTY-THREE

I woke to a buzzing cell on my chest.

Before I even sat up and looked at it, Stanley said, "Who is it? Who's that?"

"Geez, you're impatient," I said, struggling to sit. When I was upright, I didn't look at the cell since the foreign landscape caught my attention. Clearly, we were in Mexicali. "Wait, we crossed the border already?"

"Geez, you're a snorer," he said. "Could barely hear myself think up here. And, yes, we crossed the border with no incident. It was just like the Tijuana border, a cattle call of cars crossing over without stopping."

Nodding, I looked at the cell.

"Well, who texted?" Stanley asked.

"Mick, he actually drove the man all the way back to California. He's currently questioning him at his storage unit, and so far, he's been unsuccessful."

"What about the others? Did any of them text back?"

"Not yet," I said.

"That's not good."

I called Ramona, but it went straight to voice mail. Looking at my watch, I knew she was due to land any minute. The drive to Mexicali was approximately five hours, which was the same for the flight to Arlington. I left a quick voice mail and told her to call back as soon as she landed.

"We're not going to the station," I said, "until I hear from Diaz or Ramona."

"I guess we're waiting then."

"Why?"

Stanley pointed ahead. "Because we're here. That's it there, I think."

"Really?" We were in a concrete jungle where three freeways intersected. There were two large overpasses, and in the distance, I could see a Home Depot and a Walmart. "Where is it exactly?"

Stanley motioned over one of the freeways, toward a large concrete, nondescript building. After circling back and forth over two freeways, we finally found some parking a few blocks from the police station. As soon as we parked, Ramona called back.

"Just touched down," she said. "We're currently taxiing to our gate."

"Did Diaz text back yet?"

"Not yet."

"To clarify, he never responded to your earlier text about the catering evidence, did he?"

"Nope."

"Well, we're outside the police station in Mexicali right now. And I'm not sure it's wise I amble in there until we hear from Diaz."

"Hmm," she said. "You know, he has a partner—or maybe a junior detective underneath him, not sure—that I worked with just as much as Diaz. He was in the room during our conversations; he speaks good English and is bright. He knows I'm supposed to be coming back with Stanley."

"What's his name?"

"Johnny Jimenez. The detective referred to him as JJ a few times."

"Have his contact info?"

"No, I don't."

"You trust him?"

She laughed. "No. But I have trust issues. To be fair, this JJ person has given me no reason not to trust him."

After briefly discussing her plans to follow Ernesto, I hung up.

"Well?" Stanley said moments later.

"She hasn't heard from Diaz yet, which is concerning since it's been about six hours since she first communicated with him."

"Okay, so what do we do?"

"I think you head in there alone and feel out the situation."

"Feel it out? What's that supposed to mean? And alone?"

"Go in there and ask for Diaz's associate, a detective named Johnny Jimenez. According to Ramona, he knows the plan and is expecting you. Immediately question him about Diaz and his unresponsiveness."

"Okay, but I don't feel comfortable walking in there without you, or with my laptop."

"Leave your computer with me, and I'll keep the thumb drive, too. If you feel good about the situation, and get an idea of what's happened with Diaz, come back here and we can discuss going in together."

He thought about that. "Okay, will do, sounds fairly safe." Before I knew it, Stanley was strolling toward the police station.

While waiting on his return, I left the FJ and grabbed a couple of tacos at a street cart I could see not too far away. When I got back to the vehicle, a text from Ramona came through. She told me that Diaz had just communicated with her; that he'd been out of cell range. She said Diaz would contact me very soon.

Sure enough, minutes later, after polishing off my tacos, Diaz texted:

Garrison Chase, sorry I'm not there, been chasing a lead and out of cell range. Please work with Detective JJ. He can give you and Stanley access. See you soon.

Just as I finished reading, I saw Stanley in my periphery. As he got closer to the FJ, he started waving me out. When I didn't leave the FJ, he swept into the back seat. "Can you not see me waving at you?"

"What's the story?" I asked. "I'd like to hear it first."

"Detective Jimenez is there, and he seems very nice. Apparently, Diaz has been a few hours south in San Felipe working some tip he received. And the road there and back to San Felipe is terrible for cell reception. Anyway, Jimenez got approval from Diaz for us to start accessing some databases. Let's go."

I pulled the bucket hat tight to my head, then left the FJ. Stanley led the way with his laptop tucked under his arm. Inside the station, there was no metal detector to go through, though we were given a decent pat down. Eventually, we were led to a windowless room at the back of the station. It wasn't an interrogation room. It was a computer server room.

Detective Jimenez was waiting for us there, typing away on a keyboard at a wooden desk in the corner of the room. He looked up and smiled. "Nice to meet you, Garrison Chase. You can call me JJ." He stood and extended his hand. "You can take off the hat and sunglasses. You're fine."

I did, then shook his hand. JJ was dark-skinned and young, maybe late twenties. Smooth, freshly shaven face and close-cut, jet-black hair. Though he looked slightly babyish, he did have a three-inch scar over his right eye that gave his overall appearance some mystery. Like maybe he wasn't so innocent looking.

He offered me coffee straight off, so that put him in my good books. Typically, I didn't like to drink coffee in hot climates. But because the room held a variety of computer servers, it was kept icy cold by a pumping air conditioner. I'd only been in the room under a minute and already felt the chill.

While I palmed the warm paper coffee cup, Stanley and JJ got to work. Stanley was busy hooking up a cable to his laptop. I think it was an ethernet connection, but I couldn't tell for sure since computer technology wasn't exactly my strong suit.

Before they got going, I interrupted them. "JJ, quick question: The catering evidence you sent Futurum, where did it originate?"

"Originate?"

"Yeah, was it found with the victims' bodies? Or was the glassware, napkins, et cetera, found somewhere else? Or perhaps sent to you?"

"Oh, I see what you mean. No, it wasn't sent to us, it was found on the bodies at the crime scene."

With that, he turned and went back to work with Stanley. Stanley gave me a quick nod, understanding what that meant, then turned his attention to the computer setup.

I grabbed a chair and watched them work. From what I could gather,

Stanley was downloading some databases onto his laptop and feeding them into the Futurum software. With every new database, Stanley would turn the laptop toward JJ, and JJ would enter the log-in information. Apparently, they'd worked out a system where both Stanley and JJ felt comfortable that no unnecessary software, password, or database problems would arise.

As they worked, I thought about what the detective had said. Finding the evidence on the victims seemed to absolve the CEOs of involvement. They wouldn't have hired a hit man to kill the members of The Family, then left evidence with the bodies that implicates them. Unless, of course, they hired a terribly incompetent sicario. However, *El Cameleon* was quite the cunning killer so far, and he wouldn't have made repeated mistakes like that.

Stanley suddenly exclaimed, "There it is!" He and JJ exchanged high fives.

I rushed over. "What'd you find?"

Stanley pointed at the screen. "Only one unknown profile left. The other unknown profile was a CEO of Mexican nationality." He beamed.

"So, wait," I said. "We have The Chameleon's DNA profile then?"

JJ and Stanley both nodded in unison.

My mind spun. "How many databases have you accessed so far?"

"Three so far," the detective replied.

"And obviously you've run the killer's profile through them and come up empty."

Stanley snorted. "Obviously, Chase. What do you think we've been doing?"

I ignored the barb since I was simply thinking out loud. I looked at the detective. "Do you have a criminal DNA database like CODIS?"

He nodded. "Yes, but not nearly as extensive as CODIS. It's been in development over the past decade, but really made some improvements in the past year."

"And you've run The Chameleon's profile through it?"

He hung his head. "No, was waiting on Detective Diaz to give access to that. He told me to have Stanley run all the databases that Ross had access to, and Ross didn't have access to that. We were planning to do that with Ross, but then he went on the run and was killed."

"What's Diaz's ETA?"

"Not sure," the detective responded.

Stanley asked before I could. "Shoot him a text and ask for access."

JJ shrugged, then complied.

It seemed like it took forever for Diaz to reply, which sent my mind down a conspiratorial path. Like maybe these detectives only wanted Stanley to get to the point where he currently was. That maybe they didn't want us accessing the criminal database and pinpointing the killer's identity.

Why is that? Because they want all the glory? Or do they want to protect the killer's identity?

When the beep came through on JJ's cell, the two men stopped what they were doing.

JJ turned and smiled. "Diaz granted access."

Guess I'm wrong.

There was some debate between Stanley and JJ about how to quickly get the process going, but they finally agreed after a few minutes. Then we waited on results, which took close to ten minutes.

"Here it is," Stanley said, looking back at me.

I walked over. Before I saw the screen, or before they said a word, I knew the results, just based on their slumping disposition.

"No match," JJ said, pounding his fist on the desk.

Surprisingly, Stanley stayed upbeat. "What other databases, Detective, can we look at? This is how it works, by the way. Just because we didn't get a hit, doesn't mean we're doomed. We at least know something, that the killer hasn't been arrested lately."

That seemed to refocus the detective.

While they went back to work, my cell buzzed. Nosy Stanley asked me right away who it was. Fortunately, the text was short, and I'd read it before responding.

I lied. "Ramona, just giving me an update."

When Stanley turned back to his screen, I read the text again. It was from Detective Diaz. It said: *Make an excuse and get out of there. Too many eyes and ears in that station.*

I sat there for some time, staring at the text, mulling it over in my mind. Suddenly I thought about Detective JJ, about his somewhat innocent look. Deciding to test him, I shot Diaz a text back, asking if the catering evidence was found on the victims' bodies.

He replied within a minute:

No, not found on the bodies. Sent to us by an unknown party.

FORTY-FOUR

"You DRIVE," I said, handing Stanley the keys to the FJ as we left the station.

"What's going on? Why'd you yank us out of there like that? A bit abrupt, wouldn't you say?"

I didn't respond. Instead, I was glancing over my shoulder, seeing if maybe JJ was coming after us, or sending some other cops to tail us.

"Chase!" Stanley snapped his fingers.

"We'll chat in the car." To give Stanley an idea of what was going on, I handed him my cell, opened to the text exchange with Diaz.

He gulped. "Oh, I see. You think that detective was misleading us?"

"Good possibility," I said. "We have conflicting answers on the catering evidence, don't we?"

By the time we reached the FJ, I felt confident nobody was following us. But I wanted to be cautious, so I said, "Drive around like we did when we first got here. Do a couple of circles. I'll see if I can detect anyone following."

Just then, a text from Diaz came through. He said he was en route to his house. He was going to shower and change and asked us to meet him there.

He followed up with an address, which I plugged into the Google Maps app.

While Stanley navigated a few confusing loops, then proceeded to the address, I kept my head turned and watched for anything unusual. But I didn't see anything suspicious during the ten-minute drive.

"It's up here on the left-hand side," Stanley said.

We were in a somewhat middle-class-looking neighborhood. The homes on the street were brightly colored. In front of each place, a large iron-barred gate stretched across the driveway. There were no picket fences on this street. Instead, every home had a cinder-block perimeter that enclosed the front yard. On the top blocks were jagged pieces of broken glass, sticking straight up from the base, discouraging anyone from climbing over.

Stanley pulled in front of a bright red-and-blue home. "Here we are," he said. "What exactly do we know about this guy, anyway?"

"Not much. Ramona says he's been a detective for close to twenty years." I laughed thinking about her description. "Apparently, he's suave but dated."

"What's that mean?"

"From what she texted, his hair is like Guy Fieri's, platinum blond with dark roots, and he dresses like a young Ricky Martin."

"Who's Ricky Martin?"

As I got out of the vehicle, I said, "Never mind. Ramona likens Diaz to an old Mexican pop star. He wears skinny jeans and silky button-ups that he keeps tucked into his pants."

After closing the door, I briefly inspected the iron gate. To its left was an intercom. Above the keypad was a black-and-white label that read, *G. Diaz*. I pushed the call button and waited.

Twenty seconds later, the gate disengaged and began rolling back, screeching on its rusty wheels. I waved Stanley inside the semi-circular driveway. Once he parked, we approached the front door together. Before we reached it, the door swung open.

A robed Gerardo Diaz looked left and right, then eyed me. "Anyone follow you?"

I shook my head.

"Come in, come in," he said, waving us in fast. "Sorry for the rush, this case is coming to a head and tensions are mounting. I don't want you standing outside for longer than need be. Eyes and ears are everywhere in this country." He flashed some pearly white teeth. "Sorry for the robe, just got out of the shower. San Felipe is one dusty town."

Diaz wore a long and baggy cream-colored bathrobe, which was tied tightly at the waist. His hair was indeed platinum blond with dark roots. Since it was still wet, it was plastered straight down. I wondered if he normally styled it like Guy Fieri did. Though his hair was identical to the famous chef, he looked nothing like him. Diaz was lean and above average height. The man reminded me more of a blond Enrique Iglesias than a young Ricky Martin.

After some brief introductions, Diaz said, "While I finish getting dressed, have a seat at the dining table. There's more room in there."

Diaz's house had an odd smell, like nail polish remover or something similar. The house was a basic structure. Nothing more than a collection of walls and chopped up rooms. No big open areas that flowed into each other like you'd see in contemporary American homes. The dining room was twice as big as the living room. In between the rooms, I glimpsed a small kitchen. Beyond the kitchen, I saw a short hallway with one room on either side. There was no décor, no pictures or artwork. Though it looked like there had been at one point since there were several nails still sticking out of the wall.

Once seated, Diaz asked, "Would you like something refreshing like an aqua fresca, or something with a caffeine kick, like a café con leche?"

I was going to say aqua fresca, but Stanley jumped in and asked for a café con leche. Since I didn't want the detective wasting time making two different drinks, I went with coffee, too.

"Let me change first," he said, "then I'll work on the coffee. Would love to know what you've found out."

Stanley couldn't help himself. "We isolated the killer's profile, detective. We're right where Ross left off."

Diaz beamed. "See, I knew it. I knew we'd get here again." He held up his pointer finger. "Be right back. I can't wait to hear all about it."

As he swept out of the room, I said after him, "And I'm interested to know why you suddenly wanted us out of the station. Seems like you received some new intel and can't trust your colleagues maybe?"

He shouted over his shoulder, "Yes, there's been some interesting developments since my trip to San Felipe, for sure."

While we waited on Diaz to change, Stanley booted up the laptop and asked for the thumb drive. He wanted to share all the evidence with Diaz, including the visuals.

Five minutes later, Diaz was back in the kitchen, but he didn't come into the dining room. "I'm so excited to hear what you found out," he said, "and what you know about this profile. Why don't you tell me everything while I brew some espresso and warm the milk."

"Sure," Stanley said.

Since the kitchen was right next to the dining room, we didn't have to shout. Stanley went into too much detail about what databases he and JJ had used. I made some rolling motions with my hand to speed him along.

"So," he said, "we have The Chameleon's DNA profile, and we ran it through your criminal database but found no hit."

Diaz popped his head out. Looking at Stanley, he said, "That would be too easy, right?"

Stanley snorted. "I know. It's never that easy."

Diaz went back to work in the kitchen. You could hear the espresso maker heating up and porcelain clinking as Diaz gathered the cups. Stanley continued, "All we really know for sure is that the killer isn't part of The Family."

"That can't be," Diaz flatly stated.

"What do you mean?" Stanley said.

"I mean," he responded, "everything I know so far points to this being an internal feud. I'm not sure of the American CEO involvement in all this, but it sure looks internal to me, like an extremely disgruntled family member."

"Right," I said, "but couldn't one branch of The Family have hired *El Cameleon* or a hitman to pretend to be The Chameleon?"

He popped his head out again. "Maybe. But it seems so personal, you know? And they're not the type of people that ever hire outsiders to get a job done. They're so private and family focused."

Before I could respond, he disappeared into the kitchen again. Stanley looked exasperated. As I sat there staring at him, looking at his narrow little head, I thought about what Diaz had said. From what I knew, his assessment seemed correct. This family probably wouldn't have hired an outsider. Still staring at Stanley, I had a sudden thought.

And I blurted it out. "Adoption! What about adoption?"

"What are you talking about?" Stanley said. "Has the heat gotten to you?"

It was probably a long shot, but the thought got me excited. "No offense, Stanley, but you sort of look adopted, I've always thought that. I mean, you're so different looking than your dad."

He blinked, pushed up his glasses, and said, "I'm not, you know, just for the record."

"I know that. It's just that the evidence points to someone outside the Salazar family. But Detective Diaz insists it's an insider, someone within their family. How could both be true at the same time? Think about it."

Stanley lit up. "Adoption! You're right, that could be. If the killer was adopted by The Family, he wouldn't share any of the genetic markers. Does The Family adopt, though? Doesn't seem like they would."

I asked Diaz. "What do you think?"

"I think we're making progress," he said from the kitchen. "You two are doing well, very well indeed. But I must agree with Stanley, this cult is deeply family-based. Not sure adoption is something they'd ever consider. Drinks are almost ready."

Immediately I made a call.

"Who are you calling?" Stanley asked.

"Mick, see if he's still working on that cult member."

He picked up straight away. I asked, "You still at the storage unit?"

"Yup, just finishing up. Without violating the Geneva Convention, I won't get this guy to talk."

"So nothing useful?"

"Nope."

"You're going to let him go?"

"Yeah, no choice."

"Before you do, make a deal with him. Tell him if he answers one innocuous question, you'll let him go."

"Okay, what question?"

"Whether *La Familia* adopts or has ever adopted a kid? It's a long story why, don't ask."

"Fine. Will call you back soon."

When I hung up, I saw that Diaz had taken a seat across from me at the table. He was wearing one of those tight silk button-ups that Ramona had mentioned. He was sipping a café while Stanley was asking him if he could get access to any state adoption databases. Stanley had turned the laptop toward him and was showing him the huge genealogy tree.

There was a cup of espresso with milk on a saucer in front of me. As I went in for a sip, Stanley said, "Careful, it's hot, just burned my tongue. What did Mick say?"

I backed off and put the saucer down, then addressed Diaz. "We have a member of The Family in our care and a colleague of mine has been trying to get intel about the cult from him. He's asking the man about adoption right now, gonna call back any second, in fact."

Diaz blew milk foam across the table.

"You okay?" I asked.

"Yeah," he said, wiping his mouth. "Like Stanley said, it's a little hot. Gonna get some more milk to cool it down."

As he started to leave, Mick called back. I turned away and answered it. "Well, anything?"

"Sure, he gave up that info no problem. Like you said, it probably seemed innocuous to him. He said that adoption was rare but has happened. And only by the third-branch members. A third-branch family would only adopt if they didn't have many male descendants, just so that particular family had more workers, you know."

I said thanks to Mick and hung up, then beamed at Stanley. "We might be onto something here."

Stanley held up his small espresso cup and thrust it toward me. "Cheers."

I clinked his glass. As Stanley went in for a sip, I couldn't help but notice Diaz standing still in the doorframe to the kitchen, staring at us. For a second, he had a weird look on his face, then he immediately smiled when he saw me looking at him.

He took three strides toward the table, holding a milk pot in his right hand, but I wasn't focused on the pot. I was focused on his legs, on those skinny jeans of his and how they fit so tightly. They showcased his legs. His bowlegs.

El Cameleon!

Instantly, I dropped my cup. Brown liquid splashed everywhere, all over my shirt and chest. My eyes flicked to Stanley. He was halfway through a sip. I lunged toward him and slapped that cup from his mouth as hard as I could.

"What the hell!" he screeched.

The cup flew across the room and smashed against the kitchen door-frame. White porcelain bits shattered and dispersed across the room while foamy dark liquid dripped down the wall.

Looking left, the killer was moving forward, fast. He dropped the pot of steaming milk, and it crashed against the table's edge, sending foamy white liquid shooting across the table and into my lap.

Meanwhile, his left arm was flying forward. In his hand, he grasped a fat syringe with a long tip. Like a tomahawk, he chopped it straight down at my exposed left shoulder.

I tried to intercept, but he was too fast, so the needle sunk deep into my skin. My right fist did manage to smash his hand away, just in time, too, since The Chameleon only manage to plunge it halfway down. The syringe snapped at its base, leaving the needle inside my arm, along with an intense pain.

El Cameleon had stumbled back, looking at his empty hand, wondering what his next move was.

Ignoring the pain, my momentum had me moving forward, so I crawled on top of the dining table and used my palms to pull my body across the wooden surface. But I felt woozy and collapsed onto my chest; my head dangled over the table's far edge. I started losing control of my bodily functions, including keeping my eyes open.

Pentobarbital? Damn.

To my right, I heard a thump. But my head felt so heavy I couldn't lift it and look for the source of the noise. I could see, in between long blinks, Stanley's head in my periphery, which rested against the ground.

Is he dead?

Right below me I saw the syringe body, with the plunger still halfway down. With my waning strength, I managed to pull my shoulders over the table's edge. At that point, momentum carried my body crashing to the ground. In the process I smothered the syringe.

I flopped onto my back as I grasped the syringe.

All I heard was laughing in the background.

Before I shut my eyes, I jammed the plunger end onto the floor. The last thing I saw was a thin squirt of clear liquid loop into the air and land on my chest.

With my eyes closed and my breathing labored, I felt a body hovering over me.

The last thing I heard was, "It doesn't matter. It doesn't even matter."

FORTY-FIVE

I CAME to and immediately felt incredible pressure on my lower stomach. For a second, I wondered if my insides had ruptured.

Am I about to die?

Soon I realized I was strapped tight at my waist and my upper body was twisted and bent to the left. When my eyes finally focused, I saw a seat in my field of vision.

I stayed still to get my bearings. Eventually, I understood my hands were tied behind my back, and the pressure on my lower stomach was a tightly cinched lap belt. Feeling motion, I knew I was currently speeding down a freeway in some car. I also heard two things: the blasting of an air conditioner; and someone muttering in the front seat.

When I felt lucid enough, I sat up. Immediately I saw the back of the driver's head, which showcased the platinum tips and dark roots of *El Cameleon*. He was eyeing me in the rearview mirror, shaking his head.

We held eye contact for five long seconds. He was fuming at the sight of me.

I swallowed and said, "Guess I ruined your plans, huh? Emptying that syringe and knocking the cup out of Stanley's hand. Or did he sip enough of your poison and now he's dead?"

The man scoffed. "You've meddled and ruined a lot, no doubt, but nothing you did in Diaz's house thwarted my plans. You think I would kill two Americans and leave the bodies to be found? No way, not making that mistake again. Where you two are going, nobody will ever find your bodies."

"Stanley's still alive then? Where is he?"

He didn't answer. Instead, he started listing off names: "Rogan Ross, Gerardo Diaz, Raoul the gardener, and Silvio Garcia. You forced my hand." He narrowed his eyes further. "Damn you, Garrison Chase. That's unnecessary death."

I held his stare. "Says the serial killer."

He stabbed his finger at the rearview mirror. "And Stanley's employee in California, her death will be on you as well. And maybe this redheaded Santa Claus friend of yours, and the FBI agent, too. Oh, and this colleague of yours, Mick is his name, right?"

"Where's the kid? Trunk?"

The man didn't answer. Instead, he said, "How'd you know, anyway? What tipped you off? I know you and Stanley were on the right path with the adoption angle, but what did I miss? I thought I had Diaz down perfectly. The clothes, the hair, even his theories."

I liked that he wanted info from me. "Tell me who you are first."

He studied me in the mirror for a stretch, then said, "My given name doesn't matter. I go by Leon, have for a while. That's all you need to know."

"Fitting," I replied, "short for chameleon, I assume."

He repeated himself. "What tipped you off?"

I debated not answering. But since I wanted to knock this guy down a peg, I said, "Seemed a little off that there were no pictures on the wall, but there were still nails protruding out. The smell was weird, too. Thought it was nail polish at first, but now I know it was from you dyeing your hair. Those two things didn't tip me off per se, but you could've done better. You could've spent more time on the minute details. What tipped me off was something you can't control."

When I didn't elaborate, he said, "Which was?"

I smiled. "Your bowlegs. Those tight jeans made it real clear. Looks like you're straddling a hula-hoop when your legs are together."

Leon ignored the jab. "And where'd you learn I was bowlegged?"

"From my red-headed colleague you set up and tried to kill. He'd spoken with that addict across the street from Ross's hideout. All that guy could remember were your bowlegs."

"I'll be damned," Leon said, nodding, "it's the little things that get you. Don't they?" He mulled that over for a bit, then looked away.

"Where you taking us? Where are we going?"

No response.

I thought about the situation. "Let me guess, Stanley's in the trunk. This is a small car, and we couldn't both fit in there. Even if we could, you'd be hard-pressed to haul my big body into a trunk, right? Probably hard enough to get me into the back seat on your own. No offense, but you're a little guy. Smart, I'm assuming, but not that strong. What did you do with the real Diaz?"

He sighed. "Sure are talkative for a man who's about to meet his demise."

"Why didn't you tape my mouth shut then?"

"Believe me, I debated it. Looks a little suspect if someone glanced in and saw a big piece of tape over your mouth, no? I'd rather hear you jabber than get pulled over. Like you said, I'm smart, I guess."

Just then, I noticed we passed a sign that said San Felipe.

"San Felipe, huh? Were you lying about being down here earlier?"

"Here's some parting wisdom for you, Chase. When you can, stick to the truth as much as possible in any story. Only lie when you absolutely have to. Less problems and inconsistencies that way."

"You did come to San Felipe then. How'd you get the jump on Diaz?"

"I lured him down here with the promise of intel that would help him crack the case. He was desperate to solve this, and I used that to my advantage."

"The development in San Felipe that you mentioned was dumping Gerardo Diaz's body here, I imagine. That's why Diaz was unreachable for six or seven hours. That's quite the escalation for you."

"Escalation?"

"Killing a cop."

He eyed me in the rearview. "You're right, but Diaz had made too much progress. He was on the right track and had to be stopped. I had no choice."

"So, his partner, Detective JJ, was telling the truth about the catering evidence then?"

Leon nodded.

I kept at it. "And you lied about that in your text to me to keep the CEO involvement in play?"

"No. To get you suspicious about JJ. I knew you'd ask the catering question to JJ, and that he'd tell the truth. And I wanted you not to trust him so you'd leave."

"Tell me about the CEOs and their involvement. I'm confused."

He sighed. "Listen, no more questions. I have plans for you when we get to our destination. I need you awake and to do some work, so you'll figure out soon what's happening. You're a smart man, too, no?" He broke into a maniacal laugh.

To be honest, it was slightly unsettling.

Leon continued. "You'll definitely understand soon enough." He turned the rearview mirror away and gave a final cackle.

I thought about him saying he stuck to the truth as much as possible, figured I'd push him on that. Why not since he just told me he needed me alive to do work, which I assumed was something akin to digging my own grave.

"In the kitchen," I said, "you mentioned the killer was likely a disgruntled family member. Is that the case? Are you an adopted Salazar and know you're at the bottom of the family food chain? A mere step above the women. Is that it? Or are you just greedy, and you're a hired hand by some American and Mexican CEOs?"

Instead of responding, he cranked on the stereo. Ranchera music blasted in my ears, stifling any conversation. Knowing he wasn't going to talk, I settled back and focused on the surroundings. Minutes later, we passed the town of San Felipe and drove straight south for another forty-five minutes, eventually pulling off Highway 5 and taking a compacted sandy road toward the Gulf of California, aka the Sea of Cortez. The more we drove, the more worried I got since I saw zero signs of civilization. All I saw was miles of desert in every direction. On the horizon were low-lying mountains. There was no vegetation anywhere. Only thing covering the sandy soil were tangled, dried bushes of tumbleweed. Just looking at the landscape made me thirsty.

The sandy road eventually turned into a small, pebbled driveway, which ran about a half mile to the beach. As we approached the sea, I couldn't help but notice the beauty of the white sand beach juxtaposed with the greenish-blue hue of the water. Seemed ironic that I was coming to such a beautiful place to face death.

Leon finally turned off the radio as we approached a tiny shack on our left. I studied the property; it looked like a small fishing camp. Aside from the shack, there was only one other outbuilding, which was down by the water. It wasn't a large structure, more of a shed, really. No doubt whoever owned the property kept fishing rods and reels in there, maybe some boat supplies, too.

Out front of the shed, in the receding water, was a center-console fishing boat. It was stuck in the murky, wet bottom of the gulf. Use of the boat was entirely dependent on an incoming tide. At the front of the boat was a thick, long rope that stretched about fifty yards and wrapped around the only palm tree on the beach, which was just to the right of the shed.

Leon parked the car next to the shack. Almost as soon as the engine shut off I felt the stifling heat creep into the vehicle. Leon left, entered the shack, then returned thirty seconds later with a silenced pistol.

Not good.

I studied his movements. He popped the trunk, then opened the far passenger rear door and tentatively leaned inside. Leon wasn't a stupid man. A stupid man would've opened my door and reached across my body to unlatch the seat belt, which would've resulted in me headbutting the man as hard as I could.

Leon, however, kept the pistol—which I could now see was an HK 45 with suppressor—trained at my chest with his left hand while his right quickly pushed the seatbelt release button. He motioned me out his side.

"Nice and easy," he said.

I had to shimmy left across the seat. By the time I was out of the vehicle, I was already dripping sweat.

Keeping his distance, and the pistol trained on me, he commanded, "Turn."

I did.

Then he cautiously approached from behind. My hands were tied with plastic zip ties. It only took him a fraction of a second to slice my hands free. By the time I turned to face him, he'd backed up a safe distance and was tucking his knife away.

The Heckler & Koch was still pointed at my forehead.

"Now Stanley." He jutted his chin toward the open trunk. "Take him to the beach."

Stanley was curled up in the trunk, still passed out. His hands were also zip-tied behind his back. He was a sweaty, sopping mess. Thankfully, as I approached him, I saw his chest rising slightly.

I scooped the kid up, then headed toward the beach. Leon kept a safe distance behind me. His right hand held the HK 45, and his left held Stanley's laptop. He only spoke when necessary. I could tell he was deep in thought and calculating every move. Which made me think the best strategy was getting him out of his head so he couldn't be so thoughtful and calculated.

So, I tried to engage in conversation by asking what we were doing. What the plans were, how he thought he'd get away with everything, things like that. He didn't bite, ignoring every question I threw his way.

All he said, by the time we were at the shoreline, was, "Over there by the rope."

I walked to his pointed location.

"Set him down here."

I did, placing Stanley on the wet sand directly underneath the semi-taut rope.

"Take everything out of his pockets," Leon commanded. "Start with his front pockets."

I took my time doing that, which was a good thing because I felt the thumb drive in his front left pocket, so I didn't immediately pull it out. Instead, I left it in there, wondering how it got from the laptop to his pocket.

Leon asked, "What do you have? Show me."

I held up Stanley's wallet and the FJ keys.

"Toss them here, then turn his pockets inside out so I can see they're empty. Check his back pockets, too."

When I pulled out his front pockets, I clasped the thumb drive between my thumb and palm. Then, as I reached around to check Stanley's back pockets, I pulled his pants out a little and dropped the thumb drive into the top of his underwear. Leon was behind me and couldn't see my movements.

"Anything in his back pockets?"

"Just this." I tossed him the cowboy's cell. He asked me to move aside while he walked around and quickly patted Stanley's back pockets to make sure I'd gotten everything.

"Now you." Leon wiggled his fingers.

I handed him my wallet and burner cell.

He made me pull out my pockets and spin around. Then he pointed the pistol at the shed. "Move."

When I was thirty feet from the shed, the smell hit me. I paused in front of the door.

He commanded me to open it. When I did, I instinctively put my forearm across my nose. There was a dead body in the middle of the shed. It was a man. I knew it was Gerardo Diaz because of the tight jeans and frosted tips.

"Take him to the boat," Leon said. "Put him at the stern."

I scooped up Diaz after Leon jabbed the pistol at me. While I brought the body to the boat, Leon was ten feet behind me, carrying a large anchor he'd taken from the shed.

By the time I'd made it back to Stanley's position, the kid was sitting up, holding his head and moaning. Before I could ask if he was okay, Leon interrupted me.

He said, "Take this." He pulled out a long zip tie from his back pocket and tossed it toward me. "Loop it through the other zip ties on Stanley's wrists and then around the rope. But not tight, leave some slack around the rope."

I hesitated.

Stanley looked up, confused, pushing up his glasses. "Where are we? What happened, Chase? Whose body were you carrying?"

"Chase," Leon said. "Either you comply, or Stanley dies right now, doesn't matter to me. You'll simply have to carry another body to the boat."

Since I figured he'd pull the trigger, I did as instructed.

"Good," he said, backing up. He pulled out another zip tie and thread it into a loop. "Your turn. Turn around and clasp your hands behind your back."

I did. As I got into position, I thought about making it hard for him to tie me up. But that thought died pretty quickly. I had a good idea what Leon had planned, which was to get us in the boat, shoot us, then dump our bodies in the Sea of Cortez. If I made a ruckus now, he'd simply shoot me, then probably wait for the tide to rise to help float my body, which would make it easier for him to get me into the boat.

"No funny business," he said, jabbing the suppressor into my back. With his free hand, he quickly zipped the tie tight. Then he followed it up with another tie and thread a third between the two and looped it around the rope.

"I'm so confused," Stanley said, still rubbing his head. "Aren't you a detective?" He blinked a few times. "Wait, I get it. I think. You're a corrupt cop and a serial killer?"

"Just serial killer," I said. "The body I was carrying, Stanley, was Detective Diaz. And Diaz was not a corrupt cop."

Leon started walking to the boat. He had our possessions, including the laptop, in his hands. Over his shoulder, he said, "You guys talk it out. You have some time before . . ." He cackled the rest of the way to the boat.

While updating Stanley, I watched Leon position the anchor near the transom, then remove a cover from the outboard motor, bail some standing water, and lastly, fill up the tank with a medium-sized gas can. Once I had Stanley up to speed, I said softly, "I dropped the thumb drive into your underwear when he asked me to check your pockets."

He whispered back, "That's what's down there. I was wondering."

"Tell me about the thumb drive. Last I saw it was in the laptop and you were crashing to the floor."

"I don't think this guy, what's he call himself, by the way?"

"Leon."

"I don't think Leon spotted the drive since it was on the other side of the laptop when we were sitting at the table. I was feeling woozy before you slapped the cup out of my hand, so I knew something was up. Leon was hyper focused on you as he rushed to the table, so before passing out, I manage to pull out the drive and pocket it."

I couldn't help but smile. "You really are better at this than you look."

He didn't smile back. "Not sure if that's a compliment or not, but thanks anyway."

I motioned to Leon. "He might think the data he saw is still on the computer, but it's not, right?"

"No. Data is only on the thumb drive."

"We can't get on that boat. We can't. Understood?"

He swallowed. "I think so."

"The moment we get onto that boat is the moment we're shot, then we'll be dumped into the sea with Diaz. Dragged down by that big-ass anchor, never to be found. Got it?"

His bug eyes went wide, then he slowly nodded.

There was enough slack in the long rope that we were able to sit on our butts in the sand.

Stanley said, "He's gonna order us onto the boat by gunpoint. Any moment now. We resist, he shoots us. What's our plan?"

"Not sure quite yet, but we have time to think. He's not going to order us onto the boat soon."

"Really?"

"Really. Tide has to come up enough to float the boat and take our weight. An hour or so, I think." As I contemplated that length of time, I looked back to the shore. "Let's shimmy our way to the palm tree. Palm trees have some ridges and grooves on their exterior that could maybe saw away at these plastic ties."

"Is he going to let us move, though?"

"Can't hurt to try." I stood and shouted at Leon. "There's a little patch of shade in front of the tree. We're going to move there."

He didn't say anything for a second, then shrugged.

When we made it to the tree, I tried to contain my excitement when I saw a ridge on the tree bark a couple of feet off the ground. I instructed Stanley to sit in front of me to block the view, then I eased to a cross-legged position with my back against the tree. Though Stanley blocked a good portion of my body, I still moved slowly and deliberately so I didn't draw any attention. Soon, I got into a decent rhythm sawing away at the plastic tie.

Stanley asked, "It working?"

"Too early to tell. My skin is taking most of the rubbing, and it stings like hell. I think I'm bleeding, too."

"Oh, geez, look what he's doing now," Stanley said.

I focused on Leon. He was standing behind the boat's console. The laptop was flipped open to the left of the steering wheel. We were too far away to hear what he was saying, but he was clearly frustrated. Suddenly he slammed the computer closed, grabbed his pistol, and hopped out of the boat.

"Damn, he's coming." Stanley said. "He knows there's no data on it."

For ten long seconds, I sawed as slow but as hard as I could. As Leon neared, I stopped the sawing motion and tried to break my wrists and hands apart. Straining with all my power, the tie just didn't break.

Leon marched up to Stanley, holding the laptop in the air and announced, "Password. I need your password."

Stanley didn't respond right away, which prompted Leon to point the Heckler & Koch at his face.

"Deoxyribonucleic acid," Stanley said. "All one word."

Leon seemed satisfied. As he turned back to the boat, he suddenly stopped and stared at me. "You're in the shade. Why are you so red-faced?"

I swallowed. All I could think to say was, "Not used to this heat, I guess."

He was about to turn again, but his eyes flashed down and to my left. Suddenly the gun was in my face. "Up now! Away from that tree. Move!"

Dejected, I slowly stood. As I did, I glanced to the spot where Leon had been looking. There was a small, sticky pool of vibrant red blood in the sand.

FORTY-SIX

ONCE I WAS AWAY from the tree, Leon commanded, "Down on your knees."

Sensing death, I took a deep breath, then eased onto the sand. Stanley was to my right, a few feet down the rope. We made eye contact as Leon moved in behind us.

"You too, Stanley," he said.

I gave the kid a quick nod, then looked away in case he took the first bullet. Didn't want that to be the last thing I saw. While looking straight ahead, I formulated a plan. If Leon intended to shoot me at close range, or place the suppressor against my body or head, I was prepared to move and make it hard for him.

Seconds ticked by as Stanley and I held our breath.

I was listening intently, hoping to sense if he was moving in close or not. There were sounds behind me, but I couldn't quite make out what he was doing.

I glanced over my shoulder, then returned to looking straight ahead.

He's moving forward. What's he doing?

Closing my eyes, I felt him nearby. I was ready to throw my head back and hope for a connection, but then I heard a familiar sound, and it wasn't the pistol's slide engaging.

It was the zipping sound of a plastic tie. When I opened my eyes, I saw Leon cinching another zip tie around Stanley's wrist as a precaution, he did the same to me, then he ordered us to stand. Breathing a sigh of relief, we shimmied down the rope until we reached our original spots.

"This is where you stay," Leon said as he headed back to the boat.

When he was out of earshot, Stanley said, "I thought that was it, Chase. I thought we were goners. What now?"

"Not sure," I said, looking around. For a few minutes, I stared up and down the long expansive stretch of beach. To the south, quite a distance away, I saw the tiny outline of another boat moored in the sand. I figured there were several fishing shacks around this area. The problem was the distance between them. I also realized that Leon carried a suppressed pistol because a gunshot could be heard for miles. There was absolutely nothing around to muffle any sound. Leon had planned well.

Stanley sighed and snapped me out of it. "He's realized there's nothing on my computer."

I looked toward the boat and saw Leon marching in our direction. "Appears so."

"Nothing," Leon said, ten feet away. "There's nothing on that laptop of yours."

I didn't respond. Stanley shrugged.

"You two oughta consider being more cooperative," he said.

Stanley beat me to the response. "Why? Why would we? I mean we're dead men walking."

"Dead men sitting," I corrected.

"True," Leon replied, "but it's not about you two at this point. Is it?"

"Then who's it about?" I asked.

"Colleagues, friends, that's who." Leon looked at Stanley. "And your employee or employees at your company."

Stanley looked incredulous. "You're going after them? They don't know anything."

Leon jabbed the pistol at him. "Convince me that's the case then.

292

Convince me you two are the only ones who know my identity. Convince me that the data I saw at Diaz's house for a brief minute doesn't lead to me. Show that to me again."

I scoffed. "So that's how we spend our final hour? Convincing a madman who will just go out and kill these people we care about anyway? Thank you, no."

"I get it. I see why you wouldn't trust me. Contrary to what you think, I'm not some crazed madman. I'm not a serial killer like BTK or the Zodiac. Those men enjoyed killing and taunting the police and bragging about their exploits and sending notes to the press. That's not me. Everything I've done has a specific purpose. Hell, I've barely shed blood. Right?"

Neither Stanley nor I responded.

He continued. "The truth is, gentlemen, I don't want to risk exposure and travel to DC and Phoenix and Central California to kill people and tie up loose ends. I really don't. I—"

Stanley interrupted. "You've killed thirteen family members, not to mention Detective Diaz and my colleague Rogan Ross, and—"

"Collateral kills," he said. "They weren't ever part of my original plan. I prefer not to kill now, especially since my plan has been a success. I appreciate that you may not believe me, but honestly, what do you two have to lose at this point? Why not take a chance and convince me? Which just may save a friend's life."

"Even if we did tell you something," I said. "You'd simply take our word for it? Really?"

"Fair enough," he replied. "I can be honest here. If you make a good case that others aren't onto me, I will definitely follow up after your deaths and see if I could confirm any intel you provide. Seriously, think about it, why travel around the country and risk exposure like that? Why risk killing an FBI agent and an innocent girl in California if I don't have to."

Sensing I had some bargaining power, I said, "Convince *us* then."

Leon eyed me. "What do you mean?"

"You want us to convince you our colleagues know nothing. Fine, but first convince us what you're saying is true, that you wouldn't harm them if they truly know nothing. That you're not an unstable serial killer. Otherwise, why should we tell you a single thing?"

"And how do I do that?"

"You said your plan was a success. Start there. What does that mean?"

Leon didn't say anything.

I used his line: "What do you have to lose at this point, Leon? Seriously, why not?"

"Well done, Garrison Chase," he said, smiling, "well played."

He backed up a bit, rested the HK 45 on the rope, then said, "I was adopted at a young age and don't remember much about my birth mother and father. I remember abuse at the hands of my dad—that I remember—but not much else. Then I recall a year or so of abuse at a foster home until being placed into a large family. The hands-on abuse stopped. For a while, most of my childhood, in fact, I believed I was in a better place.

"As I grew older, I realized the truth, though: I was adopted into a toxic family. The worst part was probably the lack of hope. Very little hope for the third-branch male members, and zero hope for the women. The women were treated like they were less than human. They existed for sexual pleasure and to give birth to male sons. I was sickened by how my family viewed women.

"So, I vowed to put a stop to it, to end the vicious cycle. My plan was to pick off the male members in the first branch, who were the heirs to this continuing empire of degradation. I wanted those men to die and the family to implode. But I couldn't just start killing the most prominent members first since that would cause immediate scrutiny, so I started lower down the chain and worked my way up."

When he paused, I asked, "Can you explain why you planted evidence framing the CEOs?"

He nodded. "The Family knew right away their men were being targeted, but the authorities didn't know what was going on and who was connected to who. Which was exactly what I wanted in the beginning. I needed to buy time so I could work my way through the kill list. For years, I'd been working these catering jobs with The Family, and I realized these

America CEOs were just as bad as the men in my family. So, they were the perfect scapegoats at the beginning."

"Ultimately, though," I said, "you took credit for the serial killings. Right? I mean, you left the calling card at the mansion with your logo on it."

"Exactly," Leon said. "The final three brothers who died in the fire ended the first branch. Before that, The Family already suspected it was an insider, and I wanted to make that known without question. In order to breed distrust and war within the family. It was never about the Americans. I just used them as a tool to cause confusion and keep the heat off me, so the cops made no progress. In the end, the scrutiny brought to the Americans by me framing them, and by Ross's podcasts, brought their horrible actions to light. I trust they're going to pay some sort of price for throwing those degrading parties. Which seems just in my opinion."

I shook my head. "You're making your work out to be some sort of honor-type killings. Yet you took out innocent people like Diaz and Ross."

Leon nodded. "You're right, but I had to. Diaz was close to the truth and a real bulldog. And rumor was that Ross had my DNA, which was tied to the killings."

"Why frame me then?" I said. "More confusion? You see your opportunity with me leaving the complex after you murdered Ross. Did you use that to your advantage?"

"Confusion, multiple suspects, rabbit trails, it all helped point away from me until I neared completion of my kill list. It all served that purpose."

"Posing the bodies that way, was that for confusion, too?"

He didn't answer that question, so I tried another one. "What about Silvio?"

"Silvio was a good man, one of the only males who had ever successfully left the cult. He was disillusioned by *La Familia* as well, especially with their treatment of women. I respected him. But his sudden involvement also worked out well for me. Really well, in fact."

Stanley finally spoke. "How so?"

Leon grinned ear to ear. "I floated the rumor that Silvio was *El Cameleon*. That he'd hired some Americans to help, and that proof of their involvement with the mansion fire could be found in the rental car. With the first-branch males wiped out in the fire, The Family believed Silvio and the third-branch members were rising up. Next on the list for them would be second-branch males." Leon flashed the grin again. "That was who came after you at the rest area."

And we wiped out a ton of them. I asked, "How many second-branch males are left?"

"Plenty," he responded. "More than enough to take on the third-branch males. My hope is that they wipe out each other. Even if they don't, there will be zero trust and respect between them. Just hatred and animosity, which effectively ends The Family's rein and breaks the cycle. And that's the point: to stop this vicious cycle."

There was a brief moment of silence as Stanley and I processed everything.

Leon interrupted the quiet. "I just want this family wiped off the face of the earth. I don't have ill will toward your colleagues. I'm telling the truth. At this point, almost everything is wrapped up nicely. The Family is nearing its end. And *El Cameleon*—poor, poor, Silvio—who started all this, is dead. I just need to make sure your colleagues don't have my DNA. Because that profile wouldn't match with Silvio, would it?" He broke into another round of maniacal laughing.

I interrupted it. "Sounds like a tight story, Leon, but I don't fully buy it."

"How come?"

"CEO involvement, that's why. It's more than you just framing them and using them as scapegoats. Stanley's father is involved and has been working with the top American CEO in Palmera. Plus, he's hired men to monitor and kidnap his own son, not to mention bribing an agent in the Phoenix field office. Or was that you? Your story doesn't account for any of this."

He shrugged. "Honestly, I can't explain it. I'm not sure what's exactly going on there. I framed them and used them at first, yes, but they're not involved with any deaths. All I can tell you is I have no relationship with any CEO, or an American law enforcement agent, or the Attorney General's office. I assure you."

I pushed him. "I don't believe you."

There was silence. We'd reached an impasse.

Quietly, though, I heard, "Well, I do. I believe him."

Glancing at Stanley, who was wringing his hands, I asked, "You do?"

He winced. "I wasn't exactly forthright with you about my father, Chase. I'm sorry."

"Forthright?" I sighed. "You mean you lied, Stanley?"

He stared at me without blinking.

"Say it, Stanley," I seethed. "Say you lied."

He reluctantly nodded. "Okay, I lied, Chase. I definitely lied."

FORTY-SEVEN

I took a second so I didn't explode on Stanley.

"Fathers," Leon said, chuckling. "Am I right?"

I ignored him and glared at Stanley, then commanded, "Explain."

He took a long breath and said, "In the car with my dad, he let on more than I told you. He explained a lot. And I, uh, well I still have the recording on the cowboy's phone. He tried to, but he didn't delete it."

I seethed. "What's he's involved with?"

"Tax evasion." Stanley swallowed. "We're talking massive evasion, Chase. I mean, billions of dollars owed to the IRS by these major American corporations in Palmera. The companies were working hand in hand with Mexican authorities to hide income and avoid foreign taxes. An American watchdog group had found out about it. They'd researched it, and during the investigation also discovered the horrible abuse of the local women by these CEOs. To make a long story short, an indictment was filed, which was sealed. This was all going down before the election."

"Let me guess," I said. "These corporations tell the aspiring president they'll put their support and finances behind her campaign, just as long as she supports their idea for attorney general if she gets elected. Of course, the CEOs had already spoken with your father and said that if they helped get him appointed, he'd have to make the indictment go away."

"Pretty much," he said. "Dad didn't want me digging up anything about these CEOs. That's why he went to the lengths he did."

"Not to protect you from the killer, Stanley, not at all. He only wanted to stop further stories and scrutiny about these men in Palmera in case the tax evasion and abuse issues came up with the media, and his involvement with burying the indictment."

Stanley didn't say anything.

Leon did. "Fathers are the worst. Was he at least there for you, Stanley?"

The kid screwed his face up.

I said, "What kind of question is that?"

Leon paused, then spoke. "My birth father beat the tar out of me, and my adoptive father was really no better since he was rarely present. There were thirteen kids in our family. When I was young, I thought he cared for me, at least somewhat. I had these terrible nightmares every so often—from the beatings, you know—and my adoptive father would come into my room and comfort me. He'd stroke my hair, shush me and tell me, 'night night.' Over and over until I calmed down and feel asleep."

Stanley and I exchanged glances.

Leon continued. "That was it, that was the only time he spent with me. Ever. Just a few minutes, a few times a month. I craved his attention so bad I started faking nightmares to have him visit. Eventually, he moved rooms in our house, to the one farthest from mine. And he stopped visiting. Never came into my room again. That was when I realized he wasn't concerned about me, not once. He used to visit my room to get me to calm down, just so the bastard could get a good night's rest."

Leon shook his head. "The men in my family, unbelievable. For the rest of my childhood, I can remember clasping my hands under my cheek and rocking myself to sleep, saying, 'night night' over and over and over, pretending it was my father saying those words. Pretending he cared. Posing the bodies like that, no, Chase, that wasn't confusion. That was deeply personal."

Silence ensued. There were no further words, and no sentiments expressed by Stanley or me, just the sound of tiny waves lapping against the boat's hull.

Leon spoke first. "Enough reminiscing, no? Tide's coming in. Now's the time, gentlemen, to convince me. Your turn."

Of course, Stanley and I hadn't discussed a game plan about what to do next. We exchanged looks but didn't say anything.

"Oh, really," Leon said, "that's how you're going to play this?"

We remained silent.

"If that's the case, then, on your feet, gentlemen." We didn't move. Leon lifted the HK and pointed it at Stanley. "You know how this goes."

Once we were on our feet, he said, "Stay right there." He ducked under the line, then approached Stanley cautiously. I watched him cut the zip tie that was looped around the rope, but not the two around his wrists. He did the same with me, never getting too close, and keeping the pistol level the whole time.

He said, "To the boat then."

With no point in running off, Stanley went first, then me, then Leon. We slowly waded through the now knee-deep water. Stanley kept glancing back, willing me to say something. But I was thinking about a specific plan and whether it was smart or suicidal. The boat was both our death sentence and our only chance. It was a small, confined spot, and I gambled that Leon wouldn't shoot us right after boarding. I convinced myself that he'd put us in place first, probably cross-legged or kneeling at the stern, before shooting us in the back of the head, then connecting us to the anchor and dragging our dead bodies into the watery depths.

That was what I'd do, anyway. It was the least amount of work.

When Stanley looked back again, I mouthed, "Follow my lead."

At the bow, Leon commanded Stanley to board. The kid couldn't help himself. He looked back at me and said, "We're not supposed to get on this boat, Chase. That's what you said."

"Just do it, Stanley," I replied.

But he didn't. Instead, Stanley started blabbing to Leon. "My employees know nothing. I promise. The evidence I showed you only exists in a secure cloud account, nowhere else. I don't keep it on the laptop, and for their safety, my employees don't have access to the account. Neither does Slim or Ramona. And even if someone had access, we only put this together in your presence. Right? Nobody knows of your involvement and your adoption into the family. We have names of CEOs and an extensive Salazar family tree, but that's it. Your name is nowhere, you're not part of the tree, nobody knows your identity. I promise."

Leon didn't respond, just said, "Get on the boat."

"But I'm telling the truth," Stanley pleaded.

I turned and added, "For what it's worth, he is."

Leon gave his trademark maniacal laugh. "Come on, you two, please. Remember what I said to you in the text, Chase? That there were eyes and ears in the police station. That's very true. Just so happens those eyes and ears are mine. It's easy to buy cops in Mexico."

"So," I said, "what does that prove?"

"You're telling the truth that my name isn't out there. I'll give you that. But I know I left some trace evidence at one of the many scenes, and you, along with Detective JJ have isolated my DNA profile."

I thought about that, deciding to stick close to the truth since that was what Leon preferred. "You're right, we did. But it's useless. You're not in any criminal database, and you're not in the family tree."

Stanley piped in. "And I'm positive you've never given a sample to a private company to trace your ancestry. Or ever would."

Leon used the gun to point. "In the boat, both of you."

Stanley refused. Though I didn't necessarily believe it, I mouthed to him, "It's okay, go."

Reluctantly, he did, and I followed. Though our hands were still tied behind our back, the fishing boat was shallow and low, so we were able to enter via the bow without trouble.

Leon didn't board right away. Instead, he said, "To the stern."

Exactly where I didn't want to go. But when I heard Leon sigh, and saw his finger tighten on the trigger, I complied. Stanley and I walked back, stepping over the anchor and its chain and Diaz's body. We stopped when we came to the transom.

Stanley muttered, "What's the plan, Chase?"

"No more talking," Leon said as he hopped onto the bow. He stood behind the center console with the HK 45 pistol pointed at Stanley.

"Turn and kneel," he commanded. "Both of you."

"Wait," I said.

He stabbed the gun again. "Turn!"

Before I did, I blurted, "We have the evidence on us. We'll show it to you, then you can decide about our friends."

Brief silence, then, "On you? What do you mean?"

Stanley looked at me. I shrugged and said, "Stanley has a thumb drive on him with all the data on it. I dropped it into his, uh, underwear when I was rifling through his back pockets."

Leon scoffed. "So, he lied, or now you're lying." He shook his head. "Not surprising."

"His undies," I said. "Check them." I didn't think Leon would be stupid enough to get close and do it, but you never knew, it was worth a shot.

As Leon stepped from behind the console, I tried to hide my excitement. But he proceeded no further, unfortunately. "Turn and back up," he said.

Damnit, damnit.

While Stanley backed up, Leon said, "I'm not touching you, Stanley. Your hands are by your butt. I think you can figure this out on your own."

Stanley looked at me, and I nodded.

He used his fingers and tugged at his underwear, jiggling until the thumb drive dropped from the bottom of his left pant leg.

Two more chances, I thought.

After ordering Stanley to the stern and picking up the drive, Leon opened the laptop, which was still on the console.

I said, "It's fingerprint access only." Leon examined the drive but looked dumbfounded. Since he didn't believe me, he stuck the drive in and tried himself.

"Get back here, Stanley," he said.

"No," I said, "it's my thumbprint it needs."

Leon sighed and didn't say anything for a moment. Then, "Alright, you back up, but slowly."

I did, but I turned forward when I neared the console.

"No," he said, "turn back around."

"But you need my thumb on the flat part of the drive, and the drive needs to be inserted."

Leon stood still. I knew he was thinking about the complications.

"Cut my hands free," I said. "You can back up, and I'll unlock the drive, then you can rezip my hands. You have a frickin' pistol, Leon."

While he thought about it, I envisioned it happening. My plan was to grab the laptop, thrust it in front as a shield, and hope that it would deflect the bullet or bullets.

"Nope, no way," he said. "Not going to happen."

One more shot, I thought. But it was by far my least favorite option.

"Fine," I said, turning and kneeling. "Use your knife and cut my thumb off then. That's what you'll have to do."

He gave his annoying cackle. "Not a bad thought, not bad at all."

I listened to him moving behind me, hoping he'd get close and go for it. Nothing happened for what seemed like minutes. Finally, I turned to see if he was moving close. Just as I did, I saw the end of an oar rocketing toward me. I tried to avoid it by snapping my head forward, but all it did was place the impact on the back of my skull.

I timbered like a fallen tree. With my hands behind my back, I smashed against the deck with my chest and chin. Dazed was an understatement. I saw blackness in between blinks, not stars.

Fighting a losing battle, I was just about unconscious as I felt Leon slice my hands free. Following that, I felt a sharp, searing pain. It was probably the worst pain of my life. It stopped me from passing out, though; it brought me alive, in fact.

He's doing it, he really is. He's sawing off my thumb!

Sensing Leon was straddling my body to do the work, I swung my lower leg up like I was doing a calf curl. My heel connected squarely with his balls.

Leon dropped to his knees. The knife skidded away.

And Stanley leapt into action.

It was a blur, but I witnessed the kid bent at the waist and charging forward. He smashed into Leon's midsection. Leon had been on his knees, holding his crotch. The two flew backward and collided with the console.

Now on my back, I watched Stanley stand and use his elbow to sweep the HK off the console. It landed with a dull thud to my left. Leon had collapsed onto his butt, his back pressed against the console. He lifted both arms and hauled Stanley to the ground by his shirt.

Since my hands were now free, I scrambled to get the gun, confused for a moment as to why the deck was so slippery and I couldn't grasp the weapon. When I blinked a few times and refocused, I saw all the blood.

My blood.

Trying not to think about that, I lifted the pistol above my head with both hands. I just about passed out again when I saw my right thumb, dangling straight down, hanging on by a flap of thin skin. Blood pumped from the wound, which dripped and flowed down my forearm like a snaking red river.

The lights started turning off in my head, but I thought about Stanley. Looking over, I saw that Leon had knocked him flat and was now straddling him, reaching with his right hand toward the bloody knife.

I swung the pistol left. Fought to aim. Fought to stay awake. Each blink got longer and darker. Longer and darker.

Focus, Chase, focus!

In between blinks, I saw Leon draw the knife back, high over his head, arching his back. Just before thrusting the blade into Stanley's chest, everything came into focus.

As the knife plunged downward in a vicious arc, I pulled the trigger.

And remembered nothing after.

FORTY-EIGHT

I'D BEEN awake for a few minutes, wondering where on earth the nurses were.

I sat in a somewhat lumpy bed in a Mexican hospital. My private room wasn't run-down or dirty, just basic. There was Spanish writing on the IV pole next to my bed, which tipped me to the fact that I was still in Mexico.

My head pounded and my right hand was immovable, wrapped in so much gauze it looked like a white boxing glove. Had no clue if I still had a thumb or not, which was what I mainly wanted to ask the nurses about.

Since I wasn't hooked up to any monitors, I figured I wasn't in that bad of shape. My pants were next to the bed, so I stood and put those on one-handed since I didn't like the drafty gown. My shirt was nowhere to be seen. I imagined it'd been soaked in blood and found its way to the trash.

Clearly, I'd had visitors since three chairs had been scrunched together at the foot of my hospital bed. After climbing back in bed, I played back the final moments of the confrontation with Leon in my mind. Like my thumb, I had no idea of the outcome. Unsure whether Leon was dead or alive.

While thinking, I noticed a collection of newspapers on my bedside table. For the next hour, I read through the stack of papers, learning everything I could about the preceding day. Just as I was finishing the last article, I heard voices in the hallway. They were familiar voices.

Immediately I put the paper back on the stack, laid straight, and closed my eyes.

A door creaked open. I heard a soft voice say, "He's still out." It was Ramona.

"No need to whisper," Slim said. "He's gotta wake soon. I'm surprised he's still out. Maybe the smell of these burritos will wake him up."

"Think we should've gotten him one?" It was Stanley. "Pretty sure he likes burritos."

"Pretty sure," Slim replied, "that a fat burrito isn't part of his post-op meal plan."

Ramona chimed in. "From what I know, Chase will eat anything, any time. Pretty sure he'll be ticked we didn't bring him one. We should eat fast."

I could hear them taking their seats and unwrapping the burritos. The smell was intoxicating. With my eyes closed, I said, "Pretty sure Ramona's right, you should've brought me one."

Silence for a moment. I added, "Somebody's only eating half their burrito."

"You devil," Slim said, laughing. "You're awake."

Ramona was first to my side. She slugged my shoulder, gently, as I sat up. "How long have you been awake? You feeling okay?"

"Feeling fine. Been awake long enough to get some light reading done." I motioned toward the newspapers.

"Here," Ramona said, tearing her burrito in half and handing part to me.

I took two big bites.

She shook her head. "You and your appetite are unbelievable."

Slim had already sat down, more concerned about his burrito than me being awake. Stanley swept to the other side of my bed. "So glad you made it, Chase. You lost a lot of blood. And I mean a lot."

I winced. "And my thumb, too?"

Collective silence. Everyone took a bite except me. I said, "Guess so."

"Not exactly," Ramona said in between chews. "They sewed it back on. The doctor isn't sure it will take, though. Time will tell."

I nodded, then moved the conversation elsewhere. "Thanks, Stanley. Apparently, you raced the boat to the docks in San Felipe and got help. That right?"

He nodded. "Yeah, both of you were bleeding out and slipping all around that boat. I used your wristwatch and clamped the band as tight as it would go. For a tourniquet."

"Smart," I said. "I read Leon made it, too."

He snorted. "Yeah, he's in the same hospital, if you can believe it, just under police surveillance and handcuffed to his bed."

"Where'd I hit him?"

"You don't remember?"

I shook my head.

"Outer left pectoral muscle." Stanley laughed. "Blew his whole nipple right off. Part of it landed on me."

As we continued eating, Stanley told details of how he managed to get me to the hospital and explain everything to the Federales. Apparently, he called in Detective JJ, and JJ turned out to be a great help. There wasn't a corrupt bone in that young detective's body.

When I finished eating my burrito half, Ramona put her hand on my forearm and said, "Obviously, your name's been cleared." She squeezed my arm and kept her hand there.

I liked that.

"It's already apparent to the authorities," she continued, "that Leon was responsible for Diaz, and Rogan Ross, and the gardener, and members of The Family."

I cleared my throat. "What about the rest area?"

"Don't want to know anything about it. Don't say a word. Tucson office is attributing that to The Family. Let's leave it at that."

"Fair enough," I said.

I turned to Stanley. He'd plunked down on a chair to eat his burrito. "Papers mentioned a Senate investigation into the CEOs and their alleged treatment of women at their parties. Nothing about rampant tax evasion, or your father, though."

He stopped chewing and looked up at me with wide eyes.

When he didn't say anything, I said, "Where's the recording, Stanley? Where's that cell phone?" I felt Ramona's and Slim's eyes boring into me, which told me they had no idea that Stanley had a recording of his father.

Stanley didn't respond.

"Kid, come on, talk. You hoping I wouldn't remember? Where is it?"

Eventually, he tapped his pocket. "Right here. Your stuff is in the top drawer, by the way." He motioned toward the bedside table.

I pushed him. "What are you doing about the recording? That's what I mean. That's the important question."

Both Ramona and Slim leaned in a little. Stanley blinked and pushed up his glasses, then wiped his brow, but he still didn't say anything.

So, I did. "Obviously nothing since you haven't told these two. Right?"

Stanley pleaded. "He's my father, Chase. My dad."

"I get it, Stanley, I do. It's tough. I don't envy your position. I appreciate that he's your dad, but he's also our nation's chief law enforcement officer." I paused. "And he shouldn't be."

Stanley reluctantly nodded.

I drove my point home. "He hired men to illegally monitor your home, then to kidnap you at gunpoint. He received one of the most important positions in our country for failing to uphold the law, for looking the other way, for protecting men of incredibly immoral character."

By this point, Stanley's head was low, so I stopped.

Slim asked, "Just to clarify, you have a recording of your dad admitting to these things?"

Stanley nodded without looking up.

"What does the recording exactly say?" Slim said, "as it relates to the tax evasion indictment. Did he mention names?"

"He did." Stanley finally lifted his head. "Apparently, it was the Senate majority leader who orchestrated it, who went to school with Alvin Berba-coa, by the way. As I'm sure you know, the Senate leader is in the same political party as my father. And the president isn't, which makes it hard for the president to push her choices through."

"I get it," Slim butted in, "the Senate leader agrees to push one of her nominations through if she gives them the AG position. A tit-for-tat."

"Yup," Stanley said. "It's my understanding the president wasn't involved with the deal between my dad and the Senate leader to bury the indictment charges."

I rested my head on the pillow and blew out a deep breath. "Typical Washington. Man, I hate that place."

"My dad's gonna claim this is how things are done, especially since it's a divided government."

"I'm sure he will," I said, looking up to the ceiling and shaking my head. "Sure he'll have all sorts of excuses."

"I already confronted him," Stanley continued, "and he made several excuses."

"Like what?" Ramona asked.

"Like what he did was wrong, but that the American companies were employing thousands of Mexican workers and giving poor people decent-paying jobs. And that our government didn't need all the tax money, anyway. A basic ends-justify-the-means argument."

Thinking about Leon and Ernesto, I felt disgusted. I muttered a famous quote under my breath.

"What's that?" Stanley asked. "What are you saying?"

I quoted, "We humans, you see, have an infinite capacity for self-rationalization."

"Who said that?"

"Charles Wendell Colson," I replied. "He was Nixon's advisor, his political hatchet man. Colson was the first to go to prison for Watergate. If anyone knows about self-delusion and rationalizing one's behavior, that man does."

Stanley nodded. "Exactly what my dad's doing. Is that what you're saying?"

"I am. Leon, too. He wanted to stop his family's cycle of degradation, so much so he justified in his mind murdering his own family. He claimed he wasn't a madman, but he was."

"True," Stanley said, "complete mad thinking on his behalf. To the point where he even justified collateral killings."

A momentary pause. I said, "One thing about Leon, though. One thing he had right."

"He had something right?" Stanley said. "What?"

"How important it is to stop a vicious cycle. Stanley, you have a chance to stop the cycle of corrupt government and immoral leadership in our country." I motioned toward the cell in his front pocket.

He sighed, then stood. "You're right, Chase." He pulled out the cell and handed it to Ramona. "Do whatever you will with the recording." She nodded and took the phone.

"I know this move will fracture our relationship," Stanley said, "probably beyond repair. Will he go to prison?"

"Doubt it," she said. "He'll immediately be removed from office, though. Senate leader will be out, too. Who knows what happens to the president."

Stanley shrugged. "All good things, I guess."

"Not just good things," Slim said, "the right things."

Stanley nodded and moved toward the door. "I need some air. Excuse me."

When the door closed, Ramona said, "Poor, kid."

Neither Slim nor I had anything to add, so I pulled the sheets back, then pivoted and put my feet on the floor.

"You're dressed," Ramona stated.

I had my pants on but no shirt.

She asked, "What are you doing exactly?"

"No sense sticking around here." I opened the bedside drawer and pulled out the burner cell and my wallet. "I mean, nurses haven't checked on me for over an hour. I'm not getting the quality care here."

"Stay put," she ordered.

I stood. "I can't. Have stuff to do."

"Oh, you do, do you? Like what?"

"For starters, I should probably visit a doctor in the States and get a second opinion on this thumb."

"Chase, come on, please lay back down. At least get doctor's approval to leave."

I didn't move. Slim laughed. "He's not going to listen. He should, but he's not going to."

"Fine, then," Ramona said. "At least cover up with the gown." She handed it to me. "And grab that IV pole. We'll pretend you're getting some exercise, then make a run for the car."

I smiled as I put on the gown and grabbed the IV. "I like your style."

Slim held the door open. "Only thing you have to decide, pal, is who you're driving with. We both have cars here."

An awkward moment followed. I shuffled toward Ramona.

"I get it," he said. "Makes sense."

"Sorry, buddy, don't mean to offend you." Ramona took my hand and escorted me toward the door.

Slim glanced at our clasped hands. "Now it really makes sense."

"It's not like that," I replied.

"Oh, it's not, is that right?"

"That's right, buddy, she has my dog." I grinned. "And I have to go with her."

AUTHOR'S NOTE

Dear Reader,

Thank you for taking the time to read my book. I hope you enjoyed NIGHT NIGHT KILLER. If you did, I'd be grateful if you left a review on Amazon.com and/or Goodreads.com. Reviews are extremely helpful!

If you'd like to learn more about me, the Garrison Chase thriller series, or sign up for my newsletter, please visit my website at:

craignhooper.com

I'm also giving away a free ebook to all my fans! FALLOUT, the prequel to the Garrison Chase series, is FREE when you sign up for my newsletter. Please visit my website to get your free copy.

If you have any questions or comments, please don't hesitate to reach out at craig@craignhooper.com. I absolutely love hearing from fans!

Thanks for being a reader.

ACKNOWLEDGMENTS

A huge thanks goes out to Kristen Weber. Kristen's my developmental editor, and she's been with me since the second book of the Garrison Chase thriller series. I'm so happy to have her in my corner. Her insights, edits, suggestions, and encouragement have been invaluable to my writing career and the development of this series. You're the best, Kristen!

Thanks also to Elaini Caruso. Elaini's been my copy editor for the past two Garrison Chase books. I'm extremely grateful for her corrections, edits, and suggestions. She does a fantastic job polishing my writing.

Finally, I applaud the work of Jovana and the team at Deranged Doctor Design (DDD). DDD has been with me since the very beginning. They've done incredible work with my book covers. They've also helped with creating content for advertising, social media, and my website. I appreciate the whole team at DDD.

ALSO BY CRAIG N. HOOPER

Fallout (FREE!)

The Greatest Good

A Thin Line

All the Good Men

The Baja Directive

The Garrison Chase Series (Books 1-3)

Made in the USA
Monee, IL
05 January 2024

51264944R00177